DEAD MAN'S HAND

DEAD MAN'S HAND

JAMES J. BUTCHER

ACE
NEW YORK

ACE
Published by Berkley
An imprint of Penguin Random House LLC
penguinrandomhouse.com

Library of Congress Cataloging-in-Publication Data

Names: Butcher, James J., author.
Title: Dead man's hand / James J. Butcher.
Description: New York: Ace, [2022] | Series: The unorthodox chronicles; 1
Identifiers: LCCN 2022001556 (print) | LCCN 2022001557 (ebook) |
ISBN 9780593440414 (hardcover) | ISBN 9780593440421 (ebook)
Subjects: LCGFT: Fantasy fiction. | Thrillers (Fiction). | Novels.
Classification: LCC PS3602.U848 D43 2022 (print) | LCC PS3602.U848 (ebook) |
DDC 813/.6—dc23/eng/20220114
LC record available at https://lccn.loc.gov/2022001556
LC ebook record available at https://lccn.loc.gov/2022001557

Printed in the United States of America
1   3   5   7   9   10   8   6   4   2

Book design by Daniel Brount

*This book is dedicated to good fathers,
both those whom we are fortunate enough
to have with us and those whom we would
give anything to have with us again*

DEAD MAN'S HAND

PROLOGUE

Leslie Mayflower glowered out between the dusty blinds of his darkened living room, watching the street. The morning sun made him squint his bleary eyes, bringing forth a pounding in the back of his head.

He wasn't sure which to curse harder, the sun or the empty bottle of whiskey in his grip. Or maybe the other empty bottle on the couch behind him. Or perhaps the broken one he'd thrown against the fridge the night before.

It was simpler to just curse himself.

The phone rang, brash and blaring. He hardly recognized the sound. The assault on his head redoubled, but at least he was certain what to curse above all else.

He pawed at the receiver without taking his eyes from the window. The base fell to the floor and he left it there. He held the plastic handset to his ear.

"Yeah." His voice croaked. He couldn't remember how many days it had been since he'd last spoken.

"Damien Grieves, calling for Les Mayflower, please." The voice was calm and authoritative. And familiar.

"Bastard," Mayflower growled.

"Ah, it is you," Grieves replied.

"Not interested."

"Les, just listen—"

Mayflower didn't listen. He dropped the handset and stomped on the base until the tinny sound stopped. He turned his attention to what really mattered.

Across the street, Sarah was pruning her roses. The kids were at school for the day, and she had Thursdays off. She usually spent her days off in her garden, enjoying the empty street until the rest of the neighborhood returned in the afternoon. He sometimes watched her live her quiet morning out, peacefully, and found something like peace in that for himself.

The front pocket of his flannel robe began to buzz, and he twitched his stance a few inches wider on instinct. He grunted and withdrew his confounded cell phone from his pocket, glaring at the small screen on the front. It read simply **Unknown**.

"Unknown my ass," he said. He snarled and snapped the phone open. "Go to hell." He swigged one last time from his whiskey bottle, receiving only a couple of drops for his trouble. He sat it alongside the others that lined his coffee table and opened the front door. He went outside, his passage disturbing countless days of accumulated dust, which swirled in the blinding beams that poured into his house.

"Mayflower, please," Grieves said, his voice smaller and more static on the old cell. "It's important."

The sun seemed very upset that Mayflower had left his hideout, redoubling its efforts to split his head in two from front to back. He focused his annoyance on Grieves. "I'm in the middle of something," he lied.

"It can wait."

"You don't know that."

"Whatever it is, it can wait. I've got something bigger."

"Handle it yourself. I'm retired." He made as though he was inspecting the stability of his paint-peeled picket fence. He confirmed it was just as rickety as the letters he consistently received from his neighborhood association of asshats claimed.

"Men like us can't retire. You know that."

Mayflower stopped cold. He felt his teeth grind and his old heart begin to thrum. Not faster, but harder, like it was suddenly wrapped in taut wires. The pumping blood made his muscles tense and ache. "Men like us?" he said, his voice a whisper. "You and I are nothing alike, witch."

"I disagree—"

"Go to hell, Grieves."

He snapped the phone shut and popped out the battery, shoving them both back into the pocket of his robe.

Across the street, Sarah looked up and saw him. She smiled beneath the wide brim of her sun hat and waved a dirt-stained glove at him. He managed a tight-lipped smile back, but his stomach twisted and he retreated into the dark of his hollow home.

He shut the door behind him and leaned back against it. He growled, ripped a cigarette from the crumpled pack in his robe pocket, and lit it, drawing in a deep breath of scorching heat. He held the smoke in his chest for a moment before letting it slip out, then went toward his diminishing liquor cabinet to fetch a new bottle of whiskey.

He stopped in front of the fridge, his feet crunching on broken glass from the bottle he had smashed against it last night. The icebox was a blank white canvas save for a single sun-bleached sticky note at its center. The adhesive had long since failed, so he had used a magnet to keep it in place.

The magnet covered up the top half, but the bottom read, *Take care of yourself*, in a painfully familiar and feminine hand.

He read it, over and over again. Then he took a deep breath and ground the cigarette out on the heel of his palm. It hurt, and all he could think was *Good*. He put the cigarette back in the pack, got out the broom, and swept up the broken glass.

He started toward the liquor cabinet again, before stopping himself. "Hydrate, idiot," he croaked at himself. He filled a tall cup with water from the sink and forced himself to down the whole thing.

Then, and only then, did he go to the liquor cabinet and withdraw his second-to-last bottle of whiskey. He cracked it open and took a swig before he settled back in at the window. There was little else to do but watch the day slip away.

Just then, the sound of an engine came. It wasn't the throaty rumble of the old mail truck that patrolled the neighborhood, nor the quiet rush of the usual suburban sedans. It was smooth and quiet, hardly a whispering breath as it came closer. If the street hadn't been silent, he might never have heard it coming. But he did hear it, and he also recognized it.

"Bastard," he growled, slamming the blinds closed until only the thinnest slat of light eked through. He watched the road, waiting.

When the car came within sight, he saw it was sleek, black, and mirrorless. Even the windows were imperceptibly dark. It reminded him of a black-shelled beetle. The car slipped down the street slowly, as though studying. Finally, it reached Mayflower's house and pulled into his driveway behind his beat-up tank of a jeep.

A jeep that could crush the black plastic bug car flat, he noted proudly.

The car's door opened, and out stepped a man clad in a fine and expensive black suit. He wore a pair of stylish open-rimmed glasses on his hawkish nose.

Mayflower spat a curse and took a deep, deep swig from his bottle.

"Grieves," he muttered over the burn of the liquor, "you son of a bitch."

Grieves walked up to Mayflower's door and knocked in three precisely identical motions.

Mayflower thought about not answering. About staying in his

darkened living room, glaring out the window until the witch left, but that wouldn't be the end of things.

Three more knocks, exactly as the last.

"I know you're home, Les. I just called you."

"I'm coming," he barked, stomping to the front door and throwing it open. "What are you doing here?"

Grieves offered him a polite smile. "I called you while I was on my way. Figured you'd throw a tantrum and hang up on me."

"You want to see what a tantrum looks like?" Mayflower asked quietly.

Grieves straightened his tie, annoyingly unperturbed by the threat. "I'm not here to fight. I wanted to tell you myself before you found out."

He stopped. Something was wrong. "What?"

"Samantha is dead."

Mayflower heard something shatter at his feet, and he numbly looked down to see it was his bottle of whiskey. He stared at the mess of broken glass and splattered liquor for a long moment before looking back to Grieves.

"How?" he asked. In her line of work, it was inevitable; he knew that. But Samantha Mansgraf was tough, the toughest witch he'd ever met, and he'd been half convinced she'd outlive him despite already being his senior by a century or more.

"We're not sure yet," Grieves said. "But it was . . . unpleasant."

Mayflower's lip curled in a grimace. "How many did she take with her?"

Grieves frowned. "Hers was the only body we found."

He glared. "That's not right."

"My people were very thorough."

"If someone tried to kill Mansgraf, she'd tear their throat out with her teeth. If several people tried, she'd start using her hands."

"Well, you know her better than anyone else."

"Not better than you. You were her student. Until you screwed her over."

Grieves ignored his comment. "You were her partner," he countered. "She's hardly said a word to me since you quit."

"Retired," Mayflower said.

"I didn't approve it."

"Fortunately, I didn't work for you or the Department, so your approval was unnecessary."

Grieves shrugged and held up his hands in a defusing gesture. "Fine, fine. In any case, now's not the time for this."

"Why are you here, Grieves?" he asked.

"To tell you the news."

"You could have sent a lackey. What are you, Department director by now?"

Grieves twitched a brow in annoyance. "Assistant director."

"Fine. Assistant. You still could have sent a peon. Why are *you* here?"

Grieves took a deep breath and straightened the collar of his jacket. "To ask for your help. You knew her best. If she left any clue or sign, you'd be the best one to find it."

Mayflower studied the assistant director for a long moment. The man was a couple of promotions shy of frequenting the White House. He could have sent someone to make contact—Lord knew he had the people. Yet here he was himself.

That was telling. Though of what he wasn't yet sure.

Grieves's face was a mask as impenetrable as those worn by his Auditors. "I'm just seeking the counsel of a friend."

"We're not friends," Mayflower said.

"Of a former colleague, then," he amended. "Will you come?"

Mayflower turned and walked to his smoke-soaked, sunbleached armchair, leaving Grieves standing in the open doorway. He reached below and found the old, heavy revolver. He then dug out his box of homemade ammo. He clicked open the six-chamber cylinder, revealing a single lead slug. It was a round meant to kill men, not monsters. He tapped it out of the chamber and put it in his pocket before loading six custom rounds. They were crafted with cold-hammered iron bullets and his own mixture of a gunpowder based on silver fulminate. Iron and silver, tools his kind had used for centuries. He clicked the gun shut, pocketed a few more rounds, and loaded the weapon into his shoulder holster.

The weight of it gave him a sudden sense of security, of power, but it was fleeting and quickly replaced with bitter nausea and doubts. He let the witch see none of this.

"You won't be needing that," Grieves said, eyeing the weapon coolly.

"That has never once been true."

He sighed. "Very well. I'll drive."

"So will I," Mayflower said, trading his robe for the tattered suit jacket on the hook beside the door. It was much heavier than it looked and didn't match his whiskey-stained slacks or leather boots, but he didn't care. "I'm not riding in your plastic death trap."

"Fine," Grieves said, climbing into his black beetle with ease. "I'll lead the way."

Mayflower only growled and slammed himself into his jeep.

It grumbled to life after some practiced coaxing, and Mayflower began following the dark, mirrorless car toward the north end of Boston.

The drive was calm, although Grieves drove at a teeth-grindingly slow speed, despite the roads being relatively open after the midmorning traffic rush. Even so, Mayflower found himself gripping the wheel tighter with every mile, until his fingers grew numb.

Mansgraf was dead.

Back in the old days, he was uncertain such a thing was even possible. But that was a long time ago. Things had changed, and they simply refused to stop.

When Grieves's vehicle finally led Mayflower to the scene,

however, there was one thing he was certain of: Mansgraf hadn't gone down without a fight.

The warehouse Grieves took him to was identical in nearly every way to those around it, aside from the atrocity that was that damned Unorthodox-themed kids' restaurant a few blocks away. The only difference was this one looked like it had been cored out by a flaming auger from the inside. Each of the windows had been blasted outward, scattering scorched shards of glass for hundreds of feet. Blackened outlines of flame flared from the broken windows, searing ashen plumes that fanned out along the metal roofing. They were like a dozen wide, horrified eyes wearing too much mascara.

Grieves parked beside the dozens of Department vehicles, and Mayflower pulled over beside him. He got out of the jeep, eyeing the scene.

"We think it happened sometime early this morning, before dawn," Grieves said, stepping beside him. "Why she was here, we're not sure."

Mayflower glanced around. If it weren't for the rings of yellow tape, scuttling Department personnel in white clean-suits, and white-masked Auditors standing guard, the place would have been empty.

"She must have known someone was after her," he said. "Lured them here so she could use her big guns away from bystanders."

Grieves nodded. "She was never one for using anything less subtle than a fireball."

"Saw her use a knife once," Mayflower said. "The fireball is kinder."

Grieves began to reply, but a voice cut through his own.

"Grieves! What is that man doing here?" A man approached, his own Department suit of a less well-fitting style than Grieves's. His blond hair was balding, and his scalp flaked aggressively in the empty patches.

"Department Director John Peters," Grieves said coolly, "this is Les Mayflower, a consultant—"

"I know full well who he is," Peters said. The acid in his voice could have scrubbed the pavement white. "He's the Huntsman."

"Not anymore," Mayflower said. "Now I'm just a man."

"I doubt that." Peters turned to Grieves. "I asked you what he was doing here."

"Outside consultant. Thought he might see something we missed."

"I said no unauthorized personnel allowed! Need I remind you of the"—he glanced at Mayflower—"the sensitive nature of our situation?"

"Of course, sir," Grieves said, ever composed, "but I think it would be prudent to at least get his take on things if we're to find out what happened here."

Peters glanced between them. "Fine. Five minutes. Then he's gone."

"As you say, sir."

Peters shook his head and muttered something before storming off.

"Nice guy," Mayflower said.

"He's an irate asshole. But he gets the job done, in his own way."

"Rather than in your own way?"

Grieves shrugged. "No one is perfect." He gestured to the warehouse. "This way."

He led Mayflower in through the bustling mass of manpower that combed the scene. Each and every one of them stepped instinctively out of Grieves's way when he passed. Everyone knew the man's face, and likely even more so his reputation for surgically thin patience.

Inside, the building looked like a broken observatory. The ceiling, walls, even the floors, had been scorched as black as a starless night. Dozens of stacks of wooden and steel crates had been disintegrated or melted into formless piles of slag and ash, creating an alien landscape of rolling darkness. Scattered across the landscape were pools of still, hard puddles that looked like ponds of ice.

"What are those?" Mayflower asked.

Grieves bared his teeth in a bitter, wolfish smile. "Molten metal."

"Weapons of her attackers, maybe? Where are the bodies?"

He shook his head. "At those temperatures, flesh and bone would be incinerated. We're analyzing the residue now."

Mayflower nodded, then felt a chill as he came within sight of the room's center.

There, he saw a perfect circle of bright gray concrete, like someone had shone a spotlight into the middle of the darkness. But the circle was spattered with pooling blood. And at its center was a prone form underneath a tarp.

Mayflower felt his grinding heart clatter in his chest. His hands clenched into fists so tight that he felt his short nails gouging into his palms. He and Mansgraf hadn't been friends. They hadn't even particularly liked each other. But they had been partners.

That was a bond as deep as blood.

Now, with that blood spilled so generously at the center of the otherwise empty scene, it looked like some grotesque painting that Mary would have found interesting but not living room appropriate.

His legs felt heavier with each step he took toward Mansgraf's body. It felt unreal that she could be dead. She had always been so powerful, so sure, so wise. Not to mention so paranoid that she did her own dental work.

How could this have happened?

Grieves stopped just beyond the ring of unburnt concrete. "Problem is," he said, looking around at the flame-scoured husk of the building, "she was so . . . thorough that we can't figure out who or what did this. The only clues we have are her wounds and these."

He drew Mayflower's enraptured eyes to the side. There, in the scorched ground, were thin, sliding marks that scraped furrows in the ash.

"Claws?" Mayflower asked.

"Would hardly narrow it down, but could be. Or maybe a blade. Or even ice skates for all we know. The only thing that's certain is that these marks were made after the place was half burnt down, and Mansgraf never left the circle."

"So, her attacker lived," Mayflower said, finding himself staring at the spotlight of gray again.

"We think so," Grieves said. "But we can't be sure of anything until we get this in a lab. After that, we can maybe figure out who or what it was that got her."

Mayflower's lips peeled back in an unconscious grimace.

The blood had begun to darken already, with long, thin lines of it strewn around the concrete as though with a manic painter's brush.

Then he saw a few lines that stood out to him. Lines that were in places they shouldn't have been.

He traced them with his eye, trying to place how they might have come to be there. Then he found a single trail of blood, dribbling all the way back to Mansgraf's body.

"You said something about her wounds?" Mayflower asked.

Grieves nodded. "Lacerations. Long and deep. Could be any number of things. We're having them analyzed as I speak."

"Show me."

"Les," Grieves said, drawing an eyeful of ire from Mayflower for using the name. "You don't need to do that to yourself—"

"Show. Me."

Grieves sighed. "Very well." He gestured to one of the clean-suited figures in the circle. "Raise the tarp."

They obeyed and gently peeled back the blood-flecked cover from the corpse.

Mayflower felt his whole body grow taut with revulsion and rage, like someone had coiled every spring of muscle in his body.

If it hadn't been for the bloodied patchwork robes she had always worn, Mayflower would have hardly known it was her.

What was left of her looked like a ham that had been spiral cut while riding a roller coaster. Her limbs were covered in long, trailing slashes that cut down to the bone.

Her gray eyes were sightless, staring in fury at nothing. Her timeworn face was locked in a grimace of pain and defiance.

Mayflower forced himself to tear his gaze away from her expression.

He turned his attention to her hand. Sure enough, the odd trail he had noticed led to the index and middle fingers of her right hand, which were coated thoroughly in her own blood.

He traced the marks again with his eyes and realized what they were.

Mansgraf had left a note.

It wasn't much; she'd likely had a small window in which to leave her message while bleeding to death.

Mayflower dug in his dusty memory for what the symbols might be. Then he recognized the writing. It was ogham. Old ogham. A script once used for carving into stones with tools that could cut only straight lines. But hers hadn't been straight. She had flung streaks of her own arterial blood in long, winding curves, like writing in a fun-house mirror. It was probably why the others had yet to notice it in the gory commotion.

He wracked his brain, pulling out old information he hadn't used for years.

Finally, he managed to piece it together.

Mayflower turned away and headed toward his jeep.

"See anything?" Grieves asked.

"No," Mayflower lied.

He did see something, something small and simple.

A request, drawn in the blood of his dead partner with the strength of her dying breath.

Kill Grimsby.

ONE ✳

I 'M NOT SURE WHAT I DID TO DESERVE THIS," GRIMSHAW Griswald Grimsby said, "but I'm sorry."

He stared at his tutu in the cracked mirror. It was *pink*. Not just calm, natural, happy pink. Aggressively pink. The kind of pink that made infants cry and attracted bees. The fabric was drawn taut overtop his T-shirt, pulling the material tight until it scratched uncomfortably against the faded burn scars that marred much of his left side.

Carla, the restaurant manager, shrugged her broad shoulders. "Taco Tuesdays aren't pulling in the folks like they used to," she said. "We need something shocking to get people's attention."

"I do magic," Grimsby said, turning his back to the mirror to examine the handmade taco-shell wings that had been stapled haphazardly to the back of the tutu. "*Real* magic. How is that less shocking than this?"

"People can see magic anywhere," Carla said. "You're not the only witch in the world, Grimsby, and you're far from the best."

"Then why hire me at all?"

"You're the only one who applied. Now, if you want to continue working for Mighty Magic Donald's Food Kingdom, turn around and let me fix the back."

Grimsby most definitely did *not* want to continue working for Mighty Magic Donald's Food Kingdom, but he turned around anyway, his eyes falling to the floor. The lacy skirt didn't bother him as much as the clutching, constricting fabric did. He danced uncomfortably from one foot to the other, trying to dislodge things from places where he preferred no lodging take place.

Carla had suggested he exchange his jeans for tights, but he had decided that was not going to happen. The last thing anyone needed to see were his pale, skinny legs. Well, perhaps second to last.

"It's just once a week," Carla said, "and only until Taco Tuesday picks up again! Although, if it does really well, we could just make it Taco Fairy Tuesday. After all, Wizard Pie Wednesday is a hit . . ."

Grimsby tried to imagine wearing the outfit once a week for the foreseeable future. It hurt him the same way it hurt when he had found his first gray hair more than a year ago. At nineteen. It was a deep hurt, with a pain that held every indication of only getting worse with time.

"I will quit."

"And go where?" she asked, picking at a crease in the eye-punching-pink cloth.

"There's lots of places hiring the Unorthodox," Grimsby said, his tone defensive.

She scoffed. "Sure, but they're not being hired to *be* Unorthodox, Grimsby," she said. "They're being hired *in spite* of being Unorthodox. Therian accountants. Vamp security guards. Outside of the Department or maybe private contractors, no one's looking to hire a witch."

Grimsby felt his throat go taut, but he clenched his jaw. "You are."

"Not a real witch. Just—one like you," she said, the words without malice, but that somehow made them hurt worse. "After all, you're barely licensed to use magic at all. You've got, what, spinning plates and that magical duct-tape trick?"

"They're not tricks," Grimsby said quietly. They were real magic. *His* magic.

"Whatever. Look, no one who doesn't want a witch will hire you, and anyone who does want a witch can find a better one. You're stuck with me, and I'm stuck with you."

He wanted to argue, but she was right.

He had spent most of his childhood training to join the Department of Unorthodox Affairs. After they had denied him entry, he hadn't had many options. It had taken him nearly a month just to get this job. People weren't exactly banging down the doors to hire failed witches. Or any witches, for that matter. Outside of normally strict Department utilization, magic was heavily regulated. So why hire a witch when any Usual would do?

So he couldn't just up and quit, despite how much he wanted to. He needed the work. Bad. Badly enough that he let himself be dressed in costumes three days—make that four—a week. And that didn't include holidays, though after last year's lawsuit he doubted Carla would make him portray Santa again. He didn't have the build for it anyway. What kind of Santa Claus is five six and a hundred and thirty pounds?

The not-so-jolly kind, that was for certain.

He glared at the wings again. Carla had glued thin, brightly colored fabric in the curvature of the shells to replicate taco fixings. She had even liberally applied red, green, and brown glitter for seasoning. Where would anyone find brown glitter, anyway?

"Toad's teeth," he cursed quietly.

"Why do you always swear so strangely?" Carla asked idly, pinning a faltering wing back into place. "It's off-putting."

Grimsby shrugged. "My mother didn't like cursing," he said.

"Must be a witch thing," Carla said without any real interest. "Nearly done. Here." She placed the final, knife-twisting touch into his hand. It was a plastic tube with a rubber avocado hot-glued to the end.

"Is this a pencil eraser?" Grimsby asked, staring forlornly at the avocado.

"You noticed? Darn! I was hoping it was more subtle than that. It's a wand anyhow. Don't you need to use a wand for your tricks?"

"They're not tricks," Grimsby snapped.

"Well," Carla said with a tone and head tilt that insinuated that they were, in fact, tricks.

He sighed. "No, I do not need to use a wand."

"Oh. Have you tried? Maybe it would help with your . . . you know." She gestured vaguely to all of him.

He took a deep breath, stretching the pink cloth to the limit. "Yeah. Maybe it'll help," he said mechanically.

"Good." She stepped back as much as the cramped janitorial closet allowed and examined him one final time. "So, how do you feel?"

He tugged at the constrictive tutu. "Like I need to pay rent," he said.

"That's what I like to hear!"

Grimsby only grumbled.

Tutu, taco wings, and avocado wand. By these atrocities combined, he had changed from Grimsby, mild-mannered children's magician, to an abomination whose name could only be uttered in horrified whispers: the Taco Fairy.

Now it was showtime.

Grimsby sidled out of the closet, ducking under the barrage of reminders Carla shouted after him as she tidied the makeshift dressing room. He let the door shut behind him and leaned against it for a moment, taking a deep breath. He had hoped the air would be fresh and bracing. Instead, it just smelled like burnt cheese and was exhausting.

There was a flushing sound from across the hall and a man

stepped out of the restroom, wiping his hands on the front of his pants. His eyes locked with Grimsby's for a brief moment, before they fell upon the tutu and wings. The man nearly choked as he tried to stifle his laughter. He shook his head and continued past Grimsby toward the dining room without saying a word.

Grimsby puffed out a breath through his cheeks. He could handle embarrassment well enough. He wouldn't have made it this long at MMDFK unless he could. He occasionally flubbed his lines or jumbled up his spells. He was a human, after all, and not even a particularly good one.

But he would have appreciated it if people laughed at him because of his own mistakes, not the crimes of others. Then, at least, he might have deserved it.

No one was so low that they deserved the Taco Fairy.

Yet Taco Fairy he would deliver upon them, though it would come at a terrible price.

Minimum wage.

He straightened himself up. Pride was a luxury, but it was also relative. If he was going to wear a pink tutu and taco-shell wings, he was going to *wear* a pink tutu and taco-shell wings, dang it.

He straightened himself and strolled into the dining area of the restaurant, which was hardly more than a dozen booths and five or six tables. There was a handful of adults scattered around the seats, quietly conversing or staring at their phones. Most were the usual crowd of clean-dressed, casual adults, but one man stood out. He was skeletally thin and of a towering height that made Grimsby feel like a child. He stood in the corner, chewing on an unlit cigarette, his eyes shadowed by a pair of dark glasses.

At Grimsby's entry, a few patrons looked up and were instantly aghast, but not all.

Not enough.

"Ladies, gentlemen, and the guy with damp jeans," Grimsby bellowed, making every head snap his way. "Welcome to Mighty

Magic Donald's Food Kingdom! You find yourselves having the great fortune of arriving to our fair land on this Tuesday of Tacos, where the purchase of but one single taco will deliver upon you the bounty of two, that's right, two tacos! Purchase, purchase the tacos and consume them! As I, the Taco Fairy, am empowered by your sated taco lust."

There was little more than stunned silence in the room. The man in the corner quietly chewed his cigarette, his hidden gaze never wavering.

A willowy woman with a prominent monobrow rose from her seat, her hands on her hips. "Where the hell have you been?" she demanded in a tone that was more appropriately aimed at a child than a working adult. "My son's party started ten minutes ago!"

"Ah, but you see," Grimsby said, "I was delayed."

"By what, creep?" she demanded.

Grimsby winced slightly at the word and bared his teeth in an expression that would only pass for a smile in a court of law. With a good lawyer. He felt all need to be reasonable float away.

He imagined it did so on taco wings.

"For Taco Fairies have no wings, madam, but shells," he said, "useless husks full of meat and other, more odious contents. Our life is a waking nightmare. And at night, the bears come."

"Jesus Christ," the woman said, rolling her eyes, "are you a nutjob or just an idiot?"

"Signs generally point to the latter," Grimsby said, "but only generally. Don't worry, ma'am, I'm the best tutu-clad magician in at least a two-mile radius."

"Whatever, I'm not paying you to mouth off."

"Technically, you're not paying me at all, ma'am. My services fall wholly under the purview of the Mighty Magic Donald's Food Kingdom Birthday Package: Extravaganza Level. Terms and conditions may, and certainly do, apply."

She glowered. "Then don't expect a tip from me, fairy boy."

"Of course not, ma'am. I've worked here over a year. I know the drill."

She snorted, revealing a tall gumline yellowed with nicotine. "A year here? I'd kill myself."

Grimsby again donned his most technical of smiles. "We're always hiring. Now, if you'll excuse me, I've got a show to put on."

He strode past the monobrowed mother, doing a clumsy, yet dramatic spin that left her covered in taco-seasoning-colored glitter. She sputtered angry stammers at his dismissal, and he hurried his step before she could form actual words.

Before he reached the door that led to the massive warehouse turned playroom, a cool hand rested on his shoulder.

"Mr. Grimsby," a gravelly voice said, "a moment of your time."

Grimsby turned to see the skeletal man from the corner standing before him. And a good deal over him. The man seemed like he was a scant few inches shy of seven feet, though perhaps it was partly just how he carried himself. He wore a wrinkled suit jacket that was several different shades of sun-bleached gray. His slacks were an unfashionably dissimilar shade of blue. His face was gaunt, as though he was sick or starving, and his cheeks were covered with white and black stubble, like television static.

Grimsby wasn't sure what to say, so he simply paused and tilted his head. "I'm, uh, kind of in the middle of something."

He saw the man's eyes glance over the tutu even through the dark shades he wore. "Clearly. But this is important."

"Oh, all right. Just make it fast?"

"My name's Mayflower. I'm . . . with the Department. I've got a few questions for you."

With the Department? The last word he had gotten from the Department was a letter of preemptive denial for any further applications to join, and a license for basic magic. That was more than a year ago. "Questions? About what?"

"About who. Samantha Mansgraf."

He shook his head. "Oh no, I want nothing to do with her. Last time we spoke she ruined my life. I don't want to know what she'd do if we spoke again."

"It wasn't a request." The man seemed to grow a few inches taller, though it was likely in Grimsby's imagination.

Grimsby felt himself bristle up, foam wings and all. He had never taken well to bullies. "You sure? Because it sure sounded like one to me."

"You're mistaken." The man's voice was like weathered stainless steel, cold, timeless, and inflexible.

Grimsby's voice by comparison was closer to a creaky swing set in a harsh wind, but he didn't let himself back down. "No, I think you're the one who's mistaken if you think you can come in here and just make demands of me. The Department had its chance to ask me questions, and instead it just sent a letter. I'm done with it, and so I'm done with you."

The man's face darkened, though his expression didn't change.

"Now I'm going to work. I've got bills to pay."

"I think your bill's about due."

Normally, the words might have made Grimsby chuckle in appreciation, but the man delivered them in a way that rendered laughing somehow impossible.

He did find the courage to be flippant, however.

"Oh, scary," he said, rolling his eyes. Though it took some effort. The man was impossibly tall, lean, and oddly terrifying. But he refused to let it show. "But you forgot to dramatically take off your sunglasses when you said it. Really deadened the punch line." He turned and stepped through the glass doors to the playroom.

The man started after him. "I'm not going to ask again—"

"Whoa," Grimsby said, holding out a hand. "Did you even read the sign?"

Mayflower scowled. "Sign?"

Grimsby pointed to the cardboard cutout of King Donald that

was fixed against the wall. The king, who had a waffle for a head for some reason, was holding out his royal scepter at about chest level. A sign on his chest read, YOU MUST BE THIS YOUNG TO ENTER. Grimsby had set the height himself, and it was just low enough to brush the top of his head.

Mayflower paused. "You're kidding."

"Sorry, it's not my rule," he said, pointing to King Donald. "It's the law of the land."

"You—"

"Law of the land!" he shouted, stepping over the threshold and throwing the door shut behind him. As he walked away, he glanced over his shoulder to see the silhouette of Mayflower in the glass of the door. Even through the frosted glass, the man's eyes seemed as steady as a rifle's scope.

Grimsby shuddered. What could he have wanted? He hadn't expected to ever hear from the Department again, unless it was to issue him a fine for misuse of his magic. Whatever Mayflower wanted, he was certain it would bring him nothing but trouble. Though a part of him did want to know more. Despite what he had told Mayflower, he'd like nothing more than to have another shot at joining the Department. But that was never going to happen.

Mansgraf had seen to that.

He shrugged the questions and doubts away and looked around the playroom. It was time to get to work.

TWO

MMDFK, A POOR ALPHABETISM FOR ANYTHING, LET alone a children's party restaurant, had been rezoned from an industrial location during its construction. What had once been a broad three-story building stacked high with boxes and pallets had been emptied, and within it had been constructed the abominable Food Kingdom of Mighty Magic Donald.

Concrete had been covered with rubberized tiles and fake grass. Electrical conduits had been boxed in with plywood painted to look like fortress turrets. The glass-paneled ceiling had been layered with gaudy paints the shades of primary and secondary colors. The gray light of the cold autumn day was marred into nauseating hues as it poured down over the Astroturf that filled the play area below.

Constructed at the center of the warehouse, likely by some architect or engineer who was either really hurting for business or clinically insane, was the Food Kingdom Castle. The castle was the reason parents drove to a nearly abandoned industrial park a half hour outside Boston and paid for food that tasted like recycled cardboard. And not the filling, double-corrugated stuff, either.

Surrounded by a ball-pit moat, the gingerbread battlements of the mad Food King's castle rose fifteen feet in the air. Ice-cream cone parapets rose in spirals nearly to the ceiling, their points adorned with a limp flag bearing MMDFK's logo: a pizza sporting a bejeweled crown. A drawbridge shaped like a half-eaten cookie extended over the moat, leading to the castle's inner sanctum.

But as Grimsby entered the kingdom, he saw the castle was under attack.

Children crawled over its battlements and stormed its bridge. They swam in the moat and clambered over the spring-mounted horses set into the ground, knocking down the costumed mannequins that formed the Food King's court. Chaos, anarchy, and treason in the Food King's ignoble realm.

Grimsby could not let this stand.

It was in his contract, after all.

He was the marshal of this realm, the spandex-clad enforcer of safety regulations, and, most of all, he was responsible for any harm that befell the kids in this room.

Fortunately, he was also a witch, and that was sometimes useful.

He took a breath to brace himself for what came next. He could show no fear, no hesitation, and most of all, no pride. You can't have pride and appropriately handle kids at the same time. It was some kind of universal, or perhaps cosmic, rule.

He bellowed out with his bracing breath, shouting, "Gentle-boys and ladygirls!"

The children stopped and dozens of tiny eyes turned from their ravishing of the Food Kingdom to this pink newcomer and his wings of tacos.

There was a pregnant silence, until Grimsby finally uttered, "Who wants to see some magic?"

The children roared, shrieked, and screamed in reply. Some odd child in the mix even trilled like a bird. They descended the battlements with frantic, graceless ease and rushed toward him over the fields of emerald plastic.

He stood steadfast as they charged him. Some skidded to a halt an acceptable few inches away. Others crashed straight into his legs. He managed to catch anyone who tripped or stumbled, and settled them around him in a growing semicircle of sticky hands and curious faces.

They were all talking, of course, whether at him, to one another, or just for the sake of it. There was no such thing as silence, not in the Food Kingdom.

He waved his avocado wand about, saying, "Children, children," over and over. He managed to draw numerous eyes and make many of the kids forget their mouths for a moment. Finally, when the room was as close to quiet as it might ever be, he spoke. "Which one of you is the birthday boy?"

A sizable chunk of a child stepped forward, shoving the smaller kids out of his way. He had a familiar monobrow and a prominent scowl line at the center of his shiny forehead. Together, they formed an upside-down *T* on his brow. He wore a white T-shirt emblazoned with a picture of his own face adorned with a digitally added party hat. Below it read the words HAPPY BIRTHDAY, RICHIE!

Richie crossed his plump arms and glared. "Which dildo wants to know?" he demanded.

Grimsby forced a confused smile, trying to maintain verbal stride. "Why, the Taco Fairy, of course. I perform magic for the esteemed King, Mighty Magic Donald, and all subjects in his kingdom, and I've come to wish you a happy birthday—"

"Boring!" Richie declared, drawing a smattering of giggles from the kids. He looked around, pleased with himself. "This whole place is boring! Boring as dildos!" he said.

More giggles.

There was a tug at Grimsby's skirts and he turned to see a young girl who was wearing an outfit very similar to his own, though her wings were much more tastefully made of something close to gossamer. If it were a contest of who wore it better, Grimsby would have lost, albeit barely.

"Mr. Taco Fairy," Little Miss Tutu said in a quiet voice, "what's dildos?"

Grimsby open and closed his mouth several times before he finally answered, "Ask your mother." He didn't really consider the implication of his suggestion until it was too late. He winced and hoped it would go unnoticed.

The girl nodded thoughtfully and stepped back into the crowd.

Meanwhile Richie had withdrawn some melted chocolate from his pocket and was consuming it with one sticky paw while glaring at Grimsby. "My mom thinks I'm just a kid. But I'm ten now. That's *two* numbers. I'm too old for this baby castle and the dildo fairy. And *way* too old for magic tricks."

Grimsby's face twisted uncomfortably at the imagery of such a fairy. As if the taco version wasn't disturbing enough. The wings alone . . . He shook his head. "Most definitely. Any ten-year-old should be bored of magic tricks."

"No doubt," Richie said. "Bored as dildos."

"Ah," Grimsby said, realizing what must be happening. Richie must have recently learned the word and, more important, that he wasn't supposed to use it. Thus, he felt the irresistible urge to find room for it in every sentence, as any young boy would. "Well, you'll be happy to hear that these aren't tricks. I happen to know *real* magic."

The children gasped and murmured among themselves, and Grimsby nodded around to them as though such whispers were only proper.

Richie's eyes only narrowed in doubt. "You mean you're a real witch?" he asked. "Is that why your skin is so ugly?" He pointed to the left side of Grimsby's neck.

Grimsby found himself subconsciously covering his scars with his hand. He felt them itch and burn nervously all the way down to his fingertips. "No. That's something else."

"What about your outfit? I didn't think witches wore such dumb clothes."

Grimsby shrugged. "Real witches can wear whatever they want."

Richie shook his head vigorously, his cheeks flapping. "Nah-uh! My uncle works at the Department, the one with witches and other creeps. He says they have to wear masks and suits or they go crazy."

"The Department of Unorthodox Affairs," Grimsby said with the same technical smile he had given the boy's mother. "And your uncle's only part right. The masks are practical, but the suits are voluntary."

"Then where's your mask?" Richie demanded.

The children all muttered their own doubts as to Grimsby's legitimacy. Well, some did. Others got bored and wandered off to fall into the ball-pit moat.

Grimsby tapped the abnormally large round spectacles on his face. "Masks can have many shapes. These are mine." It was true. The glasses were the only thing between him and peering into the Elsewhere.

"So without those you'd go crazy?" Richie asked.

"Eventually," Grimsby said. *If I lived long enough*, he added internally.

"Take them off!" a child in the back shouted.

Grimsby shook his head. A brief flicker of the Elsewhere flashed through his mind, and he shivered. "That would be . . . a bad idea. But don't worry, I can still do magic with them on." He began purposefully walking as he said, "Follow me!"

The children began swarming around him even before he started to move. They ran in circles, jumped up and down, and found other means of releasing their atomic levels of pent-up energy after having stood still for nearly two minutes.

Grimsby waded gently through them, trying to avoid knocking anyone down. In the whirling mass, he saw Little Miss Tutu fall beneath the stampede, like a little pink doll in a dryer filled with sticky bricks. He stooped down and parted the kids that might have stepped on her and hauled her up onto his hip. She was wide-eyed but unharmed aside from a small tear on one of her wings. Her eyes were brimming with tears and her lip was trembling dangerously. A meltdown was imminent.

"Here," Grimsby said, handing her the avocado wand, "why don't you take this? I'll bet you can use it better than I can."

Her eyes widened even more and her mouth fell into a shocked circle, brimming tears forgotten. She seized the wand and began waving it vigorously. She waved it at Richie and mumbled something about bubbles and trouble.

Grimsby found himself smiling as he carried her and shepherded the others to the courtyard of the plastic castle. They crossed the cookie drawbridge, the dozens of small feet like thunder on the hollow structure.

He had set up the courtyard scene over the weekend, and it had somehow remained mostly untouched by the kids. A half dozen mannequins, dressed as lords and ladies of Halloween surplus, stood along the walls overlooking two figures waiting in the courtyard. These two were dressed in cloth and rubber armor, one silver, the other black: two knights squaring off against each other in an eternal showdown, each daring the other to make the first move.

"Behold," Grimsby said, "the battle of the ages! Silver Knight versus Black Knight, good versus evil."

"Dildo versus cool guy!" Richie said.

Grimsby continued as if he hadn't been interrupted. "Today, I will bring them to life with magic, and we will see who triumphs!"

The kids made consonantless sounds of interest and excitement. Little Miss Tutu stopped wand waving for a moment, her wide eyes focused on the still and silent knights. Grimsby took the opportunity to set her down among the others and turned to his show.

He raised his hands dramatically in concentration.

He began to chant, keeping his tone measured to a simple beat, "Blackened steel and silver bright, when one and one two knights shall fight, who will triumph, dark or light?"

The mannequins shuddered, almost imperceptibly.

The kids stared in earnest, and even Richie failed to feign disinterest.

Grimsby grinned. "Come on," he said, "I need your help. Say it with me! 'Who will triumph, dark or light?'" He repeated the words a couple more times.

Within moments, the kids joined in. Though many of the younger children mangled the phrase, their hearts were in the right place even if their mouths were not quite up to the task. An avocado wand waved excitedly from somewhere in the crowd.

Grimsby made his arms start to shake, as though he were gathering all the power of the universe. But magic didn't run on universe juice.

He summoned his Impetus, feeling its warmth well up within him, like a font that enveloped his heart. It spread through his chest, surging with radiant energy.

He winced as it began to flow through his limbs. Where it touched the old, weathered burn scars that covered his left side, it began to sear. He spotted a few sparks leaping from the weathered scars. He pushed the pain away with practiced effort, driving the Impetus toward his other hand instead. It wasn't easy, like scooping water uphill, but he managed. He soon felt his right hand grow warm with Impetus, ready for his command.

He turned his focus to the Bind spells he had positioned all over the mannequin knights. He could sense them, like spider silk against his skin. He extended his Impetus toward the Binds, feeling his way through them until he found the first pair in the chain.

Then he did the only verbal part of the spell that was actually necessary: he muttered a single word.

"Bind."

And, at his word, the scene began.

The first pair of the numerous Binds he had placed flared to life. Thin blue strands of light, like crystalline spiderwebs, crossed between the runes, drawing them together, pulling on the mannequins like marionette strings.

The knights' swords rose in rickety salutes, the result of Binds between the knights' arms and the ceiling. Another pair of runes turned them first toward the statue of Mighty Magic Donald, next to the gathered nobles and children, and then, finally, to each other.

Grimsby pulled at the strands of his Impetus, plucking the Binds again and again, each time pulling new pairs, giving the knights a jerky semblance of life. If the children noticed the thin strands of glimmering magic, they didn't seem to care, instead focusing on the show.

The knights lunged forward, their wooden swords clattering against each other with a deafening crack that made the children wince. More blows, dealt by the Black Knight, lashed outward with reckless, crudely choreographed abandon. The Silver Knight parried them all.

The children clapped and cheered. Richie, and a few of the older kids gathered around him, shouted encouragement to the Black Knight. The rest simply cheered for the show.

The Black Knight then swung high, a cleaving blow, and the Silver Knight raised its blade to block it as it had the others. But as the blades ground against each other, the Black Knight reached into its armor, drawing a dagger.

"Look out, mister!" Little Miss Tutu shouted.

The Black Knight lashed the knife forth, sending the blade flying with another Bind, this one linked between the knife and the Silver Knight's stomach. The wooden blade drove deep and stuck, held by the tensed strand of magic.

The children gasped as the Silver Knight fell to his knees. Grimsby severed his Impetus to the thread between the knight's hand and sword, and the wooden weapon clattered to ground.

The Black Knight loomed over him, turning his sword downward in preparation for a killing stroke. That particular flourish had actually been the most difficult part of the whole show, but the collective gasp of the enthralled children made the many hours of trial and error worth it.

"Get up, get up!" they all shouted. Even Richie's gang of big kids had joined in. Everyone loves the underdog.

Except Richie, apparently.

The porcine lad was shouting, "Finish him! Fatality!" Again and again.

Then, as the Black Knight drove the blade down, the Silver Knight shifted to one side, drawing the knife from its own stomach as it did. The falling blade missed, and the Silver Knight drove the dagger up into the chin of the Black Knight.

The kids all drew in a hushed breath as both knights froze.

Then the Black Knight fell.

The kids roared in approval, clapping and shrieking and shouting so loudly that Grimsby winced.

"The Silver Knight wins!" he proclaimed.

More shouts and applause, but he turned to see Richie standing in front of him with his plump arms crossed and his lips drawn in a pout, his monobrow particularly thunderous and moody.

"I wanted the Black Knight to win," Richie said.

"Sorry," Grimsby said with some small measure of satisfaction to have disappointed the birthday boy, "but today belongs to the Silver Knight."

"It's my birthday," Richie said. "I get what I want. Make the Black Knight win."

Grimsby shook his head. "The good guy always wins," he said.

"Nah-uh! My dad says nice guys finish last and deserve it. Good guys are dumb. They never win."

Grimsby frowned. Richie was right, of course. Sometimes, maybe most times, good guys might not win. But that was in the real world. "They do in this Mighty Magic Kingdom, kid," he said.

"I said no!" Richie shrieked.

"Well, when it's called Mighty Magic *Richie's* Food Kingdom, then you can be the boss. Behead the Silver Knight. Enslave the mannequins. Lead a reign of diabetic tyranny. Until then, the verdict belongs to King Donald." He turned and shouted at the statue above the play palace, "What say you, Your Majesty?" Then, under his breath he muttered the catalyst word one last time. *"Bind."*

The last spell should have made the statue nod. But nothing happened. Not even a stoic, waffle-headed tilt of his crown. The statue remained motionless.

The kids all waited, staring at King Donald, but he remained still, as though inanimate. While that was fortunately true, it wasn't a part of the show.

And it really killed Grimsby's momentum.

Richie puffed out a breath in a snort. "He's not even a real king! He's just a stupid statue!"

The others murmured in agreement.

Grimsby's frown deepened. Had his Bind failed? They had occasionally broken or faded, especially with age, but he hadn't had one fail altogether since he first learned the spell all those years ago. To date it was one of three spells he could manage without a grimoire. It was practically a reflex to him.

And it had just failed.

He felt something small and tense in his gut twinge, something not unlike the pain in his scars. His mind assailed him with memories of his final trial to join the Department, to become an Auditor.

He had failed then, too.

"I—uh—" He stumbled, staring at the king as though something might happen any second. Nothing did.

"Uh, uh, uh!" Richie shouted at Grimsby, likely having sensed his weakness. "Stutter Fairy is more like! Go cry into your dildos, Stutter Fairy!"

Grimsby shook his head; he'd have to figure it out later. The kids would tear him apart if he let Richie get any more momentum. He turned back to the boy. "You really shouldn't use that word in front of—"

He was interrupted as the birthday boy suddenly clawed the glasses off his face, throwing them to the ground. Richie said something snide, but Grimsby couldn't hear him. Him or anything else. At least, not anything else in the waking world.

His heart skipped. His mask was gone. The one thin layer between him and the Elsewhere. He screwed his eyes shut on instinct but felt the undeniable urge to open them.

When he did, the world had changed.

THREE ✳

Suddenly, without his mask to shield him, Grimsby was surrounded by the Elsewhere.

Gone was the familiar plastic and grease of Mighty Magic Donald's Food Kingdom.

Instead, he stood in a ruin. Where the false castle had been, there were now crumbling battlements of weathered stone. The mannequin court had become elegant watching statues that moved in the corners of his sight. On their clothes and joints he could see the small blue pinpricks of his Bind runes, waiting to be empowered by his Impetus.

High above, much higher than Grimsby remembered the room being, loomed a solemn statue of a king, uniquely unchanged among the rest of the setting, like a giant's timeless and long-forgotten toy abandoned in a ruined wasteland.

Gone was the colorful skylight. Instead there was only a cracked, glassless dome, like some great greenhouse that had been shattered. Beyond was a cloudless red sky and a black sun. Or was it a moon? Light seemed to emanate from everything except the looming orb above. Instead, it seemed to devour the light, like a dark, cosmic maw.

In the distance, Grimsby could make out some kind of broken cityscape of crumbling buildings, shrouded in ashen mist, like a ruin that had been shelled of all life. Except it wasn't lifeless. Figures moved among the distant structures. Some were flying things the size of hounds. Others were large enough that they were silhouetted against the red sky as they slipped between towers. Tall, skeletal figures with limbs long enough to claw out the stars, if the scarlet above had held any.

Grimsby stood in shock, the sudden surrealness that was the Elsewhere bearing down on him.

He told himself it wasn't real, and in one sense it wasn't. But in the rest of his senses, it *was* real. Very real. Without his mask, he could see it and the creatures that roamed it.

More important, they could see him. Even though he was only partially within the Elsewhere, they could now reach him.

They could *get* him.

He needed to return before it was too late. He wasn't prepared to defend himself, not here, not now.

He looked around wildly, searching for his mask.

The children were gone, replaced by small, flitting shadows. They were formless, nearly shapeless Figments, hardly more than passing smoke. He could barely tell where one started and another ended, let alone which of them might have been the thief who stole his mask.

Then he saw something. A glimmer of gold and glass. His glasses. His mask.

The shadow that held it was drifting away, floating over the moat of frozen blood that surrounded the ruined castle. Grimsby gave chase, sidestepping the other Figments as best he could. Though he could hardly see or feel them, he knew his body was still in the same world as them. The children they represented could still be harmed by him if he wasn't careful. But caution came with a steep price: time. And time in the Elsewhere was a deadly thing.

He had to act. Now, before something caught wind or sight of him.

He called forth his Impetus, feeling it flow through him. This time it was no mere warmth, but a cauldron of fire that burned in his chest. He could see the flames seethe forth and wreathe his body, blue-green fire that harmed neither cloth nor flesh.

However, when they reached the scars of his left side, they sparked and hissed orange, spewing gouts of smoke and ash. He tried to redirect them as he had before, but the Elsewhere made his Impetus too powerful to finely control. The eerie flames turned red as they reached his scars, igniting his clothes in outlines that perfectly matched his marred flesh, like hot branding irons beneath his skin. He recoiled on instinct, his Impetus flickering as he lost concentration. The fire in his apartment that had left its mark, so long ago, was suddenly hot against his face.

He heard his mother's screams.

He wailed and forced the memories away, clutching at his head as though it might split apart. He could feel his Impetus draining away as his scars burned and smoldered. He ignored the feeling, instead focusing on the glimmer of his mask. The shadow that held it was climbing the broken drawbridge of the castle, making its way toward the inner sanctum.

Richie's umbral form was too far away for Grimsby to reach him, let alone place a Bind rune on him. The only two other spells he could manage would be either useless or too slow. He groaned in frustration, wishing desperately that his magic wasn't so limited. Then glimmers of blue light caught his eye.

Richie had no Bind rune on him, but nearly every nearby mannequin did, on either its body or clothing.

Grimsby spotted one on the castle walls, a guardsman in rubber armor. Faint lines of blue light linked its runes to the castle gate, where he normally made the mannequin patrol, but the runes were idle and dull, the strands loose like cobwebs caught in the wind.

Grimsby quickly moved, putting Richie's shadow directly between himself and the mannequin, then focused on its Binds. He took a deep breath, feeling his chest swell like bellows on a forge, before kneeling and placing his palm firmly on the ground. After a moment's concentration, a glowing Bind rune formed under his hand, looking like it had been painted on the wind-scoured stone in molten cobalt.

Grimsby focused the full extent of his Impetus into his fingers, stretching them over the rune. Within seconds, their tips burst into unearthly flame.

"*Bind*," he said in a choked voice of gritty fear.

Thick bands of azure flared to life between the new rune and the runes on the mannequin, making it jerk forward and fall from the wall. It skittered across the floor like it was being hauled by a fighter jet, moving directly toward Richie.

In the distance, one of the towering skeletal figures turned its gaze toward Grimsby, as though it heard his lone word. It stopped its ceaseless wandering and began striding toward him, crossing what seemed like miles with every step. Its motions made the earth churn and tremble. Its silhouette darkened the scarlet sky.

Grimsby tore his gaze away and focused on the spell, throttling the Impetus that flowed through his palm and into the rune just enough to slow the mannequin before it collided with the amorphous shadow. He then tightened the Bind once more, like a fisherman would with a catch on the line, and the mannequin's limbs ensnared the shadow before they were both dragged toward Grimsby.

The skeletal giant drew closer, its strides paced like it was running through thick oil. Its arms, hundreds of feet long, extended out toward Grimsby, carrying with them a chill, dry wind.

The mannequin and shadow came to a grinding halt at his feet, the numerous small Bind runes all competing to press into the larger rune on the ground. Grimsby spotted his mask, twisted and bent in the grip of the shadow, and quickly wrested it away.

The skeletal titan was reaching for him, its hands larger than the world, ready to wrap around him and snuff him out. Without hesitation, he shoved the warped spectacles onto his face.

The Elsewhere vanished.

The colossal figure was nowhere to be seen, though Grimsby felt a chill reach through him in a sudden wave. He was back in Mighty Magic Donald's Food Kingdom, surrounded by aghast children, standing over Richie, who was sobbing hysterically, pinned beneath a dime-store mannequin in nickel-store armor.

The Bind spell was crushing the boy beneath the dummy so tightly into the ground that his face was growing red to the sound of creaking wood. Grimsby waved the spell away, and it dissipated with a snap, leaving the mannequin to roll onto the cold stone.

Only then did he notice the scorched patches in his tutu and through his shirt beneath where his knotted scars had leaked power from his Impetus. It had burned broad, ugly shapes through the cloth, leaving his skin blackened with soot, the gnarled, grotesque swathes of scar tissue seething with painful heat.

Now freed, Richie squealed and rolled over, crawling desperately away. He scrambled through the ring of frightened and enthralled children, yelping in fear at the sight of every costumed figure. However, he was in such a rush that he didn't see the ball-pit moat and plunged face-first into it.

Nobody laughed; they only stared at Grimsby.

He forced his shaking limbs to freeze. He had to stay calm in order to keep them calm. Though that was easier said than done when his heart was coursing with adrenaline and his clothes were still smoldering.

He took a shaky breath and went to Richie, reaching down to

help pull him from the pit, but the boy only scrabbled frantically up the other side and sprinted through the frosted-glass doors and into the restaurant.

Grimsby watched him go, then looked around at the other children. There was a long moment of silence, and he felt the irresistible urge to break it, even if it meant saying something stupid.

So, with a wave of his hands, something stupid he said.

"Ta-da . . . !"

FOUR ✳

I SWEAR TO GOD I OUGHT TO BURN THIS PLACE TO THE ground!" Richie's monobrowed mother screamed.

Grimsby winced under her verbal barrage. She was so close to him and so venomously angry that she was spitting with nearly every syllable. He hesitated to wipe the accumulation off his glasses, worried it might prod her to redouble her efforts. A small cluster of gathered parents stood behind her, not quite as furious but upset nonetheless.

"I'll tie you to a damn stake myself and use your fruity outfit as kindling!" she continued.

Grimsby shuddered at the thought. He hardly remembered the fire that had left him with his scars, but he remembered the pain. Both that of seared flesh and that of a lost mother. He felt his own anger begin to build within him, but he pressed it down.

The woman was angry, and she had fair right to be. Richie had been out of line, but Grimsby's reaction, while necessary, was only made so by his own incompetence.

Still, he felt like fifteen minutes enduring the woman's shrieks was fair repentance for his actions. Mother Monobrow apparently did not agree.

Her words faded to a furious blur in Grimsby's ringing ears. He glanced over at Carla, his face pleading for her to intervene. His manager looked up for a brief moment from the stack of papers she had busied herself with, saw Grimsby's gaze, and hurriedly returned to her work.

Maybe she figured he couldn't see that the papers were blank.

He was on his own, then. So be it.

"Ma'am," he said, speaking for the first time since she had begun her tirade, "I think that's enough."

He saw her mouth curl into a bitter smirk, as though she had been waiting for him to speak up. "How dare you?" she demanded. "I will decide when it is enough!"

"Because you're so emotionally removed from the situation?" Grimsby said.

She scoffed and took a half step back as though he had struck her. "You *creep*. You think just because you can wave your hands about and make some sparkles happen that you're better than me? Look at you; look at this place." She gestured all around. "You're nothing. You're not even human."

He bit back the first few replies that came to mind. "Ma'am, that's inappropriate."

"I don't care what's appropriate!" the mother said. "It's my child; I'm not obliged to be reasonable."

There was a buzz of agreement from the crowd.

Mother Monobrow seemed spurred on by the others. "What do you have to say for yourself?"

Grimsby felt his stomach twist. They were right. He had made a mistake. He had to own up to it.

He stood there and said the only thing he could say. "I'm sorry. I panicked and made the wrong decision."

Mother Monobrow scoffed with disgust. "You think an apology means anything to me? Nothing you can say or do will ever make up for what you've done."

Grimsby paused, his brow furrowing; then he asked her, "Then why are we having a conversation?"

She balked at that, her righteous tirade stumbling for a moment. Behind her, the chime to the restaurant's front doors went off, but the crowd was too thick for Grimsby to see who had entered.

"I want justice!" she finally said.

A woman's voice cut through the roiling crowd like a knife of ice. "Then perhaps we can lend a hand," she said.

The crowd turned, and the room fell into a cemetery silence.

Standing in the doorway were two figures, dressed in sharply pressed and well-fitted suits of gray. They wore featureless white masks of hardened Kevlar that hid their faces, save for their eyes.

"Auditors," someone murmured.

Grimsby felt the blood drain from his face and race into his accelerating heart to hide. Auditors were the enforcement agents of the Department. Government-sanctioned witches who dealt with Unorthodox affairs. If a Usual murdered another Usual, you called the police. If either party was an Unorthodox, you called the Department and its Auditors. And there was only one Unorthodox in the building: him.

His mind raced. Had someone called them? Had the Auditors come in response to what had happened with Richie? It seemed too soon for that. Maybe they knew he was toeing the line his low-level license allowed with his magic. Had he violated the law that badly? Or maybe that man, the one who looked like an abandoned scarecrow, had called them after Grimsby's less-than-cooperative responses.

What was his name? Mayday? Manfred?

Grimsby shook his head; the name hardly mattered. What mattered was that the Department was here. And they could only be here for him.

His beating heart was stretching his veins thin with blood and adrenaline, but he had no way to use it. He couldn't run, and he certainly wasn't going to fight. That would just make things much worse, assuming he even survived. He could do nothing, nothing at all. All he could do was try to remain calm, a task adrenaline was not ideal for.

Mother Monobrow finally seemed to gather herself. "Yes, um, good. You're here," she said, regarding the unreadable masks with apprehension. "This *creep* assaulted my boy with some devilish spell, and I want him arrested!"

As the woman said the word *creep*, the second Auditor, a tall and muscular man, tensed. The female Auditor, however, seemed implacable. She only nodded after the mother had finished speaking.

"I see," she said finally. "And you want to take this to trial?"

"I'll take this as far as it can go!" Mother Monobrow said. "I'll get a damn billboard if I have to. Justice for Richie!"

"Of course, ma'am. I'll even file my report with a priority flag. It shouldn't take longer than a few months to process."

"A few months?"

"Quite fast for misdemeanors. So long as the defending witch"— she gestured to Grimsby—"wasn't acting in self-defense, it should wrap up only a few weeks after that."

Mother Monobrow faltered. "Self-defense?"

"Well, naturally. If the defendant was acting to, oh, I don't know, say, recover a mask that had been stolen, it would be firmly within the limitations of the Statute of Unorthodox Liberties. In fact, it would then be the prosecution who would be on trial for assault. Perhaps even attempted murder."

Mother Monobrow's face was so white that the thick makeup around her eyes looked like a clown's face paint. "Murder?"

The Auditor nodded, withdrawing a notebook and scribbling. "And since the boy in question is only a minor, responsibility for the event would then pass on to his legal guardian. The court might even find it reasonable to take him into government-mandated care for a time while the proceedings took place, to ensure that guardian was of sound mind."

"Oh." The word was the same shape as Mother Monobrow's mouth.

"Listen to me, droning on," the Auditor finally said, her voice sounding like she must have been smiling. She turned to Grimsby. "Come along, now, sir. We've got a report to file."

"Wait!" Mother Monobrow said. "Maybe I was a bit hasty. Let my inner momma bear get the best of me."

"You did?" the Auditor said, tilting her head. Despite her inflection, it wasn't a question.

"Yes, I think so. No one was hurt. Perhaps we'd better call this water and let it go under the bridge."

"Perhaps we'd better," the Auditor agreed. She turned her attention to the rest of the parents, letting her gaze linger on each of them. "Does anyone else have an incident they wish to report?"

More grave silence.

"Oh good. Have a wonderful day." Her tone indicated that it was time to part ways, but she didn't move. She simply waited.

The Auditor behind her held open the door for the next few minutes as parents hurriedly gathered their children and ushered them out. Before long, MMDFK was nearly empty, save for Carla, Grimsby, and the two Auditors.

The female Auditor spoke again, this time her voice not quite so professional. "Miss, may I borrow your employee for a few minutes? We need to speak with him."

Grimsby frowned. Without the air of cold authority frosting off her voice, she almost sounded familiar. Like the tune of a song he'd forgotten.

Carla nodded hurriedly. "Yes, of course. If you need anything, I'll just be . . . here." She shut tight her office door. A moment later, Grimsby heard the dead bolt click.

"That's a bit better," the woman said.

He stared at her hard for a moment before his eyes widened with recognition. "Rayne?" he asked, his chest suddenly feeling like it was a hornets' nest.

"Call me Auditor Bathory, please," Rayne said. She looked around for a moment, her piercing blue eyes visible through the eyeholes of the otherwise blank mask. "You work here?" she asked in a measured tone.

Grimsby became suddenly and acutely aware that he was still wearing taco-shell wings and a tutu, and that it wasn't even in good shape since his last spell had burned out several holes in the fabric. He unconsciously tried to smooth out the fabric but only succeeded in brushing small puffs of ash into the still air. He opened his mouth, but the hundred excuses that flooded his mind all came out as a single, stuttered, "U-unfortunately."

The man beside Rayne snorted. "It suits you," he said. His voice was also recognizable, though it took Grimsby a few moments longer.

"Wilson," he said, not trying to keep the disgust from his voice.

"*Auditor* Hives, please," Hives said, flaunting the title. Grimsby could hear that damned smirk of his through his mask.

Grimsby looked between Hives and Rayne for a moment, his stomach dropping. "So you two are . . . partners?" he asked.

Hives began to reply, but Rayne cut him off. "Yes," she said. "Assistant Director Grieves assigned us both to come interview you." She withdrew a pen and pad from the inner pocket of her jacket.

Grimsby's nauseating jealousy was overshadowed only by his dubiousness. "Interview me? Why? Are they making a documentary on what not to do during Department training?"

"Not . . . exactly," Rayne said. She made a few notes, the pen moving gracefully in her limber fingers. She had played piano for him once, and it had been masterful. "Mr. Grimsby, could you please tell us where you were yesterday?"

"Where I was?" he asked. "Why?"

Hives took a step forward, lording his size over Grimsby's just like he always had. "Just answer the questions, Grimsby."

He scowled up at Hives. "No, I don't think I will." The Auditor was nearly a foot taller than him and twice as wide, but he had learned back during training that Wilson had little beyond bulk to his name.

He had also learned that bulk still counted for a lot.

"I could make you," Hives said simply.

Grimsby smiled. It was a genuine smile of amusement.

Even before his employment at MMDFK, he had been bruised and battered by Hives and other classmates during their shared apprenticeship. His time in the Food Kingdom had made that seem like a distant, fond memory.

"No," he said simply, "you couldn't."

Hives's eyes narrowed through his mask. "You wanna bet?"

He shrugged at Hives. "One of two things would happen, big guy. The first is you get embarrassed by a guy in a tutu. The second, and admittedly more likely, is that you beat up a guy in a tutu. Neither paints you in a particularly flattering light. More importantly, neither one of which ends up with you making me do a thrice-cursed thing."

Even through his mask, Grimsby could see Hives's eyes bulge with anger. But before he could say another word, Rayne stepped in.

"Grimshaw," Rayne said in her earnest voice. "Please."

Grimsby turned away from Hives, although it took a while. The guy seemed to take up half the room. He locked eyes with Rayne and saw there was something else in her stare. Something she wanted to tell him but couldn't.

He sighed, trying to think of even a single time when Rayne

had been wrong about something, but not one came to mind. "I was here," he finally said. "Mostly. Monday through Friday and every other Saturday I'm here from nine to nine."

She noted this on her writing pad. "Are there any cameras here that can confirm that?"

"Cameras? Of course not. The Food King's 'treasury' isn't exactly overflowing. But there's dozens of parents and twice as many kids."

"Any of them witches?" she asked.

Grimsby scoffed. "No self-respecting witch would step foot in here."

Hives snorted. "And yet you work here."

"And yet I work here," Grimsby confirmed without looking at him. "Self-respect is expensive."

"What about other Unorthodox?" Rayne asked. "Someone who can verify your information?"

"I said no. But there's at least fifty Usuals that could."

Hives leaned over to Rayne. "Usuals can't see anything that matters, and even an Unorthodox would be questionable. Their testimonies wouldn't mean a thing to the investigation."

"Investigation?" Grimsby asked. "What investigation?"

Rayne took a deep breath. "Mr. Grimsby, do you know a woman named Samantha Mansgraf?"

Grimsby's gut twisted, and his face matched it. "You know I do."

"Please elaborate."

"Why? I didn't tell the other guy anything. Why should I tell you?"

Rayne frowned. "What other guy?"

"I don't remember his name. Something about flowers. He said he was working with the Department. Asked me earlier about Mansgraf."

Her face was unreadable behind the mask, but Grimsby could tell that something was off.

"For completion's sake, let's just get your information down. Please elaborate your relationship with Samantha Mansgraf."

Grimsby sighed. "She was our final administrator when we tried to join the Department. It was just us three left from a class of fifteen. She passed you and Biceps over there." He gestured to Hives.

"But not you?" Biceps asked, his tone smug.

Grimsby felt a flare of compressed anger. "You know full well she didn't. She had me disbarred altogether." His hands curled into fists tightly enough that the burn scars on his left arm grew taut. "She ruined my—"

"Mr. Grimsby," Rayne interjected, cutting him off altogether. "Are you aware Samantha Mansgraf was murdered last night?"

The hard shards of anger that filled his guts shattered, leaving his innards dusted with cold, deflated fear. "What?"

Hives stepped forward. "Rayne! That information is classified and part of an ongoing investigation."

Rayne turned toward Hives, locking down his gaze for a long moment.

"Her body was found this morning, on the other side of this very warehouse district," she said without looking away from Hives, as though daring him to stop her from speaking. "Do you know anything about that?"

Realization struck Grimsby like a baseball bat to the back of his head and a blowtorch to his spine. That was why the Department had such a sudden interest in him.

They were here to see if he was involved with the murder.

"Of course not! I would never—I could never—" He found the words missing from his tongue as his mind reeled. Mansgraf dead? How? She was the oldest and most venerated witch in the Department. And also likely the deadliest by a wide margin. Who would want to kill her?

Even more terrifying, who could have?

"Mr. Grimsby," Rayne said, tearing the paper from her note-pad, "we'll be in touch." She held out her hand to him in a professional gesture, eyes still locked with Hives's; he seemed unwilling or unable to look away.

Grimsby, still stunned, mechanically reached out to shake her hand. Her skin was distant electricity that any other day would have made his heart race, but at the moment his heart was already working overtime.

It was running for its life.

Mansgraf dead, and Department Auditors here questioning him. That meant only one thing.

He was a suspect.

"Thank you for your time, Mr. Grimsby," Rayne said.

When he looked up, she was staring at him now. There was something in her blue, nearly teal, eyes, even behind her mask. Some kind of fear or warning. He had never known Rayne to be afraid of anything, and that made her fear infectious.

Hives was massaging the back of his head, grumbling and apparently having lost whatever staring match for dominance the two Auditors had been having. "Come on," he said. "We need to report back."

"Of course," Rayne said. "Mr. Grimsby, good luck with your endeavors."

Grimsby's head was pounding and spinning and reeling all at once, so much so that it was a miracle when he managed a nod.

Him, a murder suspect for the death of the most respected witch in the Department. A witch he was on record for having bad blood with. And to top it off, he had no way of corroborating an alibi for where he had been when she was murdered. In fact, he had been close by and had freely admitted it.

He numbly watched Hives and Rayne leave and load into one of the sleek black Department cars with no mirrors and impossibly dark windows. He watched them drive off until he was standing alone in the restaurant and for several minutes more before he realized there was something in his hand.

It was a piece of paper.

He opened his clenched grip to see it was the kind of paper in Rayne's notepad. She must have slipped it to him when they shook hands. How had he not noticed? Probably because he had just had a two-ton pile of life-changing, and possibly life-shortening, bricks dropped on his head.

He flattened the crumpled note and unfolded it. It was damp from the sweat of his own palm. It read simply:

Be careful, the Department is out for blood on this one. Don't resist, don't be suspicious, and please, please don't be guilty.

—R.

"Puppy dogs' tails," he mumbled to himself. "I hate Tuesdays."

FIVE ✳

GRIMSBY'S GUT WAS A MIXED STORM OF EMOTIONS. He felt like lying on the ground and curling into a ball. He felt like punching a wall. He felt like breaking something beautiful.

But mostly, he just felt like crap.

The last hour had been a whirlwind of confusion, fear, and pain, and he needed a break.

"Grimsby?" Carla said, poking her head from her office door. "Are the Auditors gone?"

"Yeah."

"Good." She breathed a sigh of relief, then looked at the clock. "We've only got an hour until the next party arrives. I want you to clean up the bathrooms and the castle and—and Jesus, clean yourself up while you're at it."

He took a deep breath. He wanted to scream and throw something heavy at her, but where else could he make a living on his magic? Instead, he only said, "Yeah. Fine."

"And don't forget to water down that disinfectant; last time you used too much. I'm not made of money. Oh, and—" Carla continued to call after him, but he tuned her out.

He made his way to the men's restroom and let the door slam shut behind him, blotting out her voice to a muffled mumbling. He went to the sink, leaning on the cold porcelain and staring into the hard mirror. He pushed down the natural anxiety he felt around the reflections. Mirrors were about as close to the Elsewhere as they were to the real world. But as long as he was careful, he would be fine.

He looked at his face and realized what a mess he was. His dark hair was short enough that it was usually not a hygienic concern, but right now it looked like someone had half skinned a black cat and glued it to his head. His burning scars had scorched through both T-shirt and tutu, leaving several patches of skin bare along his left shoulder and arm. In the gaps, ash had painted his gnarled skin a sickly shade of gray. His eyes were red and bleary, each with a line of semiclean skin that cut through the ash on his cheeks. He realized that at some point he had been crying. Probably in front of Rayne, no less.

He would have been embarrassed if he had any room left inside.

"Odd's Bodkin, Grimsby," he cursed himself. "Get it together."

He ran the tap and splashed cold water on his face. It came away in a murky gray color. He grabbed a handful of paper towels and dampened them to start cleaning off the ash. It was some minutes and many handfuls of paper later before they came away mostly clean. He looked vaguely more human, even if he didn't feel it.

Just as he had scooped the blackened paper towels into the garbage, the door to the restroom swung open, the sudden creak of its hinges shattering the hushed silence.

He looked over his reflection's shoulder to see the skeletal man—Mayflower, that was his name. His narrow face was gaunt, shadowed, and thunderous. Grimsby expected that the man wasn't pleased with how their last conversation had ended.

Mayflower stood for a moment, regarding Grimsby through dark glasses.

Grimsby felt his already tense nerves fire with annoyance. "I guess I shouldn't have said Long John in the mirror three times," he said.

The man bared his teeth but didn't smile. Maybe the joke had slipped between the half inch of space between his head and the ceiling.

"Great show today," Mayflower said.

Grimsby rolled his eyes and felt his shoulders dip. And he had thought the harassment was over. "What are you doing here?" he asked.

"I haven't decided yet."

Grimsby didn't like the ominous tone he had spoken with. "Who the jabberwock are you?"

"I told you."

"You lied to me."

"Did I?"

"Yeah. Those Auditors had no idea that you had been here. And come to think of it, your suit looks like it was salvaged from a time traveler's dumpster. You're not Department, so who are you?" He glared hard at the man in the mirror.

He watched in the reflection as Mayflower opened one side of his jacket, revealing the shoulder holster of a firearm against his side.

Grimsby felt a sharp pang of shock. He whirled around, pressing the small of his back against the cold porcelain sink. He forced himself to stay still, although he felt his heart already rattling his ribs.

Mayflower seemed to linger, making certain Grimsby had seen the weapon.

He lifted his eyes from the holster to Mayflower's face. "Who are you?"

"My name is Leslie Mayflower," he said. "Some call me the Huntsman."

Grimsby sucked in a sharp breath in instant fear.

"The Huntsman's not real. He's a myth."

Mayflower said nothing, and it was the most convincing thing he could have done.

Grimsby had been told stories about the Huntsman by his mother. Sometimes they were to help him sleep. Other times, they were to make him behave.

The Huntsman was sometimes a hero and sometimes a monster.

But he was always a killer.

"The Huntsman—he has to be a myth."

"I sometimes wish I was."

Something in the man's eyes told Grimsby that he wasn't lying. Whether or not what he said was true, he believed it to be true. And he had a gun, which offered a certain layer of practical indisputability to his claim.

"Wh-what do you want?" he asked.

"Samantha Mansgraf."

Grimsby frowned as confusion was mixed into his fear, creating a cocktail that was growing all too familiar. "Maybe you didn't hear the news. She's dead."

"I know. What do you know about her death?"

"What? Nothing! Why does everyone assume I know something?"

Mayflower withdrew a photograph from his pocket. He held it out, revealing something that looked like impressionist art done in red and black on gray.

Grimsby took it and looked closely. "Is this a riddle or something?"

"You tell me. You did Auditor training. Read it."

"Read what?" Grimsby began; then he looked closer. The lines had a rhythm to them, some kind of system. It took him a moment to recognize it—ogham, the old stone-writing method. He wouldn't have noticed if Mayflower hadn't said anything. "I—I can't make it out. Been a while."

"Two words. *Kill Grimsby.*"

Grimsby felt his body grow numb, aside from the thousands of needles that suddenly seemed to try to escape from his veins. "Wh-what?"

"Written in Mansgraf's blood by her own hand with her dying breath," Mayflower said. Then he drew his gun. The weapon looked old, like it had been forged in another century, in a time when the world was simpler and colder. "This is loaded with cold-forged, blessed-silver, hollow-point rounds," he said. "It can fulfill her last request."

Grimsby stared numbly at the weapon in the Huntsman's grip. As frightened as he was, his brain fixated only on one thing. "H-hollow-point rounds?"

It hardly seemed the time for such a thought, but he was a little proud nonetheless.

That pride evaporated when Mayflower sighed and leveled the gun at his heart. "My partner's dying wish was for me to kill you. Give me one good reason not to."

Grimsby's grip tightened on the sink as the world seemed to start spinning. He tried to say words in a heart-wrenching plea, but they came out less eloquently than he intended.

"I'm—uh—me—good! Grimsby?"

The room was growing dark. His head felt like it was spinning so fast that it might float away. It was all very inconvenient.

The Huntsman loomed over him, the barrel of his weapon big enough to swallow the world. Grimsby stared into its depths.

Then, suddenly, he was staring at the ceiling.

A moment later, he was staring at nothing at all.

SIX

MAYFLOWER STARED DOWN AT THE UNCONSCIOUS punk in his tattered pink tutu and foam taco-shell wings. Then he aimed his gun at the boy's heart.

But it felt oddly heavy. He was surprised to find his hand was shaking.

This was the guy who had killed Mansgraf?

He shook his head. There was no way. He had seen Mansgraf torch fourteen men in as many seconds. She'd killed a revenant using the silver fillings in her own teeth. He once watched her strangle a vampire to death with its own severed hand.

And she'd been killed by a kid in a tutu? A kid wearing foam wings? A kid who had passed out at the mere threat of death?

It was impossible.

And yet her last words, written in her lifeblood, flashed before Mayflower's eyes. Long, ragged red streaks in a script as dead as his partner.

Kill Grimsby.

Her last request. Why else ask if not to avenge her death? What reason could she have had?

He shook his head. Something was off.

He couldn't trust his instincts, not like he used to, but they told him something was wrong. Very wrong. And this time he was inclined to believe them.

"Goddamn it," he muttered. Things had just gotten more complicated.

He longed for the days when things were simply monsters and slaying. Black-and-white. But that was a long time ago. Now everything was more muddled gray. He was starting to think maybe it always had been; he just couldn't see it.

Not until after Mary died.

He growled and shook his head. He had hoped to shake out the memories, but they just settled to the bottom of his mind instead, like shards of glass floating in a whiskey bottle.

He needed time to figure things out. But he didn't have it. The Department already had an interest in Grimsby. It wouldn't be long until they deciphered Mansgraf's message themselves. Especially after the kid had blabbed to them about seeing him. If they took him in before Mayflower could find out the truth of things, he'd either never get the chance to avenge Mansgraf, or some punk would take false blame for her death.

This really complicated things, and he hated when things were complicated.

His pocket began to buzz. He holstered his gun and drew his phone instead, flipping it open and growling at the confounded device as he fumbled to press the button to answer.

"Yeah?"

"Mayflower," Finley's slightly husky voice chimed over the tinny speaker. "I've got something you might be interested in."

He grunted. Finley was a Department tech who owed Mayflower some favors. A lot of favors, actually. She had been the one who had given him Grimsby's info from the Department files. She was a good kid, and he hated to cash in with something like this.

She could get burned for it if she wasn't careful. Maybe even flagged. But he had little choice. All he could do was try to settle this quickly.

"Spill," he said, nudging Grimsby's arm with his boot. The kid had some strange scars that marred his skin, like old, old burns. He seemed too young for scars so old. Somehow they had burned through his outfit, leaving it a mangled mess.

"I've scrounged up some footage of Mansgraf over the last few days. Nothing major, just street-cam vid."

"And?"

"And there's something missing."

He waited. "Are you going to make me guess?"

"No, we'd be here awhile. In all these clips, she's got a suitcase with her. Simple, black. The most recent one dates to maybe an hour or two before her death."

He grunted and waited for Finley to continue.

"Well, there was no suitcase found at the scene."

He frowned. "You think whoever, whatever got her took it?"

"Maybe," she said. "It's hard to say."

"I'll keep an eye out for it."

"Les," she said, her voice hushed, "there's something else."

"Tell me, Finley."

"I—I shouldn't be telling you this. Hell, I shouldn't even know it myself. But I think it's important."

He waited quietly. He wouldn't push her to give him the information. If it was as sensitive as she suggested, it could end her career to pass it along. Maybe worse.

"The Department has been trying to keep it quiet, but . . . Mansgraf had been black-flagged."

"What?" Mayflower demanded. "For how long?"

Black flags were reserved for Department Unorthodox who had gone rogue. Top-priority security liabilities and threats. He had hunted down a few himself. Hell, so had Mansgraf. They were often an alive-or-dead kind of deal, and more often the latter than the former.

"Nearly two weeks. Department's kept it real quiet."

"Hell," Mayflower muttered. This changed things. Again. If Mansgraf had been black-flagged, that would have made her hunted by both the Department and whoever got her. Assuming they weren't the same party. She was on the run, with no allies, and God knew what on her heels.

She had been alone.

And she'd died for it.

He felt his teeth grinding before he realized he was clenching his jaw. She should have come to him. He could have helped.

Except he'd told her not to. They had been the last words he'd spoken to her. He'd made her promise to leave him alone, and she had. Even though it meant her death.

It was just one more death on his hands.

"Goddamn it," he whispered, so quietly that he wasn't sure he'd spoken at all. Mansgraf should have come to him, promises be damned. She'd needed his help, and he would have given it. Every damn time. Although maybe she didn't because his help wouldn't make the difference.

He caught a glimpse of himself in the bathroom mirror. The water-spotted glass was not flattering. When had he gotten so old? Hell, when was the last time he'd eaten? The man staring back at him looked like he was halfway through being embalmed. The Huntsman, the one some people still whispered about—he was nowhere to be found.

Maybe that's why Mansgraf hadn't come to him for help. Maybe she thought the Huntsman was already dead.

Maybe she was right.

Mayflower shook his head. Time to doubt later. Time to grieve later. Time to work now. "Do you know why she was flagged?"

"Not exactly. Something to do with an operation out in Salem. Some kind of recovery op. I'm working on the details."

"Don't," Mayflower cautioned. "You've stuck out your neck far enough."

"True," she agreed. "So why stop now?"

"Finley, I don't want you getting flagged, too."

"I'll be careful. If it makes you feel better, I can *not* tell you what I find. But I'm gonna dig until I find it, one way or another. I'll die of curiosity otherwise."

He shook his head. She was a smart kid. Too smart for her own good.

"Just be careful," Mayflower said. "Keep me in the loop. If you need my help, you call."

"Sure thing, Les. You find any leads of your own?"

He glanced down at the still-unconscious kid on the floor. He'd begun to stir but was likely still going to be out for a couple of minutes. "Unknown."

"Well, be careful. You don't want whatever got Mansgraf to get you, too."

He shrugged, even though she couldn't see it. "Maybe. Fin, one more thing."

"Yeah?"

"The Department is crunching the data from the scene, analyzing whatever they can, right?"

"Yeah. They've got a few dozen techs going through it now."

"There's a note in the blood. Any chance you can delay them figuring it out?"

She made a pondering sound. "What's it written in?"

"Ogham. Old-school stone writing."

"Yeah, I think I can misplace the reference directory for that particular script for a few hours."

He had no idea what most of that sentence meant, but only one part mattered. "How many hours?"

"Say, until midnight? Anything beyond that might draw suspicion."

"Do it. I need some time before they catch up."

"All right. Be careful, Les."

He grunted and snapped the phone shut. Little ever got done by being careful.

He knelt down and hauled the kid up from the floor to sit him against the wall. It wouldn't do if he choked to death on his own vomit. Last thing Mayflower needed was another dead-end lead.

Or another dead kid, a secluded part of his mind reminded him.

As he moved Grimsby, the bathroom door creaked open, and a paunchy middle-aged man stepped into the restroom. He looked from Mayflower to the tutu-clad Grimsby, then back to Mayflower.

The man spoke like he was watching a particularly absurd scene from a play he'd never seen. "Uh, are you—are you mugging a tooth fairy?"

Mayflower arched a brow at him. "Bastard owes me thirty-two quarters."

He then stepped over Grimsby and strode past the flabbergasted man.

Things were getting complicated. He needed to do some scouting.

SEVEN

GRIMSHAW GRISWALD GRIMSBY PEDALED HARD DOWN the road toward his home. The Torque enchantment he'd put on the rear wheel of his bike assisted him, sending solitary green sparks skittering every few feet, but he needed to put his legs to work to ease his mind. Sweat soaked his skin, half freezing in the chill autumn air. His breath was hoarse and dry, but he wheezed onward without slowing.

When he had woken up from his encounter with Mayflower, the man was nowhere to be seen. He was uncertain he'd been there at all. But whether the Huntsman was real or imaginary, Grimsby had had little choice but to go back to work.

The evening shift at MMDFK had been miserable, but he had stayed even later than he needed to. He figured it would be better than sitting at home, his mind eating itself alive with worries. The bathroom toilets had never been cleaner than they were when Grimsby finished with them that night.

But now he had little recourse. No menial task to hammer his slowly building nerves into. The only thing waiting for him was the ride home to an empty apartment.

The gears on his bike suddenly caught, and he felt the skirt of his tutu rip away. In his haste to flee from the unusually insane day at MMDFK, he had forgotten he was wearing it. He skidded to a halt, nearly stumbling in the process. The churning of his Torque spell on the rear wheel grated hard against the handbrake, making the rubber squeal as green sparks ground out of the gears. He tried to dismount the bike, but the tutu was stuck, growing more so with each moment as his Torque spell tangled the fabric in the gears.

He growled and pulled at it more and more desperately, pouring in the excess energy that had been pooling inside him all night.

Finally, he tore the fabric free from the mechanism, his breaths coming out as wheezy, panicked sobs. Frustrated tears dampened his cheeks, making the cold air feel all the more harsh. He dropped the bike to the sidewalk, his spell making the rear wheel slowly spin. He ripped what strips of fabric remained of the tutu skirt from his waist and dropped them on the concrete. After the beating it had taken, what was left now looked like a wrestler's one-shouldered leotard. A sudden gust blew the discarded strips away into the dark of the night. He felt a chill run through him, like cold fingers tracing his vertebrae. The feeling of being watched struck him as acutely as the wind.

He shook off the sensation and climbed back aboard his bike, telling himself to ignore the nerves, but when that failed, he used the feeling as an excuse to exert himself. He pedaled so fast that he would have been worried about getting a ticket if the worrying parts of his brain weren't already working overtime. His legs pumped fiercely while the rest of him was just glad to have menial work to attend to, letting his mind go blank.

Twenty minutes later, he came to a sweaty halt just past Saul's Sandwiches and dismounted once more. He sprinted his bike into the alley and fumbled desperately with the chain that secured it to the metal staircase, propping up the perpetually spinning wheel so it wouldn't wander. Taking the stairs three at a time, he hurried to his apartment and managed to get the key into the lock on the third try. The door flew open wide under his frantic weight, and he fell inside, kicking it shut behind him. The cold tile of the kitchenette felt wondrous on his sweat-slicked back, and he let himself lie there, his chest heaving.

His heart was racing. It had been for hours, and it seemed hellbent on continuing its manic pace. He stayed on the floor for several long minutes, giving his lungs time to get backlogged oxygen to his brain.

He climbed to his feet when his heart finally slowed to a reasonable rate. He tried to flick on the light switch but forgot his bulb had been burnt-out for weeks.

He groaned, rubbing at his suddenly pounding stress headache with his left hand. With his other, he pointed across the room. He reached out and felt his senses extend beyond the ends of his fingers. He fumbled through the cold emptiness until he found the thread he was looking for, like a single strand of a warm, dusty cobweb.

"*Bind*," he muttered, urging the tiniest spark of his Impetus into the filament of latent magic. It flared for a moment, turning from a cobweb into something more like a guitar string drawn taut.

The lamp in the far corner of the room jerked forward an inch as the Bind rune on its drawcord was pulled toward its opposite on the floor, clicking the lamp on. The tiny spark of power ran out almost immediately, and the gossamer strand of magic snapped and withered away to nothing, letting the lamp settle back into its original position.

The warm light revealed his apartment in all its glory, if glory was a heavy mixture of empty take-out containers, half-empty plastic cups, and a floor carpeted with dirty laundry. He stared at the mess, almost surprised. This was the first time in a week or two that he had been awake enough after his shift to do anything other than collapse onto the couch and go to sleep. His place was even more of a mess than he was normally comfortable with.

He shook his head. He had bigger problems. Problems like the only person in the world he'd prefer to see dead had coincidentally been murdered. He was thinking of something more like heart attack or, more thematically, being crushed by a flying house. But not murder. And certainly not murder he was suspected for.

But even at his worst, he hadn't wished for her to die. Not really.

He had just been so furious that she had been the last obstacle between him and his dream of becoming an Auditor, and she had stopped him. It had been her personal assessment that had ended his career before it started, a career he'd spent years, his whole life, preparing for. He was certain it was because of the weakness his scars left him with. While skin and muscle had healed from the fire, his magical ability never had. Yet even with that impediment, he had outpaced most of his classmates through time and effort. In the end, though, that hadn't mattered to Mansgraf. She had failed him all the same and made certain he would never have a second chance.

He doubted he'd ever forgive her, but in time he had come to realize it was his fault more than hers. He had thought that he could beat out the best witches of his generation despite the magical handicaps his scars left him with.

She had decided he was wrong.

And she had been right.

Grimsby couldn't even manage pyromancy, the most basic of magics. Some said the first magic, even. He couldn't even manage a spark, save for when his Impetus slipped through his control and into his scars. It had only been his knack for the more obscure spells, and finding new ways to use them, that had managed to keep him in the running. But it hadn't been enough. It hadn't mattered.

Maybe none of it mattered. Not anymore. Not after tonight.

If the Department decided he was responsible for Mansgraf's murder, they wouldn't waste time taking him in. He'd be arrested, quietly, and imprisoned or, worse yet, silenced.

He shivered despite the sweat that soaked him.

He had to do something, anything, but what could he do? Hide? They would find him. Run? They would catch him. Find the real killer? He almost laughed. He was a children's magician. A party clown, except even most clowns were self-employed. He was no Auditor; Mansgraf had seen to that. He didn't have the tools, the training, or the spells to go vigilante.

No, he couldn't do something so drastic. Yet he couldn't do nothing.

So what was left?

He looked around his apartment, and the sudden urge to scrub the place to the bones filled him. That, at least, was something he could do. And, more important, he could do it *now*. He had to do something, anything, and it seemed as good as any.

"Live like a psycho killer, get psych evaluated in court as a psycho killer," he muttered to himself, and that, more than anything else he'd been through that day, made sense.

So, he cleaned.

He gathered the trash onto the three-legged coffee table at the room's center. When it began to tilt, he leaned down and put a little extra Impetus into the Bind that held the odd third leg to the ground, causing a faint glow to pool beneath the leg, and kept piling. He sorted out his laundry all into one heap, separate from the trash. He'd have to go to the laundromat later.

When he had gathered the last of the rubbish, he began to do what he always did. He summoned his Impetus and extended two fingers on his right hand.

Trash service was expensive, and since the nearest recycling center was two blocks away, he had come up with his own solution. Although he was technically not allowed to do so without

Department approval, which he would never receive, he had made a new spell, one that he was proud of and yet could show nobody.

He reached out in front of him and pressed his twin fingers hard onto the wooden floor. The spot almost seemed to warp, the light shimmering like air off a hot sidewalk or starlight bending around black holes. Then, slowly, he drew his fingers into a circle about the size of his head.

"Chute."

And suddenly, there was a dark spot. A gray disk where he had drawn the circle. It was flat, featureless, and still. Like someone had left an obsidian plate on the ground and forgotten about it, ready to be peeled up by some cartoon character or another.

He picked up some trash and tossed it through, only a little nervous. So far, the spell had done exactly as he wanted it to: ferry stuff one way into some hole in the Elsewhere. But this spell was a homemade contraption compared to the time-tested spells he had learned from his mother's grimoire as a child, Bind and Torque. He had been using them since before he even used complete sentences.

But so far, Chute seemed to do its job. The trash went through without complaint or backlash. Grimsby grinned and began shoveling the rest in as well. When he finished and the apartment was clear of refuse, he waved his hand, severing the disk's ties to his Impetus, and the circle simply popped out of existence like a soap bubble, leaving the bare floor.

He continued his cleaning spree, tending to his numerous spells as well by putting just a touch of Impetus in each of them. Handymen were even more expensive than trash service, and frankly magic was easier than a hammer and nails, which his lease prohibited anyway.

So, whenever something broke, Grimsby fixed it himself.

His coffee table, couch, and bookshelf would likely have long since collapsed if not for the Binds he had placed on them. Even the ceiling fan was busted; its motor had burned out, so Grimsby had put a Torque spell on it to keep it spinning like his bike wheel. Aside from the occasional spark of green magic, he could hardly tell it was broken. These weren't like the panicked invocation he had used to catch Richie earlier. They were enchantments. They took a bit longer to set up, requiring him to physically mark the spell's runes, but were much more efficient.

Every spell he cast drew upon Impetus for fuel. Fast spells, invocations like the one he had used when he lost his glasses, used his Impetus like gunpowder more than anything. They were short, powerful, and quickly exhausting. But enchantments had something almost like a battery. He could store power in the spell itself, which it would slowly expend to perform its function. So long as he topped them off occasionally, didn't overuse them, or didn't accidentally sever them, they should hold for days or even weeks.

Should being the keyword.

Once, the neighbor above had been vacuuming and the wire to the machine had shorted. The electricity messed with the Torque spell Grimsby had put on the fan and instead of spinning slowly for a long time, it spun very fast for only a few moments. *Very* fast. One of the broken blades was still lodged in the drywall like a DIY enthusiast's Excalibur; it refused to come out of the wall but would no doubt be coming out of his deposit.

Other than that, though, it had all worked out well enough.

He smiled absently, the world of worry forgotten for just a moment.

Above all, he was a witch. Using magic just made him *happy*. It was what he was born to do. He wanted to be like his mother and join the Department and use magic to help people, but that was never going to happen.

So this was what he was left with.

Magical gears and enchanted duct tape.

His smile tinged bitter on his lips and fell away as fast as it had come.

He took a deep breath, determined not to let it come out as a sigh, and eyeballed his laundry pile. It was too much to carry to the laundromat in a single trip. He pulled out an armful of things he could manage instead. He left his costumes, including his outfit for Wizard Pie Wednesday: a blue robe and pointed hat that were adorned with yellow stars. He smelled it, determined it was clean enough, and tossed it on the couch. Then he shoved the rest into the tiny closet beside the entrance to his apartment. The closet door was eternally creaky and refused to stay closed. He shut it two or three times, only to have it open again. Finally, just as he was tempted to use a Bind, it stayed shut.

He looked around the apartment. It wasn't neat, but it wasn't a sty, either. He was fairly certain he had gotten it right in the margin between psychopath and sociopath.

The sweet spot known as normal.

Grimsby began to scoop up the dirty clothes into a linen laundry bag, paused, and stripped off the scorched leotard, which was all that was left of his accursed tutu, and tossed it in as well. Now, dressed in a simple black T-shirt and blue jeans, he kicked open the door and stumbled out onto the staircase, letting the door close behind him.

He had just reached the bottom of the stairs when something caught his eye. It took him a moment to even realize what it was. His bike was loose from its chain and had somehow ended up ten feet deeper into the alley, its wheel spinning ominously.

He glared and looked around. Sometimes the neighbor kids would try to steal the bike, but they had never managed to undo the chain. Had they finally gotten it, only to lose their nerve after a few feet?

He grumbled and moved toward his bike. He couldn't simply leave it in the middle of the alley. He couldn't afford to replace it if it was damaged or stolen for real. He slung the bag over his shoulder and wrestled with the bike for a moment to get it facing in the right direction so that he could walk it back to the apartment stairs.

A car passed on the road outside the alley, its bright headlights illuminating the dark for a brief moment. In the sudden light, something on the brick walls caught his eye. Lines where they shouldn't have been, but by the time he turned his head, the car had passed and the alley was dark.

Curiosity getting the better of him, he moved closer to the graffitied wall, holding back his bike from inching forward on its own. When his eyes finally readjusted to the dimness, he saw there were words on the wall, scratched into the brick and mortar over-top the layers of built-up paint from years of tags. Three simple words, manically scrawled in the dark with some kind of chisel.

THIS ISN'T OVER

Grimsby shuddered. The words looked fresh.

"I liked it better when they used spray paint," he muttered.

He shrugged away a shiver and turned back to deal with his bike.

The alleyway grew bright once again with the lights of a passing car. Grimsby focused on the ground to protect his vision. It was then that he noticed the chain on his bike hadn't been undone or unlocked.

It had been broken. The metal links were scattered over the concrete, twisted and shattered.

A shadow spilled over him where there hadn't been one before.

He whirled around to see someone standing in the alley entrance, between him and the street.

They were tall. Even taller than that Mayflower man had been, and shrouded in rags that obscured their form.

They loomed in the alley, so still that Grimsby was uncertain they were real.

"H-hello?" he called out.

They said something, but the voice was so low and distorted that he couldn't make it out.

Then the stranger extended a hand out to their side. A hand with three fingers that reached to their knees, tipped with chipped blades almost a foot long.

Grimsby's breath caught in his throat, his numbed grip tightening on both bike and bag.

The *thing* took a long, lean step forward.

Grimsby didn't wait for it to take a second. He screamed and hurled his laundry bag at the thing in a panicked, slightly pathetic gesture of self-defense.

With a blur of claws, the bag was shredded to ragged scraps before it even struck the figure, sending flayed bits of cloth fluttering across the alley.

Grimsby felt a sudden pang of loss for his ruined clothes, but the feeble attack had bought him sparse moments. He whipped his bike around and straddled the seat, pedaling madly, making his way deeper into the darkened alley. He reached out and poured Impetus into the Torque spell on his rear wheel, feeling the energy draining from him quickly, but the spell's strength redoubled. Green sparks streaked out like a flaming pinwheel, and the enchanted wheel lurched him forward with sudden and reckless speed.

His wheels ground hard over damp concrete, and he somehow managed to maintain frantic control to keep from careening into a wall or dumpster, but behind him he heard heavy, wrenching steps, like a car dragging a skittering steel bumper over the road.

The noise was screeching and awful. But it was moving at a steady gait. And drawing closer.

The thing was fast. Too fast. Even at his pace, it would soon catch him.

Grimsby had no time to think, no time to rationalize. He

didn't know what this thing was; he only knew the crazed primal instinct that he needed to get away from it. A frantic glance over his shoulder told him it was on his heels, its long, clawed hand reaching out for him.

He couldn't outrun it on flat ground; he had to improvise.

He neared an intersection in the alleyway. He would have only one chance.

His Impetus welled, flowing through him. He had no time to efficiently direct it, and he felt energy build up in his scars, making his skin grow hot. In the dark dank of the alleyway, he could see his scarred skin smolder with a subtle glow as sparks trailed in his wake.

He dug his right thumb into his left palm, placing a Bind rune, leaving the mark like a stamp coated in shimmering ink. Then, as their chase reached the intersection, he reached out and placed the second rune on the corner of the building to his left.

Between gasping breaths he wheezed his spell, *"Bind!"*

Taut strings of blue light appeared as the bond formed, and he felt his arm jerk back as the strands pulled the Binds toward each other. Instead of fighting the force, he leaned into it, swinging his body and bike around the corner with the momentum of his anchored arm.

As a result he went from full speed in one direction to suddenly changing his angle sharply to the left. The Bind nearly tore his arm from the socket, but he managed to keep his balance. Without losing more than a touch of speed, he cut loose the spell and continued flying down the intersecting alley, the dangling strands of the severed Bind drawing azure sparks on the concrete before withering away.

Meanwhile, the thing behind him proved not so nimble. It was fast, terrifyingly fast, and it was much larger than Grimsby. So much so that its considerably larger mass couldn't shift directions nearly so quickly.

Grimsby heard it screech over the concrete as it tried to follow him. It sounded like a car wreck a scant dozen feet behind him. Trash cans clattered and glass shattered. He glanced quickly back, unable to help himself.

For a moment, he thought the thing had given up.

Then its claws wrapped around the corner of the building, crushing the bricks to rubble beneath its grip. Its shadowed, rag-covered head leered around the corner for a heartbeat before it gave chase once more. It was disturbingly silent as it pursued him. Aside from the sound of its body in motion, the thing didn't cry out or scream. He couldn't even hear it breathe.

It was deadly silent.

Grimsby's attention turned ahead. The alley was long, and there were no more intersections to use to his advantage. He was in a dead sprint, maybe literally.

Ahead, the alley gave way to the open night. He saw street-lights and distantly hoped that the light would be his sanctuary from the thing behind him. Part of him thought that the idea was ridiculous. The rest of him knew it was his only chance.

He pushed all his strength into his legs, suddenly grateful that he'd never had money to afford a car. His knees and shins were alive with pain, but the muscles in his thighs and calves were strong from biking and desperate to run. His Torque spell made the gears squeal as he sailed forward, leaving a green trail in his wake.

The end of the alley drew near, as did the clatter of claws on concrete.

He neared the dawning streetlights, his breath held, his body leaning forward as though to cross a finish line.

That's when the second shadow appeared before him, almost as tall as the first.

EIGHT ✳

G RIMSBY SCREAMED.
It was all he could do, really. That, and keep pedaling
straight into the thing blocking his path.

He quickly resolved that if he was going to get torn apart, he
was going to give these things a few bruises for their trouble. Besides, his adrenaline firmly asserted that anything that wasn't
moving as quickly as possible was not an option.

That's when the one in front of Grimsby raised its arm. Its
hand was not armed with claws, but with a gun the size of Grimsby's forearm.

The figure before him raised the gun, as silent as the beast in
the alley behind him.

Grimsby screamed again and quickly lost his balance. His bike
wobbled before the front wheel jerked as it caught the curb. The
handlebars twisted and the wheel wrenched sideways, causing the
whole frame to tip forward and send him flying forward in a chaotic jumble of limbs. He bounced hard, rolling into an unsightly ball
that careened into the gunner's legs.

He felt his ribs crack into shins, and the wind was banished
from his lungs. Shattered thunder echoed across the alley, making

his ears ring. Then the gunner fell upon him. He felt limbs moving around among his own, angrily kicking and striking to break free.

A gruff voice swore, "Goddamn it!" as the stranger struggled loose and stood.

Grimsby, dazed and breathless, rolled over and looked up to see Mayflower give him a glare as sharp as knives before sprinting down the alley toward the creature. In the shadowed corridor of brick and grime, Grimsby saw a gleam of claws and a flutter of cloth. Then the thing vanished deeper into the dark.

Mayflower pursued it, leaping over the fallen bike, gun held ready, but as he reached the intersection Grimsby had used to evade his pursuer, he looked around dubiously before spitting bitterly into the garbage-laden gutter.

He returned down the alley, though he walked backward, his eyes scanning the dark and even the rooftops and fire escapes above. His gun was held low, but his finger rested a bare millimeter from the trigger.

Grimsby recovered enough to sit up. His ears were ringing painfully. White smoke powdered the air, making his lungs stutter as they sucked it in. The lone gunshot had smelled like molten metal. The strange odor burned the inside of his mouth and nose, making his wheezes mix with ragged coughs.

Mayflower finally reached him, but instead of stopping, he continued stepping back until he could watch both Grimsby and the alley without moving his head.

He was quiet for far too long, his sunglasses propped up on his brow to reveal gray-blue eyes that refused to waver from the darkness.

Grimsby tried to speak several times, frantic, worthless efforts, before he finally managed something that resembled human speech. "H-help."

"I did," Mayflower growled. "Now tell me why I'm not wasting my time."

"I—I don't— What was that thing?"

"You tell me," the Huntsman said, eyes as cold as gravestones.

Grimsby felt the panicked confusion abate enough to be re-placed by growing anger. "How the toil and trouble should I know? You think I get chased down alleys by monsters often?"

"I've seen a lot of scum die to their accomplices."

"Accomplice?" Grimsby said, voice cracking. "You think that not only do I know what that thing was, but that I have a personal relationship with it? Who do you think I am?"

Mayflower didn't answer for a long moment.

Grimsby climbed to his feet while he waited, the burning in his limbs slowly thudding into a dull ache laced with sharp pains.

Finally, the Huntsman spoke. "I think it's likely that's the thing that killed Mansgraf."

Grimsby felt himself perk up. "That's great!"

"It's what?" he said in a low, deadly voice.

"No, I mean it's not as great as nothing killing Mansgraf, but it's better than people thinking *I* killed her, you know?"

"Then tell me, witch," he said. "Why did she write your name in her own blood?" He swung the revolver down to point at Grimsby's chest. "Tell me why I shouldn't."

The pains of his body faded away as he stared down the barrel of Mayflower's gun. His legs tensed to start sprinting again, but where would he go? Biking routine or no, he couldn't outrun a bullet. Nor could he fight; it was the *Huntsman*. He'd be dead before he could manage a spell. He could only hope to reason with Mayflower.

But as the Huntsman's face hardened into a stone-carved glare, that seemed less and less likely.

"Look, Mr. Mayflower, sir," Grimsby said, slowly raising his hands. "I don't know why she named me. Maybe her real killer is trying to use me as a scapegoat?"

He shook his head fractions of an inch. "No. The angles

wouldn't add up. The message could have only been left by her. Try again."

"Then maybe she didn't mean me? Maybe she was losing her head as she died and made a sanguinary typo."

"I've seen her dig a living bullet out of her own guts with just a spit-polished spoon and soup tongs. Try again."

"Well, I don't know, man!" Grimsby said, his voice thready. "Maybe she just wanted me taken down with her! She failed me during my testing for no reason; why not have me executed for the same?"

"She always had reasons."

Then Grimsby thought he saw the Huntsman's hand shake, almost imperceptibly. It almost felt like . . . hesitancy.

"You're—you're not sure, are you?" he asked carefully.

Mayflower didn't reply.

Grimsby kept pressing. "Do *you* think I did it?"

"It doesn't matter," he said. "If Mansgraf wants something done, it's for good reason."

"Is it, though? I mean, I know she was dangerous, but does that make her flawless? Hasn't she ever made a mistake?" He tried to lock down the Huntsman's eyes with his own. "Haven't you?"

Mayflower's whole body stopped, and for a moment, Grimsby thought the man had frozen in time. Only the slight downcast of his gray-blue eyes showed any sign of life. Finally, the Huntsman let his gun fall slowly to his side.

"I don't know what that thing was," Grimsby said, pointing back to the alley. "But I promise you, I had nothing to do with it, and I had nothing to do with her death."

"Damn it," Mayflower cursed. "Goddamn it, I believe you."

"Oh jeez, thank you!" Grimsby said, his body half sinking back toward the ground. He could barely keep his shaking legs beneath him. "I can't wait for this to all be cleared up."

Mayflower's face didn't soften. "What do you mean?"

"Well, you can just make a call to the Department, right? Tell them I didn't do it and everything will be back to normal?"

"No."

"Why not? You're the *Huntsman*. Aren't you supposed to work for the Department?"

"I don't work for anybody," Mayflower growled.

"Work *with* them, then. Don't you work with them?"

"Technically speaking," Mayflower said, with something that on a human might be called embarrassment, "I'm here unofficially."

"You're *what*?"

"I retired years ago. Any Department clearance I may have had evaporated when I did."

"So what is this, like a hobby to you? What in the name of Oz are you doing here?"

"I needed to know if you did it."

"Why? Why not leave it to the Department?"

"Because," he said, his knuckles cracking as they tightened on the butt of his gun, "they might have let you live."

"Oh." Grimsby gulped. "So, uh, how did you even find out about me?"

He glowered. "A former . . . colleague called me onto the scene of Mansgraf's murder to see if I saw anything they missed. I did."

Grimsby's jaw dropped an inch as he understood. "And you saw the note she left."

"Yes. And it won't be long before the Department does, too."

"Can't you just tell them that you checked me out and I'm clean?"

"No one is clean," he scoffed. "It wouldn't do any good anyway; they'd just assume I was dirty, too. We'd both be arrested for the murder."

"Then—then what do we do?"

"*We* don't do anything. I suggest you find a ladder and the darkest, deepest hole you can and climb in until this is all over."

"I can't do that! I've got work and—and—"

And what else?

"I've been to your work. You'd be better off in a hole."

"But wait—what if that thing comes after me again?"

Mayflower shrugged. "Better keep up on the cardio."

"But why? Why did it come after me at all?"

"It's probably some beast on a random killing spree."

"That started ten minutes from where I work, with my old teacher, who left a note with my name on it. Does that seem random to you?"

Mayflower's brow furrowed into canyon-deep crevasses on his forehead.

"Look, I don't know what that thing is or why it's after me. But I do know two things. The first is that I'm terrified. The second is that if it took down Mansgraf, I don't stand a chance."

The Huntsman didn't speak. His face was stony, as though he were doing ancient calculations behind his sea-granite eyes.

Grimsby took a breath, trying to summon his courage. He was about to say something that was likely very, very stupid. But it didn't seem like he had much choice, not if he wanted to live to see another Tuesday.

"Please," he said, "I need your help."

His adrenaline had finally subsided, and the chill night soaked into his sweat and damp clothes, making him shiver. If Mayflower didn't agree to help, he didn't know what he'd do.

Finally, the grayed man growled in frustration. Then, he holstered his gun and spoke. "Come on," he said. "My jeep's this way." Without another word, he turned on his heels and strode off, his eyes combing the night.

Grimsby felt his relief surge as he scrambled to his feet. He stopped and glanced down at his bike, reluctant to leave it behind. He thought about hiding it, but the only place nearby was the alley he had come from, and he was not going near that again. He felt a pang of regret, then left his bike and scuttled after the Huntsman as fast as he could, his aching legs having to work hard to keep up.

With the Huntsman's help, things would work out. They had to. Didn't they?

He shook away the cloying doubt and tried the same with the fear that gripped deep in his chest. The doubt subsided, for the time being. The fear didn't.

They reached a darkened parking lot not far away. Mayflower led the way to a rusted old jeep that looked like it might have actually seen the last world war. Maybe the first, too. And was just maybe tough enough to live to see the next as well.

Mayflower opened the back and dug in it for a moment. Then he gestured over his shoulder to Grimsby. "Come here."

Grimsby did so.

"Give me your hand."

He did that as well. His exhaustion aided neither his curious nor his defiant nature. He probably would have started singing carols if it was asked of him.

Mayflower glared at the knotted scars on his hand for a moment and then slapped an iron cuff over Grimsby's wrist.

"Hey, what—" he began, but before he could react, Mayflower seized his other wrist and did the same, leaving his wrists locked in front of him. "What do you think you're doing?"

"Insurance," Mayflower said. He gestured to the cuffs, which were engraved with symbols Grimsby didn't recognize. "With those on, you can't get your magic up."

"Why? What if you need my help?"

"*Your* help?" he said, with enough derision in his tone that it hurt like a punch in the gut. "There's two options here, kid. The first is that you really are innocent, and this thing wants to kill you, too."

"Right, so how can I—"

"In which case, you're as likely to kill me as anything else when you inevitably panic."

Grimsby didn't reply for a moment. The man might be right. He certainly hadn't handled himself elegantly before. "And the second option?"

"The second option is that you're not innocent, you helped this thing kill Mansgraf, and it's either turned against you or you're trying to play me. In which case, you not having access to magic will also help me."

Grimsby frowned, but he couldn't argue much. The Huntsman's logic was sound, but that didn't mean he had to be such a jerk about it.

He opened his mouth to argue anyway but saw in Mayflower's face that his stance was as firm as stone. Protesting would likely just make Grimsby seem even more suspicious. He growled in frustration but didn't push the issue.

"So, what now?" he asked.

"I may know of a safe place for you to lay low. Assuming it hasn't been compromised."

"Where is it?" Grimsby asked.

"Mansgraf's lair."

NINE

L AIR?" GRIMSBY ASKED. "WHAT KIND OF PERSON HAS
a lair?"

Mayflower opened the back seat of the jeep, half guiding, half
shoving Grimsby inside. "You didn't know her very well."

The back of the jeep smelled like cigarettes and dried leather.
Most of the upholstery had been bleached and peeled away by the
sun, leaving bare pitted steel and pocked cushion foam. He saw
more than one bullet hole punched through the metal.

"I guess I didn't," Grimsby admitted. "She tested us for a
month and barely said a word the whole time."

Mayflower grunted. "Sounds like her." He shut the door.

It was only when the door closed that Grimsby realized there
were no handles on the inside, and that a cage of bars separated the
front and back.

Mayflower climbed into the driver's seat and dug a cigarette
from his pocket.

"Hey, uh, what's with the cage back here?"

"It's to contain dangerous assets."

Grimsby shifted uncomfortably; the bars must have threaded

straight through the seat cushions, encasing the whole back of the cab. "You already got the cuffs on me; can't I just sit up front?"

Mayflower flicked a glance over the top of his glasses at the rearview mirror, giving Grimsby a hard glare. "No."

"There's not even a seat belt back here!"

"Seat belts are designed to prevent occupants from jettisoning out the windshield during a collision," Mayflower said as though reciting the knowledge from a manual.

"Yeah, which is why I'd really like one."

"That'd be redundant. The cage will keep you in the car just fine."

"'Just fine' is not how I'd describe it."

"Better not distract the driver, then," Mayflower said, coaxing the jeep to life. It sounded like it should be in a hospital bed surrounded by its loved ones, but it started moving somehow.

Grimsby bit back a curse and tried to find a place on the seat that was comfortable, but there was none. The cage's iron bars made certain of that.

With little warning, the Huntsman kicked the jeep into gear, and the old beast rasped a roar before jerking forward.

Grimsby braced himself as he was flung from side to side with sharp turns and sudden accelerations. He screwed his eyes shut; his stomach was growing uneasy with the jeep's unpredictable motions. Mayflower drove like hell was on his heels, and Grimsby was certain he left rubber on the sidewalk more than once.

He tried to focus his thoughts elsewhere to steady himself.

"So let me get this straight," he said, trying to ignore the building nausea in his stomach. "Mansgraf had a lair?" It didn't help that all he could smell was whiskey and cigarettes, and whatever the opposite of that new-car smell was.

"Basically," Mayflower growled after a moment. "More like a safe house."

"No, you said 'lair.' Like she's some kind of supervillain."

"Call it what you want. It may be the safest place in the city for you, if we can get inside."

"And the Department doesn't know about it?"

"No."

"Great. And I'm supposed to stay there until this blows over?"

"Yes."

"Okay, so my problem is this: if it's Mansgraf's safe house, and Mansgraf is dead, how safe is her house?"

"Is this a bad joke?" Mayflower asked, his voice cold.

Grimsby shrugged. "Depends on your punch line, really."

"The thing that killed her did it outside of the safe house for a reason. If we can get you inside, you can stay there until I figure the rest of this out."

"What do you mean *if* we can get inside? Don't you have a key?"

"It's not locked. It's hidden and it's trapped to hell and back."

"Then why there? Why not, oh, say, anywhere else?"

Mayflower didn't reply, and Grimsby made himself crack open his eyes despite the objections of his stomach.

"You're not telling me the whole story, are you?" he asked.

He heard the Huntsman mutter a curse under his breath. "I'd be going there even if you weren't with me. I need to find out more about what Mansgraf was doing when she was killed, and it's the only place that might have answers."

"Then how about you drop me off somewhere else on the way?"

He growled. "Because Mansgraf was a witch. That means I probably can't see whatever traps she left behind. You can."

"So you *do* need my help," Grimsby said, a small measure of satisfaction creeping into him.

It faded quickly.

"I need your eyes, witch. I'd leave the rest behind, if I could," Mayflower said. He then tapped his grayed sunglasses. "These let me see some magics, but not as much as one of you can. You see. I'll do the rest."

Grimsby's rapidly deflated ego made his tone grow sour. "You don't care about helping me. You're just using me to break into her lair."

"And you're using me to not be torn apart by a monster. We're using each other. It's what people do." His glare might have burned a furrow in the road if it grew any more intense. "If we can get inside, I find what I need, and you can stay there until this is over. It's mutually beneficial."

"You mean codependent."

Mayflower grunted. "Maybe, but you don't have much of a choice, kid."

"What do you mean?"

"If the Department thinks you got Mansgraf, they won't bother looking for anyone else. So if I don't find the real killer and set this straight, you'll be hunted until the day you die. And with your survival skills, I wouldn't bother putting in a two-week notice."

Grimsby gulped and fell into silence.

The Huntsman had a point. If he didn't get the real killer, Grimsby was going to be out of luck no matter how things shook out. It was in his best interest to help out, even if it meant going to a less-than-safe house.

Even so, he felt his skin grow clammy at the thought of breaking into Mansgraf's lair. He had no idea what to expect, but his imagination summoned images of gothic spires, gargoyles, and limping henchmen named Igor. The more reasonable part of him imagined the thought of stepping in the wrong place and being incinerated, or crossing an invisible barrier and coming out on the other side as mush.

Of the two, he preferred Igor and company, hands down.

He fell silent, dredging up more awful images with every passing minute, and Mayflower seemed content to let him stew. It wasn't long until the jeep found its way to the highway, and its motion became predictable enough for Grimsby's stomach to settle.

The runed bars of the cage blockaded the windows as well, leaving him trapped in a box of iron. Small engravings and carvings from dozens of old languages or more had been etched into the metal. He recognized many of them: Latin, Hebrew, some druidic runes, even old ogham. He might have been able to even read a few of them, but he was suddenly exhausted.

He supposed it was reasonable. He had narrowly evaded a monster, been threatened by a vigilante, twice, and also worked a twelve-hour shift. He had a right to be tired, though his mind was still reeling. It was hardly believable that it had all happened in such a short span, and he wasn't entirely certain he wouldn't wake up in bed any minute, ready to start another shift wearing some ridiculous costume.

And he also wasn't entirely sure which scenario would have been the nightmare.

He let himself slump down into the seat, his body aching thankfully at the rest, uncomfortable though it was. He found himself listening to the sound of the wind cutting through the holes in the steel chassis, its bittersweet song oddly soothing.

Soon, his consciousness wandered away, leaving him blissfully numb.

TEN

GRIMSBY WOKE UP SOME TIME LATER, HAVING NOT EVEN realized he had slept. There were no streetlights or other vehicles in sight as Mayflower guided the jeep down a darkened road.

"Where are we?" he asked through a stifled yawn.

"Nearly there," Mayflower said.

He pulled off the road into an empty lot of cracked, sun-bleached pavement. The lights of Boston shone on the southern horizon, and the tallest of the city's structures were just barely visible through the treetops and deep curtain of night. The sound of the highway was nearby, but any traffic was beyond sight.

Mayflower climbed out of the jeep and opened the back door for Grimsby, who climbed stiffly out onto the concrete. He tried to stretch, but the cuffs made it impossible.

What struck him more than anything was how empty the entire lot was. There were no walls, no towers or fortresses or gargoyles. Not even a ditch that might serve as a moat. It was just . . . empty. It looked like a commuter parking lot that had been abandoned sometime in the distant past.

"Wow. Nice place. Fort Knox would be jealous," Grimsby

said. The cool autumn wind cut through the trees around them in a sudden gust that pierced easily through his T-shirt and jeans. He shuddered and clutched his arms around himself, at least as much as his chains would allow.

Mayflower was already pacing the pavement, searching around with an old flashlight that looked heavy enough to club a man to death with. "It's beneath us," he said. "An old safe house left over from when the Therian Liberation movement died out, forty years back or so."

"Wait, she lives in a werewolf Mafia den?" Grimsby asked.

"Therians, not werewolves."

"What's the difference?"

"Werewolves have some degree of discipline. Either way, it's a former Therian Mafia den; we made certain of that." His voice took on a tinge of nostalgia for a moment before he shook it away. "Though it may be more dangerous now than it was before. Stay close, and don't touch anything."

Grimsby jingled his handcuffs. "That'll be hard. Can't you take these off?"

"Not happening."

"Why not?"

Mayflower pressed a pair of fingers to his brow in exasperated annoyance. "Because I don't trust you, Grimsby. You're a witch. You're young. You're stupid. Any one of which is reason enough to give me doubts. All three is likely to get me killed."

"Then why cuff me if I'm so incompetent?"

"Those could keep even a witch like Mansgraf from managing a spark of magic," Mayflower said. "With them on, you're only young and stupid."

"I'm not stupid!" Grimsby said.

"You let a man with a gun who had most of a mind to kill you just a couple hours ago drive you into the middle of nowhere, alone, in the middle of the night," Mayflower replied.

Grimsby opened and closed his mouth a couple of times, failing to find a cutting reply.

"Well, I'm not *that* young," he said.

Mayflower muttered a curse under his breath and gestured to a patch of asphalt that was just beyond the light of his flashlight. There, barely visible, was the round shape of a manhole.

The Huntsman went to it and pried it open with disturbing ease. He was oddly casual, as though he weren't about to delve into the hidden lair of a paranoid witch that happened to also be the former lair of a syndicate of criminal Therians. He shone his light down within.

Grimsby peered over Mayflower's stooped shoulder to see nothing but iron rungs sunk into the wall of a concrete shaft. They descended below the light and into the darkness beyond. Decades-old claw marks marred the walls of the shaft and bit deep into the decayed rungs.

"I don't like this," Grimsby said.

"You wanna try the Marriott instead?"

"I mean, if you've got a secret witch lair in one of those, I wouldn't argue."

Mayflower rolled his eyes under his gray sunglasses. "This place is safe because it's remote and because you'd likely die trying to get inside. If it were easy for us to get into, it'd also be easy for anyone else."

"I thought you knew Mansgraf. Don't you know, like, a password or something?"

"Yeah. The password is shut up and don't touch anything."

Grimsby grumbled. "I still don't like this."

"Good," Mayflower said, "you'd be insane if you did."

"Well, you sorta look like you're having a good time. What's that say about you?"

Mayflower only glanced at him with a cryptic expression. And something almost like a smile.

"Maybe I should wait here," Grimsby continued. "Keep watch, you know?"

"For what? Nobody has any idea about this place. With luck, it'll be weeks before anyone manages to find it. If they ever do. Besides, your sight might make the difference down there."

"Are you sure? Your glasses are probably good enough, right?"

"Mansgraf was a witch, and a damned good one." He pointed at the shaded glasses he wore despite the dark of night. "I can see some of what she might have left behind, but only enough to kill it. Anything more subtle than an invisible bear and I'll miss it. That's where you come in."

Grimsby swallowed a lump of hard fear in his throat.

Mayflower was right; he had nowhere near the perception a witch did of the Elsewhere. It was part of what made witches so essential long ago, when folks had much darker things than witches to be scared of, and that hadn't changed much. Technology could replicate at least as much, if not more, of the destruction witches could manage, and even some of the utility. But so far, nothing could see into the Elsewhere like a witch could. He could see things no Usual could, and that made him useful.

However, at the moment, he did not feel like being useful.

He felt like being useless and crawling into a hole in the ground. But not this one. One that was safe. Although he was beginning to believe safety wasn't an option. Not yet. If he wanted to have someplace safe to wait out this insanity, he had to make it for himself.

"All righty-roo," he said, voice cracking as he said that particular word for the first time in his life.

Mayflower grunted. "You first."

"Wait, what? Why me first?"

"You can see. We just went over this."

"You have the gun. Why don't you go first?"

"Because I have the gun," he said simply.

"This is seeming less and less like a safe house and more and more like a 'Let's Kill Grimsby House.'"

"Again, you're free to walk away. You asked for my help."

"You need me, too!"

"I really don't; I'm just trading back pain for headaches at this point," Mayflower said.

"Fine," he grumbled. He stretched his taut and nervous fingers in their chain confinements and wiped at his brow. "All right. Here I go," he said, without moving at all.

Mayflower waited for a few breaths before sighing. "Any time now, witch."

"Yeah, right." He edged cautiously forward, peering into the pit.

"I'm going to push you down in ten seconds," Mayflower said.

"Then you won't know if anything's down there or not."

"I will if I hear you land on something other than concrete."

"But you—"

"Six."

"Six? I don't think that was four—"

"Three."

"Oh, fine!"

As Mayflower grimly continued to count, Grimsby dipped one foot down and alighted on one of the rungs. It creaked in a manner that would have wholly uninspired confidence if he had any to lose but otherwise didn't give way under his weight.

He inched down farther, feeling for the strength of the rungs below him before trusting them enough to descend again. It was a slow, nerve-wracking process, and after what felt like half an hour, his head descended below the surface of the pavement.

"Keep going, witch," Mayflower said. "I'm putting my light away."

"How am I supposed to see anything?"

"Use your damned second or third sight or whatever you have."

"Oh, right." Grimsby clung to the rungs with his left arm and closed his eyes as he reached up and fumbled off his glasses with the other. An impressive feat in handcuffs.

When he opened his eyes, the world had changed.

The scarred walls of concrete looked more like claw-slashed mud and stone. The steel rungs were something closer to bone, almost riblike as they descended beneath him. The air smelled of wet dog, burning oil, and blood. Up above, he could just make out a black moon in a red sky, while down below, it was a roiling cloud of white shadows that bubbled thicker than fog, obscuring the depths. He glanced at Mayflower, but the Huntsman had faded to a bland, detail-less Figment, a shadowed silhouette of himself. It would have been near impossible to tell him apart from anyone else.

At least, had it not been for the gun in his hand. That item was disturbingly clear.

Mayflower spoke, but his words were blurred, like whispers through cotton and rain. "Keep going," he said; at least that's what Grimsby heard.

Reluctantly, Grimsby descended, deeper and deeper into the dark. As he neared the writhing fog, it receded, letting him see a few yards farther into the pitch of the depths below. It was more of the same for a long time. At least, it felt like a long time. Between the strangely slow and fluid motion of the Elsewhere and Grimsby's own nerves, his internal clock was going mad.

Then there was a deafening crack, the sound of splitting bone. Grimsby looked up to see a pair of large, goatlike eyes and a grin of dozens of sharp teeth staring out from a recess in the stone. A frantic heartbeat later, the rung he was clinging to wrenched from the wall under his weight.

He tried to catch himself with his other hand. He would have been able to reach, if not for the shackles. His grasping fingers came up short, the chains around his wrists pulling as taut as one of his Binds.

He fell backward, both hands scrambling numbly at the walls, but his limbs were slower than his senses. It felt like he was clawing his way through molasses. He tried to brace his back against the far side of the shaft, but he was too short, and it was just out of reach. His feet slipped, and he began careening down the shaft into whatever was lurking in the twisted shadows below.

At best, it would be solid concrete.

At worst, it would be something *else*.

Neither was likely to be survivable.

Which made the fact that he was falling all the more inconvenient. He twisted in the air, managing to peer downward, waiting for the inevitable parting of the fog and the hard impact of solid ground.

But it came far sooner than he expected.

The roiling mist vanished suddenly, revealing the ground only five or six feet below. When he crashed into it, it hurt, but it was hardly lethal. He lay on the ground, stunned for a long moment, his ego bruised more than his body, though not by much. The thin layer of mist that remained dried up and disappeared with a strange giggle.

He thought he saw that same face in the dark, grinning and inhuman. Then it was gone.

He looked up at the rung that had broken beneath his grip, about six feet above him, and groaned. "I hate Tuesdays," he muttered, though it was probably Wednesday by now.

He climbed to his elbows, twisting awkwardly in his cuffs, and rolled over, staring down a single long hallway ringed with scars of claws and fire. In the darkness, he saw a flicker of movement.

Mayflower was right; there was something down here.

ELEVEN

GRIMSBY STARED HARD INTO THE DARKENED HAZE UN-til Mayflower dropped behind him with a soft grunt.

"See anything?" he asked, his voice distorted by the Elsewhere into near static.

Grimsby nodded slowly. "Maybe? I think there was something in the dark, but I'm not sure." Even with his sight in the Elsewhere, he could see no further signs.

"There's always something in the dark," Mayflower said. "Best be sure of that. Come on. Her lab is this way." His Figment led the way down the hall, the shadowed figure's steps wary.

"Lab?" Grimsby asked.

"If Mansgraf left some kind of clue as to what the thing that killed her was, it'll be there."

"Like what?"

He shrugged. "Notes, signs, anything she might have left be-hind, either incidentally or for me to find."

Grimsby nodded and continued, but before he could take two steps, Mayflower seized his arm.

"Stop!" he hissed, voice hardly audible.

Grimsby took a step back and replaced his glasses to see Mayflower kneeling on the ground. His fingers were gingerly extended and tracing some invisible line toward the wall.

Except it wasn't an invisible line.

Without the Huntsman bringing attention to it, Grimsby never would have seen it, but there was a thin thread of wire running a couple of inches above the floor.

Mayflower traced it to the wall and felt at the bricks before finding a trio of them to be loose. He very carefully removed them, working so slowly that Grimsby wasn't sure if he was moving at all. Sweat ran down the man's brow by the time he was done, but he set the bricks aside, revealing a hollow in the wall about the size of Grimsby's palms side by side.

Mayflower drew a knife from his boot, and after a moment of careful prodding, he let a great breath of relief escape. He reached into the hollow and withdrew something that looked like a gray brick that had been flattened and slightly curved.

On the curved side, raised letters read: *FRONT TOWARD ENEMY.*

Grimsby felt his heart skip a handful of beats. "Is—is that?"

"Land mine," Mayflower said. "Claymore. One-direction explosive. Mostly one-way, at least. Would have killed us both and collapsed the tunnel."

"Good thing you spotted it, or I would have—" He shuddered, not wanting to think of what would have happened. Then he stopped, staring at Mayflower in disbelief. "What are you doing?"

Shock forced its way into his voice as Mayflower put the claymore into his jacket.

"What?" he asked.

"You're just gonna take it? And put it in your *pocket*?"

He paused in thought for a moment, then said, "You're right. Silly of me." He pulled the mine from his pocket, examined it for a moment, then made certain *FRONT TOWARD ENEMY* was pointing away from his chest. Then he replaced the mine. "That's better."

"Better?" Grimsby demanded. "You're carrying around a land mine that you *just* said would have killed us both!"

"Relax." He held out what looked like a short rod the size of a key. "It's harmless without a detonator—or a trip wire. Well, relatively harmless." He frowned and glanced back to the alcove the mine had been hidden in. "For some reason she had this one rigged to both. Don't know who could fit in there to detonate it, though. Wireless, too . . ." He trailed off, brow furrowed in thought.

Grimsby barely heard him, instead shaking his head, never taking his eyes from the claymore. "You've got to be kidding me."

"What? Plastic explosive is surprisingly stable. For an explosive."

"So, you're all right with having a land mine in your pocket, but you won't even take the cuffs off me?"

He shrugged. "The land mine doesn't give me any lip."

"Neither of us will have any lip to give when it blows our faces off!"

"If," he said simply. "Now, get to seeing, witch."

Grimsby shook his head. Mayflower must be insane. Of course, maybe he wasn't alone. Grimsby had followed the Huntsman here, after all. He had told himself he was looking for safety, and yet even after nearly breaking his neck from falling and narrowly avoiding a land mine, he didn't feel the urge to turn back.

In fact, he felt nervously compelled to go deeper.

"I must be crazy." He sighed as he removed his glasses again.

The Elsewhere was a logical and welcome sight after what he had just seen. It looked like a sewer system a couple of centuries out of date. It was all old brick, cracked mortar, and dripping water. Shadows and mists gathered in mixed black pools of glassy stillness as red light seeped through the chinks in the tunnel walls.

Grimsby looked around, but before he could fully orient himself, there was a skittering in the dark. Mayflower must have heard it, too, as he froze, his silhouette hand raising the all-too-clear gun in its grip.

The sound came from around the next bend, and they crept quietly up to the corner. This time, Grimsby kept his eyes out for trip wires, hoping the Elsewhere wouldn't hide them from him. They reached an intersection in the tunnel and Mayflower stepped past him and glanced back. He slowly nodded, holding up three fingers.

Then two.

Then one.

The shadow of the old Huntsman burst around the corner, weapon drawn, and Grimsby fumbled his way behind him, uncertain how he'd help to any degree with his hands bound. He tried to look menacing, but it probably looked closer to constipation.

Sitting in the center of the hall, under one of the few functioning lights, was a clean black cat. Its fur was long and silken, though it licked at a paw that was stained crimson. It fastidiously ignored them, choosing instead to focus on its bathing efforts. At its feet was a gutted rat, nearly half as big as the cat itself. Its body was twitching, but its eyes were distant and lifeless. Its spilled innards seemed to wriggle and crawl as though fleeing a sinking ship.

Grimsby shuddered as his stomach recoiled at the unnatural sight, and he shook it away as best he could, trying to justify it as an Elsewhere illusion. It didn't help much. Despite the scene, though, he breathed a sigh of mild relief. "Must be Mansgraf's pet or something," he said.

Mayflower, however, did not relax. He kept his gun trained on the cat.

Grimsby frowned in confusion. "You allergic or something? It's just a cat."

"It's not a cat, Grimsby. Put your glasses on."

He shrugged but donned his large spectacles. When he did, the world of bricks, mists, and cracked red skies became a much duller one of concrete and fluorescent lighting. It was all quite mundane.

Except for the cat.

Everything in the Elsewhere had looked so strange that he hadn't considered that such a normal-looking creature should have been warning enough. With his earthly vision restored, the cat's true form was revealed.

The only part that was actually cat was its head. Or, more accurately, its bleached white skull.

The creature before him had the skull of a cat, but its body was almost mechanical, though not like any robot Grimsby had seen in science fiction movies. It looked more like a junkyard sculptor's work than an engineer's. It was long and lean and mostly metal, but it looked to be forged of hammered scrap. It had no gears or pulleys or obvious mechanics, yet it moved all the same. Its teeth were old nails and its claws were literal razor blades. It had no tongue, yet it still continued to mimic licking at its paw in some eerie pantomime of life.

The blood on its paw and the dead rat at its feet, however, were both very real.

Grimsby felt his stomach rebel again, and he had to force it back into line. A cat hunting a rat was the natural order of things, but there was little natural about this creature.

"What is it?" he asked.

"It's a familiar," Mayflower said.

Grimsby felt a flash of recognition at the name. He had heard of them before in his studies but had never seen one up close before. They were companions and servants to witches skilled enough to craft them. The Department even deployed them on occasion, like the police might use dogs. "Maybe it's Mansgraf's?" he suggested. "I imagine I'd like some company if I were down here alone."

Mayflower grunted. "Probably safest to take it out," he said, aiming his gun carefully at the creature.

At that, the familiar ceased licking its paw and turned to look at Mayflower. Its long tail of chain links began to flick in a rattling imitation of an agitated alley cat.

"I don't think that's a good idea," Grimsby said.

"Why not?"

"Well, for starters I think it understood you. Which means it's at least partially intelligent."

Mayflower gritted his teeth. "It's a familiar, not the real thing. Magic programmed through a skull and given a body. It's closer to a toaster than an animal."

The cat's tail began to clatter faster.

"You're making the toaster mad," Grimsby said. "Look, there's no way it wasn't Mansgraf's. And if it's smart enough to understand you, it was smart enough to understand her. Maybe it can help us."

"Maybe it can't."

"Even if it can't, Mansgraf was your friend. Do you really want to honor her memory by blowing away her pet?"

Mayflower turned a baleful eye toward him. Grimsby struggled to suppress the chill that passed over him. The barrel of the Huntsman's gun was only a short arc from bearing down on Grimsby's chest, if he had the inclination.

For a second, Grimsby thought he might actually do it. However, he instead spat a short curse under his breath and lowered his weapon.

The cat flicked its eyeless gaze between them, turning its whole skull to do so, before tilting its head at Grimsby in a disturbingly unnatural gesture. Then it unceremoniously picked up its vanquished prey and clinked off into the dark.

"I hate those things," Mayflower said. "Abominations. A hairsbreadth from necromancy."

Grimsby shrugged. "If I remember right, they don't animate the actual spirit that inhabited the skull. They just use the departing spirit to shape the magic and make it imitate the creature. Like—music being pressed into a vinyl record. You just have to use a lot of spirits before you actually animate the thing, then have the spell imitate the creature, like a needle in the grooves of the record. It doesn't trap the spirit, which is a lot better than the alternative."

"And the alternative?" Mayflower asked darkly.

"Well, if you did it wrong, pieces of the spirit can get sort of—stuck."

"Enslaved spirits," the Huntsman spat. "Necromancy."

Grimsby held up his hands defensively. "Hey, I don't approve of it, either. But familiars aren't the same thing."

Mayflower grunted. "Witches." He shook his head. He looked down the hall, past the red pool on the ground where the familiar's prey had been. At the far end was a set of large metal double doors that looked like they had been transplanted from a meat freezer. "That's her lab. What do you see, Grimsby?"

Grimsby pulled off his glasses to reveal the Elsewhere. He hadn't noticed before, but the hall beyond emanated an eerie red light, one that was a deeper, more sanguine shade than the skies had been. The sound of ominous wind filled the tunnel, like an autumn gust full of dead leaves, yet the air was still. Shadows flitted over the walls, pausing to turn featureless heads toward him before vanishing again. He shivered. The Elsewhere was always full of shadows. Most of them were harmless.

But most was not all.

"It's . . . different than before," he said. "There's something I can't quite make out."

The silhouette of Mayflower turned toward him, hardly more than a shadow itself. When he spoke, it was a distant whisper. "Then get closer, witch. It's your job to see."

Grimsby gulped. He felt sweat begin to form like dew on his

scalp. Even with his sight, a skilled witch could hide traps and worse in the Elsewhere. Not to mention the more mundane but still looming worry that he'd stumble upon another land mine.

He didn't want to go any farther, but he couldn't just stand there, either. Every moment that passed was one in which the Department got closer to finding him and one more Mansgraf's killer had to disappear. He took a deep breath and made his way forward, inch by inch. His feet scuffled along the ground; his knees hardly able to bend enough to move.

The hall seemed to twist and shrink, and Grimsby was uncertain if it was his own nerves or if the Elsewhere was playing tricks on him. The fickle realm was unnerving that way. The pipes that ran along the walls seemed to slither like steel snakes burrowing deeper into the earth with arterial pulsations. The ambient red light grew darker and yet more intense, making Grimsby squint through it.

Suddenly, he felt himself cross some kind of threshold. The floor beneath him felt as though he was standing on thin glass. Then it shattered.

He fell.

Cold pressed against him, smothering his screams and numbing his skin. It was like plummeting down through an ice storm. A keening wail filled his ears, louder and louder until he vainly, breathlessly, screamed back just to hear anything else. The sound grew so loud that he nearly forgot he was falling. He clutched at his head in an effort to keep it from splitting apart.

Then it was suddenly still. Nothing left but black and silence. The world was now lightless, as though the thousands of red lightbulbs around him had all burned out at once. He whipped his head around in a panic, but he could see nothing. In fact, he couldn't see, hear, or feel anything at all. His body gave him no sensations or signs. He wasn't even certain he was moving. He fumbled for his glasses, but they were nowhere to be found. The dark was all around him, either devouringly large or gravely small. Grimsby wasn't sure which frightened him more.

A skittering began to fill the dark, like claws scrabbling over dried bones. The black began to boil with gray mist, but in the plumes and contours, Grimsby saw crowded and starving faces. The mist surged around him, encircling him. The forms inside it rasped and keened, though they remained hidden.

Finally, it was all around him, a scratching, snatching fog of cold that crept in on him. A tendril touched his arm, and pain flashed through him, the only sensation in the still blackness. Fingernail-shaped scratches appeared in his flesh, weeping bright red blood.

Grimsby shrieked and withdrew his arms and legs, curling into the smallest ball he could as the mist drew closer.

He was suddenly fairly certain he was about to die.

Then, like a starving avalanche, the mist surged forth.

TWELVE

GRIMSBY SCREAMED, THROWING HIS ARMS OVER HIS eyes. He hunched into himself, feeling more raking scratches covering his body, each digging a little deeper than the last.

Then, just as he felt himself inhaling the razor mist, it receded. It was as though someone had pulled its leash, like a rabid dog. Tendrils still licked at him here and there, but on their own they were more like thorns than teeth. Grimsby felt the cold dissipate, though the pain remained. He lay there, quivering in a huddled mess, and heard only his own sobbing moans.

Then a voice sounded in the dark, like the croak of a toad large enough to engulf the earth.

"Little lost boy, come to the gingerbread house with no crumbs to guide him home."

Grimsby flinched and made a noise that, even in his agony, he was ashamed of. It was a gargled, pleading, and desperate cry for help.

"But quite a Gretel you've found." The voice was oddly cheerful, despite its guttural sound, like a child home from school with strep throat and ice cream. "Though he cannot help you here in the dark. But Wudge could."

The mist receded more, just barely, but enough so that Grimsby no longer felt the edges of its cold claws clamoring against his skin. He could feel it nearby, like a morgue freezer's breath rolling over his flesh. He took in a shuddering gasp, and it came out as a pained moan. He slowly peeled back his arms and opened his eyes.

The world was still an utter blackness, with a ring of the gray mist swirling, sharklike, around him. Just a few feet away, he saw the glow of a pair of familiar eyes. The mist intermittently obscured his sight of the eyes, moving too fast, like storm-drawn clouds over twin full moons. The howling faces were just barely visible in its depths, seeming furious that they couldn't reach him.

He tried to focus on the eyes that lay on the other side of the mist. "Wh-who?" Grimsby managed, his throat still trembling from fear.

"So rude to ask, yet ruder not to tell," the voice said, the eyes rolling in an invisible skull. "You should be thanking Wudge, not asking questions."

"Wudge?" Grimsby said, straining to be heard over the screaming blackness. "You're Wudge?"

The hovering eyes rolled again. Grimsby could see now that they were yellowed with irises like a goat's, the same he had seen when first descending into Mansgraf's lair. "The little witch does not listen well. Perhaps Wudge was wrong to let it live."

At its words, the whirling wall of faces began to inch closer, grinning menacingly. Grimsby felt a sudden surge of pure panic. "No, no, wait! I'll be quiet. I mean, I'll try to, at least."

The gray receded slightly. "Good, good." Below the eyes, two wide rows of dozens of needle teeth revealed themselves, glimmering in the dark, though they didn't move with the voice. "Why have you come to the she-bitch's lair? She didn't say you'd come here."

Grimsby couldn't help but stare at the teeth. The smile was far wider than the thing's eyes. "I, uh, I'm here looking for a place to hide."

"Little boy has come to the lioness's den, looking to hide? It is she who you should be hiding from."

"You mean Mansgraf?"

Eyes glared and mouth twisted, spitting a stream of green sparks that faded into the dark, his voice changing to a mocking song. *"The she-bitch, the she-witch, the absolute stitch in my snitch. Duck in a ditch if you seek the she-bitch, or she will bewitch you and pitch you into a hitch."*

Grimsby's brow furrowed with the creature's furious singsong rant. "Yeah, that's Mansgraf, all right."

The eyes and mouth shook from side to side. "Why seek refuge with the woman of men's graves? Seems a dangerous thing to Wudge. Even for a little, tiny half-witch."

Grimsby gritted his teeth and ignored the odd insult and tried not to bring up the fact that he had a class D permit that said he was, technically, a full witch. "She's not dangerous anymore. Someone killed her, and I'm with the guy who's trying to figure out who."

The eyes grew wide. "What? What does the half-witch say?"

"She's dead. Mansgraf got killed last night and—"

"What?!" Wudge demanded, but before Grimsby could reply, the face vanished. For a long, dreadful moment, he was alone in the vortex of mist and shadows. And it was shrinking.

His mind raced. Had he upset the voice? Had he scared it off? He hoped not. It seemed like Wudge, or whatever it was, was the only thing between him and the hungry fog.

For the briefest moment, he missed the simpler yesterday of Mighty Magic Donald's Food Kingdom. At least there all the scars he got were emotional and from people he could see.

Echoing, toadish groans sounded in the distant darkness. They came closer and closer until they were a maddening, rattling chorus of giant bullfrogs.

Then the eyes appeared, and beneath them frowned a wide, wide mouth full of needle teeth. Grimsby wasn't sure what Wudge was, but he definitely wasn't human, nor any Unorthodox Grimsby had ever seen.

"The she-bitch is dead—it can't be true!" he shrieked. The face turned and paced in place, like a hovering mask with no wearer. "How dare she die and leave a bargain scorned?"

Grimsby, desperate to keep Wudge from leaving again, asked, "What bargain?"

The frown faced him again, the yellow goat eyes narrowed in anger, but the voice's ire trailed off into defeated sadness. "Nothing. Nothing, nothing, nothing. Wudge should have known. Never trust witches. Never, never, especially not she-bitches." His voice was growing even more froggish, like his invisible throat was straining.

"I—uh, am sorry?"

Wudge turned and glared reddened, watery eyes at Grimsby. "Wudge thinks he will let the Geist eat you now."

This time, it was Grimsby's eyes that widened. He could only assume the Geist was the hungry mist. "What? No! Wait!"

His protest was drowned out as the Geist swirled around him and began to keen and wail, like a cloud of iron wires screeching against one another. It closed in on him, the flickering shadows drowning out Wudge's face.

"And why should Wudge wait for you?" His voice called, quiet but piercing through the sound of the mist, "Nobody ever waited for Wudge."

The Geist closed in, the cloying, pressing presence of it collapsing upon Grimsby like a blender of ash. It was going to tear him apart—he was certain of it. He felt the dull dread in his belly as surely as the manacles on his wrists.

"Please," Grimsby pleaded, "I just want to go back!"

There was a long pause.

"So does Wudge."

Suddenly, the eyes closed, the face vanished, and even the mist around Grimsby seeped away into blackness.

Then Grimsby opened his eyes. He hadn't remembered closing them, but he opened them all the same. He stared in confusion for a moment. How did the ceiling get up there? Wait. He was lying on his back. When did that happen? And why did his head hurt? Why did everything hurt?

Suddenly, a shadow emerged above him and seized his arm. He struggled in wild, aimless panic, but its iron grip on him did not loosen. It hauled him to his feet and another hand shoved something onto his face.

And then the Elsewhere was gone. He was staring at Mayflower and his head was thundering in a slightly less literal sense.

"What the hell happened?" Mayflower said.

Grimsby blinked a few times before remembering he had a voice to use. He felt pains all over, especially on his arms. "I don't know. Maybe it was some kind of trap Mansgraf left? What did you see?"

"You just passed out and dropped like a rock," Mayflower replied. "Then started moaning and wriggling around in the dirt. Couldn't tell if it was a really bad dream or a really good one."

"Bad," Grimsby said. "Definitely, definitely bad."

Mayflower finally loosened his grip. "I figured that when you started bleeding."

Grimsby winced as a sudden, sharp pain struck him where Mayflower's grip had been. He looked down to see his own blood soaking into the black cloth of his T-shirt in long, thin streaks. He gently peeled back one short sleeve to reveal his shoulder. The fabric was perfectly intact, but the skin beneath was covered in shallow rakes, like those from dozens of sharp, child-size fingernails. He felt them all over his back as well, throbbing and stinging, though he found no trace of them on his scars.

"I don't think it was wholly a dream," Grimsby said.

Mayflower's gaze turned from the scratches to the ground by the wall. "Looks like you weren't the first to fall into this one." He knelt and reached out, picking up something small and white. He held it out to Grimsby, revealing a rat's skull. It was covered in scratches, some so deep they cracked the bone. "I think you were lucky it didn't last long. Otherwise you'd have lost a few pounds."

"Maybe all of them," Grimsby said, staring at the skull, his head unconsciously nodding. "Right. Um, excuse me."

He turned and stumbled a few feet back down the hall in the direction they had come from before he began to retch. He hadn't eaten much that day, so it mostly spilled out as acrid bile over the concrete floor, darkening the gray dust to yellowed black slime. He stood there for several minutes, his cuffed hands pressed against the wall to brace himself, before he finally spat out the last strands of bile and turned back to Mayflower.

The Huntsman was standing, waiting with surprising patience. "You all right, witch?" he asked.

Grimsby half shrugged, the motion stretching his skin painfully.

"Good. Because now we get to go into her lab. The real dangers may yet be ahead."

"Oh good. I'm getting tired of these fake dangers, only almost killing me. Back in my day—" Grimsby rambled, desperate to talk to calm himself, but Mayflower had already continued down the hall.

Grimsby shook his head. "Yeah, I'm definitely the crazy one," he muttered as he followed the Huntsman.

THIRTEEN ✺

MAYFLOWER GESTURED TO THE HEAVY SLIDING DOOR that led into the lab. "See anything?"

Grimsby, still reeling from Mansgraf's last trap, removed his glasses, studying quickly and nervously. The steel door shifted to old and weathered wood, like the door of an old ship's cargo hold. He looked for subtle changes in light or sound but found none. Nor did he find any runes or signs of movement. Finally, satisfied, he replaced his glasses and shook his head. "Nothing there."

Mayflower nodded, seized the door handle, and pulled it open wide, gun at the ready.

The room beyond looked to have been some kind of cistern once. It was circular, about twenty feet across, with both a floor and a ceiling of metal gratings. A spiraling staircase at its center both climbed up and descended. Through the metal links of the grates, Grimsby could see more levels above and below like floors in a tower, but the structure was tall enough that he saw no end.

This level was relatively bare. Mostly full of barrels and crates stacked on wheeled pallets. Some were labeled in obscure languages and dialects Grimsby couldn't even recognize. Most of them, however, read simply POTABLE WATER or MRE.

"Is . . . is this a doomsday shelter?" Grimsby asked.

"It's an everything shelter," Mayflower said. He looked up and down. "Her notes are up above, I think, and her lab down below. You take the lab; I'll check the notes."

"Wait, why do we have to split up?"

Mayflower rubbed the bridge of his brow. "I don't have time to babysit you, witch. I can read notes, but I've got no clue what is going on in a lab anywhere, let alone hers." Then, after seeing what must have been a terrified expression on Grimsby's face, he added, "She wouldn't have put traps in her own lab to stumble over while she was working. Probably."

"Probably? Why did you have to add 'probably'?"

"Mansgraf was volatile and unpredictable. Plus paranoid as hell. Nothing's beyond her. Just help me find something that I can use to end this mess."

"Eyes aflame," Grimsby cursed, looking down into the dimness below the grating. "I don't like this place."

Mayflower growled in frustration. "Look, you've only got to hide here for a few days. Then you can go back."

Back, Grimsby thought. *Back to what?*

He felt his stomach twist at the thought. It was like someone had reminded him he had been starving, except it wasn't food that he lacked.

It was much more.

He tried to shake the feeling away, but it clung to him. He was forced to ignore it instead.

"Fine, I'll go look downstairs. But if I don't make it back, tell my girlfriend I—"

"Don't bother. I know you don't have one."

"Fair. Well, in that case, tell my friends—"

"Try again."

"Ugh, fine. Just tell my landlord I'll be late this month."

Mayflower didn't reply and was already climbing the central

staircase, grumbling about punks or something similar as he did. Grimsby tried to cover his nerves and unease with a grin but didn't do a great job of it. He felt like he was mostly just baring his teeth.

He was about to delve into the laboratory of a powerful, paranoid, and possibly insane witch who had just been murdered. Whatever he might find, it was unlikely to be pleasant, or conducive to his overall health.

And even if everything went perfectly, and Mayflower went off to find the killer and clear his name, Grimsby wasn't sure he liked the idea of going back to his old life.

The last few hours had been terrifying, to say the least, but they'd also been more than that.

They'd been different. They'd been exciting. And they'd been the closest he'd ever been to what it might be like to be an Auditor.

He took a step down the stairs toward the dimness below and found himself hesitating as instinctive fear gripped him. He shook his head firmly and took a deep breath through his teeth. This was the closest he had ever been to doing something a real Auditor might do, and this was how he was handling it?

Maybe Mansgraf had been right about him. Maybe he wasn't Auditor material.

His misshapen grin turned to a grimace as he ground his teeth.

No, he wouldn't be afraid. Well, at least not so afraid that he wouldn't follow through.

She had been wrong about him, and he had a chance to prove it. Even if it was only a chance. Even if it was only for today.

Even if it was only to himself.

He clanked down the metal staircase, feeling it rattle with his own steps as well as Mayflower's above. As he passed each level, he studied it, searching for a place to begin.

The first level was covered in shelves lined with old books. Some of them were scattered over the numerous tables that crowded the floor, but they were coated with a thin layer of dust, meaning Mansgraf hadn't used them recently. Grimsby glanced at the ones that had been left out, but their titles were in languages he didn't recognize.

There were pages of notes as well, scribbled on torn notepads, scattered around the books, but they were even more of a mess. He glanced over them for a moment, not daring to actually touch them, but found them written in some ugly script unlike any he'd ever seen. It was either very obscure or Mansgraf's own cipher. Either way, it would be of little use.

The next level down smelled of chemicals, and he found something much more like a laboratory than he was really expecting. In fact, it almost looked like a morgue. Stainless steel shelves and counters ringed the circular concrete walls. Sheet plastic had been laid down over the grated floor to prevent drippings. Vials, burners, tubes, and more were organized in impossibly neat fashion, starkly dissonant with the crazed book pile above.

He glanced at the lines of vials. Some of them were simple, viscous fluids; others had things floating in them. Lizards, rodents, insects, and other, less pleasant creatures and parts of creatures, as well as liquids that swirled and moved without ceasing. They seemed to be gathered for brewing elixirs. He grimaced. That particular area of witchcraft had always eluded and disgusted him.

One final level down, it was surprisingly barren. The reinforced concrete walls were lined with stainless steel shelves, carefully packed with containers of various sizes and shapes. Boxes, chests, barrels, even a briefcase or two. They towered all the way to the plastic-layered grating of the floor above.

Although they were a motley assortment of containers, they were arrayed at meticulous distances, their outlines measured out by lengths of silver duct tape denoting a very specific space for them to be placed, with not one touching any of the others. Their old surfaces were all marked with symbols, draped in chains, and even bound in fitted iron cages. It took Grimsby only a moment to recognize the symbols as being very similar to the ones May-flower's jeep-cage had.

It must have been some kind of binding magic, he thought, though not like his own Bind spell. His magic brought things to-gether; this magic trapped things within.

Finally, he noticed a door set into the concrete wall of the cis-tern. It was wood, oddly enough, old wood that was more gnarled than the bark of any tree. It was dark from ragged age, and just looking at it made him feel like he had splinters in his eyelids. Burned into the frame around the door were symbols similar to those on the boxes and other containers. At the top was a small indent, like a knot in a tree, though it looked to have once held something geometric inside. Now, however, it was empty.

He quickly slid off his glasses, delving into the Elsewhere to see what he could glean, but he saw it was all disturbingly similar to the waking world. In fact, the door and each of the boxes had remained unchanged in every detail, as though the warping nature of the Elsewhere could not faze them as it did all other things.

"Stupid half-witch," a familiar voice behind him croaked.

Grimsby whirled, arms raised in a moot defensive gesture that any martial artist would have found insulting.

There, hidden beneath the curving metal staircase, was a pair of yellow, horizontally slitted eyes in the shadows.

"Wudge!" Grimsby hissed. He flexed his fingers nervously. He instinctively summoned his Impetus, but the heat in his cuffs grew to a painful glow and sparks spat pitifully from his scars.

Wudge half scoffed, half snorted. "Very stupid half-witch," he said.

"What are you doing here?" Grimsby demanded.

The eyes narrowed, as though annoyed at the idiocy of his question. "Sitting."

Grimsby, oddly enough, felt his nerves ease at the reply. Last time they had met, Wudge seemed to hold Grimsby's life in his hands. He had little experience dealing with that. But smart-mouthed quips? That was more in his realm. "No, I mean why are you here? What do you want?"

"It doesn't matter," Wudge said, his croak strangely solemn. "The she-bitch will never give it to him now."

Grimsby stared for a moment before he realized that Wudge was actually . . . tiny. The space below the stairs from which his eyes stared couldn't have been more than a foot tall. "What do you mean?" he asked, arms still raised defensively.

The creature sighed, too despairing to be annoyed anymore. "The she-bitch had something Wudge wanted more than anything. She told Wudge she'd give it to him if Wudge watched over her home. But now she's gone, and she took it with her. Wudge will never have what he wants now."

Grimsby felt a twinge of sympathy for the creature. Perhaps even empathy.

"Yeah, Mansgraf has a way of doing that," he said. "She took what I wanted most, too."

Wudge's yellow eyes widened in surprise. "She did?"

Grimsby nodded, feeling his unease fade away. "What does she have that you want?"

Wudge reached out from his tiny alcove, revealing a thin and spindly hand that was as long as Grimsby's, but only half as wide. The tips of his gray-green fingers were covered in bulbous pads, giving him an almost cartoonish look. Grimsby wasn't sure if he should be amused or creeped out, so, just to be safe, he was both.

Wudge pointed past him toward the door.

"What's through there that's so important?" Grimsby asked.

"Everything," said Wudge quietly, withdrawing his hand.

"Ominous. But what's actually in there?"

"Wudge—isn't sure."

"Why not open it, then?" he asked. "Something tells me she won't mind."

"Only her key can open her locks, and one of her locks holds the door closed. But she doesn't keep the key here. It's too dangerous. Too near the boxes."

"So where's the key?"

The fingers of the spindly hand drummed along the steps, though Wudge himself was still hidden in the shadows. "Wudge doesn't know. She-bitch is clever. She cursed the key. When it is used, it vanishes and reappears in the worst place it can find."

"And where's that?"

"That depends on who is looking for it."

"So without the key, you can't get to everything that's inside there."

Wudge's eyes nodded.

"Well, if you ever get it open, and you find my career in there, let me know, would you?"

"Wudge might."

Grimsby snorted and shook his head. Despite their earlier encounter, he was starting to like Wudge, whatever he was. "Why don't you step out and show yourself, Wudge? I feel like we should have a proper introduction."

Wudge's eyes narrowed suspiciously. "Why?"

"Because that's what reasonable people-ish things do. And I don't know about you, but I'm a reasonable people-ish thing."

"Wudge is not reasonable, and Wudge is not people-ish."

"Well, I don't suppose I can argue with that too much. But maybe you could do it as a favor to me?"

Wudge pondered silently for a moment. "A favor for a favor?" he asked.

Grimsby shrugged. "Sure, buddy. A favor for a favor."

"So be it," Wudge said, the words having odd weight to them.

Grimsby watched as Wudge began to crawl out from his cave beneath the stairs. His long, thin arms were almost disturbingly gangly, like an emaciated child whose limbs had grown overly fast.

His gnarled hands pulled and he grunted as he heaved himself forward, emerging from the shadowed recess beneath the stairwell.

For a moment, it looked as though he had a bulbous, pale head covered in wrinkly white hairs. It took Grimsby a moment to realize that it wasn't his head at all.

It was a large onion, or at least part of one.

It looked to have been hollowed out, with eyeholes gouged in place by spidery fingers. Wudge seemed to be wearing it as a helmet.

It took some angling to squeeze his large, onion-helmed head out of the gap between steps, but once he had he tumbled forward in a wild somersault.

He landed in a sprawled spread, like he was about to make a snow angel in the concrete.

He climbed to his feet, which were as long and thin as his hands but wrapped in strips of ratty leather. He brushed off his only other garment, a burlap loincloth around his waist, and then turned to Grimsby, puffing up his sunken chest until his ribs looked like they might cut through his skin. He stood proud at his full height, which might have been a foot and a half tall. On his long tiptoes.

He regarded Grimsby with goatlike eyes through the two finger-dug holes in his onion-helm, and spread his wide, wide mouth in a grin full of needle teeth.

"Behold Wudge!" he proclaimed. "Last of the Wudges. Dweller in the dark and guardian of the she-bitch's lair." His long, leathery ears dangled on either side of his head, flopping nearly to his elbows, making him look a bit like a hairless rabbit.

A hairless rabbit with *a lot* of teeth.

Grimsby stared for a moment, taking in the admittedly unexpected sight. Most Unorthodox could pass for normal humans in dim enough lighting. Vampires, Therians, and even selkies and many others were hard to tell apart most of the time.

Until they weren't.

But there were even more things that he had heard of yet never seen, things that no one could ever confuse with a person. And they were often terrifying. More monster than Unorthodox. He had seen a gargoyle once on the news, just a few seconds of footage. In that time, it had killed six officers and collapsed a building before Auditors brought it down. It had taken him a week before he could sleep without thinking about one being in his closet. That was only a couple of years ago.

And yet he'd never seen anything quite like Wudge before. No one would mistake him for human, but he wasn't exactly a monster, either. Perhaps something more in-between. Though he supposed that was where most Unorthodox fell.

He shook away his surprise and held out his hand to the small creature.

"Grimshaw Grimsby, court wizard of Mighty Magic Donald's Food Kingdom," he said. "Nice to meet you."

"Their pizza tastes like newt gizzard," Wudge said with distaste before squinting at Grimsby's offered hand, tugging idly at his ear as he pondered. "Wudge can't give you his hat," he said firmly, wrapping long fingers protectively around his helmet.

"What? No, I don't want your hat. I just wanted a handshake."

Wudge's toadish mouth turned into a frown that was wider than his head. "Half-witch is gross. Shake your hand yourself."

"No, it's how people say hello. You just grab each other's hands and shake."

"Why?"

Grimsby frowned. "No idea, but it's how it's done."

Wudge grumbled and tentatively took Grimsby's offered hand. His fingers were wiry and surprisingly strong. Grimsby couldn't help but think they'd have no trouble strangling him. Instead of conventional shaking, however, Wudge rattled his hand from side to side like a seizure from the wrist.

"There," Wudge said, still dubious. "It is shook."

"Close enough," Grimsby said, prying himself from Wudge's fingers. "Now, what favor can I do for you?"

Wudge's lips upturned in a smile that made Grimsby shiver for a moment. "Later. Later Wudge will ask."

"What if we don't ever meet again?" Grimsby asked.

"Wudge will find you. Wudge can find you now."

"Oh. Well, um, good, I suppose?" Somehow, something told Grimsby it wasn't all that good at all, but he shook away the concern. One problem at a time. Though he supposed he already had more than one problem at the moment. More correctly, he decided, not one more problem right now. "Do you think you could help me, Wudge?"

"Wudge doesn't know. Can't make you taller, if that's what you want."

Grimsby scowled and stood up slightly straighter. He was exactly average in terms of height. Globally speaking. "No, not what I mean. I need to help my, um, friend find out what happened to Mansgraf."

"Why?"

"Because I think whatever got her is after me. And because, if I don't, her friends are going to assume I'm the one that killed her."

Wudge croaked with a low, froggish chuckle. "Puny witch could never kill the she-bitch."

"Believe me, I know it. But they're looking for someone to blame, and that'll be me unless I can give them a better option."

"A tough bite of steak would be a better option," Wudge muttered under his breath.

Grimsby pretended not to hear. "Was Mansgraf doing anything strange in the last couple of weeks?"

Wudge tugged at his leathery ears in thought, balling them both up in one spidery hand. "Why should Wudge help you? You already owe Wudge a favor."

"Well, that's true, I guess. But can't you just help me as a friend?"

"Wudge not your friend. And you not Wudge's." His tone was matter-of-fact, as though Grimsby had suggested they both had blue skin.

Grimsby thought for a moment. "Well, you somewhat owe me, too."

Wudge's large eyes narrowed like twin lunar eclipses. "How?"

"You didn't know Mansgraf was dead until I told you. If I hadn't, who knows how long you would have stayed down here waiting for her?"

Wudge thought for a moment. "Who *would* know?" he asked, as though contemplating a grand question.

"No—I mean, you owe me for saving you time."

Wudge's eyes narrowed and his teeth bared at the word *owe*.

"Not a lot!" Grimsby added hurriedly. "Just enough to tell me what you know, I think."

The tiny creature groaned. "Oh, fine. But only because Wudge is getting bored of talking. Three questions, half-witch."

Grimsby frowned. "Why three?"

"Because it is the best number. Now, two."

"Are you kidding—" he began, then quickly stopped himself. Wudge was more literal than he had anticipated.

Wudge only grinned his many, many teeth, waiting.

"Okay, fine, Wudgey-boy. Where has Mansgraf been?"

Wudge grinned, his croaking throat emitting a surprisingly childlike singing voice. *"A towny-town, all sleepy-sound, where she dug deep in the ground. But you'll never guess what she found!"* The words echoed unnaturally, making Grimsby's skin crawl. He thought he heard instruments coming from somewhere, but they weren't like any he'd heard before.

He shivered, almost not wanting to press further. "What did she find, Wudge?"

Wudge smiled his biggest smile and said, "Something she already had two of. Goodbye for now, Grimshaw Grimsby."

Then he vanished.

Grimsby blinked. Wudge was simply gone. Like someone had flipped off a light switch labeled *Wudge*. He reached up to take off his glasses and search for him in the Elsewhere, only to remember he'd had them off all along. Somehow, the tiny creature had just disappeared.

He had never seen anything like it before, or perhaps more accurately, never *not* seen anything like it before. All sorts of things could become invisible in the mortal world; it was why witches' extra sight was so useful. Usually invisible things were just inside the Elsewhere, and without a mask a witch should be able to see them, for better or worse.

And yet Wudge was gone, as surely as if he'd never existed at all. For a moment, Grimsby was uncertain if he had imagined the strange creature or not. He blinked hard several times, replaced his glasses, and blinked some more, but nothing changed.

"Grimsby!" Mayflower shouted from above, as though for the hundredth time. "You find anything?"

He glanced up to see Mayflower making his way down the staircase.

"Uh, maybe?"

FOURTEEN ✳

GRIMSBY FINISHED EXPLAINING HIS ENCOUNTER WITH Wudge, watching Mayflower's scowl deepen with every syllable he uttered. By the time he finished, the old man's frown was deep. Mariana Trench–deep.

"You saw a short, onion-hatted . . . thing, and it told you a riddle about Mansgraf?"

"Yeah, basically. Well, half song, half riddle. He actually could carry a tune, which surprised me."

"*That* surprised you?" Mayflower asked.

Grimsby shrugged. "Tiny guy had some pipes."

Mayflower glared at him; the only readable emotion in his expression was annoyance.

"You don't believe me."

"I believe when you fell, you landed on your head harder than I thought. Or maybe not hard enough."

"I spoke to him. He was Mansgraf's . . . security guard."

"Her security guard."

"Well, it's not like Brink's is hiring out secret-witch-lair night guards. To protect you from Unorthodox things, you need something Unorthodox."

"I never have," Mayflower said. His hand twitched toward his gun in an absently fond gesture.

Grimsby eyed the weapon, unconvinced it was an average gun. "Still," he said, "even the *great* Huntsman can't be in two places at once." He used air quotes liberally as he said Mayflower's title.

The great Huntsman grunted. "The part of this that's strangest to me is that you believed this . . . Wudge. Even if it was real, a creature of Elsewhere would never surrender information freely."

Grimsby ran his scarred hand through his hair, feeling a small prickle of sweat on his scalp. "What—what do you mean?"

"I mean that Elsewhere things are hungry. And people are stupid. When they make deals, it usually ends up with the people dead and the monster full."

"Well, those require, like, contracts and stuff, right? Like a shady time-share?"

"No. The old-fashioned creeps might. Those are the real scary ones. But even a willing agreement from your own mouth is enough to seal a simple deal."

"So, hypothetically—" Grimsby began.

Mayflower interrupted him with a weary sigh. "You didn't."

"I just agreed to do him a favor—"

"What favor?" he asked sharply.

"Well, I don't really know yet—"

"You didn't even say what it is you'd do? All for some useless song?"

"Well, technically the song was a freebie."

"So what did you ask for the favor?"

"I, uh, got a handshake," Grimsby said.

"A handshake."

"Yeah. Hardly worth it, though. It was a bit clammy, no eye contact, six out of ten, as far as handshakes go."

"Dumbass," Mayflower said, taking a half-burnt cigarette from his pocket and sticking it in his lips to chew on the filter.

"Well, it's not like I—"

"Stop. Just—just stop." Mayflower pinched the bridge of his nose and screwed his eyes shut. "You better pray that . . . Wudge thing doesn't cash in on that favor while you're still alive. Sometimes they forget mortals are, well, mortal. He might forget until you're long dead."

"You mean hope he'll forget it for, what, sixty years?"

"Sixty years?" Mayflower asked. "So you're an optimist, then?"

Grimsby began to reply but stopped halfway through. "Wait—was that a joke?"

"Depends on your answer, really."

He couldn't help but smirk a little. "Either way, it's done now, for better or worse—"

"It's for worse," Mayflower said.

"For worse, then!" Grimsby threw his cuffed hands in the air dramatically, then winced as he tugged open a half dozen scabs from his earlier encounter with the clawing mist. "It's still done. Look, what are we going to do about what Wudge said? Mansgraf found something, and it was right before she disappeared. That can't be a coincidence."

"No," Mayflower said, glaring around at the shelves of containers. "No, it can't."

"Wait, you agree with me?" he asked, hardly believing the thought.

Mayflower only growled as he flipped through the handful of manila folders in his grip and tossed one to Grimsby.

Grimsby promptly fumbled it, scattering papers everywhere. "You can't just throw something to me without some kind of warning!"

"Jesus," the Huntsman said, shaking his head. It sounded like half curse and half plea.

Grimsby mumbled to himself as he stooped to gather the fallen papers. He shuffled them into a rough order and began to skim. It was some kind of proposal or report. Most of it was in a technical jargon that took forever to say nothing. But one thing on the page stood out to Grimsby.

And furthermore, it is my belief that the Hand can be found at these coordinates in modern-day Salem, MA.

Salem. It was a place with a checkered history for witches. He looked up to Mayflower.

"I don't get it. Is this a report of some kind?" Grimsby asked.

"No. It's a request to excavate some site in Salem. An old burial ground."

"Wait—a dig in Salem, you said?"

"Yeah."

"*A sleepy town*,'" Grimsby quoted, pointing to the map of Salem in the file. "'*Where she dug in the ground.*'"

Mayflower scoffed, but not in total derision. "Maybe there's something to this Wudge story after all."

"You think Mansgraf was there?"

"I do."

"This Hand, whatever it is, must be what she found," Grimsby said. "'Something she already had two of.'"

"Seems likely."

"But what is it?"

"I don't know. But I know it can't be good."

"How?"

Mayflower pointed to the lone space on the looming, crowded shelves that was missing a container. "Because a Wardbox is unaccounted for, and I happen to know Mansgraf had a suitcase with her before she died."

"So, this Hand, she put it in that suitcase. But why?"

"To protect it."

"From what?"

"From everything," he said, chewing on his cigarette in thought. "Some objects are so powerful that they draw everything from the Elsewhere for miles around. Like chum in a sea of invisible, hyper-intelligent, magic sharks. Some things in our world can sense it as well."

"You think the thing that chased me—the thing that got her—sensed it, too?"

He frowned. "Not if it was in the Wardbox. It had to have known about it some other way."

"So if she had the Wardbox before she was killed, where's the suitcase now?"

The Huntsman didn't answer and instead only raised an eyebrow as though awaiting Grimsby's answer to his own question.

"Oh. Because whatever killed her took it."

"That's my guess."

"How do we know it didn't just break it open and take whatever's inside?"

"Wardboxes aren't some dime-store notions. They're made to keep what's inside in, and what's outside out. If someone wanted to break into one of these without the key, they'd have to be a damn sight better witch than Mansgraf, and I'm unconvinced such a person exists. Even if they did, I doubt that creature is one."

Grimsby shook his head. "I don't understand. Why didn't she just go to the Department? They could have protected her."

"Because Mansgraf was black-flagged."

"Black-flagged? What does that mean?"

"It means she was being hunted by the Department. That's why she vanished, and that's why she was alone."

"What? Why?"

"I think that thing's song is right. I think Mansgraf was there, at the dig, but I think she took the Hand they dug up—before the Department could get it."

"Took as in . . . she stole it?"

"Yeah."

"But that doesn't make any sense. Why would she steal something that the Department was going to get anyway?"

Mayflower said nothing; he only raised an eyebrow that encouraged Grimsby to go on.

"Unless she didn't want the Department to get it at all."

"That's my guess."

"Okay, so this Hand." He glanced at the request again. "She beat the Department to it and bailed. But why?"

"Could be any number of reasons. Mansgraf was a paranoid old bat. She's thought someone was out to kill her ever since I've known her."

"Well," Grimsby said, hesitating, "in fairness, you're only paranoid if you're wrong."

Mayflower's face darkened, but his tone stayed level. "True enough."

"So what's the Hand? Some kind of weapon?"

"Most likely. Something no one should have."

"So she didn't want the Department to get their *hands* on it, then," Grimsby said, grinning.

Mayflower glowered. "These aren't jokes, boy. Some of the things in these boxes could twist a man's mind to horrors you can't imagine. We once found a knife that drove a man mad. It made him kill his whole family and flay them to the bone. He had three kids."

Grimsby shuddered. "Right—sorry." He suppressed the tumbling of his stomach, albeit barely. "I tend to handle stress with jokes."

"I noticed. Bad ones." Mayflower shook his head and looked around at the Wardboxes, his brow furrowed deep. There were dozens of them.

Grimsby gulped, suddenly feeling uncomfortable surrounded by so many boxes of who knew what. "So, what now?"

"Now that I know about the Wardbox, I just have to find a way to track it."

Grimsby felt his excitement begin to rise. They had found something, something that might actually lead to settling this whole nightmare. "Because if we find the box, we can find both the Hand and the killer!"

Finding the killer would clear his name.

Finding the Hand might do much, much more.

He felt a dangerous hope rise in him for the first time in a long time. Mansgraf had stopped him from becoming an Auditor, but Mansgraf was gone.

Maybe there was a chance to undo what she had done.

Maybe there was a chance for *him* to be something more.

It was only maybe, but that was more than he'd had in a long, long time.

It took Grimsby a long moment to realize Mayflower was staring at him.

"What?" he asked.

"We?" the Huntsman finally said.

Grimsby winced and dug his toes into the dusty concrete. "I—I didn't mean . . ." He trailed off. Not because he was embarrassed, but because he realized he was telling a lie without knowing it.

"You didn't mean it?"

"Actually, I did. I was . . . thinking you could use some help."

The Huntsman's face was as implacable as stone, and just as emotive. "You don't think I could manage alone?"

"No—I mean—look, the faster we find this Wardbox, the faster we find the real killer, and I can—I can go back to my life."

Mayflower studied him for a moment, the checkered lighting from the grates above shadowing his face. "In a hurry to get back to the grease trap?"

"Y-yeah."

"Don't lie to me, boy," he said simply. "It'll get you hurt. And it'll get me killed."

"I—well—okay, fine!" Grimsby threw his hands in the air. "I

was thinking that if this Hand thing is so important to the Department, I could—"

"You could turn it in to them for another shot at joining."

Grimsby winced but nodded.

"You know Mansgraf died keeping that away from everyone. Them included."

"I know, I know!" He pressed on earnestly. "But with her gone, what are we going to do? Stick it down here and hope no one finds it? The Department is the safest place for it to go."

"And you just so happen to get a job out of doing this good deed."

He groaned. "Yes, okay? Oz forbid something good happening for me. That would make it opposite day for the first time in, say"—he glanced at his watchless wrist—"forever. Look, Mayflower. You need to find who killed your friend. I get that—"

"Do you?" he asked sharply.

Suddenly, Grimsby felt like he might be skirting the most dangerous trap he'd encountered since entering Mansgraf's lair. "I get it enough," he said firmly. "But this is my only chance, and I've got to take it." He felt his voice begin to crack as he struggled to say the words. "I've—I've got to."

Mayflower glared hard for a long moment. He stared, and Grimsby could have sworn he saw some kind of recognition flash over the man's face. Then it was gone.

"So how do we find the Wardbox?" the Huntsman finally asked.

Grimsby opened and closed his mouth a couple of times.

Before he said anything, there was a slithering of chains, and they both turned to see the cat familiar standing on the stairs. Its large, empty eye sockets regarded them imperiously. It made a strange, mewling noise and stared at them.

"Uh," Grimsby said. "You speak cat?"

"I'm a dog person," Mayflower said.

The cat mewled again, in a repetition so exact that it was disturbing. Then it turned, bounded up a few steps, and mewled again, just the same.

"What is it, Lassie?" Grimsby asked.

The familiar's tail twitched in a lifelike expression of annoyance, and it continued up the stairs until Grimsby could no longer see it through the grated floors.

"Accursed thing," Mayflower spat. "I still think I should have blasted a hole in its—"

He was interrupted as the familiar returned, razor paws clicking down metal steps, with something glimmering gold in its mouth.

It set the gold object down on the ground a few feet from Grimsby, then retreated to the steps and mimed licking its razor-blade paw.

He looked to Mayflower, then to the object. He shrugged and went to pick it up.

"Well, what did the monster find for us?" the Huntsman asked.

"It's . . . a fancy compass?" Grimsby said hesitantly.

He leaned down and picked it up. It was solid and surprisingly heavy in his hands. The ornate face was arcane, and not in the witchy way. It looked more like the work of an engineer with an artistic streak.

Mayflower said nothing for a moment. Then: "Bring it here."

Grimsby did so and handed the gold device to the Huntsman.

He examined it thoroughly. "Son of a bitch," he muttered.

"What is it?"

"Mansgraf's astrolabe. I remember seeing her use it before, tracking things no one should be able to track. She mentioned once to me that it was a . . . ." He frowned, trying to remember. "A dowser?"

Grimsby eyes widened. "A dowser? Are you sure?"

Mayflower nodded.

"If that's true—it might be just what we need. Good dowsers can find almost anything."

"Can you use it to find the Wardbox?"

"I think so. I've used a spell like it once before in training. Well, something sort of kind of like it, at least." He turned to the familiar, which sat waiting on the stairs, pretending not to notice them. "Good, uh, kitty?" he said.

The familiar mewled, though he was uncertain how. He nervously reached out toward it and petted its bleached skull. To his surprise, the cat allowed it, even deigning to lean slightly into his palm. Then it flicked its tail, batted at his hand, and darted away.

"Good thing you didn't blast it, huh?" Grimsby said.

Mayflower grunted. "What do we need for the spell?"

"We need to tie what we're looking for to the astrolabe, show it what we want. It's like telling your compass which way is north. I, uh, need part of whoever made the box."

"So some hair or nail clippings?"

Grimsby shook his head. "Not quite. Those are organic, sure, but hair's just a protein and nails are keratin. To have a connection to its owner, it needs to be more than organic. It needs to be something that is or was once alive."

"What about blood?" Mayflower asked, his eyes smoldering.

Grimsby's face twisted in slight disgust, though he supposed there were fouler choices. "Yeah, that could work. If Mansgraf made the boxes, we could just go to her death scene and collect some of her—"

"Mansgraf didn't make them. Probably for this exact reason. Anyone who killed her could use her body to find the Wardboxes."

"Darn. Well, without that, I don't think we can—"

"Mansgraf didn't make them," the Huntsman repeated. "But I know who did."

FIFTEEN

G RIMSBY CLIMBED TO THE SURFACE AND FELT A COLD
gust of autumn wind touch his sweat-dampened brow. He
hauled himself up onto the cracked asphalt and lay on his back for a
moment, staring at the cloud-strewn night sky, catching his breath.

A moment later, Mayflower grunted his way up the ladder as
well, climbing to his brown-booted feet and rolling his shoulders.
"Ladders are a young man's game."

"Not to mention chutes," Grimsby said. He felt a small flutter
of power as he used the word, which was normally reserved for his
spell. He quelled his Impetus with a slight effort. "So, you think
this— What did you call him?"

"Ashmedai," Mayflower said, half spitting the name.

"You think this Ashmedai guy made Mansgraf's Wardboxes?"

"I know he did."

"All right. And you think he'll just, what, give us some of his
blood?"

"No, I don't think he will. But that doesn't mean we can't take
some."

"I think that's illegal."

"The thing runs an underground sex-cult nightclub. Taking

some of his blood will probably be the most legal thing to ever happen there."

"So, is he human?"

"No. He's an incubus."

"An incubus?" Grimsby asked.

"A male version of a succubus. A sex demon."

"Demon? There's no such thing."

Mayflower nodded. "Not as a species, no. It's more of a category. Immortal things from the Elsewhere. They often feed on human vices. In this case, lust."

"A demon," Grimsby mused, shaking his head to hide the shiver that rolled through him. "I don't even know if demons can bleed."

"I do."

"Oh."

It was all Grimsby could manage to say as Mayflower went to his jeep, opened the back hatch, and began digging around.

"How are we even going to do this?" Grimsby asked. "Walk in and say please? I feel like that's dangerous even when it's not a demonic sex cult you're dealing with."

"With this," Mayflower said, finding a box and opening it to reveal dozens of charms and talismans. He selected one—it looked like a charred bone wrapped in a leather cord—and held it up.

"We're gonna fight a demon with dollar-store goth jewelry?"

Mayflower sighed. "It's a talisman. Dates back to old days. Very old days. Ash is scared of it."

"Why?"

"Because it's his own pinky bone. The last mortal to defeat him used this to do it. Historically speaking, every time he gets his ass kicked, it starts with this thing."

Grimsby found a grin curling itself over his lips despite his nerves. "Do you *pinky* promise?"

Mayflower only growled and draped the talisman around his neck.

Grimsby paused. "Wait, couldn't we just tie the dowser to that? I mean, it's a part of him, and bone is, or at least it was, living tissue."

The Huntsman frowned. "I doubt it. The thing's been torched for a long time, and fire has a way of purifying any magic that's left in something."

Grimsby felt at the burn scars on his arm. Nothing about them felt purified. In fact, they felt warped, even wrong, though he'd lived with them so long that he didn't notice as much anymore.

"So, we, uh, just walk in and threaten him with it?" Grimsby said, suddenly finding breathing a little difficult as Mayflower's plan unfolded.

"Yep. This could char him to cinders inside his own domain. It'd take him months to heal back from a pile of ash. Years more if I scattered those ashes from a jetliner."

"Ash to ashes, we all fall down," Grimsby muttered, his nerves forming into meaningless quips. He suddenly wondered when he had started sweating so much, and who had set his head spinning. "S-so we got the demon kryptonite. That's good."

"It's not all demons. Just him. Would barely slow down anyone else."

"Okay, Ash kryptonite. Just as good. Just as good. Just as good . . ." Grimsby said hurriedly. He was having trouble standing at this point.

Mayflower nodded and closed the hatch. He went toward the driver's door but paused when Grimsby didn't follow.

"Well?" the Huntsman demanded.

Grimsby tried to stay calm. He tried not to speak fast. He failed on both counts. "So, let me get this all straight. We're just going to go on a quick errand run to get some demon's blood, use it for a spell to track down a stolen Wardbox that contains something so hideous that the most dangerous witch alive was willing to stop being alive just to keep it out of the hands of everyone, and then we're going to try and bring down the thing that killed the most dangerous witch formerly alive?" He sucked in a desperate breath, having expunged his lungs for his rant. "Does that about cover it?"

"Sounds about right."

"Cool. You know, a few hours ago I was performing for a bunch of kids next to a plastic castle while wearing a tutu."

"And?"

"And? And? This is insane. I must *be* insane."

"It's your idea to come along, witch. You wanna climb back down that hole and wait for me to come back? Be my guest."

Grimsby found the option tempting. Down there, with a bunker around him, plotting to go and find the Wardbox and Mansgraf's killer had felt like wistful daydreaming. Now, up here, with Mayflower waiting on him to hurry, it felt all too pressing. He tried not to think of how much harder it would be when the time came to actually do it.

"Well, witch?"

Grimsby glared at the ground and clenched his fists so hard that his knuckles cracked. If he wanted to be an Auditor, he needed to act like it. He needed to earn it.

"No, I'm fine."

"No, you're not."

Grimsby thought for a moment, then nodded. "No, I'm not. Let's go."

The Huntsman regarded him for a short moment, then nodded. "Good." He led the way to the jeep and gestured to the back. "Get in."

"What? Not the back again!"

"The back. Again."

"Can't I just ride shotgun?"

"Do you even know how to handle a shotgun?"

"Why would that matter? It's just a figure—"

Mayflower reached over into the glove box and pulled out a sawed-off that was hardly over a foot long. "A figure of speech?" he said, finishing the sentence.

"Fine." Grimsby climbed into the back seat and slammed the heavy door shut behind him.

Mayflower got into the driver's seat a moment later and coaxed the jeep to life.

"So where's this demonic, underground"—Grimsby cleared his throat and felt his face redden awkwardly—"sex cult even at? Seems like something that wouldn't be on a GPS."

"A what?"

"Never mind. You know where you're going?"

"How else would I get there? Hold on."

Mayflower revved the engine, and the coughing jeep sputtered as though it was at death's door, then loosed a surprising roar. Apparently, the high gear got a lot of use and was well broken in. He half jumped the curb as he careened onto the side road that led to Highway 93, merging north shortly after to head back toward the lights of Boston.

"Don't you have any music?" Grimsby asked, feeling motion sickness well up in his stomach.

"Of course," Mayflower said. He rolled down the window to let the wind roar into the jeep.

"I meant like a radio!" Grimsby said, having to shout over the cold air.

Mayflower only shook his head and accelerated.

Grimsby gripped the bars of the back seat's cage, bracing himself against Mayflower's sudden lane changes and turns. He tried to gather his thoughts while he had a moment, but his head was swimming.

So much had happened in such a short time, he wasn't sure if it could even be real. The last year had passed by in a haze, each day more or less the same drudgery as the one before it. It had all felt like nothing would ever change, like his life was a boring, immutable script.

Yet, suddenly, here change was, and Grimsby didn't feel relieved, as he might have expected. He felt a little excited, sure, and even a bit anxious.

But mostly, he just felt sick.

He wasn't sure he was cut out for this. Even when his training had been fresh in his mind, more than a year ago, he wasn't the most promising of students. He had managed the challenges that Mansgraf and other instructors threw his way, but it had always been by the skin of his teeth and other bits. Despite his best efforts, his scars had always slowed him down compared to the others in his class. Even some of the simplest tasks for most students had proved to be a challenge for him, and now, with a real challenge before him, he doubted his own readiness.

And why shouldn't he?

He had failed the *tests* to become an Auditor. Why would he be any more prepared for the real thing? It was a profession that dealt with this kind of hectic madness as a matter of course, and required a calm and competent head.

Grimsby didn't feel like his head was either, let alone the rest of him.

Maybe he could have managed if he had spent the last year training or studying, or even doing something as simple as going to the gym. But he hadn't had the time.

No, that wasn't true. He could have found the time; he could have made it.

He hadn't had the will.

He had been oddly content in his melancholy slump. It wasn't a good life, but it was consistent. It was safe. And while it hadn't been easy, it had been habit, which was like easy but a lot more dangerous. He had wished for a year for things to change. He just had never suspected it might happen. Now that it had, he wasn't certain he was ready for it.

Especially not if it meant going to steal demon blood in order to hunt down a witch-killing monster.

Yet if someone had asked him, even a week ago, if he would want to do this, he would have jumped at the chance. It sounded like such an *adventure*. He would have thought it would be exciting and fulfilling.

But he wasn't excited, and he certainly wasn't fulfilled.

Mostly, he was just terrified.

One wrong step, one wrong move, and it might all end. Everything, in a single moment.

And that scared him so badly that he felt it in his bones. It scared him so badly that he *hurt*. His stomach felt like he'd eaten week-old MMDFK pizza. His head was a building pressure cooker. Even his joints, which usually only troubled him on his left arm, all felt like they were full of coarse sand, as though he had some kind of flu.

He had always thought this was what he wanted. That it was what he was meant to do, and only cruel fate had kept him from it.

Now he wasn't so sure.

But even demons and monsters weren't what scared him most. What really frightened him, down to his deepest core, was a simple question.

If he failed at this, what else was left?

The question, and perhaps the answer to it, might have scared him more than everything he'd faced in the last twelve hours combined, and he didn't dare dwell too long on it.

Focus on the task at hand, he told himself.

Help Mayflower find the killer. Get the Hand Mansgraf stole and return it to the Department. Then figure out what the blue blazes to do next.

It was almost a relief to think that he might not live long enough to even worry about that last part.

But the relief was short-lived, and he just felt sick again.

Mayflower's voice shocked him out of his focus. "We're close."

Grimsby tore his eyes from the rusted patch of metal that he'd been staring at for what must have been half an hour.

Mayflower was guiding the jeep at an unusually legal pace. The winding streets of the city wrapped around them, curling off into the dark around apartments and businesses that were awkwardly built by necessity. Many of the roads around the city had been there since horse and cart were the preferred method of transit, and they were appropriately chaotic as a result. He could smell the Chelsea River nearby, and the heart of the city stood tall, just visible to the south.

Mayflower took the jeep down a knot of side roads that had Grimsby's head spinning. The rugged wheels rattled over peeling asphalt and the battered bricks beneath. He wasn't sure how a whole city could feel so Gordian and ancient, but Boston managed.

"When we go in, stay close. Don't stare at anyone or anything. And most important, if somebody offers you anything or asks you anything, you say 'no,' got me?"

"No."

Mayflower flicked a glare into the rearview, and Grimsby thought he saw the passing of a smile, an actual human smile, on the man's lips. Then it was gone. "Punk."

He found a secluded alley that was just wide enough for the jeep and slipped inside, parking in a hollow surrounded by forgotten dumpsters.

Mayflower climbed out and cracked the back door for Grimsby to do the same. He shivered in his blue jeans and black T-shirt, but it wasn't just because of the cool air. Sweat had dampened every inch of the cloth and he struggled to shove his matted, dark mop of hair out of his face. He screwed his eyes shut for a moment, peeling off his glasses to clean them on his shirt. When he replaced them, he opened his eyes to find he had only made the smudges worse.

Meanwhile, Mayflower drew his pistol from within his coat and clicked open the cylinder, mouth moving as he counted silently. Inside his jacket, Grimsby caught a glimmer of what looked like silver in the streetlights.

"What's that?" he asked, gesturing at the Huntsman's jacket.

Mayflower glowered, but his stony face relented by the narrowest of margins. He peeled back the coat to reveal script stitched within the lining of his coat in what looked like silver thread. "Huntsman ward," he said. "Half the time, I'd prefer Kevlar, but this at least can do something against magic."

"I've never heard of that before."

"With good reason. If every witch knew about it, it wouldn't be long before one of you came up with a work-around."

"So why are you telling me?"

Mayflower frowned, doubt shadowing his face. Then he shrugged away the question. Instead, he tested the hammer and, satisfied, returned the pistol to the holster hidden in his jacket.

"Ready?" he asked.

"Are you gonna at least undo these cuffs?" Grimsby asked, holding up his shackled hands and clinking the inscribed chains.

"No."

"Come on. What if it goes bad in there?"

"Goes bad? This isn't a drug deal on television. It's not going to 'go bad' unless you make it go bad, and the odds of doing that are lower if you have the cuffs on."

"Oh, come on. How bad could I really make it?"

Mayflower only raised a brow.

Grimsby sighed. "Fine. But fair warning. If anyone asks about the handcuffs, I'm going to tell them it's a weird sex thing."

Mayflower's eyes narrowed a fraction of an inch before he lowered his gray-lensed shades.

"Come on. And keep quiet." He strode down the alley with long steps, making Grimsby scurry to keep up with him.

They had traveled half a block when the thrum of deep, bass-driven music began to resonate in Grimsby's chest. As they got closer, he could see a crowd formed on the sidewalk, a rough line of a couple hundred people all buzzing with chatter and energy. They were all waiting to enter a pair of double doors that looked like they were stolen from a cathedral. Manning the doors were two women; one wore a dark suit, while the other wore skintight leather so well fitted that the only thing it left to the imagination was whether she had any tattoos.

The suited woman was broadly built and tall, almost Amazonian, but without much in the way of litheness. Her shoulder muscles looked like they might tear the fabric if she gave any effort, though her face was oddly petite, with a button nose and slender jaw. She wore a pair of dark sunglasses, despite the night, and stood stoically behind her partner.

The second woman was built in a manner that made Grimsby's face redden. Her ample bosom was barely contained in her bodysuit, and the zipper had been tactically positioned a considerable distance below her throat to distract any- and everyone. Her slim waist and long legs drew the eyes of most every man in the queue, and Grimsby saw more than a couple of women sharply jab or tug at their preoccupied dates. A few more of the women were as entranced as the men. She had a long braid of dark hair that bounced around perkily as she moved along the line. She ushered some guests forward while sending others away.

Mayflower disregarded the line, crossing the busy street with unflappable confidence. Grimsby, meanwhile, flapped an apologetic gesture at the drivers who were forced to brake to allow them to pass.

Mayflower approached the steps that led to the club doors but halted. He met the eyes of the dark-suited woman at the door and nodded. She gave him a terse nod back, then focused her gaze on Grimsby, who could see her soft features darken, though what she saw, he didn't know.

The tightly dressed woman returned to the door, guiding a pair of couples who looked like they should be busy in photo shoots, not wasting their time at a nightclub. She passed by Mayflower and Grimsby without pause, gesturing up the stairs.

"Four more VIPs, Rora," she called up to the other woman in

a strange accent that lingered over her syllables. "Let's see if we can't make them regulars."

Rora nodded and stepped aside, allowing the guests in.

Only then did the dark-haired beauty turn to Mayflower and Grimsby. "My stars, if it isn't the Huntsman himself," she said to Mayflower, tilting her head in a manner that was appealing with no effort. "I thought you were dead."

"Aby," Mayflower said. "Been a while."

"More than a while," Aby said. "What do you want?"

"I need to talk to Ash."

Aby's expression settled into something like painted glass: opaque, cold, and beautiful. "Why?"

"I'm calling in a favor."

"I think you burned all those up," she said. "Along with the last club."

Mayflower shrugged. "I told Ash what I'd do if he didn't stop. He didn't stop."

"You know, some good girls got hurt in that fire."

"And Ash stopped buying those girls from overseas and started hiring them instead. I told you both what I was going to do, too. Blame Ash for the rest."

"I do. For his part."

"Good. Now take me to him. We need to talk."

Aby's icy expression cracked enough to reveal a wicked smirk. She glanced at Grimsby. "Who's the boy?"

"No one," Mayflower said curtly.

Her smirk widened, and she leaned in to look at Grimsby. As she leaned forward, he did all that was in his power not to examine the area around her suit's zipper. He found himself staring straight up into the cloud-cast night.

"I like him," Aby said with a smirk. "He's innocent. Not at all like you."

"He's not your type, creep," the Huntsman said.

"No, but I could make an exception. Or I believe I've a few girls that'd be interested. Some boys as well. What do you say, young man?"

Grimsby was uncertain whether he'd ever felt so uncomfortable and yet flattered at the same time. He didn't trust himself to speak, so he just shook his head vigorously.

"He's not on the menu," Mayflower said. "Now take me to Ash."

Her dark eyes shifted and became blackened pools with stirring fire deep below, like twin campfires on a new moon. "Everyone is on the menu," she said. Then her expression melted, as though she'd caught herself, and she settled into a languid shrug that reminded Grimsby of a stirring panther. "But have it your way. That *is* our business, after all. Follow me, Huntsman, follow me." She led the way up the stairs, her hips swaying in an entrancing rhythm.

Grimsby took one step and his foot missed the stairs, making him stumble. Mayflower's iron grip took hold of his shoulder and kept him from falling face-first.

"Jesus, Grimsby," Mayflower hissed as he caught him. "Get yourself together."

Grimsby blushed, knowing he'd let himself be distracted, though he didn't exactly regret it. "Right—right. Sorry."

He glared down hard at the stairs as he fell into line behind Mayflower. The one time he risked glancing up, he caught Aby studying him. While he initially felt a hot rush when he saw her, the look in her eye suddenly made him shiver.

It was hungry, and not in the good kind of way.

"Rora," Aby said as they passed the dark-suited woman. "Take over, would you? I'm taking them to see Ash."

Rora raised a brow that was as thin as a crosshair, but something in Aby's face kept her from pursuing the subject further.

Aby opened the doors, turned to Mayflower and Grimsby, and gestured in a mockingly gracious fashion, her voice almost lost in the thrumming music. "Welcome, boys, to the Lounge."

SIXTEEN

THE LOUNGE WAS DARK—DARK ENOUGH THAT GRIMSBY'S eyes strained and took a moment to adjust. The room felt like an arena, with a sunken pit at the center that was crowded with people, all moving sinuously to the driving rhythm of the music. Lights pulsed from the walls of the pit and across the floor, illuminating very little. Grimsby saw people dancing in tightly packed groups, but in the thready light he also caught glimpses of couples, and sometimes more than just couples, doing things that made his face redden. He hurriedly looked away.

Aby led them across raised catwalks that crossed over the writhing dance floor like bridges over seas of flesh. Hands reached out from below, drawn in her wake like rippling tides. Their fingertips brushed against her ankles, and she let herself linger for a moment under their touch before continuing onward. As she passed, the hands receded, like a crashing wave.

One arm reached toward Mayflower's boot, and the Huntsman casually stomped on it and ground it under his heel as he passed.

Grimsby scuttled awkwardly away from the few remaining limbs that reached toward him.

The catwalk wrapped around a bar that was raised above the

dance floor. Waitresses, all wearing dark dresses that were low-cut and short skirted, collected brightly colored drinks from the bar before nimbly weaving through the crowds. As they passed through the dancers, more fingers reached out, brushing against them as they had Aby. They weren't aggressive; instead they gave the impression of surrendering to the instinct to touch soft fabric as it passed by. Grimsby wasn't sure the entranced dancers even realized they were doing it.

In the flickering lights, Grimsby saw the waitresses' eyes reflect in a way that wasn't quite human, and just as Aby had, they lingered under the guests' touch for a short time. Their eyes quickly became half lidded, like lionesses after a full meal.

The catwalks were oddly labyrinthine. They split and spread into other corners of the large room, some occupied with booths full of people who were oddly close together, others leading to bays of nearly opaque glass where silhouettes of lithe women performing intricate and impossible poses were sharply projected against screens, like living art.

Grimsby felt a sharp jab on his arm and looked over to see Mayflower had elbowed him.

"Keep the hormones under control, boy," he whispered, "or you won't make it out."

Grimsby nodded hurriedly and tried to focus. He looked down, hoping to find something uninteresting to stare at. On the dance floor below, a woman and man in the crowd had been given a small ring of space and had decided they no longer needed clothes for the kind of dancing they were doing.

Grimsby bit his cheek, hard, and tore his eyes away to stare forward. There, he could only see Aby's swaying hips. He clenched his fists harder and dug his nails into his own palms. He stared straight up at the darkened ceiling, fully expecting to see some naked people doing adult gymnastics in the rafters for no obvious reason.

To his relief, there were none.

He stared into the dark and clenched his fists tightly. Only then could he focus on moving forward.

He was so focused that he nearly ran straight into Aby when she stopped before a velvet curtain, but Mayflower's cool grip seized his shoulder and pulled him back before he made contact. When he looked down, Aby looked a little disappointed.

"I'd like to ask you to stay close," she said. "These are private chambers, and I'd prefer our guests to not be disturbed."

Mayflower made a disgusted sound.

Grimsby only nodded, feeling like his eyes were wider than was strictly necessary.

Aby led them through the curtain, and the music suddenly ceased. The throbbing, trendy beat of the nightclub fell away, and soft, alluring violins suddenly laced the air with dulcet tones. They were in a long hall, the floor covered with plush red carpet, and the walls dotted with art that depicted more unbridled anatomy than Grimsby was used to seeing.

A woman approached them, Aby's extreme opposite in dress. Where Aby was clad in a parallel skin of opaque leather, this new woman was dressed in draping finery that was all but transparent. She curtsied lightly, but before she opened her mouth Aby waved a hand.

"Not now, Marion. I've got guests for Ash."

The woman raised a brow but did not argue. "As you wish. Do you desire anything else?"

Aby began to shake her head but then paused and glanced back at Mayflower and Grimsby. "Have Arienette meet us outside of the master suite."

Marion curtsied again and slid away, her sinuous body slithering beneath thin silks.

"What are you up to, whore?" Mayflower demanded.

Aby shook a finger at him. "So rude. Normally, I can see the appeal in that kind of language, but not from you, Huntsman." She donned an exaggerated pout. "I think you might actually mean it."

"Bite me."

"I've offered on numerous occasions," she said. "You aren't married anymore, after all."

Mayflower's hand rose, poised to reach into his suit. "Not another word."

She smiled triumphantly, content to be under his skin for the time being. She pretended to lock her lips closed before dropping the invisible key behind her zipper, coincidentally lowering it a few teeth as she did. She continued down the hall. It seemed impossibly long and winding. Doors lined either side of the corridor, and through some of them Grimsby heard the rapid, rabid sounds that accompanied sex. Sometimes he thought he heard four or more voices, all wrapped together in a sweaty chorus. He did his best to think about anything, absolutely *anything*, else.

He didn't do a great job of it.

Finally, they found their way to a staircase of lacquered wood. It wound upward in a spiral for a few stories. Aby led the way, her long legs flexing deliciously with each step. Mayflower followed, his glower focused on the back of her shoulder blades. Grimsby kept pace just behind him, trying to look anywhere that wasn't at Aby's legs.

He was failing at that, too.

At the top of the stairs was a landing just before a pair of double doors. A girl was waiting there, dressed much the same way Marion had been, though her attire was a touch more modest. She was young, perhaps even as young as Grimsby, though she had the sort of face that looked ageless, suitable for a mature woman or a youthful girl. She looked up, her eyes a glimmering, inhuman shade of silver, her silken hair something between bronze and gold. She smiled warmly at Aby, parting a stray strand of hair over a pin in her hair decorated with an origami crane.

"Arienette," Aby said. "There's someone I'd like you to meet."

"Of course, mistress," Arienette said, her voice like the chime of bells next to a stream.

"This is Leslie Mayflower, the Huntsman."

Arienette's silver eyes flashed, then fell flat. "Ah," she said, the word hardly a passing breath.

"Mayflower," Aby said in turn. "This is the girl you orphaned."

Mayflower's face hardened. For a moment, he said nothing; he only glared at Aby. Finally, he spoke in a voice low and harsh. "I've made many orphans," he said. There was no pride or confidence in his voice. Only quiet, hard truth.

"Yes, I imagine you have. I just thought you should know each other's faces," Aby said with a knowing smile. "Now, Arienette, I believe you have guests to attend to?"

The girl's silver eyes burned, and Grimsby thought he saw motes of fire deep within, but her face was as cool as marble in a wintered cemetery. "Yes, mistress."

She turned and slipped down the stairs, her eyes fixed on Mayflower until she was out of sight. Grimsby found himself feeling a pang of awkward jealousy that she hadn't looked his way once. It was a completely ridiculous feeling, but it was there all the same.

Mayflower bore down on Aby, his craggy eyes burning. "Why?"

"You burned down the old club," Aby said, all allure and charm drained away. "Many of the girls were hurt. One didn't make it. You killed that girl's mother. She deserves to know your face. And you ought to remember hers when you drink yourself to sleep."

Mayflower smoldered for a moment longer; then the fire in him suddenly seemed to burn out. His whole body slumped a few fractions of an inch. Not much, but enough. It took only a moment for Mayflower to recompose himself, but it was too late. Grimsby had noticed.

Aby had noticed, too. And she smiled.

Grimsby felt a cold ripple of fear roll over him. He had yet to see the Huntsman bested at anything, and yet Aby had struck a blow against him, and it had landed. And she seemed to do it with such ease.

In a sudden flurry of doubt, Grimsby realized that the Huntsman was not as indestructible as he might have believed, and he felt much less safe than he had just moments ago.

"Now then, boys," Aby said after letting the small defeat linger for a few moments. "Let's have a chat with Ash."

She opened the doors, revealing a dimly lit, lavishly appointed bedroom. A massive bed that would have dwarfed a king's dominated the room's center but still left plenty of space around the room's edge, though the only other furniture was a large armoire, a fully stocked bar, and some kind of wood and metal contraption with straps.

Grimsby didn't dare think about that last one too much.

One wall was a singular window that overlooked the throbbing dance floor below, but the dramatic shift in tone between the elegant bedroom and the club made both seem unreal. Somehow, despite the crowd's rhythmic movements to what must have been a quaking bass, the only sound he heard or felt was that of the unseen violins.

The bedroom was clean, but there was a faint trace of a rough, heady scent that he didn't recognize. It made him feel a little dizzy.

Aby closed the doors behind them. "You sure I can't interest either of you in a drink?"

Mayflower didn't reply.

Grimsby just focused on staying upright.

"Where's Ash?" the Huntsman demanded.

"Oh, he's here," Aby said, and something in her voice made Grimsby's skin shiver, and not in any way that was desirable. "He's always here, isn't that right, Ash?"

There was no reply.

Aby left the bar and proceeded to the armoire, her movements more leonine than ever, her eyes reflecting motes of light from the window overlooking the crowd. She opened the armoire, throwing the doors wide. As she did, she made a small, unconvincing gasp.

"Ah! There you are, Ash!"

It took Grimsby a moment to realize who, or what, she was talking to.

Mounted on a wooden plaque in the armoire was a severed head. It was a man's, or had been. Although it was only almost human. Short, curved horns hooked out from his brow, nearly hidden by long, glossy curls of dark hair. His eyes were closed. His mouth was covered with a metal plate that had been bolted in place.

Ash was dead, and the sinking pit that formed in Grimsby's stomach told him they had just walked into a trap.

SEVENTEEN

GRIMSBY STARED AT THE MOUNTED HEAD AND HEARD a terrified moan. He was surprised when he realized it was his own.

Mayflower, however, didn't move. He only stared at Aby and her prize, his brow furrowing. "When did you take over?" he finally said.

"A few years back," she said, reaching up and running her fingers down Ash's pale cheek. "Spend a couple centuries with anyone, and it'll be enough to make you wanna tear their head off." She smiled and dropped her touch to a wooden box below the trophy. "Both of them."

"So, what, should I start calling you Madame Aby?" Mayflower asked.

Aby shrugged. "Call me whatever you want, Huntsman. You won't be doing it long."

Grimsby felt something cold press into his arm. He looked down to see Mayflower's hand gripping the key to his cuffs, holding it out to him.

He felt himself go cold.

The only reason Mayflower would free him was that things

were about to go bad. So bad that he wasn't sure he could handle it alone. And if Mayflower, the *jabberwocking* Huntsman, couldn't handle it, what help did Grimsby have to offer?

"Eyes aflame," he muttered as he numbly took the key and began fumbling with the lock.

Mayflower settled in between him and Aby. "I'm going to give you one chance, Aby. Give us the head, and we'll leave peacefully."

"Why would you want his head?" she asked, prowling slowly toward them. "It's hardly the best part of him. Besides, who said you're leaving at all?"

Mayflower sighed, more weariness than fear in his voice. "Should I even ask if we're going to do this the hard way?"

She smirked, and her eyes began to glow like twin embers. "It's the only way I like it."

Grimsby got his cuffs loose and finally found his tongue. "What through-the-looking-glass kind of crap is going on here—"

It was right about then that Aby began to change. Her skin darkened, at first with a blush, but what became light pink slowly deepened to crimson. The leather she wore seemed to melt away, crawling over her like living skin, leaving her scarlet body bare.

She had no tattoos.

The leather pooled over her shoulders and gathered on her back in a draping cloak of roiling, fleshy darkness. Horns crowned and curled from her head in ram-like curves. Her eyes darkened until no light escaped them, save for two smoldering points. Her high-heeled boots morphed into keratin hooves. She smiled, this time revealing strikingly white fangs. She ran her serpent's tongue over her teeth in a manner that Grimsby's fear-addled brain found deeply confusing.

She swept forward in a sudden wave, the darkness at her back propelling her forth like leather sails on gale winds. Her lean muscles flexed, and her hand sprouted obsidian talons long enough to maim and disembowel.

Mayflower moved with nearly equal speed. His first motion shoved Grimsby aside; the second drew his gun from his hidden holster. He swept one leg wide, shifting his balance to roll with Aby's pounce, nearly dodging her.

But the woman, or whatever she was, was faster. Grimsby had barely managed to catch his own stumble by the time he heard Mayflower grunt with pain. He looked up to see Aby dash past him, inhumanly quick.

A long cluster of slashes had been laid across Mayflower's face. Three long cuts began to bleed freely, the middle of which had missed his eye by barely an inch.

Meanwhile, Aby had not let her momentum slow and was rushing around the room as fast as a midnight hurricane's wind. The darkness across her back propelled her forth, leaving a trail of writhing smoke in her wake. She was positioning herself for another pass at Mayflower, and Grimsby could see the Huntsman was already staggered.

He saw Mayflower raise his gun as the woman surged forward, but even when he drew his bead, he didn't fire. Grimsby saw something in Mayflower's blood-veiled gaze, something almost like indecision.

Just then, the double doors to the bedroom burst open. Rora, the guard from the front doors, stepped forward, a pump-action shotgun in her hands. She surveyed the room through her dark glasses before bringing the weapon to bear on Mayflower.

Grimsby turned, still reeling from the sudden maelstrom of violence. His heart was hammering so hard in his chest that he thought the ambient violins might have switched their tone to the thrumming bass of the club. His ears were ringing with Aby's shrieks, and his skin was coated with a sudden layer of cold sweat.

His instincts told him to run and to hide. Beneath the massive bed seemed particularly appealing. He could hide there for seconds, maybe even a whole minute, and at the moment that seemed like an eternity.

Instead, he was surprised to find himself running toward the doors. The woman with the shotgun was so focused on Mayflower that she had yet to see him. He ran at her, and he heard himself start to scream.

It wasn't a particularly flattering scream. In fact, it might have been great in the fadeaway intro of a horror movie, but he couldn't help it. The terror and fear in his body needed someplace to vent, and it seemed his vocal cords were the only parts of him currently unoccupied by massive stupidity.

Rora saw him coming at the last moment and turned. The shotgun roared, but her aim was off. Grimsby felt the air above his head crack apart. If he were above-average height, it might have caught him. The sudden shock and sound made him trip, and his charge turned into a frantic stumble in a vain effort to keep his balance.

The woman saw this and leapt back, dodging him.

He rolled into a heap on the floor just before the door. He saw the woman pump another round into the weapon and lower it at his chest.

Grimsby raised a hand, and with it his Impetus surged. He had no time to contain or control it, and wasted power flared from his scars. He ignored the sudden searing agony and raised his good hand, pointing a finger at Rora, and screamed, *"Torque!"*

A spiraling wave of green energy rushed from his finger, like a fist-size horizontal tornado full of glowing hailstone motes of light. It was strong enough that it tore down tiles from the ceiling and ripped out chunks of the carpet at its edges, pulling them into a chaotic vortex in its wake. The center of the spell struck the gun's barrel and twisted the gun in her grip a hairsbreadth before Rora pulled the trigger. The shot ripped apart the floor next to Grimsby, showering him with stinging splinters. However, without the gun's mass centered, the recoil nearly tore it from the woman's grip, and Grimsby saw her grit her teeth as her finger caught in the trigger's guard, twisting it awfully at the second knuckle.

She made no sound as she swiftly began to shift her grip to her nondominant hand, her gaze focused on Grimsby, her lips peeled back in a snarl.

Grimsby squeaked and kicked the door shut in her face, forcing her back into the hall. He fumbled numbly to his feet and clicked shut the dead bolt. Then, with his quickly burning Impetus, he shouted, "*Bind! Bind! Bind!*" again and again, using his thumbs to stamp each pair of runes on opposite doors like a human stapler. Within a few seconds, he had a half dozen bands of magical tension holding the doors closed.

A heavy slam struck the doors, followed by another, and another. The doors splintered open with each blow, revealing Rora's considerable bulk trying to batter them down, but the Binds and their blue strands of magic gossamer strained and snapped them shut again. The spells were holding, but he could feel their energy beginning to fray and weaken already.

He turned to see Mayflower with his back against the wall, Aby bearing down on him, cornering him. She lashed out, her arms a flurry of black talons, slashing at the Huntsman. Mayflower raised his arms to defend himself, and as claws raked over his flesh, Grimsby expected gouts of scarlet to rush out. Instead, where the fabric of his suit was slashed, silver light eked out from the lining. He could see the strange stitching shining in the fabric beneath, like scripture etched in thread.

Aby screamed as the light touched her. She recoiled from it, covering her eyes. The darkness on her back withered and began to burn away under its glare, sending her flying backward into a supple heap.

Mayflower shouted to Grimsby through the chaos, "Get the head!"

Grimsby, unconsciously happy to have any kind of direction in the madness of the moment, ran to the armoire, throwing it open.

The door rattled as more blows struck it. The Binds were barely holding as it was, their light flickering until they were hardly visible, and the wood was starting to split and splinter.

Grimsby came face-to-face with the mounted head, his body naturally recoiling from the macabre object. He reached forward slowly, his hands shaking and reluctant to touch the dead flesh.

"Grimsby!" Mayflower roared.

Grimsby forced himself to grab hold of the grisly trophy. It was rubbery in his grip, grotesquely unreal yet lifelike. And strangely warm. He pulled, but it stuck fast. He muttered a curse and pulled harder.

"Puppy dogs' tails, why—won't—you—!"

Then, mid-yank, Ash's severed head opened its eyes.

Grimsby shrieked, his efforts erupting from his throat in a shrill cry.

He was so shocked that he didn't realize the armoire was falling onto him until it was too late. He squealed and leapt out of the way as it toppled to the ground, its contents spilling out just before it landed, door side down.

But the head was still inside. Grimsby was less than upset about that fact, but without some part of Ash's body, they'd never manage the tracking spell.

A sudden shotgun blast made the rest of the world sound really quiet by comparison.

Grimsby looked behind him to see a large chunk of the door simply stop existing, followed shortly by another. He needed to move fast. Alive or not—he shuddered—they needed that head.

He tried to lift the armoire and turn it over, but it was many times heavier than him, and it didn't budge. He thought maybe he could use a spell to help. Then another chunk of door disappeared.

The last of his Binds flickered out, snapping like overtaut guitar strings.

They were out of time.

Then he saw a box on the ground, its lid partly ajar. He realized what was inside, and a wave of simultaneous relief and disgust flowed through him. He gathered up the box and ran to Mayflower.

"You got it?" Mayflower grunted, not looking away from Aby.

"Yes!"

"Good."

The Huntsman grabbed Grimsby by the shoulder and burst into a sprint, half carrying him. They ran straight at the massive glass window overlooking the club. Mayflower raised his gun and fired into the glass. A hole the size of a fist appeared, and the glass rippled with a webwork of sudden cracks, but it did not shatter. Thrumming music squeezed through the new gap, its rhythm heavy and driving.

What was left of the door burst open behind them. Three women, all wearing suits and dark glasses, came through. Two of them held compact handguns, and Rora still held her shotgun, though her right-hand index finger dangled limply from her reversed grip.

Mayflower fired twice more, and the cracks redoubled. But the glass didn't shatter.

Grimsby saw the women level their weapons at their backs.

They weren't going to make it.

Mayflower ducked his head behind his elbow as he charged the window, dragging Grimsby, who did something similar, behind him.

They crashed through the window. Glass rained down alongside them. The club music was suddenly blaring and pressing. Gunshots sounded, almost drowned out by the music.

Then they fell.

EIGHTEEN

THEY FELL NEARLY TWENTY FEET, THE GLASS A GLITTER-ing cascade around them. As Grimsby tumbled through the air, the world seemed to slow as the ground rose to meet him. He knew this would be the end, and he braced himself.

The gathered crowd of erotically charged dancers had ceased their movement and were all staring at them, eyes wide, mouths gaping. Even the music had quelled to the silent drone of idle speakers. The only sounds were those of distant voices above shouting, gunfire, and Grimsby screaming.

The grip around his arm sharply pulled him, and he felt May-flower enveloping him like a grumpy cloak. They landed in a roll along one of the catwalks, crunching painfully over the bed of broken glass they had made themselves. Grimsby felt sharp edges bite into his skin like teeth, drawing blood in a dozen places, compounding the welts the Geist had left him in Mansgraf's lair, but none cut deep.

For a glorious moment, they came to a stop. No falling, no running, no frantic motion at all. He raised his head and looked around at the awestruck crowd.

There was a breath of silence as hundreds of gazes focused on them: dancers, staff, and even the DJ behind his altar of electronics.

Then Grimsby saw the DJ shrug and slam his fist on the keyboard in front of him.

The bass blared in a sudden wave, and the crowd roared approvingly.

Dancing resumed.

Up above, Aby loomed in the broken window, her blackened cloak forming into smoldering, spreading wings, her eyes glowing fire.

Grimsby felt the sudden urge to stand and stare at the terrifying beauty until she descended upon him, as it would be a worthy last sight, but a pull from Mayflower jump-started the flight portion of his fight-or-flight instincts.

They ran.

Their feet pounded over the catwalk, gaining ground toward the exit. The crowd bounced in time with the rhythm of the music's driving bass, like a living sea of waving arms and neon paint. Behind them, Aby descended, her lithe body taking a graceful diver's pose. Before she struck the floor, her wings stretched out, carrying her forward and spreading smoke in a wave beneath her as she glided toward them. She was fast. Very fast. Grimsby ripped his gaze away and redoubled his own efforts to run.

Mayflower was a dozen feet ahead of him when he hit the doors, slamming them open without stopping. Grimsby was close on his tail and broke out into the cool, open night and the blinding streetlights.

The line of waiting patrons gasped and murmured as they ran across the road.

When Aby emerged, moments later, the patrons began screaming.

He looked back to see Aby, her full form bared in the mixture of moon and fluorescent light. Her red skin was wreathed with a cloak of shadows that spread wide, her horns a crown of curling keratin.

Grimsby was backpedaling without realizing it, and he col-

lided with a stalwart form behind him. It was Mayflower, staring
down the looming figure of Aby.

He was holding the talisman in one hand, the charred bone
dangling from its leather cord, and in his other was the revolver.

Aby glided across the street, ten feet off the ground. Smoke
rolled from the trail of darkness she left in her wake. It spilled over
the road, roiling in a wave. Traffic screeched to a halt as the light
was choked away. Aby's burning eyes narrowed as she neared
Mayflower.

He raised the talisman before him. White light shone from it,
like the filament of a blazing lightbulb. Where it touched Aby's
cloak of leathery darkness, the light boiled it away, making a sound
between the hiss of steam and distant screams.

She flinched from the light, but her face hardened, and she
pushed forth. The light redoubled, and her vibrant red skin began
to darken and crack, like hot coals doused with ice water. She let
loose a strained hiss of pain, and her advance halted.

"Think twice, bitch," Mayflower growled, taking a step forward. "Is it worth it?"

Grimsby looked between them frantically. "I thought it wouldn't
work on anyone but Ash!" he hissed.

"It's called a bluff," the Huntsman growled back. "It'll only
slow her down until she calls it."

Grimsby looked at the talisman in Mayflower's grip and saw
the light beginning to wane. He glanced nervously back and forth
between Huntsman and demoness, dreading that she would draw
closer and the fragile magic would fail.

But the demoness relented. She turned burning eyes to focus
on Mayflower, and her face shuddered with anger, then fell into a
placid glare. "Bastard," she said. "We're not finished, you and I."

"Yes. We are. Now, turn around and go back into your sex
dungeon before you get yourself hurt."

She smiled with her fangs bared, then stepped back into the

smoke, her red body vanishing from sight. A moment later, they heard her low chuckle.

And a series of metallic clicking noises that even Grimsby could recognize in an instant.

It was the sound of the sliding racks of guns as they chambered bullets into place.

"Shit," Mayflower hissed behind him.

Aby's voice drifted from the darkness. "Fire."

Gunshots shattered the air. Bricks exploded on either side of them, showering Grimsby with sharp shards. People screamed. Tires squealed. Aby laughed.

They dropped to the ground, crawling away. More shots cracked through the air, piercing the cloud of darkness that Aby exuded. There was a pause in the firestorm, the sudden silence as disorientating as the initial volley had been.

He felt a rough hand haul him to his feet. "Run, now!" Mayflower said.

They crunched pavement in a frantic sprint. Grimsby dared to glance back and saw the darkness had cleared. Three women with pistols were advancing after them, reloading their weapons. He turned back and focused on keeping up with Mayflower. They reached the corner of the alleyway just as the shots resumed.

Grimsby screamed as more bricks exploded and glass shattered. The welcoming darkness of the alleyway offered brief shelter, but Aby's women were advancing. Mayflower was already climbing into the jeep and slamming his keys into the ignition.

Grimsby skidded to a halt on the passenger side and tried the handle, but it stuck fast.

He looked into the jeep to see Mayflower looking at him, his face oddly calm but focused. For a fearful moment, he thought the Huntsman would leave him. Then the door clunked and the lock popped. Grimsby hauled it open, threw the wooden box into the footwell, and dove into the passenger seat.

He'd barely managed to close the door when Mayflower threw the jeep into reverse and hauled steel down the alley. Grimsby hadn't had a moment to brace himself, and the sudden momentum cracked his head against the dashboard, dazing him.

He watched blearily as the three gunwomen rounded the corner, weapons aiming down the alley. They fired. Metal struck metal. The passenger-side mirror burst into slag and glass. A new bullet hole appeared in the hood. The engine groaned but somehow kept churning.

Mayflower wasn't looking at the gunners; he was staring in the rearview as he gained speed backward. The jeep tore through trash cans and dumpsters that hadn't been emptied in who knew how long. Rancid, soggy garbage exploded in a grimy rain that coated the jeep. A smell filled the air, so pungent and terrible that Grimsby's eyes began to water.

More gunshots ricocheted down the alley. There was a sound like a popping balloon, and the jeep suddenly sagged to one side.

"Damn it," Mayflower cursed.

They finally reached the end of the alley, and he swerved the jeep in a wide fishtail, spinning out onto the road. Sparks sung from the driver's-side wheel, leaving a burning trail in their wake as they tore down the street and away from the Lounge.

After a few moments of breathless quiet, marred only by the grinding of the wheel on the pavement and the jeep's engine, Mayflower took a deep breath. Then he glanced over at Grimsby and his gaze hardened. "You didn't get the head."

Grimsby collapsed in his seat, the ringing in his ears faded and the adrenaline-fueled numbness turned to exhaustion. "No, but I—"

Mayflower slammed his hand on the wheel. "Damn it, Grimsby! We nearly got ourselves killed, my jeep's screwed to hell, and all for nothing!"

"Well, I—"

"I knew I shouldn't have brought you. You're soft. Too soft. You're going to get yourself killed, and me along with you."

"Listen—"

"We're going back to the safe house, and you're going to stay there—"

"Shut up!" Grimsby shouted, shocking himself.

Even more shocking was when Mayflower did so.

The Huntsman glared expectantly at him out of the corner of his eye.

"We didn't leave with nothing."

There was a buzzing noise in the silence. Grimsby felt the wooden box against his foot, vibrating oddly.

"What the hell is that?"

He grinned, though it was tinged with a grimace, as he picked up the box. "You remember when Aby said she took Ash's head?"

"Yeah."

"She said both of them."

"What the hell does that mean—"

Grimsby held open the box so Mayflower could see. The powerful buzzing reverberated through his palms.

"Is that," Mayflower said quietly, "what I think it is?"

"Yep. That's a penis."

"She didn't."

"She did. And apparently, she had it . . . enhanced." Grimsby felt his palms growing numb from the furious movements inside the box. "Considerably. Must have switched on when we were running."

The buzzing continued.

Mayflower started coughing, or at least that's what it sounded like. Then Grimsby realized he was laughing.

The *Huntsman* was laughing.

He choked it down into a wheeze. "And that'll work for the spell?" he said.

"I think so, yeah," Grimsby replied, trying his best not to conjure images of the Dildo Fairy.

"Not bad, kid," the Huntsman said. "Not bad."

He said it in such a way that the words carried a strange weight.

Grimsby wasn't sure what to say. For once, he felt like saying nothing was appropriate. But he did sit up a little taller in his seat.

There was a silence that might have been poignant, if not for the buzzing vibrations of a demon dildo.

"Okay," Mayflower said. "Now turn it off."

"Nope. No way I'm touching that."

"I'm serious."

"Me, too. You turn it off!" Grimsby said.

Mayflower said nothing and focused on the road.

Grimsby closed the lid and put it back at his feet, trying to ignore the sensation. The sounds of the vibrations, however, were impossible not to hear.

"Bet you wish you had a radio now," he said.

Mayflower only growled.

NINETEEN

GRIMSBY WATCHED AS MAYFLOWER WRENCHED THE nuts from the rim of the flat tire. The bullets had blown it out altogether, but it was the five miles Mayflower drove that had destroyed the rim and shredded the rubber into playground cushioning.

The adrenaline was only now fading, leaving Grimsby with a pit in his stomach so deep that it was painful, but the pit wasn't empty. It was full of anxious fear.

They'd barely escaped with their lives, and while it hadn't been his first near-death encounter in the last few hours, this time was different. This time, Grimsby had volunteered for it.

And it made him dizzy just to think about doing it again.

"How long will the tracking spell take you?" Mayflower asked through grunts as he loosened the last bolt.

Grimsby shook himself from his addled stupor, his mind still focused on the Lounge. "Not long? Maybe a few minutes."

"All right. Can we do it here?"

He shook his head. "No, no, I need to go back to my place."

"What?" He tossed the last bolt and wrench aside. "You need supplies or something?"

Grimsby paced in place, trying to get ahold of himself. "Sort of. Magic's just—it's easier at home. I don't know how to explain it. It just comes more naturally."

Mayflower nodded.

He was so implacable, the Huntsman. He had been through everything Grimsby just had and more, and yet you'd never know it from looking at him. At least, aside from the clawed slashes in his jacket and the fingernail gouges on his face.

The Huntsman was simply one thing above all others: focused.

Grimsby felt his stomach twist as his embarrassed fear grew. He caught his reflection in the jeep window. He didn't look anything like Mayflower. He wasn't focused. He was battered, bruised, and beaten. His hair was a mess, his eyes were ringed with dark circles, made especially stark by how wide with anxious nerves they were. No, he didn't look focused.

Above all else, he looked at himself and knew he was one thing: afraid.

He couldn't do this. It had been insane to think he could. He was at the end of his rope, and they'd only just begun. He wasn't brave enough; he wasn't strong enough; he wasn't smart enough.

He wasn't enough.

Mansgraf had been right all along.

He felt what little resolve he'd been able to muster begin to crumble like a sandcastle in a hurricane. He looked away from his reflection; he could no longer stand it.

He tried to keep his voice steady as he began to speak, though he did a poor job of it. "If we get moving soon, I should have time to manage the spell . . . before my next shift."

"Shift?" Mayflower said, tugging at the wheel. Even without the bolts secured, rust and time had glued it in place. "The hell do you mean your shift?"

"Well, it's almost dawn," Grimsby said, feeling cold. "I've got to go to work."

"At the pizza place?"

"We have tacos, too."

"I thought you wanted to be an Auditor. That this was your big break."

"Yeah. I did, too."

"And?"

"And? *And?*" Grimsby asked, feeling his temper rise as his nerves frayed. "I've spent the last twenty-four hours being nearly killed in so many ways. And more than one of them was by you, in case you forgot."

"I actually had. What's your point?"

"My point is that this—this—this is insane! All of it! It's absolute lunacy. Is this how you live?"

"It was. Once," Mayflower said, a strange wistfulness in his voice.

"You see how that's crazy, right?"

"Crazy is a frame of mind. To me, working in that grease trap is crazy."

"Look. I spend most of my time in a terrible costume working at a terrible restaurant performing for only mildly less terrible kids. I know crazy. But *that*?" He gestured broadly in the direction they'd come from. "Even on my worst days my job doesn't have me getting chased around by monsters, or poking my nose into succubus lairs, or stealing genuine demon-skin dildos!"

"And tell me, witch," Mayflower said with a grunt as he tore loose the tire with a hard kick. "What do you get on your best days?"

Grimsby opened his mouth, but nothing came out. He watched numbly as the rusted wheel dropped onto the cold pavement and spun to a halt.

The Huntsman wordlessly picked up the wheel and carried it to the back of the jeep, where he began to loosen the spare that hung below the rear window.

"The point is," Grimsby said, following him, "maybe . . . maybe this isn't for me. I think, once I get you the tracker, I should go back to my old life."

Mayflower was quiet for a moment. When he finally spoke, he paused and leaned on the wheel. "You sure about that?"

"What? What is that supposed to mean?"

He shrugged. "You did all right back there. Not great, but you're breathing, and that's a damn sight better than I expected."

"So?"

Mayflower focused his attention back on the wheel. Then, after a moment, he sighed, and Grimsby saw a little of the iron in the man rust away. "Look, kid," he said, not looking away from his work. "Life's a storm on the sea. You spend it drifting about, getting beat to hell one day after another. If you're lucky, maybe you find an island or two along the way." His voice grew suddenly distant, even quiet, his eyes seeing through the old jeep to something Grimsby couldn't fathom. Then they snapped back, becoming sharp and cold once more. "But the sea's always rising, and those islands don't last. The best, the absolute best, you can hope for is to choose what kind of storm you're facing."

"Inspiring," Grimsby said with a bitter taste in his mouth.

"I don't give a good goddamn about inspiring you. I need to know." Mayflower spoke without looking at him, loosening the spare tire.

"Know what?"

"Your choice. Now"—he grunted as he pulled the spare free—"is your chance to choose. What kind of storm are you facing?"

Grimsby felt his throat tighten, and suddenly he wanted to sit down. It was as though the man's words had put a weight on his shoulders. No, they hadn't put it there. They had just revealed it.

That weight was the reason it was hard to breathe. The reason it was hard to move. The reason it was hard, every day, just to get up in the morning.

Mayflower finally looked at him again and seemed to see something in his eyes. "I'm not gonna tell you which road to walk, kid. But I will say this. The road untraveled is the road most missed."

"So whichever one I pick, I'll regret not taking the other?"

He smiled, a genuine, sad smile that spoke of old pains. "Life's a bitch that way." He made his way to the bare hub of the missing wheel, put the spare in place, and began to tighten it.

Grimsby shook his head and looked at the dawning sky, uncertain now more than ever. He didn't want to keep the life he had, but this new life, it felt so unreal, so unattainable. So dangerous. It was exciting but also terrifying, whereas his current existence was largely droll drudgery. It was safe but left him feeling more hollow every single day. Maybe it wasn't all that much more survivable than being an Auditor after all.

Mayflower gave each nut a final turn to ensure they were solidly in place, then removed the jack and tossed his tools into the back. He turned to look at Grimsby, waiting. "You decide?" he asked.

Grimsby felt like he was caught in the headlights of a train. The Huntsman was awaiting his answer. What was he supposed to do?

He thought of the adrenaline, the fear, and the panic. He thought of how he'd narrowly escaped with his life so many times already and wondered how much longer he could keep it up. He thought of his scars and his weakness, of responsibility and risk.

And he came to one final conclusion.

"I—I can't do it."

He stared at Mayflower, not knowing what else to say. The words had left him empty, like they were all that was inside him, and without them he felt deflated and likely to drift away on the next breeze. At that moment, perhaps for the first time since this all started, he wasn't afraid. There was no room for it.

He was only ashamed.

He found himself looking at the ground. He wanted to break down then and there, to simply let every muscle go and give sobbing voice to the budding agony in his guts.

Instead, he just stood there, uncertain of what to say or do.

Mayflower said nothing for a long moment. Then he let out a sharp breath. Maybe it was disappointment. Maybe it was relief. Maybe it was nothing at all. Then he said, "All right. Let's get you home. If you can get me that spell, I expect we—I might be able to finish this before nightfall. You just lay low until then."

Grimsby just nodded, feeling too unworthy to look up.

Somehow, the guilt was worse than the fear. At least when he had been afraid, he had still been fighting for something. It was a panicked fight, but it was still a fight. Now, though, he felt defeated. He had surrendered. Given up.

All because he was afraid.

He said nothing as he climbed into the back of the jeep.

There was nothing more to say.

TWENTY

HALF AN HOUR LATER, GRIMSBY FELT THE JEEP COME TO a stop as Mayflower parked it in the alley beneath the stairs to his apartment. They climbed the steps in silence, and it was just more of the same as Grimsby began to prepare the spell.

He set the stolen box down at the center of a space he had cleared on his floor. Its contents were still vibrating heavily. He shook his head and took the astrolabe from his pocket and set it beside the box.

Mayflower stood near the front door, his face stern, his eyes watching outside the window in the early dawn.

"What are you looking for?" Mayflower asked as Grimsby went to the kitchen and dug around in the cupboard below the sink.

"Something very important for the spell," he said as he finally found and held up a pair of old rubber gloves. They were already heavy-duty, but he wished they were heavier.

"Necessary, huh?" Mayflower asked, his eyes sweeping the street like he was expecting an attack.

"Yes. Very much so," Grimsby said, digging around in a drawer until he found a fine-tipped permanent marker. "What about you? You looking for something?"

He shrugged. "Maybe. The Department probably won't find the message Mansgraf hid for a couple days yet, but you never know. If they do, we'll need to get you hidden before they find you."

He shuddered. "It'll really take them that long?"

"Normally, no. But I've got a friend who is slowing them down."

"Well," Grimsby said, settling down beside the humming box. "I'd better get to work, then."

"I'd say so."

Grimsby nodded and picked up the astrolabe. Withdrawing the fine-tipped marker, he carefully scribbled a replica of his Bind rune on the astrolabe's hand. This means was slower than his usual method of imprinting the rune with a touch of magic, but it would last much longer. The space was tiny, but fortunately his thin fingers let him create a close enough replica for the enchantment.

He turned back to the box, slipping on the gloves as he did. He took a deep breath, opened the lid, and gingerly withdrew the demon phallus. He felt his face curl in on itself as though he had bit into a lemon. He set the object beside the astrolabe, but it knocked itself over and rolled toward him. He retched and put it back into place, keeping it held down with one hand.

"Have you done this before?" Mayflower asked.

"Personally, no. But have I seen it done? Also no."

"Then how do you know what to do?"

"It's—it's sort of a derivative of one of the few spells I'm good at. It's a lot like my Bind spell, but instead of connecting two points, it connects two objects. And fortunately for us, this astrolabe is meant for finding things already. That's half the work done. Now it's just a matter of showing it what we want to find."

"Like giving a dog a scent."

Grimsby nodded.

He brought forth his Impetus, feeling its warmth seep through him. He carefully kept it from reaching his scars, directing it instead toward his good hand.

He reached out, both physically and beyond, feeling through the air and the Elsewhere at once. He began searching.

He could feel the threads of his own nearby spells, and even those that remained at the restaurant. A witch's magic was a part of them, so much so that they were of a single whole. They were connected, despite distances. But spells weren't the only things that worked that way. Living things had similar connections, both with other parts of themselves and with the things they created.

He reached out around the vibrating focus of his spell, searching for these threads. He couldn't sense them at first, but like eyes adjusting to a lack of light in the dark, his Impetus grew more sensitive as it was deprived of sensation. After a few moments, he felt the faintest traces of *something*, just at the edge of his touch. It was like a spider's web on his mind.

He traced the threads for a few moments, letting them grow more real in his senses. He felt some of them reach out in many directions, almost too many. The strongest of them pointed squarely toward the Lounge, likely toward Ash's severed head.

Grimsby shivered and tried to ignore that thread.

There were others as well, but they felt too similar to the first. He briefly wondered just how many pieces Aby had divided Ash up into.

Then he found a small cluster of threads that felt somehow different. Like they were made of a different weave of fiber. These pointed toward Mansgraf's lair and were so faint he nearly missed them.

Finally, he found one thread that was like the last few, but alone. He suspected this would point to the Wardbox, and hopefully the killer as well.

He seized hold of the thread and pulled. He felt nothing in the palm of his hand, but he could feel it in his Impetus. It strained against him like a fishing line around his fingers, cutting into his skin through tension alone.

He ignored the pain and pulled harder, drawing forth more of the thread until he could wrap it around the astrolabe's hand. He did so, again and again, binding the astrolabe to the Wardbox's thread, until it was strong enough to begin pulling.

He let go and looked at the dowser.

For a long moment, there was nothing.

Then the rune on the hand bloomed with faint blue light, and the hand twitched and moved around the astrolabe's edge, pulled by the Elsewhere thread of magic.

He let his Impetus fade and put the buzzing, fleshy tool back into the box, clasping the latch tight.

His hand was near numb. He removed the gloves, reminding himself to burn them later, and held up the astrolabe for Mayflower to take.

"I think I got it."

Mayflower took the golden device, his expression dubious. He turned it in his hands. "Why isn't it moving?"

"The spell isn't infinite range, but if you get within a couple miles it should lock on."

"You sure?"

"No, but it's my best guess. Still, it ought to be enough."

Mayflower grunted. "All right. Thanks, witch," he said, taking the astrolabe and heading toward the door.

"Wait!" Grimsby said, startling even himself. Seeing Mayflower walk away, it was like watching the door behind him begin to close. It was like watching his last chance to turn back fade away. His last chance to be the person he wished he was.

"What?" Mayflower said. If he heard any import in Grimsby's plea, he didn't show it.

Grimsby wanted to say he already regretted his choice. He wanted to say that he wanted to go with Mayflower and finish the job. He wanted to say that he hated himself for being the coward he was.

Instead, all he said was, "Can I get a ride to work?"

Mayflower sighed. "Yeah, I suppose. Let's go."

Grimsby swallowed the bitter taste that grew on his tongue and shook his head. This was for the best.

Then he remembered what day it was. He took in a deep breath and let out a heavy sigh. "Hold on, I have to change first."

Mayflower paused; then his eyes narrowed. "Change into what?"

TWENTY-ONE

GRIMSBY SETTLED AWKWARDLY IN THE BACK SEAT OF THE jeep, having had to remove his pointy blue hat in order to fit.

Mayflower was glaring at him in the rearview, his lips pursed into a thin line. Finally, he said, "You've got to be kidding."

"What?"

"What the hell are you supposed to be?"

Grimsby squared the lapels of his robe, which was as blue as the hat and also covered with gold stars. "A wizard. It's Wizard Pie Wednesday. Half off magic pies. Otherwise known as cardboard pizza."

Mayflower sighed and pulled the jeep out of the alley and back onto the road.

They drove in silence for a time, and Grimsby gazed out the window. He was exhausted. He hadn't had any sleep since his couple hours the night before, and his whole body was feeling like someone had coated it in cold molten iron. His muscles sagged, and every part of him wanted to find someplace dark and warm to be horizontal in for an indefinite period. But he didn't have time. He might find an hour or so of space during the day, but Mighty Magic Donald's Food Kingdom ran on daylight and inattentive parents. Besides, the day was only going to get worse until it was over.

He tried to focus, tried to make himself sharp, but the next thing he remembered was the sound of knuckles rapping against the window. He stiffened awake and blearily looked around, wiping the drool from his chin.

"Hm? Yeah? What?" he said, as if every question might earn him a few more minutes of sleep.

"Grimsby," Mayflower growled, opening the back door for him. "We're here."

"Right. Right." He felt his exhausted heart sink but shoved the feeling away. He began to climb out, but Mayflower interrupted him.

"Wait," he said, digging in his pocket.

Grimsby saw he still had the claymore stowed away inside his jacket and shook his head.

Mayflower finally withdrew a crumpled scrap of paper from his pocket and offered it to him. It might have once been a business card, but it had no name or information. At the center of the fold-scarred paper was only a phone number.

"What's this?"

"For if you need me."

Grimsby nodded. "Thanks, Mayflower."

The Huntsman grunted and looked away.

Grimsby climbed out and shut the door, and the jeep drove off, the shredded rubber of the bad tire fluttering from its fixture on the hatch. He tried not to watch the jeep go, but he couldn't help himself.

Long after it faded from view, he turned and faced the golden crown of MMDFK. He took a deep breath and steeled himself. Monsters, gunwomen, and grumpy Huntsmen, those were all new to him. But this, this realm of gilded plastic, demanding parents, and expectant children, this was his realm.

He expected to feel some small sense of pride or contentment. He would have even settled for comfort. Instead, he just felt tired and burnt up.

This, too, he shook away. "Time to get to work," he muttered as he pulled on his pointy wizard hat and made his way inside.

"Grimsby!" Carla roared before the front door's chime had even fallen silent. "Where the hell have you been?"

"Late night," he said. "Out with a fr— . . . a person."

"I don't give a damn about your social life."

"Then why'd you ask?"

Her face reddened with anger. "Just get to work. The women's bathroom is a wreck."

"It wasn't when I left last night."

"Well, that's how restaurants work. They get dirty again."

"But we haven't opened. And you're the only woman here."

Her eyes widened, then narrowed, and her face reddened again. Though this time it wasn't just anger. "Clean it."

He shrugged. "Fine," he said, shaking his head and making his way toward the restrooms.

He finished cleaning in twenty minutes, though he had to dig up a surgical mask before he started to keep from gagging, and even then it took a couple of Binds and a Torque to get the job done.

Carla popped her head in as he finished. "Better. By the way, a woman called and said that apparently the magic fairy told her daughter to ask her mom what a dildo was."

Grimsby almost slapped his forehead, then remembered he was still wearing the rubber gloves and stopped himself. "Oh jeez, no, I didn't mean—"

Carla waved her hands. "Less I know, the better. We've got enough trouble without handling a sexual harassment case. I gave her your contact information. Don't be surprised if she files suit."

"Why would that be surprising?" Grimsby muttered. "Fine, whatever. Look, since the early shift is clear today, I'm going to go, uh, meditate."

"Meditate?" Her eyes narrowed with doubt.

"Yeah. To . . . restore my magic powers. Two or three hours in a dark place, undisturbed."

It was mostly a lie, but also a little true. He needed rest or his spells might start acting funny, but that was more due to the rest of his brain acting funny already.

"Meditate on your own time. You need to get ready for your first show."

"I thought the morning slot was clear," he said, feeling the odds of rest slipping farther away.

"It was. That changed last night. We're booked full through the day."

"Oh goodie," Grimsby said. "Why the sudden change?"

"After your fiasco yesterday, the mother came to me to complain. She demanded a refund, but I talked her down to another session, free of charge."

"Wait, not the same kid from yesterday?"

"Probably, unless she popped out another brat around this time of year."

Grimsby groaned. "You know that's not how it works, Carla. I can't just change the act like that."

"So just do the same act."

"It doesn't work like that, either. You ever try getting twenty kids to sit through something they just saw yesterday? While hopped up on an IV of sugar and adrenaline?"

"Nope. Never cared, either."

Grimsby pressed on. "The younger kids won't mind. They'll watch the same show a dozen times in a row, but the older kids? They'll be bored before I start."

"So?"

"Carla. There's nothing more dangerous than a bored child. Trust me."

"Well, you'll just have to muddle through. Change the act. Mix things up."

"I can't just 'change the act'! It took all weekend to set up the mannequins and Binds on their costumes. The only other thing I could do is slam them around the room like pro wrestlers. Do you know how hard it is to magically choreograph a fight between dummies?"

"You ever watch daytime TV? Can't be that hard."

"Carla—"

"Grimsby. Shut up. I didn't hire you to complain. I hired you to keep the kids busy until their parents pay up. Now, go do your damn job. Parents are arriving already."

She left the ladies' room and let the door close behind her.

Grimsby shook his head, removing his rubber gloves and apron. How was he going to pull this off?

TWENTY-TWO

MAYFLOWER FOUND A SHADOWED ALLEY NEARBY TO park the jeep in. It was cold; the chill autumn air whistled through the new bullet holes. He'd have to patch them up alongside the others. Soon the old girl might be more holes than steel.

But not yet.

He leaned the seat back and tried to force his eyes shut. The punk was right; he needed some rest. Without it, he'd be slow, and at his age he couldn't afford any slack. It might get him killed. Worse, it might get someone else killed.

Like the kid.

Grimsby was a coward, but that being said, he was a coward who had faced down danger willingly. A real man would have done so silently, not screaming, but silence would come with age. The inner iron necessary to walk into the fire? That was something that you either had or you didn't.

The kid had it.

God help him.

At least he had the good sense to turn tail when it got rough.

Mayflower growled and tossed in his seat. Normally, the cracked leather was more comfortable than his own bed. He had spent at least as many nights on it. But right now, he was restless, and the leather was uninviting.

His breast pocket vibrated. He grumbled, tore the phone from it, and snapped it open.

"What?"

"Les," Finley said, her voice strained, "we've got trouble."

"Trouble?"

"The Department sussed out Mansgraf's message. They've put out a flag on that Grimsby guy you asked me about."

Damn it. "When?"

"Ten minutes ago. Red flag. They're looking to bring him in, interrogate him about the murder."

"They have all the same info you gave me?"

"If not more. Part of his file was classified. I couldn't get access to it. But they at least have his home and place of employment. There's already a strike team en route."

"How much time do I have?"

"Maybe twenty minutes until they get in position. After that, they'll wait until civilians are minimally exposed before they move."

Mayflower was already straightening his seat and slamming the keys into the ignition. "Can you slow them down?"

"Not without getting myself fired. But there's something else strange. Peters himself is leading the strike team."

"Director Peters? Why?"

"No idea. Maybe he took the murder personally. All I know is that he and half a dozen Auditors and twice as many Agents are on the move. If you want to get your boy out, do it now."

"So be it," Mayflower growled. "Thanks, Fin."

"Oh, one more thing, Les."

Mayflower only grunted. He was already on the road, the old jeep treading asphalt.

"I decoded some of the notes you gave me. Mansgraf's got a hell of a cipher; it's closer to her own language, but I managed to piece together her notes on this . . . Hand."

"And?" Mayflower asked, his nerves tensing. Whatever it was, if Mansgraf had locked it away in a Wardbox, it was certainly dangerous. But knowing more about it would help him find out who wanted it.

It would help him find Mansgraf's killer.

"It's literal. A severed, preserved hand. Like a hand of glory, but I'm not sure who it came from. Anyway, she doesn't give any specifics on what it is or what it does. Just one line is the best I got."

"Give it to me."

"'The Hand controls those who can't control themselves,' or something like that. I don't know what it means beyond that."

He grunted as he cut through an intersection, drawing a bevy of honks and flashing headlights. "Thanks, Fin."

"Anytime. Be careful, Les."

He hung up and dropped the phone next to the claymore in his pocket. He shifted gears and pressed his foot down until the accelerator stuck, urging the jeep to greater and greater speed.

The old engine roared a complaint but obliged.

Still more steel than holes, he thought as he made his way toward the abomination that was MMDFK.

TWENTY-THREE

GRIMSBY FELT HIS NERVES FRAYING, AND HE WASN'T quite sure why.

The skin on his neck prickled, and damp spots of sweat were growing at the small of his back and under his arms. Richie's second party had almost fully gathered, though the birthday boy had yet to show himself, and already the restaurant was crowded.

Too crowded.

Grimsby had never seen so many adults at the restaurant before. Never before had they outnumbered the children. Each parent brought a minimum of one child, but never did the parents come in pairs. He assumed that whichever parent showed up had lost a game of rock-paper-scissors or something similar, while the victor stayed well away from MMDFK. Yet today there were nearly twenty adults, and half as many kids.

That was his first clue that something was wrong.

The second was that most of the adults actually had bought *food* from the restaurant. Even more horrifying, they were trying to eat it.

Grimsby had a fifty percent discount on the food, and yet even though he ate mostly ramen and was red-lining his bank account each month, he had only eaten the food once. It was a lifetime's worth. You didn't come to MMDFK for food; you came for the plastic castle and the free babysitting. Buying the food was just a tax. Eating it was insanity.

Yet there were six or so people at the restaurant in a pair of booths, all forcing themselves to pick at their food, and none of them had brought a kid.

The last thing Grimsby realized was that they were all wearing glasses. It was a small detail, one he wouldn't have noticed normally. Glasses were the kind of thing that was the visual equivalent of background noise. The eyes hardly noticed when anyone was wearing them.

Normally, any one of these details would have been weird but not noteworthy. But all three in combination made Grimsby nervous, though he didn't know why.

He bustled around, making it look like he was busy preparing, making small flourishes at the kids and taking the sidelong gazes of parents in stride. But really, he was watching these strangers, these intruders.

It wasn't until he saw a mirrorless black car pass by outside that he realized who they were.

They were Agents. Maybe even Auditors. Each and every one of them, working for the Department. That could mean only one thing: they were here for him.

He felt his heart speed up and it was all he could do to walk casually back toward the restrooms and changing closet. He ducked inside the closet and shut the door behind him. He pressed his back to the thin wood and felt his heartbeat reverberate through the door. He tried to claw his way from the fear that fogged his mind using logic and reason.

The Department must have deduced Mansgraf's message. Grimsby was in their records, so finding him would have been no great effort. Why were they waiting? They could have seized him at any moment. He thought back to his training. He realized they were likely just waiting for civilian exposure to be minimal before making a move.

He forced a fragile chuckle.

The restaurant was the only thing left protecting him. The negative image raiding MMDFK might garner both the Department and witches as a whole was the only deterrent standing between him and imprisonment.

He had to act, and fast, if he wanted to find a way out of this. But what could he do? Should he even do anything? The Department was supposed to be an ally to all Unorthodox, a kind of diplomatic police that maintained order among the Unorthodox within the rest of society. Shouldn't he trust them? He thought of Rayne's warning from the day before, the note still crumpled in his pocket.

Trust no one, stay low-profile, and please don't be guilty.

Mansgraf was a respected witch, and her reputation was fearsome. Between the people who adored her and the people who were scared of her, if they thought Grimsby had killed her, they'd be unlikely to take him peaceably. Maybe not even alive. Even if they did, he'd lose everything. It was hard enough to get a job as a witch, but a witch who had been accused of and arrested for murder? That wouldn't do any favors for his résumé.

Of course, neither would being a fugitive.

But that shouldn't last. Mayflower had the tracking spell and should be able to clear up the case within days. Maybe even hours. Of course, that was assuming he succeeded at all. If Mayflower ended up like Mansgraf, then there'd be no one left to prove Grimsby's innocence.

No, he couldn't be captured. It was too risky. He just needed to buy time. But it wasn't as though he had many choices. He couldn't run; the Department had cars patrolling around the building. He'd make it thirty feet before they grabbed him. And the only other way out . . .

He looked at the cracked mirror. It could become a doorway, if he wanted it to be.

One of the shards was large enough that he could fit through it if he had to. Even so, he felt his guts twist at the thought. The Elsewhere might be the only place more dangerous for him than where he was. And if he tried to escape through it, the Department would surely follow.

He shook his head. It was too risky.

But what else could he do?

He certainly couldn't fight. He had a narrow margin of knowledge of witch-on-witch combat, but that was from a long time ago. Even though he'd had a few sparring matches against Hives, Rayne, and a couple of other former classmates, he had never won. Besides, these people were either Agents, Usuals who had been specially trained to bring down witches, or Auditors who had actually succeeded in their trials. He'd have a slim chance against even a single Auditor, let alone half a dozen of them.

So, fight wasn't an option.

But neither was flight.

Grimsby felt his choices quickly narrowing. Then he realized his third choice, one that he used every day. He'd dealt with aggressive parents often, and he never fought them or flew from them.

He flustered them.

If he could do the same to the Auditors, distract them and confuse them enough, it might buy him a window to escape.

He just had to think of them as belligerent customers. Ones who wanted to capture him and never let him see the light of day again. It wasn't that much of a stretch, really. They probably wouldn't even be as bad as Mother Monobrow had been.

His heart rate didn't slow, but his breathing settled into a pace that was more humanoid. All he needed to do was distract the Auditors with the most convincing blundering of performances long enough to find an avenue to escape before he was arrested and imprisoned for the rest of his life.

That was it.

He felt his breath begin to quicken again in rising panic, but he closed his eyes and forced it to slow.

That's when he heard a familiar croaking voice from in front of him. "Favor time, half-witch. Pay up."

Grimsby opened his eyes to see Wudge crouched in the shadows between an old yellow bucket and a broken broom handle. His dark, goatlike eyes flashed yellow with the reflection from the lone light above as he moved.

"Eyes aflame!" Grimsby cursed, letting out a shocked breath. "What are you doing here?"

Wudge's numerous teeth split into a grin. "Wudge wants his favor."

"Look, Wudge, now really isn't a good time for me. You would not believe the day I'm having."

Wudge frowned, his grin falling to droop wider than his bulbous head. "Why is the half-witch talking like Wudge cares what it says? You owe Wudge a favor, and Wudge has come to collect."

"What? I'm a fugitive party clown of a witch. What could you possibly want from me?"

"Wudge has found it. The key."

"The key to what?"

"All of the she-bitch's secrets."

"You mean that door in her lair?"

Wudge nodded, his dangling ears wobbling as he did. "And to the boxes."

Grimsby's eyes went wide. "The Wardboxes?" His mind began to churn. With the key, he could open the box when Mayflower found it and return whatever Mansgraf stole to the Department. Assuming they were interested in hearing him out to begin with. And that would only be after he made his hopefully daring escape.

"Look, Wudge, I'd like to help but I can't. I don't even know if I'm going to make it out of here without being arrested."

Wudge's yellow eyes narrowed, and his croaking voice drew dangerously low. "You speak as if Wudge gives you a choice." He held out his hand, the spidery fingers splayed with the pale palm upward, like an upside-down chandelier of knobby knuckles and jagged nails.

"I don't give two hoots about what you're giving me; I—"

Wudge clenched his grip, and Grimsby suddenly felt as though a hand had closed around his throat. His voice was choked to silence as he gasped hoarsely, but his lungs refused to draw breath.

"Half-witch has no choice," Wudge croaked. "Half-witch obeys. Returns what Wudge is owed, or dies."

Grimsby felt his skin grow hot as he struggled for breath. He stumbled forward, knocking over a damp plunger and mop in the cramped closet. His vision was blurring, and the lone bulb overhead looked as though it was beginning to dim. He reached out to Wudge desperately, striving for air, but the little creature was gone.

For a moment, Grimsby thought this was how he was going to die: suffocating to death in a broom closet wearing a Halloween wizard robe.

Then he heard Wudge's voice from above. "Now choose, half-witch."

He looked up to see Wudge perched on a shelf of paper towel rolls like a disturbing doll. The clenched fist loosened, and Grimsby felt air seep into his lungs.

He went limp on the floor, gasping for breath, letting the sweet feeling of air flow into him.

Wudge watched him, his spidery hand poised to clench once more.

Grimsby slowly sat up, rubbing his neck. The skin was un-harmed, but it felt like he was recovering from strep throat. "I will—I'll help you. I just can't right now. There's people outside who won't let me leave."

Wudge glared at him, the hairs on his onion-helm quivering; then he nodded. "Wudge will return tonight, when the moon is highest. You will help then."

"But what if I'm in a cell by then?"

"Then Wudge will end you, and your debt will be settled."

"But—!" Grimsby began, but he blinked and Wudge was gone.

He let out a hoarse breath, his body quivering from adrenaline and fear. Suddenly, things were both simpler and more compli-cated.

Now, more than ever, being captured by the Department was not an option. It didn't matter if they found him guilty or inno-cent. If he wasn't free to repay his debt to Wudge tonight, he was dead.

He needed to get out and get away from the Auditors, and he needed to do it before they made their move.

There was a knock on the door to the closet. Three rapid raps, followed by a voice. "Mr. Grimsby? I'd like to speak to you."

TWENTY-FOUR

GRIMSBY OPENED THE DOOR, TRYING NOT TO LET HIS nerves show on his face. Standing on the other side was a man in a sharp dark suit. He wore a pair of tinted glasses over dark-rimmed eyes.

He offered a professional smile. "Mr. Grimsby, my name is Peters."

Grimsby tried to keep his eyebrows from hitting the ceiling, and he found marginal success. Though a taller man would have had problems. "It's—uh—nice to meet you, sir, but I really should be getting back to work." He tried to sidle past the man, but Peters didn't move. He wasn't large, but his bearing gave Grimsby the feeling that trying to force the issue wouldn't be wise.

Peters continued his placid smile. "In a moment, in a moment. But first, I'm going to have to ask you to come with me."

"Why?"

"I think you know. I had a pair of my Auditors speak with you yesterday."

"Your Auditors?"

Peters's smile became genuine for the first time, though it was still cold. "Yes. My Auditors. Department Director John Peters, at your service."

Grimsby's jaw went slack. Department director. There were maybe a dozen people higher in the chain of command than him, if that. He'd be in charge of every Auditor in the state, and they were indeed *his* Auditors.

"What?" Grimsby managed. He was impressed he had gotten that much out.

"It's of little consequence. The important thing, Mr. Grimsby, is that you're going to come with me." He turned and took a single stride forward. From his stature, he clearly expected to be followed.

Grimsby stood in place, though it was more due to surprise than defiance.

Peters glanced over his shoulder with singular annoyance. It was a look that made Grimsby squirm. "*Now*, Mr. Grimsby."

He shook himself, his shock and fear turning to anger and slightly lessened fear. This time, when he didn't move, fear played the lesser of the two roles. "I don't think so."

"Excuse me?"

"I don't think so," Grimsby repeated himself, a bit less shaky than the first time.

"I don't take well to nos, Mr. Grimsby."

"Take it well or leave it rare, mister," Grimsby said, "but I've got a job to do."

"You don't want this to go the hard way," Peters warned.

"N-neither do you," Grimsby said, crossing his arms.

"What did you say?" Peters said, his eyes narrowing.

"You don't want this going the hard way, either. Even more than me. Why else would you be talking to me?" He felt his voice crack but pressed on. "I noticed your people out there. You could have arrested me at any time, but not without making a scene in front of all these folks."

"Why would I care?"

"Headlines for one. I can think of a couple right off the bat. 'Auditors Storm Children's Theme Restaurant,' or maybe 'Witches Gonna Get You, and Your Little Kids, Too.' The last thing you want is a spectacle that people will be talking about."

Peters's eyes narrowed into a venomous glare. "You are correct. Such publicity would not benefit anyone."

"Which is why you haven't made your move."

"Mr. Grimsby, you've got a choice here—"

"No. You've got a choice, Director. You can either call your people in here to arrest me, or step aside and let me do my job."

"Your job? Is that what this is?" He gestured to Grimsby's robes. "Because I call it a disgrace. To all of our kind." He said the final words with a disturbing reverence.

"The only person I'm disgracing is myself, as is my American right. Now, pick a lane, buddy. Step aside, or make the call."

Peters smiled, though the expression was one of millimeters. Then, he stepped aside. "You're only buying yourself time. My people have every exit covered. Every door, every window."

"I'm sure they do," Grimsby said, walking past Peters while trying to keep his legs from shaking. "Tell them to enjoy the show. And don't eat the tacos."

He didn't look back, mostly because he was afraid that, if he did, he might see that crocodile smile again. When he reentered the dining area, the two tables of incognito Agents looked up in telling unison.

He didn't have much time. He needed to escape, and he needed to go quickly. Peters's patience wasn't unlimited, and the majority of parents and children would soon leave. Without the numerous witnesses to exaggerate to reporters later, Grimsby would have no shield from the Department's wrath.

Yet he couldn't just walk out. The only thing standing between

him and the Department was, horrifyingly enough, the sanctuary
of Mighty Magic Donald's Food Kingdom. The moment he
stepped outside, it would be a small matter for some well-dressed
folks to slide up and escort him away into some dark-windowed
car. He'd be locked in a cell, at least for a few days, but if Wudge
was to believed, he'd be dead come midnight.

And, after his near suffocation moments ago, he did in fact
believe Wudge.

He needed to escape.

And there was only one way out left to him, though he hated
to think about it.

The Elsewhere.

But the others would surely follow him once they realized
what he was doing. He needed to create a distraction.

He forced himself not to look at the gathered Agents and Auditors, at least not any more so than the scattered collection of bored
parents. He put on his best show face and bared his teeth in a
smile. "Abracadabra, alakazam, all that kind of thing!" he said,
waving his long, loose sleeves in the air. "Welcome, ladies and gentlemen, to the illustrious realm of Mighty Magic Donald's Food
Kingdom. We are pleased to welcome you to our calorically dense,
nutritionally deficient lands."

He made his way from table to table, making eye contact with
each person for an acceptable few moments, and then one or two
more to assert dominance.

There was much confusion and awkwardness in the air. Good,
for he was a confusion-and-awkwardness-smith. "Feast your eyes,
and your gullets, on our wide assortment of morsels, from pizza
to tacos to our latest fully original delight: nacho-cheese tiramisu."
There were some unapologetically disgusted sounds, which he
capitalized on. "Yes, it is in fact legal," he said, lingering for a moment next to a table full of Agents. "Write your congressman." He
kept his face pleasant and plastic, and as he did, he summoned up

the smallest reserves of Impetus he could manage. Hopefully small enough that the nearby Auditors wouldn't notice.

"In any case, don't *bind* yourselves to just one." He imprinted a rune on the bottom of the Agents' table between lumps of dried gum. There were no cries of outrage or shouted spells, so he must have been subtle enough. Although when compared to his words and robe, nearly anything would have been subtle.

He continued his tirade, slipping several more Binds out. None were hugely powerful, but they were numerous. It would have to be enough. "Don't forget! Partake in our slop-till-you-drop buffet package. If you can finish one of every item on the menu, it's free! So long as you signed the waiver and can keep it down."

More uncomfortable gazes. He strode around the dining area and noticed a tray of nachos that were sitting on the kitchen window to be delivered. He scooped them up and set them down on the second table of Agents. "On the house! Oh, come on, dig in! Don't make me *torque* your arms like the olden days." He thumbed a waiting Torque rune onto the bottom of the tray. Before stepping away: "Bring your friends, bring your family, gadzooks, bring your enemies if you want."

He turned and bared a defiant smile at Peters, who was looming near the front door. "They'll all get what they deserve, here at Mighty Magic Donald's Food Kingdom."

Peters glared, and something twitched in his brow.

Grimsby was no social expert. He couldn't read subtle emotions or tells. But he could usually tell when he had pushed somebody until they had snapped.

Peters had just snapped.

The director lifted a hand to his earpiece and muttered a single word.

The Agents all began to stand at once.

Outside, the dark cars with black-tinted windows shuddered as their doors opened. Of the white-masked Auditors who climbed out, he recognized Rayne's lean form. Beside her was almost certainly Hives.

Behind them, a long black van's doors flung open, and four hound-like creatures leapt down. Bleached-white dog skulls mounted on metallic bodies of hammered scrapwork.

Yeah, he was pretty sure he had made Peters snap.

Normally, when Grimsby cast Bind, he would first place a pair of runes, then the spell would create a strand of magic, like an elastic band, between them. Sometimes, for more complex maneuvers, he could make three or even four runes all interconnected like a web. Regardless, those Binds were usually—although less so lately—precisely timed and coordinated. This time, however, there was no precision or control. This time, he simply activated every rune in sight.

At once.

Any one of them would have been a sudden burst of quick, violent motion. About the same amount of force as a thrown punch. But when he triggered them all at once, the room flared with blue strands of light, like a web, before they suddenly all tried to pull taut, creating a miniature hurricane.

Tables went flying; pizza launched in *shuriken*-like fashion; the plate of nachos spun like a malfunctioning merry-go-round. One Agent caught hot cheese to the side of his face and clawed at it, shouting. Another was caught in the chin by the flipping table, toppling him over onto a third Agent. The customers started screaming and panicking, adding even more motion and chaos to the scene.

One Agent drew a Taser from inside her shirt and leveled it at Grimsby. She fired, but the prongs caught in his voluminous wizard sleeve. The thick blue fabric tugged them off course enough that they missed, albeit barely.

The Department forces outside were trying to get in, but the frightened parents were barreling out the door with their kids in their arms. He heard Hives and Rayne shouting over the rest, but their words were drowned out.

Grimsby wove through the crowd, back toward his closet. It was relatively easy given his small size. He cleared the crowd and reached the hall, but in the corner of his eye, he saw Peters. The director had a strange expression on his face, almost one of satisfied realization. Grimsby felt a sudden surge of the man's Impetus, like a stiff wave of heat from opening an oven. Flames eked out of his flesh and began to wreathe his hand like a burning gauntlet. As he pointed his hand at Grimsby, he suddenly realized what the director had:

Grimsby had followed through on his threat, and the news would already have a field day with what had happened. The fleeing crowd would make sure of that. It would make little difference now if Grimsby were to be arrested.

Or to die resisting arrest.

"*Immolate!*"

Flames roared forth in a tight beam, like burning gasoline from a literal fire hose, surging straight at Grimsby.

He screamed and threw himself to the ground. The fire sliced through the drywall above his head, scorching it to a blackened wound that revealed pipes, wires, and burning studs.

The flame was intensely hot, and even though it missed him, Grimsby could feel burns on the back of his neck where his skin was exposed. His scars flared in sudden white agony, and suddenly all he could see was fire. He went cold, like someone had dunked him in ice water, and he couldn't move. He could only stare at the fire that still clung to the wall in patches and shiver. He wanted to keep running, if only to get away from the flames, but his body simply ignored him.

The fire felt hotter than it should have been and closer than it really was. His skin seemed to writhe and boil all along his left side, his scars from neck to fingertips alive with the memory of what true *pain* felt like. He hardly remembered the weeks he spent in the hospital, or the months he spent in physical therapy, the fire had been so many years ago.

But the *pain*—that he remembered.

It was so real that even now he felt it, even though Peters had missed and the fire hadn't touched him. He screamed, for it was all he could do.

Then the wall groaned and cracked. A pipe, the plastic warped by the sudden heat, shuddered and snapped, spewing water out like a lanced artery. It rained down over Grimsby, and the sudden coolness of it was like a shock of electricity amid the heat. His mind snapped back to reality, back to MMDFK, and back to the crew of Auditors closing in on him.

He saw Peters glare into his still-smoldering hand and felt another wave of Impetus, like a resonant bass in his lungs, as the flames were reignited. Peters turned his gaze to Grimsby.

This time, when Grimsby told his legs to get up and run, they desperately obeyed.

He scrambled away, half crawling the last ten feet or so down the hall to the closet. He ducked inside and slammed the door behind him.

Light flared around the seams of the frame as another beam of fire roared past. He heard the wrenching shriek of metal as the blast must have ripped the restroom door at the end of the hall off its hinges.

In a moment of numb panic, Grimsby twisted the lock on the closet doorknob. It wasn't even a dead bolt. He cursed himself for wasting time. Then cursed himself for cursing himself and wasting even more time.

Before he could let himself fall into a feedback loop, he rushed to the mirror just a couple of feet away. It was long, but part of it had been spiderwebbed by a vein of cracks, leaving only a section about a foot wide and a couple of feet tall unharmed.

If it broke any more, Grimsby wouldn't fit.

He desperately hoped the mirror would hold together as he removed his glasses, letting the Elsewhere fill his senses, and placed his palms on the mirror's surface.

In the cramped space of the closet, the Elsewhere had little to warp.

Nearby buckets were wood instead of plastic, broken broom handles were shattered lances, and the lone lightbulb was now a glass lantern with a sleeping bat made of fire within it.

But the mirror was completely opaque, like frosted glass.

Grimsby willed forth his Impetus, directing the energy through his right hand and into the glass. He felt power leaking away through his scars, but he didn't have time to be efficient. Within a second, the glass became transparent, like thawing ice. Within another, he could see a reflection of the room on the other side, though he was not in it.

After the third second, his hand passed through the glass as though it wasn't there.

The door beside him burst open, but Grimsby didn't bother to look. He pulled himself through the mirror, wriggling through the largest unbroken pane within it. As he pulled his feet through, the mirror shattered behind him.

The sound of the breaking glass was suddenly very far away.

Then it was gone.

He looked up through the crumbling stone roof to see the black sun, or perhaps moon, hanging in a red sky. He put on his glasses, his mask, and nothing changed. It was the Elsewhere. This time, however, he wasn't just seeing it.

He was in it.

TWENTY-FIVE

GRIMSBY LAY ON THE GRITTY FLOOR BREATHING HARD. The first thing he heard was a distant keening wail, its mournful cry echoing toward him. It was almost familiar, and he held his breath to listen, hoping it wouldn't draw any closer. It fell to silence, save for a whispering wind through cracks in the walls and the creak of aged timbers. The wail did not return.

He breathed a sigh in relief and accidentally inhaled a mouthful of dust. He coughed spastically as he sat up, spitting out a glob of black saliva. He was in the broom closet, still. Except it wasn't quite the same. The dimensions were wrong. It was too large, and far too tall, like a chimney that didn't quite go straight up. Instead of a single shelf, it was stacked high with rows of cramped ledges, full of disturbing knickknacks, from cloudy glass globes to wicker dolls. High above, the ceiling was cracked, and a thin scar of red light seeped through.

"Half-witch better hurry," a voice croaked behind him.

He whirled around to see Wudge sitting on a shelf beside a jar of eyeballs. He glared at the creature. "What do you want now?"

Wudge made an exaggerated expression of surprise. "So rude to Wudge! Even after all we've been through."

"You're the reason I'm in this mess! If you hadn't put a literal deadline on me, I could be sitting peacefully in the back of a Department car right now. I'd be safe."

"And helpless," Wudge said. "Wudge doesn't think that's what you want."

"Oh? Wudge doesn't think so, huh? What does Wudge think I want, then? Please, enlighten me with your onion-hatted wisdom."

Wudge's gray lips parted in a smile, one that stretched too wide. "Half-witch wants revenge."

Grimsby nearly laughed. "Revenge? Why on Earth would I want revenge? On who, even? Nobody's done anything to me."

"Oh, somebody has done much to you. Someone you know."

"Who?" he demanded.

"You," Wudge said, grinning. "Half-witch wants revenge on himself."

"What does that even mean?"

"Wudge thinks you know," he said, leaping down from the shelf and dropping easily fifteen times his own height. He landed without a stumble.

Grimsby began to reply, but Wudge interrupted him with a kick to the shin.

"Ow!" he said. "What'd you do that for?"

Wudge pointed at his wrist. "Time is short, half-witch. Especially here."

Grimsby gulped. Wudge was right; he had nearly forgotten. Time in the Elsewhere was strange, fluctuating depending on how long you were there. If you were in the Elsewhere for less than seven minutes before returning to the waking world, exactly seven seconds would have passed. Stay for longer, up to seven hours, and instead exactly seven minutes would have passed on the outside.

Grimsby had used the trick to create time and study for exams once or twice, but after nearly getting grabbed by something, he decided time management was a wiser way to go.

After seven hours, however, things got strange.

Less than seven hours was just seven minutes, but a second more would pass as seven days in the real world. Beyond that, Grimsby had heard that seven days or more in the Elsewhere would be seven years outside. Though he'd doubt anyone's ability to survive that long in the magical land. The longer you stayed, the more dangerous the Elsewhere became.

The logic made Grimsby's head hurt, and he tried not to dabble with it too much. But he had heard stories of witches coming out of the Elsewhere seven years after they vanished. He was fairly certain that's where the superstition of seven years' bad luck for breaking a mirror came from.

Most important, though, was that the rule meant that everything that would happen in the outside world in the first window of time since he left would all happen at once in just under seven minutes. Which meant anyone and *everyone* following him in that time frame would arrive. He needed to be long gone by then.

He needed a new mirror to return to the waking world. But where would he find one? The bathrooms had mirrors, of course, but popping out a few feet away from where he went in did him no favors. He needed to find another mirror to get home through, or risk staying for longer than he intended. Perhaps *much* longer.

He glared at Wudge. "I don't suppose you'd tell me where another mirror was?"

"Wudge might. For a second favor."

Grimsby rolled his eyes and turned away. The last thing he needed was to be even more indebted to the creature. He'd have to find an exit nearby. Perhaps the gas station across the street might have mirrors in their bathrooms as well.

He left Wudge in the closet and made his way into the hall. Here, too, the layout was strange and yet familiar. It was as though he had described MMDFK to an artist who was skilled but not sober, and they had done their best. The hall was too long, and oddly curved. The posters that had been taped to the walls were now stitched portraits of silhouettes who stared at Grimsby with eyes like pinpoints of darkness. Their vague forms followed him as he made his way down the hall to the dining area.

He moved at a brisk pace, tempered only by his nervousness. But as he rounded the corner, he saw something hunched in the midst of a nest of broken tables. He ducked back into the hall, his breath catching in his throat. Slowly, he peered out at the creature.

Its body was corpulent and dripping with sagging folds of skin; its flesh was pale and untouched by the sun. It was stooped over a cauldron of black iron, scooping the contents into its mouth with a flabby paw. Whatever was inside looked disgustingly similar to nacho cheese. Or maybe pus.

Grimsby didn't know what the thing was. He didn't want to move, but he had little choice. Time was ticking away, and his seven-minute lead would evaporate shortly. He had to get past the creature and out the door. Its back was turned to him, and with any luck he'd slip past without it noticing him. If it did see him, he wasn't sure what would happen. He resolved to simply hope not to find out.

He made his way toward the doors to the outside. The once-clear glass was now stained with moving images of children playing across its surface; however, the little images often fell and broke apart into pieces, or were carried off by dark creatures. Those that survived continued playing as though nothing were amiss. Grimsby felt like he could almost hear the distant sounds of children screaming in a manner that straddled the thin line between joy and fear.

As he neared the door, he heard a scuff behind him, and he turned to see Wudge. The little nuisance had a broad grin on his face as he held a glass bottle in the air over his head. Grimsby watched in confusion that quickly turned to horror as Wudge tossed the bottle high in the air.

His eyes nearly bulged out to knock the glasses from his face as he desperately lunged forward to catch the bottle. He barely managed it, scuffing his palms and bruising his knees. He juggled it for a desperate moment between his hands until he had it steadied.

Unfortunately, he had not been silent enough. There was a surprised choking noise as the creature in the room turned its head to Grimsby. Its face looked like a mask drawn taut, almost devoid of features except for black marble-like eyes and flapping jowls. It snorted and squealed, picking up the cauldron and barreling toward him.

Grimsby screamed and tried to crawl out of the way, expecting the thing to pounce on him. Instead, it continued past where he had been, shattering the glass door as it charged through it. The glass pieces fell to the ground, writhing like maggots before hardening into jagged shards of black ice.

As though in response to the breaking glass, the screaming came again, though this time it had coalesced in a single keening wail, and this time it was close. Very close. At this distance, the sound was all too familiar to Grimsby.

It was a Geist. The same thing that had nearly consumed him in the trap in Mansgraf's lair.

Instinctual, ingrained fear welled up in his guts. He remembered the chill, the clawing mist that dug invisible nails into his flesh. The wounds were still fresh enough that when a shiver rolled over him, he felt each of them twinge with sharp pain.

He began to scramble to his feet, body demanding that he start running somewhere, anywhere, but as he tried, long, thin fingers gripped his ankle, wrapping firmly around and keeping him on his hands and knees.

He turned to see Wudge's stark eyes, the horizontal pupils wide and alert. One of his gangly hands was around Grimsby's ankle, while the other held up a shushing finger over his froggish mouth.

Grimsby wanted to punt the small, inhuman thing across the

room and run for his life, but he bit back the primal fear and took a steadying breath. When it was clear he wasn't going to run, Wudge released his leg and pointed after the flabby creature that had fled out the doors.

He peered out after the cauldron-hauling monster, which had already begun to slow despite blubbery effort as it ran across a road that was unlike its counterpart in the real world. The street was long and barren, the painted lines long since bleached away by a scouring wind and the black sun. The pavement's cracks crawled and shifted like thawing and freezing ice. The road was wider across than the real one would have been. Much wider.

The blob was nearly halfway across the street when the red light of the sky dimmed suddenly. The creature looked up for a moment, then squealed again and began to lumber desperately toward shelter.

Then a living darkness swept down, like someone had cast a lasso into the sky and reeled in a storm cloud. It dropped like a swooping hawk. Faces crawled over the gray, misty surface of the shape, twisting in hunger, agony, and ecstasy all in one. It descended over the blob, the familiar wail filling the air. The only sounds Grimsby could hear over the Geist were that of the squealing, choking blob. Its cries lasted mere seconds before falling to grim silence. The wails faded shortly after. The cloud ascended once again. When it did, the creature was gone, and only the black cauldron remained, tipped over on the ground, spilling bubbling yellow ooze.

Grimsby felt his gorge rise, but he kept his stomach from totally revolting. He shuddered. Though the blob had been far from human, he could empathize with the fear it had felt, and knew all too well the pain of the Geist's grasp.

The cloud rose into the sky, vanishing from sight. Though whether it had dissipated or merely blended in among the others, Grimsby was uncertain.

It was only after Wudge took a deep breath that Grimsby felt safe enough to breathe himself.

"Eyes aflame," he whispered. "What was that thing doing here?"

"They are attracted to broken glass," Wudge said.

"Why?"

"Broken glass sometimes means broken mirror. It means yummy witches have come to play," Wudge said, making chomping motions with his fingers.

"Then what was that Geist doing in Mansgraf's lair?"

"She-bitch had trapped it. Good for getting rid of bodies."

"Did that problem come up often for her?"

Wudge grinned his bear-trap smile. "Often enough."

Grimsby shuddered and looked for the mist in the red sky, but it looked clear. He turned his mind back to trying to find another exit.

There would likely be one in what had been a gas station in the real world, though now it wasn't quite like the one he remembered. He was fairly certain the real one didn't have a clock tower rising from the top of it, or windows like an old cathedral. Although it wasn't much of a clock, as all three hands had come to rest on the seventh numeral, which might have simply been because the other eleven numbers were all missing.

The main problem, however, was that the gas station was across the street.

He watched the last of the yellow ooze drip from the overturned cauldron and could almost hear the screams of the dying blob as it was torn to nonexistence by the Geist.

"So as long as glass doesn't break, the Geist won't come?" he asked Wudge.

The tiny creature nodded. "They cannot see; they only sense from close. So long as nothing attracts it, it should stay away."

Grimsby nodded. Normally, he would have his doubts about

Wudge's honesty, but he had just helped him, sort of. Besides, Grimsby still owed him a favor. Wudge wouldn't get him killed before he could repay it.

Right?

He shook his head. He had little choice in either case. Time was short, and he needed out of the Elsewhere quickly.

He started across the street in a hurried walk, too afraid to run and draw any attention, too nervous to be slow and cautious. He realized it might have been the worst of both worlds, but it was the only option his shaking legs offered him.

Wudge kept up beside him, his relatively enormous leather-wrapped feet slapping on the shifting pavement.

Grimsby felt his stress spike into a mixture of annoyance and anger. "Why are you following me?"

Wudge shrugged. "Bored."

"Why don't you go and get the key yourself if you're so bored?"

"Wudge knows where key is. But he can't get it alone. Wudge needs a witch."

"Why me? There's gotta be some other witch you can bother with this."

Wudge shrugged. "Maybe. But half-witch already owes Wudge a favor. Besides, most witches are boring and smart. Half-witch is neither."

"Oh, how kind of you. Thank you, noble sir, for your words of encouragement."

Wudge frowned. "Half-witch is definitely neither."

Grimsby grumbled. They passed the fallen cauldron of yellow ooze, stepping around the spreading pool that seeped into the cracks of pavement. Wudge dipped a knobby finger in the substance and tasted it, but his face twisted in disgust and he spat it out immediately.

Suddenly, it began to rain. A thin, spattering drizzle that left the cold ground layered with oily black water. Or at least he thought it was water. But when he saw the liquid mixed with the yellow slop, he realized it wasn't black, but a deep shade of red.

"Is that . . . ?" Grimsby asked, trailing off as his feet squelched over the growing pool of scarlet.

"Blood, yup," Wudge said, wiping the liquid from his gray-green skin. "Be wary of the clouds, half-witch. Most stay up above, but only most."

Grimsby retched and pulled his pointy blue hat down over his head, turning his eyes upward at the growing storm clouds. There were more above than there had been before, but they seemed content to remain at their altitude. For now.

"Forecast says: cloudy with a chance of dismemberment," he muttered.

Then the clock tower across the road creaked and groaned. Its face began to turn, like a slowly spinning plate, and the hands rotated with it. When it came to a rest, the seven was where a normal clock's eight would be, and the hands all clattered as they twisted toward it.

"Seven minutes—" Wudge said, but he was interrupted.

Behind them, in MMDFK, they could hear glass shattering. A moment later came the baying of hounds. The Auditors had come, familiars in tow, shattering their own mirrors as they did.

Above, the clouds roiled. Wails sounded, too loud to be just a single Geist. They began to descend, like the red sky had broken apart and begun falling.

Meanwhile, Grimsby and Wudge were still in the middle of the road.

Wudge looked around, his eyes wide. "Good luck, half-witch," he said, and vanished.

Grimsby was alone. At least, aside from all the things that wanted to kill him.

"Puppy dogs' tails," he cursed.

TWENTY-SIX

G RIMSBY BROKE INTO A MAD SPRINT, NOT DARING TO look up as the sky fell upon him. The road grew darker as though a sudden eclipse had blotted out the black sun, and he felt a chill come along with it.

Behind him, the baying of hounds grew clear.

He risked a glance over his shoulder to see three beasts come running out of the Elsewhere's MMDFK. They did not look like the familiars he had seen in the real world, but instead were sleek, furless, dark-skinned hounds that had orange pinpricks of light burning in the hollows of empty eye sockets.

Behind them, he saw both Hives and Rayne, their masks obscuring their faces but not their identities. They took a look above at the darkening sky and decided to remain inside.

Grimsby focused on the sanctuary of the building ahead. The tall clock tower seemed to bend over him, leering like a mocking giant as the world converged on him.

The padding scratches of paws on concrete grew audible, and Grimsby felt a deep, instinctual fear take hold of him. It pounded icicles into his spine and sent his legs aflame, urging him to run faster.

So run faster he did.

The darkness was nearly complete around him as he neared the building. He looked up to see a descending Geist, or perhaps Geists, like a roiling fog of nebulous and grasping hands, all reaching toward him. He was scarcely a dozen feet from the entrance; he was nearly safe. He reached the door and fumbled with the handle to open it.

He was too slow.

They rolled over him like a damp wave full of razor blades. He felt them tug and claw at his clothes and skin, tearing at him like the thorns of rosebushes in a hurricane. It was too dark to see; he was blind. He screamed but his voice was lost. He pounded on the door, sightlessly pawing for the handle.

With a last surge of fearful strength, he threw himself forward, his shoulder leading the charge. He felt a dozen digging fingers slide over his skin, nearly drawing him to a halt. He slammed into the door, but it did not open. Again he tried, but to no avail. The Geist was pulling hard at him now, and he felt himself losing his footing. Within moments, it would carry him off the ground and turn him into red rain.

With one final, desperate charge, he threw himself into the door.

He felt it give way before him. He broke out of the darkness and tumbled to the floor, his throat hoarse from screaming, his body trembling from pain and exertion. He lay on the ground for a moment, catching his breath. Behind him, the door led only to inky blackness, like someone had curtained the frame with a silk sheet. The Geists, however, did not cross the threshold into the building.

Outside, the hounds yelped in disturbingly lifelike imitations of the real thing. He heard the sounds of tearing flesh and scrabbling paws. He felt a wincing pang of sympathy for them.

At least until one of them leapt through the door, emerging

suddenly from the dark. Its sleek hide was split apart, shredded to nothing in some places, revealing the scrapwork body it had in real life. Its jaws hung open as though panting, though it had no tongue. It had only teeth that looked to be made of shards of obsidian.

It glared at him with its burning eyes and stalked forward. Its scraps of dangling hide looked like torn upholstery. Grimsby scurried backward on his palms and bottom, his blood-dampened robe squelching over the floor, but his back quickly found a wall. As he watched the familiar approach, he saw bits of flesh fall from its form and evaporate into smoke. As they did, its movements became slower and more sluggish. It was injured, and that had slowed it a few degrees.

Grimsby might have been grateful, but he wasn't exactly in ideal shape himself. He felt cool air lick at the thin bleeding wounds on his cheeks. Blood, either from the rain or his own, had dribbled down from his forehead and was only mostly wicked away by his eyebrows, leaving the rest stinging his sight. The cuts all over his body were shallow, but they were long, and they bled enough to make Grimsby feel faint.

He tried to steel himself, but it ended up feeling more like tin-foiling himself. In either case, he still managed to climb slowly to his feet, his eyes never leaving the familiar's. The Geists outside were beginning to depart, and as they thinned, he could see the running forms of Hives and Rayne coming toward him.

He realized too late that he had let himself be distracted from the hound.

The familiar saw his attention waver and pounced immediately. Its lithe form had surprising strength, despite the wounds the Geists had left it with.

Grimsby threw up a hand and shouted hoarsely, *"Torque!"*

A sudden, spinning vortex of green light fired from his hand, whirling through the air like a glowing propeller of sparks. It missed by inches, striking the familiar off-center, but managed to throw off its trajectory just enough that instead of colliding with Grimsby teeth-first, it struck him skull-first.

Whatever its appearance, it still felt just as heavy and dense as if it were made of metal. Grimsby felt himself jerked from his feet by the force and fell into a tumbling jumble with the familiar. Its jaws snapped and growled as it tried to find purchase on his limbs, but by some miracle he managed to stay out from between its teeth.

He fell onto his back and the familiar found leverage, pressing down into him, obsidian teeth flashing toward his throat. Only by gaining panicked purchase on the thing's chest did Grimsby keep its jaws barely at bay.

He grunted as the hound bore down on him. His arms began to tremble, threatening to give way. His strength was fleeting. He needed to do something. If the hound didn't mangle him badly enough to prevent his escape, the approaching Auditors surely would make up the difference.

He summoned his Impetus, pouring the last shreds of his strength into the spell.

His fingertips began to glow as he touched one hand to the crest of the thing's chest. There, a glowing sigil appeared. Then, with a shove, he slapped its opposite on the bottom of the familiar's jaw.

His grip slipped, and the hound's fangs bore down on him. He uttered the spell through gritted teeth. *"Bind!"*

He felt sharp teeth dig into his forearm from above, but the ones below did not accompany them. The creature balked and reeled as an azure thread of light pulled its lower jaw toward its chest, distending it unnaturally. Sleek skin split and peeled like disintegrating rubber as the familiar struggled to snap its jaws shut on Grimsby's arm. The more effort it spent, the more its skin burned away.

Finally, it began to waver, as though its internal mechanisms were rusting to dust, and as its last bit of flesh turned to smoke and its orange eyes winked out, it fell into a motionless heap atop Grimsby.

He tried to take a breath of relief, but the weight of the familiar was crushing. He barely managed to wriggle out from under it. As he did, approaching footsteps on concrete told him it was no time to rest, but when he climbed to his feet, he found the room was rudely spinning around him. He stumbled deeper into the building, eyes searching for the vaguely familiar hall that would lead to what, in the real world, would have been the restroom and its mirrors.

He stumbled through the dim corridors, ignoring the sourceless shadows that scattered before him like roaches. He crashed through the door into what he was fairly sure was the men's restroom. It was empty and barren, with only a wide mirror and a wall of cold stalls. They had no toilets inside, only stone slabs, like the universe's budget had run out before it could hire a sculptor.

Grimsby stumbled to the mirror and pressed his bloody hands against the glass. He began to summon his Impetus to will his way through.

His reflection vanished, and the comforting scene of a normal restroom flickered briefly into view. Then it began to fade.

Grimsby's eyes widened and he tried to pour more energy into the mirror, but it went blank, then returned to showing only his own harried reflection.

He was out of strength. His Impetus had been burned out. It would be a barely flickering ember until he got some rest.

Echoing footsteps drew closer. Hives and Rayne were coming.

He was trapped.

TWENTY-SEVEN

H E HAD BARE MOMENTS TO ACT BEFORE THE AUDITORS caught up to him, arrested him, and unwittingly doomed him to Wudge. But without the Impetus left to escape, he was trapped. It would take a long rest to recover enough, and that was time he didn't have. The Auditors had him cornered.

Then a thought occurred to him.

They didn't have to know that.

He gritted his teeth and drew up as much desperate confidence as he could. Then he punched the mirror. Hard.

He felt his knuckles shift in sharp agony as his blow bounced off the surface, rattling the reflective sheet but doing little else.

Again he punched, this time even harder. Something popped and his hand roared with pain. Again, the mirror remained intact.

Finally, as a last resort, he hauled back his head, scrunched his eyes shut, and slammed his forehead into the mirror. Cracks webbed out across its surface before it shattered, falling to dozens of pieces.

Head and hand throbbing, Grimsby stumbled to one of the stalls, clambered up on the stone seat that passed for a toilet, and silently shut the door behind him. Then he waited.

He didn't have to wait long. Skin-thin moments passed before footsteps pattered into the room. He heard a pair of light, huffing breaths. Then a heavy foot stomped on the ground.

"Damn it!" he heard Hives say. "He beat us to the mirror. He's back in the waking world."

"Most likely," Rayne said, her voice calm and contemplative. "We haven't missed our first window. If we leave now, we'll still be seven minutes ahead of him."

"Wait, what?"

Rayne sighed and adopted a tone she had used with Grimsby more than once during their studies, and he felt a pang of mixed nostalgia and jealousy. It was a tone reserved for teaching something she thought simple to others who didn't understand it. "The first window: less than seven minutes in the Elsewhere means that seven seconds pass on the outside. Grimsby is in the second window. He'll return seven minutes after he entered. If we leave while we're still in the first window, we'll be exactly six minutes and fifty-three seconds ahead of him. You can head him off at this mirror and wait."

"Er. Right," Hives said, though Grimsby was fairly certain he didn't fully understand.

In fairness, Grimsby didn't fully understand, either. Time in the Elsewhere felt like it passed normally, but those rules changed when you returned back to regular time. He was suddenly grateful he hadn't been able to use the mirror, or he'd be running face-first into a waiting Hives on the other side.

"There's a mirror in the room next door. You use that one and cut him off."

"What about you?"

"I'll find another and be right behind you. I need to collect my familiars first."

Hives made a hesitant noise, but a moment later his footsteps departed. A few moments after that, the sound of glass shattering reached Grimsby.

Rayne's footsteps also receded, and within a couple of minutes, he heard more falling glass.

He let out a held breath and allowed his tensed muscles to sink into exhausted slumps. He got to his feet and pressed open the door, trying to figure out what his next move would be.

That was when Rayne's arm caught him across the throat.

She was a moving blur, faster than he remembered, and before he could really grasp what was happening, he was knocked face-first to the floor with a knee in the back of his spine, crushing his ribs under their combined weight.

Rayne kept atop him, patiently waiting for his hoarse coughs to subside. As they did, she clicked her tongue. "You really think that little of me, huh, Grimshaw?"

"How'd you know?" he asked, voice rasping like claws on a chalkboard.

"I figured you'd be out of juice after that stunt you pulled in the restaurant. Hell, I'd have figured you wouldn't have been able to pull that off in the first place. You've always been a magical lightweight."

His face contorted with pain, and not just from her knee in his back. "I get by."

"Stubborn as ever, I see."

"So what now, you arrest me?"

She didn't speak for a long moment. "Give me a reason not to."

"Because I don't think the Department has jurisdiction in the Elsewhere."

"Give me a reason that actually matters."

"Because I didn't do anything wrong."

"You assaulted several Department Auditors."

"With nachos! They'll recover. Besides, they started it."

"You ran from a Department task force sent to apprehend you."

"Because I don't have time to rot in a cell for a few days and trust in a bunch of bumbling morons to solve a case when they believe they've already arrested the killer."

"Morons?"

"They all got juked by a magician in a wizard robe."

"Not all of them did," she said, grinding her knee a little deeper between Grimsby's spinal disks.

"Yeah, okay, fine," he said, wincing. "Most of them did."

He felt more than heard her sigh. "Grimshaw, why'd you have to do this? Why couldn't you just lay low like I asked?"

"Would you have?"

"Of course I would have. Look, I understand—"

"No," he said, feeling his chest flare with angry heat as she ground him into the floor. "You don't. You don't understand."

Something in his voice must have driven her to silence, and he felt a little of the pressure lift from his back.

"If you were me," he said, "and the one thing you've wanted your whole life was taken from you, would you lay low? And if you had to spend your days working at a fast-food restaurant where the only thing worse than the food is the customers, would you have laid low?"

"No," she said quietly.

"No. You would have taken any shot, no matter how distant, at a chance of being something else. Something *more*. That's what I am—" He stopped, a sickening weight growing in his stomach. "What I was doing. I was taking a blasted shot at being something more."

"You won't be much more if you're dead."

"I wouldn't be much less, either," he said quietly.

More silence. Then: "Tell me you didn't do it."

"I didn't do it."

"No." He felt her knee lift as she turned him over and hauled him up until his face met hers. Her face was still masked but her eyes were wide and searching, pleading for truth. "*Tell* me you didn't do it."

"Rayne," he said, "I didn't do it. I couldn't have. I—" His voice broke and he coughed a few times before he found it again. "I don't think I could ever do something like that to anyone. Not even her."

Slowly, she nodded. "All right. I may be an idiot for believing you, but all right."

She helped him to his feet, but as he stood his head began to spin and he felt like he might tip over. He felt her grip his arm to steady him.

"You're a mess, Grimsby."

"Really? Because I feel a whole lot worse than that."

"You should get some rest."

He shook his head, but that only made the dizziness worse. "I don't have time. I'm on a deadline—"

"You really didn't pay attention when we learned about this place, did you? You have time."

"What do you mean?"

"You're in the second window. Seven minutes to seven hours on this side, it's all the same. So long as you leave before it ends, only seven minutes will have passed on the outside."

"And after more than seven hours?"

Her eyes smiled. "You'll lose time. You'll come back seven days after you came in. You can lose a lot of time if you lose track of it."

"And after that?"

"More than seven days here turns to seven years, but I wouldn't worry about that."

"Really? Because I feel like I should be worried about it."

"No, not you. You wouldn't survive a week here. Most can't. The longer you stay, the more dangerous the Elsewhere becomes."

"And you want me to stay here and take a nap? What if I oversleep? I don't want to wake up next week." *Or dead*, he thought, whether from Wudge or from something in the Elsewhere.

"Don't worry, I do overtime work in here almost every week. I'll stay with you and keep watch. And I'll wake you when it's time to go."

"Why? Why would you help me?"

"Because if I don't, there's no way you're going to make it." She laughed, but it was subdued and a little sad. "Just like old times."

He wanted to argue, but she gently guided him to the wall and pushed him down to sit against it. She was strong but soft, and resisting felt like a whole lot of work that he didn't really want to do anyway, so he let it happen.

"Just a couple hours, okay?" he said.

"Of course," Rayne replied. She began to say something else, but he lost focus and everything simply fell away to blessed darkness.

TWENTY-EIGHT

GRIMSBY FELT SOMETHING SHAKING HIM FROM A dreamless sleep. He grumbled and tried to wave a limp arm at it to ward whatever it was away, but something was wrapped around him and obstructed his movement like a loose web. His mind immediately leapt to a documentary he saw once about a spider with venom that numbed its prey so that it would be half eaten by the time it woke up.

He immediately started flailing in defense against the spider, or perhaps spiders.

"Grimsby!" Rayne shouted. "Knock it off!"

He knocked it off and cracked open bleary eyes. "Oh. You're not spiders," he said.

"Not at the moment," she confirmed.

He realized the webs he had felt were Rayne's jacket, which she had laid over him. He handed it back and stretched, his body cracking and creaking. His legs throbbed and the knuckles on his right hand were swollen uncomfortably. Mostly, though, his throat was so dry that it felt like a pencil that had been sharpened at both ends was stuck in it.

"You've got an hour before your window closes, Grimshaw. You'll wanna be long gone by then."

He nodded. "There's a place next door. Should have a couple exit mirrors there."

She shook her head. "You'll want to go farther than that. Hives will be waiting for you, and he'll have a head start. If he's close enough to hear the mirror break, he'll know it's you."

"Right, so I should go farther than—" He stopped as he noticed the breath fogging in front of his face. It was only a moment later that the chill reached him, like a slow, steady wall of shiver-inducing tendrils.

Rayne noticed it, too, and turned away to glance outside the bathroom and down the hall.

Grimsby approached her, instinctively sneaking. "What is—?" he began, but Rayne ducked back in and clapped her hand over his mouth, her skin fever hot in the cold.

She met his eyes with hers, and they were wide, but not with fear. She was alert. She was ready. She was an Auditor.

Grimsby was simply afraid, and suddenly a little ashamed of it.

He pushed both feelings from his mind as she pressed her arm against him, pushing his back to the wall beside her. Her held breath was enough to tell him to be quiet.

They stood in frozen silence for long moments.

Until Grimsby heard the first footstep.

It was barely a whisper, hardly more than the scrape of silk over stone. It drew closer, and as it did, he felt the air continue to grow colder. Before long, it began to bite and burn at his skin like a frost-ridden wind. He felt his body begin to shiver and forced it to stop.

He looked past Rayne, able to see only a few degrees through the open doorway. The light seemed to fall dimmer in tandem with the cold, but he saw a form pause outside the door.

220 JAMES J. BUTCHER

It was feminine, almost decidedly so, with curves that felt only barely exaggerated and hair that fell down in a straight curtain of silk.

But that was where the resemblance to humanity stopped.

Its skin was sleek and the shade of starless midnight, with no echo of warmth or blood to it. It felt closer to a black sky than to human flesh. It consumed the light that touched it so well that he couldn't see more than the silhouette. No dips or valleys of muscles, just a human-shaped hole in the world that revealed nothing on the other side.

Grimsby watched it stop outside the doorway and held his breath until his lungs began to burn. He wasn't sure if the room was growing darker or if it was his own oxygen-deprived vision.

Then the shape moved on, its bare feet drifting over the floor until it passed from sight.

Grimsby risked a breath, and the room began to warm, though slowly. "What the blue blazes was that?"

"I . . . I'm not sure," Rayne said, her voice betraying that not knowing was unusual to her. "I've never seen anything like it, yet it looked familiar."

Grimsby let the shivers catch up to him, both those born of cold and those born of terror. It took a few seconds to shake them all out. "I think we should go sooner rather than later. Why don't we both take the mirror in the other bathroom?"

Rayne shook her head. "It would kill me," she said matter-of-factly.

"What?"

"My window began about seven seconds after yours. That means that even if you and I return from this side at the same time, we'll both arrive exactly seven minutes later—from the moment we left."

"Yeah, so?"

"So, if we take the same mirror and you get there seven seconds before I do, you'll break the mirror we both took before I get out. Leaving me either dead or trapped somewhere between the Elsewhere and our world, which is likely the same thing."

"Oh. Yeah. Of course. I knew that."

She arched a brow at him. "So you were trying to kill me?"

"Fine, I didn't know that."

"I know." She smirked. "So whichever mirror you take, I need to take a different one."

"Right. So let's get you into the one next door and I'll find my own."

She shook her head. "No, you will use that one. Just watch out for Hives. He won't know exactly where you're returning, but if he hears the glass break, it's a giveaway. I'll find another way back. I can handle myself in here with that thing better than you can."

"You don't even know what that thing is!"

"Neither do you. So, knowledge being irrelevant, skill is the deciding factor. Oh, and what do you know, I'm the better choice there as well."

He glared at her but could do little to argue. She had always been, simply put, better.

"Fine. I'll take the bathroom mirror. You—"

She tilted her head with professional interest in what he had to say.

Purely professional.

Something in his chest twinged like a snapping guitar string.

He suddenly remembered once, a long time ago, when her lips had touched his. Now he wondered if it had just been a dream. Then he realized it didn't matter. Memory or daydream, the result was the same.

It was a long time ago; it was nothing. He shook himself, his words suddenly lost. He felt ridiculous for ever hoping that he could be more to her than a friend.

He wanted to say something, to ask her if she remembered that moment, just to know it had been real. Instead, he just shook his head. "You—stay safe. Okay?"

Her eyes crinkled in something that might have been a smile beneath her mask. "I have every intention of it, Grimshaw."

He nodded and stood, trying to draw his mind away from dusty, painful memories. He began creeping away, still feeling the chill that strange creature left lingering in the air.

"And Grimshaw?" Rayne called quietly.

He turned back, ever hopeful.

When she spoke, he dared to think there might have been some hesitation to her words. Though perhaps he just imagined that, too.

"You stay safe as well," she said.

TWENTY-NINE

GRIMSBY WINCED AND BRACED HIMSELF AS HE PASSED through the mirror.

The cloying chill fell away, and the warm air on the other side burned his skin wonderfully. He took his first step through and stumbled. His footing was spaced perfectly between bathroom sinks, and he plunged forth gracelessly. The moment his body broke contact with the mirror, it shattered behind him. Shards rained down, bouncing off his blue robes, onto the counter, and into the sinks, causing the motion sensors to trip and start spraying water over them.

The whole second-long scene must have scared the stuffing out of the two middle-aged women who had been fixing their hair and makeup in the mirror.

They shrieked and screamed, scattering toward the lone exit.

"Sorry!" Grimsby said after them, but his apology was drowned out by their departing cries.

He stood for a moment, letting his body adjust to the warmth and weight of the real world. After a few hours in the Elsewhere, the shine of linoleum and smell of disinfectant were oddly comforting.

Just as he climbed to his feet, however, the door to the ladies' room opened. But it was no woman standing in the doorway; it was the barn-broad Hives. His eyes looked wide and bloodshot through the holes in his mask, and Grimsby could see his neck and hair shine with sweat from exertion. He must have heard the commotion of Grimsby's arrival and come running.

"About time," Hives said, his breath easy and unstrained. "I was worried you'd gotten lost."

Grimsby felt his numb skin prickle with an old, familiar fear. He'd heard that tone from Hives many times during their shared apprenticeship, and each time it had come shortly before a beating.

"Hives," he said, "this isn't what you think." He tried to keep his voice calm and confident. Unfortunately, he only managed to make it cornered and brittle.

"Let me guess; you didn't do it? You're innocent, and Mansgraf's killer just framed you for it all?"

Grimsby was a little taken aback, despite the blunt sarcasm. Nobody else had thought him innocent until he'd convinced them otherwise. "Yes."

Hives's face was obscured by the mask, but his smirk still reached his eyes. "Here's the thing, Grimy: I don't care."

Grimsby gulped. So much for appealing to Hives's reason.

"Now, we can do this one of two ways: you tell me where the Wardbox is, or I beat you until I'm convinced you don't know."

"What if we just skip straight to 'I don't know'?"

Hives shook his head. "Bringing you in will be a promotion for me either way. Bringing you in with the Wardbox will be another."

"Two promotions in one day?" Grimsby asked, unable to keep the nervous snark at bay. "Wow, a couple more and maybe you'll outrank Rayne."

Hives's eyes narrowed as his smirk vanished. "Beats being a bitch-witch for the plastic king of a cheesy restaurant."

"I can't argue with you there," Grimsby admitted. "But I've

got bad news for you. I have no idea what Wardbox you're talking about."

"I think you do," Hives said.

"Nope. Honest, look." He held out the arms of his voluminous robe and shook them. "Nothing up my sleeves."

"If you don't have it, you know who does or where it is. I know you were contacted by that old pal of Mansgraf's. The flower guy. You're gonna tell me what you told him."

Grimsby couldn't help but smile. Mayflower, the dread Huntsman, being called the flower guy.

"What are you smiling at, Grimy?"

"Or what?"

Hives frowned in satisfying confusion. "What?"

"I said, 'Or what?' I'm going to tell you what I told Mayflower or . . . ? You really need to learn to leverage or you'll never make it in this business."

Hives took a pair of lumbering steps forward. "Or I'll beat your face to paste."

Grimsby felt like he could already taste a little blood in his mouth but ignored it. "Not bad. Good imagery, I'll grant you. Nice and brief. But you really need to up the ante. My face is most of the way there already."

Hives's glared deepened as he stalked forward. Grimsby swallowed the nervous lump of fear in his throat as he approached. Hives hadn't looked that big from farther away. Was he always this big? And why did he keep getting bigger?

Grimsby didn't hold back the panicked ramblings of his fear. "I mean, you would not believe the day I've had. Frankly, face paste would be a minor inconvenience compared to some of the other scrapes I've avoided."

"Is that so?" Hives asked, coming to a stop only a couple of feet from Grimsby.

Somehow, while talking, Grimsby had forgotten to back away

or flinch from Hives's oncoming bulk. "Yeah, that's so. So why don't we skip ahead a few steps? I'll give you the highlights: First, you lay into me. Second, I don't give you anything. Third, you make a mistake. And lastly, I knock your fat head out cold."

"I got a better idea," Hives said.

His meaty arm snapped out with unfair speed and seized Grimsby by the throat. His fingers wrapped most of the way around. He held up his other hand and Grimsby felt a surge of Impetus as Hives said a single word.

"*Blaze.*"

The Auditor's hand sparked to light, a blanket of fire covering it like a glove.

Grimsby felt his heart start to thrum as he stared at the fire. The heat was intense enough that he could feel it on his face already.

Hives's eyes smiled, but his voice held a tone of mock concern. "Oh, oh no. I almost forgot. You've got that whole pyrophobia thing, don't you?"

Grimsby watched as Hives inched his flaming hand closer to his face. The scars on his neck and arm felt like they were trying to crawl away. His left hand began to tremble, the creaking joints beneath gnarled skin aching with every motion.

"Let *me* give *you* the highlights," Hives said, his voice easy and confident. "I'm going to ask you some questions, and you're going to answer me. Every time you say something I don't like, I'm going to remind you why you're nothing more than a sniveling cockroach who doesn't deserve to be a witch. Got it?"

Grimsby didn't, couldn't, reply. He barely even heard Hives's words. His whole body was intently focused on only the fire.

"I said, 'Got it?'" Hives said. He moved the fire a few inches closer.

Hot air stung Grimsby's face, making him wince. He hated himself for being so afraid, but the heat, flame, and memories left him paralyzed. He could hardly breathe, even considering the grip on his throat. Although without the support of Hives's grasp, his legs might well have given way beneath him. A low squeak freed itself from the choking mitt around his neck.

Hives smiled, apparently pleased with Grimsby's reaction. "Good. Now, where is the Wardbox?"

Grimsby shook his head, finding himself pulling as far from the fire as he could, though it wasn't far enough. "I-I don't know."

"Mansgraf had it with her before she died, didn't have it after she died, and she wrote your name at the crime scene. You know."

The fire was very close now. Grimsby smelled the all-too-familiar scent of burning hair. This time, it was not just his head that shook, but the rest of him as well. "I don't! We found that a Wardbox was missing from her stash, so I made a tracking spell so we could find it."

Hives's eyes narrowed. "Where is it?"

Grimsby swallowed. He wanted to just turn into a font of words, words that might douse the fire or at least get it a few inches farther from his face. But instead he clamped his mouth shut. The spell was with the Huntsman. Mayflower had been the one ally he had, and even though the Huntsman had nearly shot him a couple of times, Grimsby couldn't let himself betray the man.

"Didn't work out," he choked. "You know me, butterfingers with magic."

Hives's hand clenched hard, cutting him off. "No, I don't think so. Where's the tracker, Grimsby?"

"Lost! Gone! Isn't that the worst when you lose the thing you use to find things? I know, I'll make a tracker to track the tracker. That'll fix everything—"

Hives's flaming hand got closer, and suddenly Grimsby's running mouth ran out of words. His whole body squirmed against the wall, as though trying to burrow inside it.

"Where is it?" Hives was shouting now, the fire flaring with each syllable. "*You will tell me.*"

The heat pulsed against Grimsby's cheek, but he clenched his teeth so hard he felt they might crack. He shook his head despite how much he trembled. He stood as tall as he could on weak knees.

"No," he said, his voice hardly a whisper. "I won't."

Then, suddenly, Hives wasn't so scary anymore. It was like a switch had flipped. Though the fire still made Grimsby want to find a well and jump down it, Hives himself seemed more of an inconvenient bludgeoning device than anything else.

And they both felt it when things changed.

Hives doubled down. He pulled Grimsby's throat from the wall and slammed him back, rattling his skull on the painted cinder blocks.

Grimsby was certain it felt worse than it really was, but the blow was jarring and made his vision swim. He distantly heard Hives's voice through his daze.

"Where is the tracker?" he demanded.

Grimsby looked up, and for a moment, he thought he saw Death standing behind Hives. Death with a capital *D*. It was as tall and thin as a dying pine, as looming and chill as a winter storm.

The strangest part was he wasn't sure if he was hallucinating. Had Hives literally knocked the sense out of him? When his vision steadied, he realized he wasn't imagining anything. He smiled.

"Where is it?" Hives demanded.

When Grimsby opened his mouth, he felt grit between his teeth and tasted blood, but he smiled all the same. "Behind you."

Hives turned just in time to receive a knee to the guts from Mayflower. His grip loosened, but the flame in his hand surged. Heat seared at Grimsby, snapping like the maw of a wolf. He squeaked and threw up the sleeve of his blue robe to shield his face.

Meanwhile, Hives had swung his burning hand in a wide haymaker at Mayflower, but his balance was off. The force was minimal, making the real danger of the blow the flames that seeped between his clenched fingers.

Mayflower caught the swing by the elbow, arresting the momentum. Hives's burning hand clenched around Mayflower's arm, but though it seethed flame, the fire rolled off the Huntsman's coat like dry ice's breath. For a moment, with their arms doubly gripped, they looked to be performing some kind of ancient salute.

Then, with his free hand, Mayflower swung his gun into Hives's jaw.

Hives's mask popped off, flying across the room like a ghost late for a job interview.

The young man dropped; the fire in his hand burned out with a hiss.

Mayflower maintained his grip on Hives's arm for a moment, making it twist in what looked like a very painful way, but as the Auditor went limp, he let the arm drop.

Grimsby stared, his heart racing, his skin still burning from the memory of the heat.

He stared in shock at the lump that was Hives just moments ago. The Auditor had overpowered Grimsby in practically every way, but two and a half seconds with the Huntsman had left him unconscious on the ground.

How?

"Grimsby," Mayflower said calmly.

"Yeah?"

"You're on fire."

Grimsby looked down to see the sleeve of his robe burning from where it had shielded his face. The flames were relatively small, the robe being closer to plastic than to cloth.

He screamed anyway, batting them out frantically.

THIRTY

GRIMSBY WAS FORCED TO HALF RUN TO KEEP UP WITH Mayflower's hurried pace. The bright glare of the afternoon sun was disorientating, as his internal clock was certain it should be dark, but the Elsewhere had eaten up those hours without letting them pass in the real world.

There were sirens approaching now, and down the block Grimsby saw a line of black mirrorless cars surrounding MMDFK.

"Eyes front, kid," Mayflower snapped.

Grimsby turned away from the scene, feeling an odd mixture of guilt and satisfaction that Richie's birthday party had once again been catastrophic.

They reached the jeep and Mayflower popped the passenger-door lock for Grimsby to get inside. Within a few seconds the jeep chugged to life, and just as Grimsby buckled in, the old steel steed kicked off with a small gout of black smoke.

Mayflower kept a sane pace. No screeching tires, no sharp turns. Just a casual, easy speed. It was at odds with his white-knuckled grip and his constant glances to the rearview.

"Thanks—" Grimsby began, but Mayflower cut him off with a wave of his hand.

"Quiet. We're not clear yet."

Grimsby nodded and let himself sink into the sunbaked cushions of the seat. They were about as soft as bricks, but at the moment the relief his body felt from being limp was wonderfully overpowering. Despite his tenuous nap in the Elsewhere, he felt ready for a second. Perhaps after eating a mountain of food.

Within a few minutes, the sirens faded, and Mayflower's tense grip on the wheel loosened. The Huntsman let out a breath, making Grimsby think he'd been holding it the whole time.

"How'd you know to come find me?" Grimsby asked.

"I've got a source inside."

"Is that the same one who said it would take a couple days before the Department could suss out Mansgraf's note?"

He nodded.

"I think your source was incorrect on that account."

"Apparently so. But without her, you'd still be getting beat to hell by that Auditor."

Grimsby thought of how desperate Hives had been to find the Wardbox, and of the heat that he could still feel in his scars, so close to his skin. He imagined how far Hives might have been willing to go, and shuddered.

"Thank you," he said, "for saving me."

They drove in silence for a few minutes before Mayflower spoke. "Kid, if I was saving you, I'd dump you at Mansgraf's lair and not look back."

"Then what are you doing here?" he asked.

Mayflower only grunted.

"Aw, shucks, were you worried about me?"

"I didn't say that."

"You didn't *not* say it, either."

"I wasn't worried about you," Mayflower said firmly.

"So I can handle myself, is that what you're saying?"

Mayflower growled.

"Well, come on, it's either one or the other," Grimsby said, his smile widening.

"Do you know the best technique for bailing from a moving vehicle?" he asked.

"Uh, no. I don't think I do."

Mayflower unlocked the jeep doors. "Then I'd stop talking if I were you."

Grimsby's smile only widened, but he still decided not to press his luck much further.

After some time, Mayflower spoke. "What was the matter with you back there, anyway? That kid was big, but I've seen you stand up to bigger."

"You have?"

"Well, you stood up to me the first time we met. I'm bigger. But I thought you were going to pass out on that Auditor. Why?"

"I . . . I don't want to talk about it."

"Well, tough shit, kid."

"What?" Grimsby asked, startled.

"This isn't therapy time. We're stuck with each other until this job is done, and I need to know what triggered you so when you freeze up next time it doesn't get me killed."

Grimsby bit back a sharp reply.

Mayflower wasn't being cruel, although he wasn't being kind, either. He was being practical. And blunt. Despite that, though, he was right. He deserved to know.

"I have a—a thing. With fire. Me and it don't get along."

"That so?"

"Yeah."

Mayflower grunted. "Why?"

"When—when I was a kid, my mother died in a fire. I almost did, too." He held up his hand and pulled the sleeve of his cheap robe back to show the scars.

Mayflower nodded. "I noticed those before. Not bad."

"Not bad?" Grimsby asked, his temper flaring. "I've got scars over most of my left side!"

"We've all got scars, kid. Some you can see." He pulled down the collar of his shirt enough to reveal the beginnings of a long-healed slash wound, and as he did Grimsby also noticed for the first time a dozen smaller scars around his hands and neck. "And some—some that you can't."

He didn't elaborate on that last, but Grimsby somehow knew the veiled pain in his words. It was the pain of loss, a pain he was well familiar with.

"Point is," Mayflower said, glaring away whatever had been haunting his expression, "you take hits when you go through life. And when you get back up after, you're stronger for it."

"I don't feel stronger. I just feel tired."

Mayflower smiled. It was fleeting and bitter, but it was a smile.

"I overheard your conversation with the Auditor. About how he was asking about me and the tracker."

"Yeah, they must know about the Wardbox."

"And you didn't consider telling him that I had the spell to find it?"

"Consider it? I was about two seconds away from giving him your middle name, if I knew it."

"But you didn't."

"No, I guess not. Hey, wait a second, how long were you watching me?"

Mayflower shrugged. "Long enough."

Grimsby rubbed the growing bump on the back of his skull. "Would it have killed you to step in sometime before he near broke my head?"

"I wanted to see what you'd do."

"What?" Grimsby asked, feeling his temper rise.

"You, the fire, and the questions he kept asking. I wanted to see what you'd do."

"I was scared out of my wits! You can't expect me to make any reasonable decisions!"

"Exactly. What you do when you're too afraid to think, that may be the truest measure of a man."

Grimsby scowled but said nothing. *Better late than never* had hardly ever been a more appropriate saying in his life than it had been the last couple of days, and while Mayflower had been late twice while saving his life, that was better than the alternative. He let himself calm a bit before speaking again.

"So. How'd I measure out?"

"You'll do," Mayflower said as he shrugged.

Grimsby wasn't sure where that rated on Mayflower's scale of punk to whatever the opposite of a punk was, but he figured it wasn't too bad and decided to change the subject before he regressed. "Any luck with my spell yet?"

"No," he said, gesturing to the astrolabe duct-taped to the dashboard. "It hasn't kicked in. In a way, it's good that you're back in it."

"Why?"

"Because if the damn thing doesn't work, I want you nearby so I can take it out of your hide."

Grimsby grinned. "Fair enough. I told you, the range isn't infinite. But get within a few miles and it should catch on."

"We'll see."

"Meanwhile, I'm starving. How about you?"

Mayflower's face bore an expression that looked like someone who had just been reminded to breathe. "I could eat."

He guided the jeep down an intersection toward a burger place that Grimsby could smell before he could see. This wasn't like MMDFK burgers. This smelled like real meat, not burnt cardboard, and his stomach felt like it might just leap out of his body and race them to the place.

He felt his mouth begin to water and his hands tremble with the sudden realization of how deprived of food he had been.

They pulled up to the window, and Mayflower grunted out an order that involved the word *triple*. Then, after a glance at Grimsby, he ordered a second of the same. They were waiting behind another driver at the drive-through window for a few minutes when Grimsby heard a clicking.

He looked over to see the astrolabe on the dashboard. It was moving on its own, the compass along the edge trembling and slowly turning.

It pointed north.

Mayflower saw it, too. Without a word, he kicked the jeep into gear and jumped the curb to get around the car in front of them. He drove straight through a hedge before swerving back onto the main road and picking up speed, using the astrolabe as his guide.

Grimsby could only look over his shoulder at the fading view of the burger place, the word *triple* bouncing around in his head.

THIRTY-ONE

GRIMSBY WASN'T SURE HOW MAYFLOWER MANAGED TO hit highway speeds on the clogged roads, but he somehow did. Even more impressive was that he hadn't drawn the attention of any police officers. He did, however, receive numerous furious honks as he nearly, only ever nearly, struck other cars. But when the astrolabe took a sudden shift and pointed directly behind them instead, he slammed on the brakes, screeching to a halt in the middle of an intersection.

Grimsby was lurched forward in his seat, but his seat belt kept him from taking a trip out the windshield, or at least cracking his head on the dash. The sudden stop made the glove box crack open, and the sawed-off shotgun fell onto his feet, making him jump and hit his head on the top of the cab.

"What in the blue blazes, Mayflower?" Grimsby asked, putting the shotgun back like it was a loose snake.

Mayflower didn't answer at first, his eyes glaring around. "It has to be close."

"Great, can we at least park? Maybe not cause a riot? I think that semitruck over there is getting up the nerve to give us a physics lesson."

Mayflower grunted and circled around, but the astrolabe jerked again, suddenly pointing in another direction. "Goddamn it," he cursed, and coaxed the jeep to speed up with a hoarse roar.

A few minutes later, it happened again. Grimsby was afraid that they might be singlehandedly responsible for several mid-afternoon traffic jams.

"Where the hell is this thing?" Mayflower growled. "Your spell is busted." He pulled the jeep underneath a railway overpass.

Grimsby picked up the astrolabe. He examined it and felt the warm pulse of his own Impetus radiate from the gold surface. "I don't think so; it should be working fine." He glanced around and felt the astrolabe twitch in his palm. Just as it did, however, he heard a groaning rattle as a train rambled along an overpass above the road.

"What is it?"

"I think the Wardbox is on a train," Grimsby said, pointing at the line of cars as they passed on the rails overhead.

Mayflower's eyes narrowed, but after a moment he grunted. "Makes sense."

"How does that make any sense?"

"Where better to hide in plain sight than a place that's always moving? Public transit is slower, but there's a lower risk of being noticed. If they stayed in one place too long, they might be found, but the train lets them keep moving, and they can jump ship whenever they feel threatened."

Grimsby nodded. "I guess that does make sense. Though what are they going to do with the Wardbox without the key?"

"I don't know. I'm still not even sure how they got to Mansgraf in the first place. But I also don't care. Whoever has that box killed her, and I'm going to find them."

He put the jeep in gear and got back onto the streets.

"Where are we going?"

"South Station. With that compass of yours, we can find the train the box is on."

"And then what? You going to gun down a bad guy on a moving train full of people?"

"Yes."

"What if you miss?"

"I won't."

"But what if you do? Or what if whoever it is is tougher than you give them credit for, and suddenly we're on a train full of civilians when he decides to toss a fireball our way?"

Mayflower was bitterly silent, his brow furrowed.

"We can go spot the guy, but we can't just walk up to him and tell him to prepare to die."

"What do you suggest?"

"Find the train, find the guy, then wait around until things clear out a bit. Keep an eye on him in case he tries to bail, but otherwise just wait. Then, when there's no one else around, you can have your showdown. Assuming you're up for it."

"Come again?"

"I'm just saying, when you tried to pull the trigger on Aby, you couldn't."

"That was a fluke."

"Is that why your hand was shaking?"

"You should stop talking."

"Look, I'm just saying, I know how it feels to be scared. Trust me."

Mayflower's grip tightened on the wheel.

"I don't know what happened to make you like that, and I don't need to. But you have to admit that you're not in total control when it comes to that gun."

"Stop. Talking."

"It's okay—" Grimsby began, but Mayflower's hand lashed out and seized him by the collar. The Huntsman pulled the fabric tight until air became scarce, never taking his eyes off the road.

"You don't know a damned thing about me, witch. Keep your psychoanalysis to yourself."

He released Grimsby, leaving him to cough and sputter for a moment as he regained his breath. Grimsby opened his mouth to speak, but a terse headshake from Mayflower advised him to do differently.

He took a deep breath and turned his attention out the window. He was just going to have to trust that Mayflower would be able to control himself when they found the killer.

Otherwise—well, otherwise he wasn't sure if he could stop him.

They arrived at the South Boston train station after a few minutes of silence. The station was an old, elegant structure. Its broad, curved facade was strewn with bays of glass windows separated by thick stone pillars, all topped by an eagle-crested clock with a weathered face of white marble. The iron hands reminded Grimsby of his upcoming meeting with Wudge. His stomach turned, and he tried not to think about missing it, let alone what it might entail.

Mayflower parked the jeep in a nearby garage, grumbling about the long rows of pristine modern cars as he searched for a spot. When he finally found one, Grimsby had to wiggle his way out of the cracked passenger door to avoid hitting the SUV beside them.

"What's the plan?" Grimsby asked.

Mayflower's face soured, and for a moment, as they passed under the garage lights, Grimsby thought he might not answer. Finally, he spoke. "Find the train he's on. Then haul him off it."

"And what if he seems reluctant to go along with the hauling?"

Mayflower grunted. "We'll . . . we'll wait for the civvies to clear out."

Grimsby nodded. "Good. That's good."

"It's stupid is what it is."

"But it's the right thing to do, isn't it?"

Mayflower shook his head. "I don't know," he said, the words seeming a bit strained. "Probably."

They wove their way through the crowds. Most folks were packed just inside the platform, sheltering in the station from the uncomfortably cold autumn wind.

Grimsby had trouble until he started walking in Mayflower's wake. The man seemed to make the crowd part unconsciously. Those who didn't make way immediately did so after meeting the man's gaze.

Mayflower glanced back to Grimsby, his hoarse voice just audible over the crowd. "Anything?"

Grimsby withdrew the astrolabe from his pocket and let the instrument settle. It was pointing to his left but slowly shifting direction. "If it's on a train, it should be approaching the station from that way."

Mayflower nodded. "Worcester line. All right, come on."

They made their way to the platform for the incoming commuter line. They waited for a time. Every few minutes a train would arrive, and Mayflower would glance at Grimsby. After checking the astrolabe, Grimsby would shake his head and they'd continue to wait.

It took him a few trains to realize Mayflower wasn't watching the lines anymore. His shaded eyes were slowly combing the crowded station.

"What's the matter?" Grimsby asked.

"We've been made."

"What? Made into what?"

"No, we've been spotted."

Grimsby's eyes widened and he whipped his head around, not sure what he was looking for.

"Keep your head down!" Mayflower hissed, not turning his own. "They'll make a move if they think we've spotted them."

"Who?"

"Agents."

"More? Already?"

"Department's probably watching all the railway lines since you ditched them. Likely expect you to try to blow town."

"What do we do?"

"Stay calm, stay still, and keep an eye on that compass. If we miss that train, we might not get another chance."

"O-okay."

Grimsby felt his knees wobble a little beneath him, but not as much as he expected. He wasn't sure if it was because he was still exhausted from the last time he had felt the surge of fearful adrenaline, or if he was starting to get a tolerance for it.

Another train came by, and he checked the astrolabe, but it wasn't the right one.

When he looked back up, Mayflower was gone.

It took every ounce of discipline in him to not look around like a lost child. He made himself move casually as he looked for Mayflower. It should have been easy to spot him—the Huntsman was nearly a full head above most of the rest of the station's patrons— but he saw neither him nor the Agents he had mentioned.

He felt the astrolabe twitch in his hand. Behind him a train slid into the station with an autumn wind at its back. He looked down at the gold face and saw the hand point squarely at the last car of the train.

Again he looked for Mayflower, and again he saw nothing.

The recorded voice above chimed, and the train's doors opened, spilling passengers out into the station. Grimsby had to fight to keep from being pushed back.

Then, on the other side of the platform, he saw Mayflower appear behind two men, each of whom was wearing dark sunglasses even in the terminal. A moment later, one man dropped. The other turned, and Grimsby could see sudden, oddly subtle movements that might have been handshakes. But something told him that they weren't shaking hands.

A voice chimed over the speakers, warning that the last chance to board was approaching.

Grimsby looked back to see the train car was nearly empty. Only perhaps a dozen passengers were aboard, and none of them looked like someone who might have killed Mansgraf. Yet the astrolabe insisted the Wardbox was on the train car.

Grimsby looked back to see Mayflower set down on a bench the man he had been fighting. The left lens of his sunglasses had been shattered and his revealed eye was closed and already swelling nicely.

The Huntsman turned to see Grimsby, and he must have seen on his face that the train was waiting. Mayflower shook his head. His message was clear: *Don't go.*

He was right. Going alone might have meant suicide. Grimsby had no idea who or what was on that train, and even less of an idea what to do about them when he got there. He didn't want to go. He wanted to drift away with the muddled crowds of commuters and regroup with Mayflower, maybe come up with a new plan, one that didn't involve him being alone and unarmed.

He knew it was the smart choice. The idling train might be a trap or, worse, an ambush. He wasn't ready for this, to be on his own. He was no Auditor, and he was certainly no Huntsman.

He was just a failed witch, a wannabe with a day job that no man would envy.

He was weak, he was foolish, and, above all else, he was scared.

He wanted to listen to that cold, pleading voice that called from both his belly and the back of his mind, and simply stay put.

But he was tired of that voice.

Tired of the sound it always made, whimpering to him throughout the day like white noise dulled gray. Tired of the doubts and dreads it instilled in him. Tired of letting it rule him.

He had listened to it enough. More than enough.

And so, just to spite that desperate voice that he knew was his own, he was getting on that train.

He turned away from Mayflower and boarded the car at the last warning from the announcer. A glance over his shoulder told him that Mayflower was, once again, gone.

He looked around the train, and among the perhaps dozen people on the car, a single man in the back was looking at him. Or, at least, he looked like he might be. The shadow of his hat hid his face well.

Grimsby coughed and straightened himself, trying to look casual. He took a seat in the corner, trying to survey the car's occupants. Just before the doors closed, however, a figure shoved its hand in to force them open. He stepped onto the train, and for a moment, Grimsby thought Mayflower had somehow made it.

But it wasn't Mayflower.

The figure was even taller than the Huntsman, and as he stepped aboard, the car creaked with his weight. His head was covered with a drooping cowboy hat and wrapped in a gray scarf, obscuring his face. He turned a head to Grimsby, and he felt the man's eyes burn into him, even though he couldn't see them. There was something about him that Grimsby couldn't place. Something all at once threatening and familiar.

The man took a seat on the opposite side of the train from Grimsby and sat motionless as the car jerked forward.

Grimsby glanced down at his astrolabe, confused. He saw it pointed to the luggage rack on the side of the train car. Resting in the shadows at the back was a plain black suitcase.

The Wardbox.

It was simply there, lying in plain sight. He had expected to find the creature that had stalked him outside his apartment, perhaps stowed away in some empty luggage car or something. But the box was alone and unguarded.

Realization flashed through him, as hot and sharp as a bolt of lightning.

The astrolabe hadn't led him to the killer; it had, of course, led him to the Wardbox.

What he hadn't counted on was that Mansgraf must have hidden the suitcase on the train for safekeeping, for all the same reasons that Grimsby had thought the killer was using the trains.

He felt his gaze drawn toward the raggedly clad figure across from him, and his skin grew cold.

If Mansgraf had hidden the Wardbox before her killer could take it, that meant they would be looking for it as much as Grimsby was. But without magic, finding it would be near impossible.

So why not simply follow the witch who was already looking for it?

And they had done just that.

He was sitting opposite Mansgraf's killer.

The only question left was how he was going to survive.

THIRTY-TWO

GRIMSBY FELT NERVOUS SWEAT PLASTERING HIS SHIRT to his skin and the plastic seat. He was alone with the killer.

Why was the man waiting to make his move? If he killed Mansgraf, he could easily slaughter Grimsby, alongside everyone else on the train.

Grimsby could only hope that it was because he didn't know his cover was blown. Maybe he hadn't seen the Wardbox yet and was waiting for Grimsby to reveal it.

If that was the case, Grimsby's luck would last only as long as the killer's patience.

He kept his eyes up, not trusting himself enough to look at the man across from him. He was afraid that if he did, he might stare. He was afraid that if he stared the man might suspect him. And he was afraid that if the man suspected him, he might start a fight that would get Grimsby and probably some other folks killed.

Basically, he was just afraid. And staying still felt much easier than doing anything else.

But he couldn't just sit there and do nothing. If he didn't act, take the initiative, the man might do it himself. He needed to do something, but first he needed information.

He slowly let his gaze wander over the train car, taking the time to let it linger on an elderly woman with a large straw hat and a young man with a torn backpack in his lap. He stared for a few seconds at the empty seat with the strange stains, and then at the single fogged window with a hairline fracture.

Finally, he let himself look at the man across from him.

He was seated alone. He wore an old suit and a coat much heavier than the weather called for. It wasn't tattered, but it was a style that even Grimsby recognized as out-of-date. His hands were covered with bulky brown gloves that seemed like overkill even in response to the chill autumn. His shoes were oddly clean, like they hadn't seen much walking, and they seemed oversize as well.

In fact, when Grimsby looked again, even the suit seemed a size or two too large. The excess cloth folded oddly over the man's body, leaving him looking like a dressed scarecrow. Finally, he wore a hat that looked like it was stolen from a southern oil tycoon about thirty years ago. The wide brim shadowed his scarf-covered face, leaving it obscured.

The brim tilted up, and Grimsby saw a sliver of darkness between the hat's brim and the scarf. He could see no eyes, but he could almost feel two cold points of sight boring into him.

He quickly looked away, staring hard at the stained and empty seat instead as his mind tried to scrabble together some sense of cohesion.

Was his pursuer a witch? Was the scarf his mask? Or was he simply wearing his disguise to follow Grimsby undetected? Why wear the disguise at all? Was he afraid of being recognized? Was he even human?

No, this was the man who killed Mansgraf, he reminded himself.

He couldn't just be a Usual. He was either a skilled witch or something else altogether. But with the scarf on, it was impossible to tell.

Although perhaps he could see past the scarf and get a better idea of what he was up against.

He closed his eyes and removed his glasses, gathering up his senses and bracing himself. After his last encounter in the Elsewhere, he hadn't planned on returning or even glancing inside it for a few days, but necessity dictated otherwise.

He opened his eyes, letting them adjust to the sudden red light, and scanned the train again.

The car's interior of plastic, posters, and uncushioned seats had vanished. Now it was all black metal, pipes, and rivets. Steam poured from broken valves, and small, skittering creatures lurked among the shadowed metal husk.

Outside, the city flitted by, tall, dark structures of beams and supports that seemed to have no purpose. He spotted a few of the colossal skeletal beings drifting down the empty streets but breathed a short sigh of relief when they seemed not to notice him.

The other passengers were gone, replaced by faint, three-dimensional shadows that drifted in and out of sight like human mist. He was alone on the train car.

Except for the man across from him.

The first thing he noticed was the suit was more stylish and the hat was now a new fedora, though the shadows of its brim were as deep as ever. His clothes were better fitted, and his build filled out and seemed toned, maybe even leanly muscled.

And feminine.

It was subtle, but after looking a bit closer, Grimsby felt certain that, at least in the Elsewhere, the killer was actually a woman.

He was also fairly sure she wasn't human, or even close. There was a kind of warmth humans and most Unorthodox had in the Elsewhere. He could feel it, even if he couldn't always see it. Like candle flames in the arctic. It was why so many things that lived in the Elsewhere were drawn toward them.

But this woman had no warmth, no fire. She, maybe *it*, was, in some strange way, hollow. In fact, she was cold, but the chill had taken its time settling over Grimsby. It took him a moment to realize he had felt it before.

Except last time, he had felt it much more keenly because he, and likely whatever this thing was, had been *in* the Elsewhere.

This creature was the same thing that had stalked him and Rayne just hours ago. He couldn't see her face, and her midnight-black form was hidden beneath her disguise. But those twin burning pinpoints of eyes, those he remembered. She stared at him with a faceless gaze, alien, inscrutable, and waiting.

Fear took him, and despite how careful he had tried to be, he couldn't help but freeze under that cold stare. Even though her face was hidden, Grimsby felt certain it had twisted with delight at his reaction.

He fumbled on his glasses; he no longer wanted to be exposed to her Elsewhere form.

He didn't know what this thing was, but he knew he needed to get away from her. As surely as he needed to eat or breathe, he needed to be anywhere she wasn't, as quickly as possible.

He felt the train slow as it reached the first stop.

His legs clenched, bracing to stand. The moment the doors opened, he was going to bolt.

He saw the doors open in the corner of his eye, unable to tear his stare away from the ghost-light gaze. But as he stood, the thing very slowly shook its head from side to side. The message was clear and simple.

No.

He was so shocked that he froze, still half standing. Several of the departing commuters stared at him for a moment, curious, before slipping out the doors. The doors, his only exit, closed. The train slowly accelerated again.

Grimsby felt himself collapse back into the seat.

Several more stops went by, but he didn't dare look away from the thing to see where the train was. It didn't matter. He needed to exit, to get away as soon as possible. But even as his panicked mind came to this realization, the thing shook its hidden head. It flexed its glove-covered hands, tilting its head around at the other bystanders with shrouded menace.

The message was clear.

Grimsby felt his skin grow cold. He knew that if he tried to leave when there were still others on the train, he'd be putting them in danger. Whoever, or whatever, this thing was, he doubted it would mind harming innocents if it meant getting to him. The only thing stopping it now was likely the desire to remain hidden.

But with each stop, there were fewer and fewer witnesses to keep it at bay. Grimsby felt his stomach coiling into tighter and tighter knots as he wracked his brain for some way of both escaping and avoiding putting the other passengers in danger. But there was none. His only choice was to steel himself and wait.

It was only two stops until the last bystander departed the train. The doors closed, and Grimsby was left alone with the monster just a dozen feet away.

The car jerked into motion, riding the rail parallel to the nearby road.

The creature stood. Slowly, finger by finger, it peeled off the misshapen glove on one hand to reveal sharpened digits longer than Grimsby's fingers. These, too, were familiar.

They were the same claws he had seen scraping over pavement as he had been chased outside his apartment.

Grimsby sat paralyzed, pinned by his own wild fear as the creature removed its other glove. It flexed bladed fingers.

He was trapped.

It began to walk toward him, slowly, almost casually. Her fingers snickered and snacked against one another as the blades rasped over one another.

He forced himself to stand, though between nerves and the rattling car, his legs threatened to give way. He looked around for anything that might help him. There, across the car, he spotted the emergency-stop lever encased in glass and big red letters. If he could reach it and halt the train, he could at least try to run.

It must have seen him thinking, as its gaze followed his to the lever, then trailed back to him. It shook its head slowly again.

No.

Grimsby braced himself with a shaky breath. The lever was just behind the monster. He'd need to get past, break the glass, and pull it. The thing was heavier than him by a great deal. That was how he'd lost it once before in the alley, after all. If he was lucky, the sudden stop might throw it off-balance enough for him to get a head start.

They both stood, on opposite sides of the train, hardly half a dozen feet from each other.

The creature took a step forward.

Grimsby made a move.

He summoned his Impetus, feeling the warmth grow within his belly and spread through his body. He hadn't eaten recently, but the sleep he'd managed to sneak in the Elsewhere had bolstered his strength enough that it didn't fizzle out altogether.

The creature must have somehow sensed his spell. It froze for a moment, then lunged forward, silent and deadly, the claws flashing toward his guts.

Grimsby forced the Impetus through his hand and into his fingers. *"Torque!"*

The spell ripped out like a spinning, invisible disk. Had it struck the creature's hand or face, it might have disorientated it, but Grimsby instead aimed for its forward foot, the one that bore the weight of its lunge.

The disk struck its mark. Had the thing been a human, the combined momentum of the spell and its own body weight might have been enough force to simply snap its ankle. But it wasn't human, and the spell barely managed to trip it off-balance.

Fortunately for Grimsby, the train happened to turn and lean in the right direction just as the spell struck.

The creature toppled to one side, colliding with the seats beside Grimsby instead of with him.

Metal shrieked and plastic snapped as the creature's weight crushed the seat to scrap.

Grimsby barely managed to dodge a thrashing claw that hadn't even been meant for him.

He grabbed the sleek silver support poles to steady himself as he rushed toward the emergency-stop lever. The space was small, and the distance short, but the jungle gym of seats and hold bars slowed him down.

Claws lashed out and gripped the rails with crushing force as the thing hauled itself to its feet in the cramped space.

Grimsby tore his gaze away and focused on moving forward, but something cracked into his calf and sent him tumbling to the ground. He managed to catch himself by holding on to a dangling leather handhold, but the force of the fall sent him spinning around.

He saw the creature had thrown a handrail torn loose in the struggle at him to trip him. It crawled up over the back of the seats, disturbingly both mechanical and spiderlike all at once, the seams of its makeshift disguise ripping apart to reveal tarnished metal beneath. It scuttled toward him with shocking dexterity.

He screamed and dropped from the handhold, crawling on the ground on all fours toward the brake lever.

In his frantic scramble, he seized the broken rod of metal,

shocked at how hot and cumbersome it was. He jabbed it at the glass, shattering it and revealing the lever. But before he could seize hold and pull, he heard the monster bearing down on him.

In a desperate gambit, he gripped the rod of slag metal tight and blindly swung it in a wide arc behind him.

The tip of the makeshift club caught on a seat, veering it downward at an awkward angle, but that angle happened to be at the exact same level as the thing's head, as it was still on all fours.

He felt the force of the blow jar his arms from fingers to shoulders as it connected.

The blow sent the creature reeling back, but it also ripped the scarf and hat away from its face, revealing what was beneath.

Grimsby found himself staring at a charred, blackened skull mounted on a metal structure that mimicked a spine. As the creature regained its footing and turned its empty eyes toward him, he realized what it was.

It was a familiar.

A human familiar.

The construct, hardly deterred by the blow, started toward him again. He needed to move, but he was frozen as he felt revulsion fill his stomach. He couldn't imagine the atrocity it would take to create such a creature.

A *human* familiar.

Although it would be the furthest thing from human by now.

A familiar made from an animal would take dozens of iterations, each a peaceful death channeled through the skull before leaving for whatever comes after this world. Eventually, you have a smooth mold that can be animated with magic, but without any true life in it.

But with a human familiar, you could never smooth out the wrinkles left behind from a real person's life. The pains, the fears. People were simply too different from one another. But you could take an imprint of one if they had just died. It wouldn't be a smooth mold; it would be more like a trap. It would catch and snag little pieces of that departing consciousness in the same way.

But what you'd be left with would be little more than an entity with a child's mind, reliving the final, crystalized moments of agony before death, over and over again. And when that tortured *thing* is given a body meant only to cause pain and destruction . . .

Well, that's how you make a real monster.

Grimsby could suddenly feel the alien *hate* that exuded from the familiar. The kind of deep, seething emotion that was so pristinely human it was unrecognizable. This thing hated him, and it was going to kill him.

Unless he did something about it.

He turned his attention back to the lever and reached out to grab it. Metal shrieked behind him, and just as Grimsby's fingers touched the lever, a mangled seat crashed into his back. The blow sent him tumbling toward the back of the car. He stopped only when his head cracked against a silver pole, and for a moment his vision blinked out altogether.

When he managed to focus his sight again, the creature was hardly a few feet away. He had somehow maintained a numb grip on the metal rod, and he held it up in pitiable defense.

The familiar loomed over him, claws clicking like a cat toying with a dismembered mouse. Its empty sockets were somehow full of pained rage and malice.

Words, as hollow as its skull, echoed from its throat like a chant spoken down a long hall. *"This isn't over."* They were warped, almost without meaning. Closer to a mantra than a statement.

Grimsby realized they could be only one thing: the former person's last words.

They chilled him to his core and rattled around his mind endlessly. Despite the words, however, he felt that it was indeed over. At least for him.

The creature raised its claw, bundling the pointed tips to spear into his throat.

He wanted to move, to run, to fight, but he was still dazed, his body fuzzily distant. Commanding it to move felt like punching Morse code through a wall of cotton swabs.

The familiar drove its hand forward, but before the blow struck, there was an explosion.

Glass shattered and rained down, and the familiar was thrown backward, spinning to a heap in the aisle between the seats.

Grimsby blinked and finally managed to climb to his feet, though the throbbing lump on the back of his head insisted that doing so would be deadly.

Cold wind ripped through the now-broken window at the back of the car, and there, making its familiar, rasping roar, was Mayflower's jeep, driving along the rails directly behind the train car.

A long, skeletally thin arm hung out the driver's-side window, a heavy revolver in its grip.

Inside the cab, Mayflower was shouting something to Grimsby.

He couldn't hear what was said, but the message was fairly clear as the jeep bumped over the rails and pulled up closer and closer to the train.

Jump.

Grimsby gulped and made his way to the back window. He dizzily climbed onto the seat, pausing as he did. There, underneath a layer of broken shards of glass, was the Wardbox. He had nearly forgotten about it.

He grabbed it, dropping the warped metal rod as he did. The box was lighter than he expected it to be. He gingerly edged one foot out onto the window's frame.

It was awkward; there was hardly any place to grip that didn't have broken glass teeth jutting out. He managed to kick clear a spot and brace his foot, then reach out toward the jeep.

Mayflower brought it in closer, the metal impact bars just bare inches out of Grimsby's reach.

Then the jeep jerked, and another explosion tore through the air.

Grimsby winced as the gun went off and turned just in time to see the familiar thrown to the side, though whether it had been hit or scrambled into cover, he wasn't sure.

Mayflower shouted something again, but Grimsby was focused on trying to get a hand on the jeep. He still couldn't reach. He heard the familiar stirring behind him, and finally fear and desperation overcame logic.

He let go and leapt out of the window, grasping desperately.

He caught the jeep's headlight a bare second before he would have been pulled underneath the vehicle and ground to paste between its undercarriage and the metal rails.

His feet dragged on the ground for a frightful moment, threatening to pull him under. He winced as his ankle caught on the gravel and his shoe was ripped from his foot. He managed to swing a leg up and clamber onto the hood, sprawling over it awkwardly, one hand still gripping the suitcase.

Mayflower holstered his gun and reached out for the case. Grimsby passed it to him, freeing his hands to brace himself.

The Huntsman kept the jeep at a steady speed, allowing Grimsby to clamber awkwardly over the hood. He pulled open the passenger-side door and fell into the seat in an exhausted mess.

Mayflower pressed the suitcase into his grip.

"You all right?"

"Yeah, I— Look out!"

He shouted his warning too late.

The familiar had made a running leap toward them, its magically animated body moving with unnatural grace.

Mayflower tried to slam the brakes, but he was too slow. The familiar hit the hood, dented it with its sheer weight, and half rolled over it to smash through the windshield.

The Huntsman tried to draw his gun, but as he did, a metal claw speared through the glass and pinned his arm to the seat.

Mayflower barely managed to keep the jeep under control as he shouted, "Grimsby! Shotgun! Shotgun!"

Grimsby kicked numbly at the dash, and the glove box fell open, revealing the old sawed-off.

He grabbed it, fumbling with it for a moment before leveling it at the familiar on the other side of the webwork of broken glass.

He went to pull the trigger, noticed there were two of them, and decided to just pull both.

Nothing happened.

"Hammer! Hammer!" Mayflower roared as he managed to wrench aside the claw that tried for his throat.

Grimsby saw a mechanism at the back of the double barrel and pulled it back until it locked into place.

Then he aimed and pulled both triggers again.

He had never heard *loud* until that moment.

The boom that assaulted his ears was so forceful that it almost kept him from noticing the recoil of the shotgun cracking into his diaphragm and knocking the wind out of him.

The shot more or less hit the mark, and the familiar was ripped from the hood and sent spinning off to the side of the rails, along with most of Mayflower's windshield and a wiper blade.

The Huntsman, without hesitation, veered the jeep over toward the tumbling body of the familiar. The vehicle cracked over the rail with surprisingly little trouble.

It rocked far more when the wheels rolled over the familiar's body.

Mayflower didn't slow or halt. Instead, after the familiar was left in the dust, he accelerated back onto the road and away from it. He pressed one hand over a trio of parallel cuts on his arm and breathed hard through gritted teeth.

Grimsby looked back and felt his stomach drop as the thing climbed to its feet. The black skull and empty sockets followed them as they drove away.

THIRTY-THREE

GRIMSBY LET HIMSELF SINK LIMPLY INTO THE PASSENGER seat, his body both burning and throbbing with his pounding heart. His head felt like he was trying to grow a new spine out of the lump that swelled from where it had cracked into the pole. His elbows and hands hurt from when he'd struck the familiar with the metal rod, his ribs creaked from cushioning his landing on the hood, and his diaphragm was still having trouble taking deep breaths after the kickback from the sawed-off. His breathing was short and ragged, but his eyes were gratefully closed.

After a couple of minutes, he felt Mayflower guide the jeep to a halt.

"Grimsby," Mayflower said, his voice tense, "put that shotgun away before you get us arrested."

He had nearly forgotten about the weapon's weight on his lap. He forced himself to open his eyes and move, shoving the gun back into the glove box.

"Be responsible," Mayflower said. "Reload it first."

He saw a box of shells in the compartment and dug two of them out, but after fumbling with the weapon for a moment, he shook his head. "Dunno how."

Mayflower grunted and took the weapon from him with his left hand, leaving his right arm to hang. There was more blood than Grimsby expected.

"You all right?"

"I'll be fine." It sounded less like an assurance and more like a statement of simple fact.

The Huntsman cracked the break of the gun one-handed, ejected the spent shells and tossed them in the back seat, then loaded it and passed it back.

"Don't cock it," he warned. "Last thing I need is it blowing my head off when I hit a bump."

Grimsby packed it back into the glove box and shut the compartment, feeling himself exhausted all the more for his efforts, but he didn't let himself close his eyes this time. "We should get you to a doctor."

Mayflower shook his head. "I wouldn't bother my doc with this." He gritted his teeth and opened his door, climbing out of the jeep and heading around the back.

Grimsby, knowing he'd pass out unless he did something or other, climbed out as well, on stiff limbs, and followed.

Mayflower tugged the back door open, revealing an old tackle box of a color that likely hadn't been used since the seventies. The Huntsman fumbled with the latch for a moment, but his blood-slicked fingers had trouble gaining purchase.

"Here," Grimsby said, pushing his hand away without thinking, "I got it."

Mayflower growled but didn't protest.

He ignored the slippery layer of blood on the latch and opened the box. Inside, the numerous compartments were stuffed with gauze, bandages, needles, pliers, and all manner of other things Grimsby didn't recognize.

Mayflower rummaged for a moment, then withdrew a spool of black thread, forceps, and a needle. He then pulled out a bottle of brown liquid, poured a portion over the wound, and swigged a long draught. He offered the bottle to Grimsby, but he waved it away.

The last thing he needed right now was hard liquor on an empty stomach.

Mayflower tossed the bottle back and sat on the rear of the jeep with a heavy thud that made the suspension sag briefly. He fumbled with the needle and thread silently for a couple of minutes, but Grimsby didn't dare try to assist him this time. He had no idea what to do anyway.

"It was a familiar," Grimsby finally said.

"Yep."

"A human familiar."

"Yep."

"What— How? Why?"

Mayflower shrugged. He had finally managed to thread the needle and was using the forceps to grab it. He prodded at the wound for a moment, a sharp breath his only indication of pain, and Grimsby had to turn his head away as the Huntsman went to work suturing.

"You asking for an answer, or just asking?"

"Both. I think. Maybe neither."

"Human familiar's useful, I imagine. Probably much smarter. Can do things others can't, and blends in pretty well."

"But it—it would be a monster!"

"You noticed that, did you?"

"I mean with a regular familiar, when an animal dies, you can channel its departing soul through the skull. It's like . . . It's like those old phonographs. The ones that scratched what they heard onto the big black disks?"

"Vinyls."

"Yeah, whatever. The point is, you don't just do it once. You do it lots of times, with different souls, until the channels scratched are all smooth and uniform. That way, you don't get the animal as much as you do an impression of the animal. Otherwise parts of the soul can get . . . stuck. You get all sorts of problems, like the animal having the same tendencies as it did in life."

"Sure."

"But with a human—you can't do it like that. It would take dozens of souls, maybe more, to do something like that. People are just too different, too complicated. Not to mention much older than most creatures made into familiars. You could do it just the once, but—especially if it was with someone who wasn't dying peacefully—it'd be—it'd be—"

"A monster."

"Yeah."

"Well. Good to know theory matches practice."

"But who would do something like that? Make something so twisted and awful?"

"I have a theory."

"What?"

"A witch."

"Well—yeah. A witch would have had to do it. Have anything else to narrow that down?"

"Nope."

"Oh great."

"We got the box, at least."

"Oh right. I had nearly forgotten." He hurried back to the cab and withdrew the suitcase, bringing it back to Mayflower and trying hard to ignore the grisly medical work he was still performing.

"It's still locked?"

There were two clasps embedded into the leather, one on either side of the hinged handle. Grimsby tried them both, and they both refused to budge. "Yeah."

A single keyhole lay beneath the handle, its brass surface etched with almost invisibly thin symbols.

"Well," Grimsby said, "we got it at least. Along with, well—the thing inside."

Mayflower dug the needle into his skin again. "For all the good it does me."

"What?"

"I don't want the damned box, Grimsby!" He spat into the ditch. "I want the head of whoever killed my partner. And even if that familiar was the *thing* that killed her, whoever made it is the one I've gotta put down." His tone grew harsher as he spoke, until he was near spitting through his teeth. His hand threaded the needle through his own flesh again and again, pulling the suture taut behind it.

Finally, he dropped the needle and forceps, knotted the suture, and cut the thread with his teeth. He poured more brown liquid over the wound and took another drink, though this time he drank much more deeply than the last. He chugged the bottle dry and shattered it on the ground with a sudden ferocity that made Grimsby jump back a pace.

"But now," Mayflower said, staring at the broken glass, "we've got no leads. Nowhere to go, no one to question, and the only damned clue I have is that whoever did it is a witch, and that it probably wasn't you."

"It's more than you had yesterday."

"And it's still nothing." He shook his head. "Without a way to track the son of a bitch who did this, I've got about as good odds of finding him as I do shooting into the air and hitting the bastard."

Grimsby wasn't sure what to say. Mayflower was right. The Wardbox had been their only lead, and even though they'd found it, it hadn't led to whoever was behind all this.

"Well, there is good news," Grimsby said.

"How?"

"If this guy was willing to kill Mansgraf, the most dangerous witch on the East Coast, to get this box, then he'll almost certainly try and kill us to get it back."

Mayflower nodded. "Yeah. Maybe so." He seemed genuinely relieved, at least a little.

"That's the spirit! We'll just have to . . . not sleep? I guess?"

"I slept yesterday. I'll be fine."

"Oh good. Well, you see, I usually like to sleep most days."

"Glutton."

"Guilty. But first, I want to be an actual glutton. I want to find the nearest place that sells dead animal and eat all that they have."

Mayflower nodded. "That's not a bad plan." He took the suitcase from Grimsby and tossed it into the back of the jeep. "Come on, I'll buy."

Grimsby felt excitement without fear for the first time in recent memory and ran around to the other side of the jeep.

There, sitting on the hood, kicking his overly large feet, was Wudge. In his hand he held Grimsby's lost shoe.

He tossed the shoe at Grimsby's bare foot. "Time to get to work, half-witch," Wudge said. "Or time to stop breathing."

"Wudge!" Grimsby said, suddenly remembering the tiny creature and their deal. "How's it going, big guy?" He collected his shoe and shoved his foot into it.

Wudge frowned at him. "Wudge not big."

Grimsby began to reply but was somewhat distracted when Mayflower leveled his gun at the back of Wudge's head from the other side of the jeep.

"Don't move," he said.

Wudge ignored him and turned around so that the barrel was dead between his goatlike eyes. He prodded the gun with one finger, then licked the finger with a long, sinuous tongue. He grinned his usual disturbing grin. "Too young. Wudge not scared of this," he said, then waved an annoyed hand at Mayflower and turned back to Grimsby. "It's time for half-witch to honor his bargain."

Mayflower shot Grimsby a glance. "So this is the thing you made a deal with?"

He tried to reply with a look that might have been confidence. It felt more like distraught anxiousness. "Yeah. Mayflower, Wudge. Wudge, Mayflower."

Wudge side-eyed the Huntsman, digging one gnarled finger under his floppy ear as he did. "Why would Wudge care who it is?"

Grimsby took a deep breath. "Look, Wudge, it's been a jabberwocky of a day. Can't we do this another time?"

Wudge shook his onion-helmed head, his long ears flopping like they believed they could fly. "No, no, no! It must be tonight, half-witch. Tonight, tonight!"

Grimsby groaned. "Why tonight? Why have the last two days been the busiest and most horror-packed forty-eight hours of my life, at least outside of that buy-one-get-one birthday special at MMDFK?"

"Who can sell birthdays?" Wudge asked, almost to himself, then shook his head. "No, must be tonight! But Wudge knows where. Wudge knows where she hid it."

"Where who hid what?" Grimsby asked.

Wudge bared his teeth in a grin. "Where the she-bitch hid her key."

Grimsby felt his breath catch. If Wudge wanted their help to get the key, that meant it was in reach. Without the key, the Wardbox wouldn't be truly secure, as whoever was after it likely could use the key to find it.

He turned his gaze to Mayflower, who was still as stone as he stared at Wudge. He slowly holstered his gun.

"Where, Wudge?" Grimsby asked. "Where did she hide the key?"

Wudge's grin widened further.

"HOW DO WE EVEN KNOW IT'S THE SAME KEY?" GRIMSBY ASKED, gripping for dear life as Mayflower took another sharp exit. The

Huntsman's arm was in an old sling, but that hadn't slowed his driving much.

"She only had the one," Mayflower said. "To all her Wardboxes and whatever else she has locked down in her lair." He looked at the scribbled note Wudge had given them. It wasn't quite an address, at least not one the post office would recognize, but Mayflower seemed confident he knew roughly where it was.

"Just one key? What if she lost it?"

"That's sort of the point," Mayflower said. "The key is cursed."

"Of course it is. Why not? Let me guess, it turns your fingers into carrots, or makes you fall madly in love with the art of erotic pottery?"

"Don't be an idiot. It's a Vanishing curse."

"What?"

"Mansgraf had one key, a single goddamned key, that could open every nasty thing she ever locked away. Think of the kind of harm that could do if someone got ahold of it and started opening every lock they could find. So she put a curse on it."

"How is that less dumb than the pornographic pottery curse?"

He sighed. "Once it pops a lock, it's gone. Poof. And it reappears somewhere inconvenient that only she knows about."

"Define 'inconvenient.'"

He shrugged. "It's never the same place, and that's what makes it such a pain to find. Last time she needed my help to get it."

"Where was it?"

"Jerusalem."

"Oh dear. That's a bit of a hike."

"Yes. So we need to get to and use it before it vanishes again."

"But—what about Wudge?"

"What about him?"

"He asked for my help to get this key from wherever it's at."

"And?"

"And—and I assume he wants it for a reason? I think there's a door in Mansgraf's lair he needs to get through."

Mayflower shook his head. "Can't let that happen."

"What? Why not?"

"Because there's two outcomes, and they're both bad news. The first is he uses the key, bails through the door, and the key vanishes, leaving us out of luck."

"And the second?"

"He opens a door he shouldn't have, the key vanishes, *and* something comes through it to our side."

Grimsby gulped. "So what do you suggest? We don't help him? You know that I owe him a Favor, right? Capital *F*? He can kill me if I back out on him."

"His favor was for you to help him get the key."

"Exactly."

"So, we do that. Help him get the key, then take it back."

"You mean steal it?"

"It's not his to have, so it wouldn't be stealing. Besides, we get you out of your deal, we get the key somewhere safe, and no bogeymen come through the door this thing's trying to open."

Grimsby squirmed in his seat. "You're talking about betraying him."

"I'm talking about doing the right thing."

"It doesn't feel like the right thing."

"Even if it's not, it's the only thing to do."

Grimsby fell silent, feeling suddenly sick.

Mayflower persisted. "We can't let that thing use the key and let it vanish again, Grimsby. Who knows where it might turn up? Besides, whoever wants that Wardbox will be looking for the key, too. We need to beat them there."

"So you're just hoping they might show up and you get another chance at revenge?"

"You're goddamn right."

Grimsby looked out the window, squinting his eyes against the wind that rushed through the open front of the jeep. His stomach was doing flips, and this time not because of Mayflower's driving.

"Can you do it?" Mayflower asked.

It didn't seem right. He had given his word that he'd help Wudge get the key, but to immediately steal it back felt the same as lying. Worse, even. Wudge was coming to him for help, and to betray someone who needed his help—he felt acrid bile in his mouth.

"Grimsby!" Mayflower barked. "Can you do it?"

He tore his eyes away from the passing storefronts and apartments. He saw Mayflower looking at him from the corner of his eye.

"We get the key somewhere safe," Mayflower said. "You give the box to the Department and maybe have a shot at being a real Auditor."

Grimsby thought wistfully of the white mask and black suit, of the implicit respect of his peers, and perhaps even their friendship. He thought of the idea of using magic every day to help people, of honing his craft in the real world. It had been his dream for so long, and for the first time it felt in his grasp.

All he had to do was reach for it.

"I—I can do it," he said.

The words made him feel sick.

THIRTY-FOUR

THE OLD JEEP CRUNCHED TO A HALT ON AN EMPTY CURB. Grimsby climbed out, his body stiff from tense waiting. But he didn't stretch his slumped shoulders; it felt wrong to stand up straight before what he was about to do. He looked up at the weathered apartment building made of sun-bleached bricks. The many windows on its face had been either boarded up or broken. Even the sidewalk was in cracked disrepair, although the rest of the neighborhood seemed more or less normal.

"What is this place?" Grimsby asked as Mayflower emerged from the jeep.

"Some abandoned dump," he said, circling around to the trunk and the shredded tire that hung there. He pointed at a sign on the front door, just barely legible through some squiggly graffiti.

It read: CLOSED BY ORDER OF THE DEPARTMENT OF UNORTHO-DOX AFFAIRS. The sign had been posted overtop an externally mounted steel barricade.

"So why does it look like it's been shut down for twenty years?"

Mayflower shrugged. "Department has bigger fish, I imagine. Besides, this place is probably foreclosed. It's probably not worth government dime to pay the Department to clean the place up from whatever's inside."

"Whatever's inside?" Grimsby asked. "You mean there's something in there, and the Department hasn't done something about it?"

"Likely so. There's a lot of creeps that are none too friendly but can't bail from their home turf. But if there's been no reported deaths in or around the place, it's cheaper to leave it there than deal with it."

"You said that like there's a lot more places around that are a lot worse."

"I sure did."

"How can the Department let something like that go on?"

Mayflower arched a brow at him, as though he'd asked how the sun rises. "It's cost-effective."

Grimsby shuddered. Bureaucracy and monsters shouldn't mix. Yet somehow they always seemed to. "So how do we get in? You got a battering ram in the jeep?"

"Yeah, but my hands are going to be full," he said as he withdrew the Wardbox and a pair of handcuffs.

"What are you doing with that?"

"You'd rather I leave it in the car, unattended? No. We've bled for this. It's coming with us."

Mayflower chained the Wardbox to his left wrist, holding the handle awkwardly with his arm in a sling. He began walking around the side of the building into a shadowed alley. Grimsby followed quickly after him.

The apartment building had a couple of exits in the alleyways on either side, probably used as fire escapes for the ground floor. Unlike the front door, these had only simple plywood caps on them.

"Make yourself useful," Mayflower said, gesturing at the door.

Grimsby immediately felt the urge to argue but then noticed

just how pale Mayflower looked. The Huntsman was leaning against the alley wall, his eyes closed. His skin had a gleam of sweat despite the cold. His breathing was faster than it should have been.

"You all right?" Grimsby asked.

"Just open the damned door, witch," he said without opening his eyes.

Grimsby bit back a sharp reply and reminded himself of how many times Mayflower had saved his life in the last twenty-four hours. He summoned up his Impetus, feeling the warmth of his magic bolster him against the cold. His old scars sparked and grew hot, so he moved quickly. He dug his thumb into the middle of the plywood, leaving a faint glowing Bind rune, then placed ones on either side. Then he placed another, larger rune, roughly the size of his hand, on the opposite alley wall, linking it to the smaller three.

"Step back," he warned.

Mayflower gave him an annoyed look but did so.

Then Grimsby pumped as much power as he could into the runes and said, "*Bind.*"

He jumped away, not wanting to be between the runes for long. Tethers of magic appeared, pulling the runes tight and making plywood creak for a moment; then a section snapped. Large chunks of wood were ripped from the door and pulled across the alley to the other rune, sticking to the wall like it was magnetized. Once the first section broke off, the rest quickly followed. It piled into a single heap against the far wall, sticking to the larger Bind like gravity had been turned ninety degrees.

All that remained around the door were a few scraps that had been nailed into the frame.

Grimsby took a steadying breath and let his Impetus subside. His scars burned, but no more than a bad sunburn. The pain would fade quickly.

Mayflower didn't even acknowledge his work. He simply pushed open the emergency door on the other side and walked calmly into the dark. His gun had appeared in his hand at some point.

Grimsby hesitated only a moment before he hurried in after him. "You sure about just walking in here?" he asked.

"As opposed to what?" the Huntsman growled. "Burning the place down and sifting through the ashes? Don't think it hasn't crossed my mind. But it'd be hours before the fire burned out and a few days before we could dig through the whole place. Not to mention law enforcement trying to intervene."

"Uh. No. That's not what I meant."

"Oh."

"I meant are you sure you want to do this with me?"

"What I want doesn't factor into much. Facts do. We need that key, and you're a walking block of incompetence."

"Gee, thanks."

"Don't take it personal, witch. Near everyone is incompetent."

"I do all right for myself!" Grimsby said with unconvincing assurance.

"Just hold this," Mayflower said, shoving a flashlight into his grip, "and try not to drop it."

"You—you try not to drop it," Grimsby mumbled, but Mayflower was already walking away down the darkened hall.

Grimsby flipped on the light and scanned around as they walked. The apartment hall was long, narrow, and nearly featureless outside of identical doors on each side labeled with plastic numbers.

"How do we even know where to start looking? There must be a hundred units in this building."

"We start in the basement."

"What? Why there?"

"Nine times in ten, if there's some spooky bastard running

around, he's in the basement. I've saved a lot of time and tetanus shots by starting at the bottom and working my way up."

Grimsby gulped. "Oh good. Can't wait."

A chill rolled down the hall. Not some idle breath, but a rolling wind that made Grimsby's skin turn to gooseflesh and his teeth chatter. More than one room number tore from the plaster on either side of him.

He managed not to fumble the flashlight as he whipped around, looking for threats, but none revealed themselves. He heard a deep, grating rasp, and it took him far too long to realize it was Mayflower scoffing.

"That was a big one," he said, shaking his shoulders like a wet dog. "I don't know about the key, but there's definitely something in here."

"What is it?"

"Take a peek, witch. See if you can find out."

Grimsby's lips curled in an unconscious sneer. "I don't think that's such a good idea."

"I'll cover you. Peek in, then get out. We'll piece together whatever you remember."

He shook his head but found no ground on which to argue. He took in a deep breath. "All right," he said, closing his eyes and lifting his glasses.

When he opened his eyes, the world had changed.

THE BUILDING WAS ON FIRE.

It wasn't true fire. It was different, somehow. It was like writhing tendrils of light. The fire moved and crawled, spreading over the wall like pulsing veins of wavering heat. It covered the walls in a blazing skin, turning the hall into a fiery tunnel.

It smelled like burning flesh.

There were screams. They echoed through the burning halls in a chorus of seven agonized voices, one of which was so familiar that it cut to Grimsby's core.

Then the screams and fire faded, as quick as they had come. The flames burned out from the core, leaving ashen, scorched walls that split like heat-cracked ribs. Within their depths was a glow, like a bed of green embers. Hands of shadow and ash reached out from the darkest crevices of the cracks, grasping at him like silhouettes come to life.

He cried out, trying to back away from the hands, but they were everywhere, and whichever way he moved, he moved into more of them. They closed their translucent grips over him, their fingers like ice. But where they latched onto his scars, they burst into flames. He tried to pry them off, but while their grip on him was iron, his hands merely passed through them like smoke.

His skin shrieked in familiar, cold agony.

He thrashed and screamed as the hands pulled him toward the wall. He felt his back press against the husk of the building, and more smoke-thin fingers emerged. They slid over his face and into his mouth, choking him and making the skin in his throat blister and crack.

Then, below him, the ground quaked. The ash-coated rafters shook and black flecks drifted down like crematorium snow.

Even through the agony, he noticed the ground beneath him burn away. The carpet crackled into sparks and dust almost instantly, leaving only smoldering wooden beams that held up charred boards that broke before his eyes and fell into the empty darkness below.

There, in the dark, he saw a form move in the light of the embers.

A new shadow appeared, reaching toward his face. He tried to push it back, but between his arm and the others, he failed.

A moment later, his glasses fell over his vision and the world returned to normal. He saw Mayflower standing in front of him. The Huntsman was batting at Grimsby's left arm.

It took him a moment to realize it was on fire.

He squeaked and dropped to the ground, flailing around in an attempt to suffocate the flames. Within a few moments, they were extinguished.

Mayflower glowered down at him, his breath heavy and his brow shining with sweat. "What the hell was that, witch?"

Grimsby climbed to his feet, poking at the holes the fire had left in his jacket. "Sorry, I—I don't know. I let down the walls and—it was too much." His voice was croaking, like he'd inhaled too much smoke. He was still shaking, but less than he had expected. Though whether that was due to exhaustion or overexposure to terror the last couple of days he was unsure.

Mayflower grunted as he stomped out a rogue ember on the carpet. "Just watch it with that stuff. This place is a tinderbox."

He gulped. He wasn't sure he could think of a worse scenario than being trapped in a burning building. Once in a lifetime was enough. "Good news is that I think our bad guy is downstairs."

"Figures." Mayflower looked around until he spotted a door with a sign that led to a staircase. "All right." He checked his gun for a moment before nodding, satisfied. "Let's go say hello."

Grimsby gulped. He wanted to shake his head; he wanted to run and jump in the nearest river. Instead, he nodded. "Let's do."

He hardly recognized his own voice, and not just from the smoke. There was something in it as he spoke, only slightly more fragile than iron. He'd never heard it before, not from himself at least.

Mayflower paused and raised an eyebrow at him, then nodded and led the way down.

THIRTY-FIVE ✳

T HE BASEMENT ENTRANCE WAS AT THE BOTTOM OF THE
main stairwell. The steps wound their way upward to the six
or seven floors above, but also down into the ground. The bare
concrete walls were oddly weathered, as though great effort had
been made to scrub them clean.

Grimsby ran his finger along the wall but jerked away. It was
disturbingly warm, like human skin. "What do you make of this?"
he asked, pointing to the scarred concrete with his flashlight.

Mayflower glanced over, then shrugged. "Probably rebuilt this
place on the same foundation. It might be three or four times as old
as the rest of the building." He made his way down the stairs with
casual caution, eyes scanning the dark.

"Any idea what we're up against?"

"Must be something incorporeal."

"How do you know that?"

"Well, corporeal monsters tend to eat folk, and that's messy
business. This place is too clean for that. So that leaves incorporeal."

"So, like a ghost?"

"No, more like a spirit. Probably a Haunt. Not born of a dead person, but from a lot of people dying at once. That kind of trag-edy can leave holes, and sometimes a Haunt crawls through. They're mean, and territorial bastards, but they rarely wander far. Probably why this place is closed down."

"What could have caused that many deaths?"

"You'd be surprised how often it happens. Gas leak, shooter, building collapse." He paused. "What's that?" he hissed, looking down the stairs.

Grimsby shone the flashlight, but his efforts revealed nothing except a heavy metal door.

Then he spotted what the Huntsman was looking at. A light shone through the gap at the bottom of the door from the other side, as though cast by a small campfire or maybe a torch.

"Turn that off," Mayflower whispered, pushing the flashlight away.

He did so, leaving them in the dark, staring at the thin line of orange light beneath the door.

They waited a few moments for their eyes to adjust before de-scending the remaining steps. Mayflower pressed against the wall on the left side of the door. Out of instinct, Grimsby did the same on the right.

The Huntsman gestured for him to remain quiet and then strained his ears to listen. Grimsby followed his lead, struggling to hear anything besides his own frantic heart.

He could hear nothing for long moments, but then he heard a crackle. It sounded like burning wood. It was constant and low, a quiet rush of wavering pressure, and an occasional pop or crack.

Mayflower gestured to Grimsby. He pointed to the door, then tapped his wrist and held up three fingers.

Three seconds.

Grimsby's heart skipped but he shook it away, trying to rein in his concentration.

That was the first second.

He tried to focus, bracing himself to open the door so that Mayflower could barrel through.

That was the second second.

Then he realized he had seen the door before.

That was the third second.

"Go!" Mayflower hissed.

Grimsby was so rattled by his recognition that when he tried to throw open the door, he failed. It rattled in its frame but held fast. The firelight on the other side flared and then blinked out. He fumbled in the dark for a couple more seconds before finally finding the latch and throwing the door open.

Mayflower barged in, scanning the room with his weapon. Grimsby followed him inside.

It was hard to see much of anything in the total darkness. His mind was still on the door. Where had he seen it before, and when? It was in the dustiest corners of his memory, and it evaded his mental efforts, as though it didn't want to be found. He was so distracted that he ended up bumping into Mayflower's back.

"Witch. Flashlight," the Huntsman said.

"Right," he muttered, manhandling the light to find the switch. When he flicked it on, even its dim light was blinding.

The first thing he noticed was the pipes. They ran everywhere in huge banks that covered the walls and ceiling. Some were simple brown, but many were a peeling fire-engine red. These all ran to a single spot at the back of the room: a massive, bulbous boiler.

The boiler looked like an iron spider, crouched at the center of a plumber's web. It looked big enough to swallow Grimsby whole. He turned the light away, unnerved by the contraption. The beam of illumination fell on a pile of junk tucked in between a couple of metal tanks of liquid.

Leaned up against the side of the pile was a copper plaque. He read it slowly and froze.

Mayflower paced the room, avoiding the piles of boxes and

bottles marked with curling labels. Likely cleaning chemicals and other maintenance tools.

His eyes fell to the floor in front of the boiler. "Grimsby," he said, "light."

But Grimsby didn't hear him. Not really. His eyes and flashlight were both focused on the plaque.

It was inscribed with three simple words: LANTERN-LIGHT APARTMENTS.

Mayflower hissed again, "Grimsby! Light!" But he hardly noticed.

His lips mouthed the words as he read the plaque over and over.

Lantern-Light Apartments.

His old home. The last real home he'd had. The home where he'd gotten his many scars.

The home where his mother died.

"Grimsby! Light—"

He was cut off as the room flared to life.

Mayflower started screaming.

This time, Grimsby heard him. It just may have been too late.

He turned to see flames raging from the open hatch of the boiler. They poured out as though from a dragon's maw and sprayed over Mayflower in a heat wave that made Grimsby's skin shrivel and his eyes burn. Mayflower had managed to throw his arm up in front of him just as the blast struck. Silver light from the etched lining of his coat poured through the holes and slashes in the outer layer, mixing with the orange light of monstrous fire to form a blinding flash.

Grimsby heard more than saw Mayflower being thrown back from the boiler. He tumbled over the piles of cardboard boxes and cleaning supplies, landing in a sprawled heap somewhere in the sudden darkness.

From the boiler, a figure began to take shape. It was as though the grated mouth had vomited forth something that was just human enough to be horrifying. Its body was near serpentine, and its almost recognizable torso had two pairs of arms. Each of the four limbs was tipped with a single glowing talon long enough to impale three or four people, and perhaps five Grimsbys.

The thing had no face, merely a hole at the center of its head that was as dark as a pupil. The gap expanded and contracted like a dog's nostril sniffing a scent. Its body seemed braided of serpentine fire, and when it moved, it did so with slithering grace.

Grimsby stood in shocked, maddening paralysis. He had never seen fire *move* like that before. Even in his nightmares, the fire might have been malevolent, even willful. But it had never *been* something. It had never been something that could chase him. It had never been something that might catch him.

But now it was all those things, plus twin pairs of fiery, lancing talons.

Somewhere, in a distant and neglected corner of his mind, he knew he'd be having some new nightmares to wrestle with. The rest of his brain, however, was much more sensible.

It told him to start screaming.

So he did.

The moment the breath passed his lips, the faceless face turned to him, the hole at the center narrowing like a scope homing in on him.

The thing moved toward him, tail and claws alike scrabbling to carry it smoothly over the floor as though it could glide. Flames grew in its wake, born on every spot the tips of its fiery limbs touched. Where they found fuel, they began to grow, and there was little shortage of fuel down here.

Grimsby turned to run. He wanted nothing more than to sprint up those steps, slam the door shut behind him, and keep running until he was hip-deep in the Atlantic. But as he turned, he saw Mayflower's body on the ground, illuminated by the spreading fire.

He was unconscious, though his weapon was held fast in his grip. Blood trickled from a gash on his brow. His arm had fallen from its sling, the Wardbox dangling from the chain around his wrist. He lay across a pile of crushed cardboard boxes, like a slumbering king lounging on a sagging throne.

Grimsby came to an instant realization. A simple fact.

If he ran, Mayflower would die.

And, for a moment, that was acceptable. A sad casualty and a price he was willing to pay. He felt some part of him grow cold, like a wet hand caught in an icy breeze.

But what kind of man would he be if he ran? What kind of person would that make him?

Whatever it was, he didn't want to find out.

When he ran, he did not run toward the stairs and away from the fire serpent.

He ran toward Mayflower, and also away from the fire serpent.

He reached the old Huntsman and stood in front of him, between the serpent and his fallen friend, and then he turned to fight.

Though what that meant, he still wasn't quite sure.

He turned his gaze to the pipes above and had an idea. It was a boiler, after all. Boiling often required water.

He raised his Impetus, hardly noticing the sparks and pain that danced over his scars amid the growing heat of the room. He extended a finger toward a cluster of pipes in the path between him and the serpent and shouted, "*Torque!*"

The force ripped out from his finger like a discus. The disk of green sparks spun through the air and struck the pipes squarely.

Metal shrieked and buckled, but for a moment, that was all that happened.

The Haunt closed the gap with disturbing speed, coming so

close to Grimsby that he could smell the burning air and hear the heat-wrenched concrete crack.

Then the pipe burst. Black, ugly water poured out, polluted by years of idle rust as it lingered in the unused pipes.

The torrent rushed straight toward the creature, but the Haunt was fast. It slipped out of the way with surprising speed and unnerving ease. Only a single splash caught its form, darkening its skin to stone gray before evaporating away in a plume of steam.

It began to move forward again, but the water pooled over the ground, creating a puddle island around Grimsby and Mayflower. The serpent tried to step through and hissed, withdrawing one flaming scythe-limb, its tip cooled to stone.

Grimsby felt safe for a brief moment.

Then the creature slid its burning body to the pool's edge. Within moments, the water began to bubble and steam, leaving charred concrete in its wake.

The thing inched closer, letting more water burn away, creating a path straight toward them.

Grimsby needed a plan, and he needed it quickly.

Then he saw it. An old fire extinguisher mounted on the wall a few feet away. He didn't dare leave the pool of water, but the thing was getting close enough that he could smell rust in the air as the dirty water vaporized.

He called his Impetus again, flinging another Torque at the extinguisher. It missed the center mass, but he managed to clip the side, tearing the extinguisher free and letting it bounce to the ground. He winced, hoping it wouldn't be too damaged to function.

It rolled toward him for a glorious moment but halted, propped up on its hose a few feet beyond the water.

It would have to do.

He looked to the creature. It was hardly a couple of feet from being able to reach him with its talons. More water poured down, but the concrete was becoming hot enough to boil it instantly.

He made a mad dash out of the safety of the water, reaching for the extinguisher.

The creature saw him move and moved to counter, lashing out with its fiery spear-tip limbs.

Grimsby narrowly avoided the strike but tripped as he did so, landing face-first in the puddle of black water. He reached out, and his fingers just barely brushed the extinguisher.

The creature was circling the puddle now, reaching for his exposed arm. He had no time to get closer, so he did the only thing he could.

He placed a Bind rune on the extinguisher's side before crawling madly back to Mayflower's body.

The creature came inches shy of impaling his legs. Its face-hole fumed in rage.

Grimsby didn't wait for it to resume its encroachment through the water. He thumbed a second rune onto his left palm. Then he closed his right hand in a clenched fist, concentrating his magic, and shouted, *"Bind!"*

The extinguisher flew from the ground toward Grimsby, but the Bind didn't have enough strength to keep it in the air. As it skipped over the ground, the cap cracked against the concrete. There was a wrenching noise, and a hiss began to fill the air. White, cloudy mist sprayed out of the extinguisher like soda from a shaken can. The pressure caused it to spin erratically as it continued to be pulled to him by the Bind.

He winced as he reached out to catch it. The speed and angle caught his fingers, jarring him all the way to the elbow. He reflexively flinched away, but the extinguisher was still bound to his palm and stuck to it like a magnet.

It wouldn't have been so bad if the crack in the casing wasn't still venting flame-retardant mist with enough force that the whole red canister was spinning against his palm like a twirling baton.

Just a few feet away, the spirit burned through the last of the water and slithered forward, its scything talons splayed out wide like a claw machine's grip in an arcade.

Grimsby screamed and tried to get a hold on the extinguisher to direct it, but it was moving too erratically. He felt the skin on his palm wearing away from the friction.

With little recourse, he braced his left hand with his right and held out his palm toward the spirit. The extinguisher was heavy, but was quickly losing weight from all the material it was ejecting, and he managed to keep it between him and the serpent.

The monster slowed to a halt, the darkened void in its head widening in something between surprise and curiosity. Then an arc of spraying foam struck it across the chest, and it squealed like a boiling lobster. When the foam touched it, its fiery skin darkened into a wide swath of charred ash.

Grimsby breathed a sigh of short relief. He hadn't been sure if the extinguisher would affect it at all. At least now he had bought a few more seconds to think.

It was right about then, though, that the spinning extinguisher began to slow. The spraying fire suppressant waned from a curtain to a sad stream.

The spirit waited patiently for his weapon to fail.

Grimsby looked around for something, anything else, that might help him.

But while he was looking away, the extinguisher ran dry.

The spirit lunged.

He was thrown onto his back in front of the boxes. The canister, still stuck to his palm, clanged against the concrete like a funerary bell. The Haunt loomed over him, its four limbs of sharpened barbs splayed wide in a killing stroke.

That was when Mayflower's gun went off.

The sound was so loud that Grimsby tried to fling his hands over his ears, and instead only knocked himself in the side of the head with the extinguisher.

The spirit froze, its face-hole widening in horror as it looked down to its chest. Dead in the center, where the chemicals had choked its fiery hide into ash, a glowing hole had appeared. It was about as wide as Grimsby's thumb, and it sparked gouts of molten liquid like hot blood.

Then the hole went dark. The skin around the wound became like cooling volcanic stone. It spread out in a cracking wave, and the creature shuddered. It clawed at itself with its talons but only left shallow scratches in the creeping rock. Within a few moments, it wracked its body in pain one final time and became a statue of igneous stone.

Grimsby stared, his heart rattling his rib cage like a loose engine block. He looked over his shoulder to see Mayflower still slumped in the boxes, his smoking revolver barrel steady on the thing's heart.

Grimsby stuttered as he spoke. "I g-guess it's a few seconds too late to say, 'Cool your jets,' huh?"

Mayflower gave him a dead-eye glare, then let his gun arm go limp.

The room was still full of pulsing orange firelight as the flames the spirit had left began to spread.

Grimsby felt a fear crawl inside him, one that was both horrifyingly new and deeply familiar. He had been in this building once before when it was aflame, and he had barely survived it.

He wasn't sure he'd be so lucky twice.

He scrambled to his feet, waving away the Binds as he did to drop the extinguisher. He hurried over to offer a hand to Mayflower. To his surprise, the Huntsman took it.

He hauled him to his feet. "We need to get out of here," he said, eyes staring at the spreading fire.

"First things first," Mayflower said. "You get the key. I'll finish this."

"I have no idea where it is!"

"Check the worst place it could be," he said. Then he leaned back and kicked the statue, hard.

The igneous rock was softer than it looked, and the Huntsman's boot tore a chunk of it out. The rest of the form wobbled and tumbled over, shattering over the ground.

After small consideration, Grimsby ran to the oversize boiler. Though still large, it seemed smaller now without the Haunt lurking within. The metal door to the furnace was ajar and full of ash, but something glinted inside.

He prodded at the contents to find them cool to the touch before sifting through them. Within a moment, his fingers found something small and hard. He withdrew it to reveal a key that was hardly different from millions of others. It was made of dull, scuffed metal. The only odd thing about it was that it had no teeth, like a fresh blank that was less than fresh.

He heard the crackle of fire, and he snapped back to the reality of being in a burning building. The heat was growing and he felt sweat rolling off his skin and soaking his clothes. He gripped the key tightly in his palm and turned back to Mayflower.

The Huntsman was kicking the larger chunks of the spirit statue to pieces. He turned toward Grimsby, and his eyes widened before narrowing. He leveled the revolver just barely to Grimsby's side.

Instinctively, Grimsby leapt back, for some reason expecting to see a spider.

Instead, he saw the minute form of Wudge staring up at him. His hand was extended, palm up, his spidery fingers gesticulating.

"Good job, half-witch," Wudge said. "Your debt is clear. Now gives it to Wudge."

Grimsby looked at the key in his palm. Then back to the onion-helmed creature. "Wudge—" he began, but a sudden, loud boom and flash of light cracked across the room. He winced, shielding his eyes from the wave of heat, and was surprised to find himself unscathed otherwise. The fire had found some chemical it liked, and wanted everyone to know about it. He gulped nervously. It might very likely find more soon.

Wudge fanned his outstretched fingers. "Key!"

Mayflower's hoarse voice shouted across the basement. "Don't do it, witch!"

Wudge's eyes turned to the Huntsman and narrowed, then turned back to Grimsby. "You told Wudge you would help him get the key. You promised him."

Grimsby gripped the key so tightly his hand cramped. He had indeed promised. It was no Unorthodox or magical obligation. There would be no curse or doom if he broke it. It would only mean that the key would disappear once more. They might never find it again, and that would leave him with no chance of redeeming himself in the eyes of the Department by recovering the Hand within the Wardbox. He would never become an Auditor.

But he had promised.

He put the key in Wudge's palm.

The wiry creature almost looked surprised, then nodded to Grimsby. "Thank you, half-witch. Goodbye."

And with that, Wudge simply vanished, taking the key with him.

The key that would unlock the contents of the Wardbox. The key that both he and Mayflower had nearly died for. The key that would have ended this nightmarish adventure.

The key that was now gone.

He turned to see Mayflower glaring at him with both eyes and gun. He let the gun fall to his side. He shook his head. "Damn it, Grimsby."

The ceiling cracked as the heat grew. Grimsby felt smoke start to burn his eyes and throat. "We need to get out of here—"

Another explosion. This time, close enough to send Grimsby flying. He cracked into the brick wall shoulder-first, just in time to see a support beam tear free from the ceiling and drop on May-flower's head.

The Huntsman dropped wordlessly, like a bag of soft potatoes.

The burning stench of chemicals filled the air, making Grims-by's eyes water and his breath catch in his throat. He coughed hoarsely as he struggled to his feet, ignoring the pain in his shoulder. He stumbled to Mayflower, who lay beneath a burning timber like a crushed bug. The only thing that had kept the beam from practically cutting the Huntsman in two was the Wardbox chained to his wrist. Somehow, through skill or fortune, Mayflower had gotten it between him and the timber, distributing the force.

Grimsby could barely think or reason. He didn't know if the Huntsman was alive or dead, and he didn't have time to check. He grabbed hold of the flaming beam and felt the heat sear into his palms and fingers instantly. He screamed but refused to let go. Instead, he pressed his whole weight against the wood. It moved the barest of inches, but not enough.

He stumbled back, eyes streaming tears from the fumes, lungs screaming for clean air. He wanted to find the stairs and ascend from this living nightmare, but he refused.

He wasn't leaving Mayflower.

His burnt right hand was curled with pain, the red skin blackened with ingrained ash. He tried to press it against the wood again, but it refused. His left hand, however, was in pain but otherwise hardly marred. The scarred skin was more resistant to the heat. He placed his left hand on the beam and braced his right on the back of it.

Then he pushed, screaming with breathless effort.

The support beam toppled from Mayflower's body.

Hardly able to move or think, Grimsby hooked his arms underneath the Huntsman's and dragged him toward the stairs, hoping that no more timbers collapsed on either of them.

He gasped for breath as he hauled Mayflower's unconscious

body toward the stairwell. The Huntsman wasn't massive, but he was tall and lean. No matter how Grimsby tried to carry him, his limp body was unwieldy. Eventually, he settled for draping Mayflower's arms over his shoulders like the straps of a backpack. He held them tight as he heaved toward the stairs, keenly aware of the drag of the Huntsman's legs over the floor.

The flames around them were now furious enough to light the whole basement with flickering, ambient orange. He heard timbers or perhaps concrete cracking and ignored the all-too-familiar chills that rolled down his neck and over his scars. He had nearly lost his life in this building once before.

He was not going to let it happen today.

He reached the door, sweat-soaked hair plastered over his forehead. He kicked at the handle, precariously balancing Mayflower across his shoulders. Finally, he caught the knob at the right angle and the door cracked open. He stumbled through it, accidentally banging Mayflower's brow against the door as he did. The Huntsman grunted lightly but otherwise did not respond. Grimsby figured if he got out with just the additional bruise on his forehead, they'd both be lucky.

His glasses were foggy with the heat and moisture of his exertion, so much so that he almost didn't see the person standing at the top of the stairs.

"Grimsby," a voice called down, "give me the Wardbox."

He looked up to see Hives standing on the landing above, his bulk unmistakable despite his mask.

THIRTY-SIX ✳

G RIMSBY FELT THE OLD SKITTISH FEAR RISE IN HIS GUT. Fear of his old rival, who had outmatched him in everything that mattered.

He wheezed an exasperated cough. "What—what are you even doing here?"

"You're not the only one who can use tracking spells. Now, the Wardbox."

Grimsby glared and glanced down to the suitcase that dangled from the handcuff around Mayflower's left wrist.

It was his last shot at joining the Department, and he wasn't going to let it go. Not after coming all this way.

Rushing heat licked at his back as another crate of cleaning supplies caught fire and burst into a conflagration. He heard something crack and fall to the floor, and the whole building groaned before settling uneasily once more.

He didn't have time to talk Hives down, and he doubted he could, even if the place wasn't on fire. Hives wanted the same thing he did, and only one of them was going to get it.

But Hives hadn't faced down crazed succubi to find it.

Hives hadn't fought off monstrous familiars to get it.

And Hives hadn't desperately risked everything for a chance to make things better.

Grimsby had, and he wasn't about to give up now.

"Go to heck," he told Hives.

Hives's eyes narrowed. "You can't beat me, Grimsby. You never could, and you never will."

Grimsby hauled Mayflower to the side of the door and set him down heavily. His shoulders were burning, his forearms tense from gripping his friend's arms. His lower back was going to kill him in the morning.

Assuming Hives didn't do it right now.

"Never could, sure," he said, adjusting his glasses as he squared himself at the bottom of the stairs. "But can't you tell?" He gestured to the scratches, cuts, and bruises that covered his body. "It's my lucky day."

Hives scoffed; then his eyes closed in concentration for a moment, and a wave of uncomfortably warm energy rolled off him, like heat from an opened forge. His Impetus was almost as hot as the fire behind Grimsby, and he felt his nerves redouble their terrorized shivers.

He pushed the feeling away and summoned his own Impetus. It was no furnace, like Hives's, but it was stronger than he expected. It projected from him, pushing back both Hives's radiant power and the fire's assault. It left him with an almost cool feeling that poured out from him, all except his scars. There, the energy flickered and spat out sparks, and the bare, gnarled skin began to glow like embers.

Grimsby winced, gripping his left arm with his right hand, as though he might squeeze so tightly the Impetus would be cut off. Instead, he only felt his palm sting as sparks embedded themselves into the burnt skin.

Hives tilted his head up in derision. "Still the cripple you've always been? A shame. I'll probably feel a bit guilty after this."

"Don't do me any favors," Grimsby said through gritted teeth.

Hives raised his hand, and he felt his rival's Impetus surge with power.

He wasn't surprised. Hives had always been the kind to throw haymakers before anything else and try to get a cheap shot in.

Grimsby had seen Hives lose only once, to Rayne. She had expertly diffused each of his spells, leaving him an exhausted wreck that could no longer stand by the end. It seemed like a decent plan.

Except Grimsby was already an exhausted wreck. He could hardly stand, and beyond that, his scars were draining Impetus from him with every passing moment. And even if he had the fuel, he didn't have Rayne's expert timing or nuance. He could deflect the first few spells, perhaps, but if a single one got through, he'd be finished.

Hives seemed to watch him go through his desperate options and came to the same conclusion he had. He raised a hand, and even as he did, his hand began to eke out flames from the palm like a pilot light. *"Blaze!"* he cried.

Fire roared out of Hives's hand in a braided torrent three feet across. The head of the flame looked like the snapping jaws of a wolf as it surged toward Grimsby. Rushing, gnashing, hungry.

He winced, face instinctively turning from the heat, and pointed with his right hand. *"Torque!"*

He felt his strength drain faster than he expected. A spinning glove of green force formed around his forearm and hand before launching forward like a whirlwind shaped into a gauntlet. The strength of it surprised even Grimsby. It tore up dust from the floor and ripped down drywall from the walls, creating a vortex in its wake.

The force struck the fiery hound square in its maw, and Grimsby heard a hissing yelp as the torrent tore it apart from the inside, dispersing the fire in a wide arc, just a few feet in front of him.

Fires caught on the floor and walls. Some of them burned themselves out, but others held firm and began to spread. Grimsby felt his eyes drawn to the embers but forced himself to focus on Hives.

The Auditor seemed almost surprised, or perhaps just annoyed, that Grimsby had deflected his spell. He raised his hand and splayed the fingers wide. "*Crush!*" he shouted.

A silvery-blue aura emanated from his hand, like an enlarged version of it, a replica of his hand made of azure-tinted mercury. It launched forward at Grimsby with shocking speed, and before he could jump aside, it caught him and pressed him into the wall.

He felt the back of his head smack onto the drywall at about the same time that his body hit and involuntarily expelled the air from his lungs. He gasped, trying to draw breath, but he was too dazed.

Hives took a few steps down the stairs, his palm still extended, pressing harder into Grimsby.

He felt the drywall crack and buckle behind him, until his shoulder blades were being pressed into the studs.

Hives reached Mayflower and leaned down to grip the chain with his free hand. He muttered another word, and Grimsby felt a surge of Impetus. The chain linking Mayflower to the Wardbox shattered, but as it did, the force of the magical hand wavered for a moment.

Grimsby felt himself draw a short, desperate breath. He lunged out and slapped a Bind rune at the wall to his side, several feet away, then pressed the other into his palm.

Then the force resumed, pulling him back into place, and he felt the air crushed from his lungs once more.

Hives didn't seem to notice his spell. He gathered up the suitcase and looked at Grimsby, his eyes hard. "You're a traitor to the Department and to your own kind, Grimsby. You don't deserve to be called a witch."

Grimsby glared at him as he struggled for breath.

Something like disgust crossed Hives's eyes as he watched him slowly strangle under the weight of his spell. He looked away, apparently lacking the stomach to watch Grimsby die.

As he did, Grimsby managed to suck in enough air to speak one word.

"*Bind.*"

The force pulled his arm painfully taut for a moment, until he finally slipped loose from under the crushing hand.

Without Grimsby's rib cage to hold it back, the mercurial force slammed into the wall.

Hives whipped around to see Grimsby had slipped free. He roared and charged, letting the spell dissipate as he did.

Grimsby's Bind pulled him to the wall, blue light glowing between the drywall and his palm, and he felt like his arm was going to snap in half at the elbow. He managed to scramble to his feet, but his right hand was still trapped. He had no time to dismiss the Bind, and desperately he raised his left arm to Hives. It was his scarred arm, the one marred so badly that it could barely manage the most pitiful magic. But it was all he had.

He shouted, "*Torque!*" in a hoarse voice. Impetus surged through him toward his palm. But as it passed beneath his scars, it ruptured forth in varying shades of flame. Red, blue, orange, black, and more. The magic vented from his arm like blood from pierced veins, and he felt his strength wane with it.

The Torque spell finally formed in his palm, but it was hardly the size of a dime, its green sparks sputtering pitifully. It launched at Hives and struck him in the chest but did absolutely nothing.

Hives reached him, and his first punch caught Grimsby in the dead center of his chest, just below his ribs, with enough force to lift him a quarter of an inch off the ground.

He was pretty sure Hives hit him some more, but after that first blow, it was difficult to keep track.

He felt blow after blow strike him, in the stomach, in the face. He dangled from the wall like a punching bag, pinned by his own spell, unable to defend himself.

He rolled with the hits as best he could. If he'd learned nothing else in the last couple of days, it was how to keep going after taking a hit. But they simply kept coming, and eventually he was too exhausted to lessen the blows. When he couldn't do that anymore, he took them all the same.

He might have been surprised to be standing if he could feel anything beyond pain. But Hives didn't relent. It didn't take long for Grimsby to feel his body falter. More strikes even made him forget just how close the fire was.

He felt his Bind finally flicker and snap, and his hand fell free. Without that last anchor, he dropped like a stone.

He landed face-first on the ground, his glasses digging into his cheekbones as his head crushed them into the concrete floor.

He heard Hives breathing heavily above him.

"You've always been jealous of me," he said between breaths. "Always wanting what I have, what I've earned. Well, guess what, Grimsby. You don't deserve it. You're a garbage person and a worse witch. And today is your last day on Earth."

"You—you wouldn't kill me," he said, his voice hardly audible. It was more of a hopeful thought than a statement of truth.

"Don't be so sure," Hives said, his tone gaining an odd edge to it.

"You're not a killer, Hives!" he said, struggling to his elbows, staring up at Hives through his skewed and scratched glasses.

Hives's face twisted in a bitter expression, one that almost looked like it had a tinge of regret. "You wouldn't be the first witch I killed trying to get this box, Grimsby."

Grimsby froze and his mind churned. There was only one other witch he was aware of who knew about the Wardbox. And she was dead.

"It was you?" he asked. "You killed Mansgraf?"

"With a bit of help from our mutual acquaintance: the Blackskull." His mask hid his face, but he had a strange look in his eyes. It was something almost like fear. "Damn woman wouldn't give up the box, though. She never even said a word to me, even after the Blackskull started in on her."

"W-why?" Grimsby asked.

"Why? Because—because I had to, that's why." He shook his head, seeming to slough off what little regret remained. "Besides, I took down the baddest witch on the East Coast. You know what that makes me?"

"A fool," Grimsby said, tasting blood in his mouth.

"A fool?" Hives demanded. He reared back and kicked Grimsby in the ribs, forcing him off his elbows and into a fetal position. "Well, I'd rather be a fool than burn to death in here. Goodbye, Grimsby."

Hives turned and started up the stairs.

Grimsby lay on the ground, feeling every inch of his body in pain ranging from ache to agony. He felt the urge to let his eyes close, to let go and embrace the painless darkness. He knew, distantly, that would leave him to burn to death. It'd mean he'd die in his old home, like he was perhaps destined to all those years ago.

And for a moment, he was okay with that.

The dark closed in around his vision, and he didn't try to hold it back.

It seemed almost poetic.

Then his eyes focused on Mayflower, still unconscious against the wall. The man couldn't say anything, but Grimsby heard his voice, saying words the Huntsman had never spoken but that somehow still rang true.

Die fighting, or die a coward.

And for once in his whole godforsaken life, Grimsby wanted to be anything other than a coward. Just once, he didn't want to be afraid.

He braced his good hand against the floor.

Just once.

He braced his bad hand against the floor.

Just. Once.

He pushed himself up to his knees. Blood leaked from his lips in a long, stringy line and pooled on the floor. He realized he couldn't see out of one of his eyes and hoped it wasn't permanent.

He looked up to see Hives ascending the steps, Wardbox in hand. The Auditor stopped and turned, his eyes burning with frustration and rage.

"You want to die like a man?" he asked, his own voice taut. "Fine."

He descended the stairs, footsteps slow and determined. Grimsby blearily drew a circle in the floor with his own blood, just a foot across. But before he could do any more, Hives reached him, dropped the suitcase, and seized him by the throat.

Grimsby felt Hives's fingers tighten around his neck, squeezing until bone and cartilage ground against each other.

He clawed at Hives's wrists, but the man was just so much bigger and stronger.

He felt his vision darken again, and this time he threw everything he had against it. He fought and thrashed, though it pained every muscle in his body to do so.

Hives growled and constricted tighter.

Grimsby felt like his head might just pop off at any moment.

He summoned his Impetus one last time. He felt its warmth rise through the cold of his body; as exhausted and spent as it was, there was enough left in it for one last spell. But he couldn't speak, couldn't utter a word for any spell.

So instead, he pressed his left hand against Hives's mask, over one eye, and pushed every last drop of power he had into his left arm.

Into his scars.

Fire burst forth from his flesh, and no small amount of it from his palm.

The heat might not have been enough to injure the skin protected by the mask, but Grimsby saw multihued flames force their way through the eyehole, illuminating the mask from within to reveal Hives's stark horror.

He howled and flung his hands to his face, releasing his grip on Grimsby's throat.

Grimsby coughed and sputtered blood, then saw Hives's foot squarely in the center of his red circle.

"*Chute!*" he hoarsely cried.

The circle faded to black glass, and Hives's foot fell through, forcing him to drop to one knee.

Grimsby clambered dumbly to his feet, seizing the suitcase as he did.

Hives looked up at him, still clawing at one side of his face.

Grimsby gripped the suitcase with both hands and brought it heavily down on Hives's head. The first strike knocked his mask askew and his hands to the side; the second took the mask clean off.

He dropped after the third hit.

Grimsby gave him two more for good measure. Then he collapsed against the wall, coughing and sucking air like it was his business, and business was agony. He dropped the suitcase to the ground and stared at Hives's unconscious body. He felt his Chute spell begin to waver and quickly extracted Hives's foot from it.

He wasn't sure if it would eject the foot when it closed, or simply take it off. And while he would find giving Hives a beating years in the making very satisfying, he didn't have any intention of making a cripple of him.

He wanted desperately to just sit and breathe, but a crack sounded from the other side of the basement door, and the building groaned once more.

He needed to get out, and quickly, before the place collapsed on them.

He struggled to his feet and resumed his awkward carrying of Mayflower. It was many degrees more difficult now than it had been before, but his body was so wracked with pain that it hardly mattered if he piled on some more.

He managed to take the stairs, one at a time, and carried Mayflower to the top. Then back out into the alley they'd come from and then onto the street.

He let himself fall against a brick wall to catch his breath.

Again, he wanted to sink to his knees and rest, but he made himself get up.

He stared at the building. The fire was climbing toward the top and was already five or six floors up. Smoke poured from nearly every window. He heard sirens in the distance, but he had no idea how far they were, or if they were even bound for his old home.

He shook his head and swallowed the aching fear.

And then he went back in.

Several minutes later, he emerged with Hives. It had taken significantly more effort than carrying Mayflower. It might have been impossible, but he'd recovered just enough strength to wrangle a few Bind runes to help him get the hulk he'd knocked out to the top of the stairs.

Then, finally, he went back one last time for the Wardbox.

THIRTY-SEVEN ✳

GRIMSBY LEFT THE BURNING BUILDING WITH THE WARD-box in hand. He was coughing roughly, and fairly certain that most of his skin was coated in a mixed paste of soot and sweat, but he had survived Lantern-Light Apartments for the second time in his life.

He returned to where he had left Hives and Mayflower to find the Huntsman sitting up against a brick wall with his glaring eyes staring at Hives. His gun was in his lap, and Grimsby could see his face slowly tightening, like iron sinews being braided together.

He didn't even look up at Grimsby when he arrived.

Grimsby set the Wardbox down and wiped his blackened palms on his pants. It didn't help much. "How's your head?" he asked, voice still raspy from his near strangulation and no shortage of smoke inhalation.

Mayflower didn't answer for a long moment. Finally, he said, "I heard him, Grimsby."

Grimsby felt his soot-suffused sweat go cold. "Heard what?"

"Don't fuck with me, boy," he said, his voice as sharp as a knife. "I heard him admit to killing Mansgraf."

"Look, Mayflower, just stay calm. We don't know anything for sure yet."

"I know one thing," Mayflower said. He raised his pistol and aimed at Hives's heart.

Grimsby was moving before he even realized it. He scrambled between the Huntsman and his quarry. "Don't!"

"Move, boy," Mayflower growled.

"No. You can't just kill him like this."

"Why not?"

"It's wrong. He's done. He's broken. He's defeated. Leave him be. The Department will take him and we'll sort this all out."

"He's a witch and an Auditor. He'll never get the punishment he deserves."

"And who are you to decide that?"

"His executioner. Now, move, Grimsby."

"No," he said, standing between Hives and Mayflower. Being the only one standing, it was largely his legs that blocked May-flower's aim. "I won't let you."

"Let me? Boy, this gun will go straight through your knees and still kill the bastard behind you. You aren't in a position to let me do anything."

"You wouldn't kill me."

"Kill you? Probably not. Shatter your kneecaps to kill the guy who murdered my partner? Probably so."

"I saved your life, Mayflower. You owe me."

Mayflower's eyes narrowed. "How many times have I saved your life in the past two days?"

"And I owe you for them all, I do. But you owe me, too. Don't do this."

His face tightened even more. "Grimsby. Move."

"No." His legs were shaking, but he refused to step aside.

When the Huntsman next spoke, his voice was hardly a whisper.

"Please."

Grimsby stopped, stunned. He'd never heard Mayflower speak that word, or with that much frank helplessness. And suddenly, he realized he had the power. For the first time, he was in the driver's seat, not Mayflower.

His stomach roiled. He was unnerved, and more than a little nauseated.

Mayflower had just *asked* him for something. Like an equal might. Grimsby wanted to give it to him, more than anything, just for the honor of being spoken to like that.

But he couldn't.

If he stepped aside, Hives was dead. And it wouldn't be Mayflower that killed him. Not really.

It would be Grimsby himself.

He looked into Mayflower's eyes. They were hard, bright, and just barely pleading. He needed to do this, Grimsby could see it. Whether it was some sense of honor, or justice, or something else altogether, he *needed* to do this.

But it wouldn't make things right. How could it?

He took a deep, shaky breath.

"No."

Mayflower's eyes dulled and he looked away. They both knew it was over. He lowered his revolver and hung his head.

Grimsby was surprised at how sick he felt. He had just saved a life. Two of them, even. Yet he didn't feel anything like pride or joy. It was a cold coal in his guts, grating against his insides and wearing them slowly away.

He was still fairly sure he had done the right thing.

So why did it feel so ugly?

"Mayflower, I'm—" he began.

"It doesn't matter," the Huntsman said.

He spoke with the same cold indifference he had always had. But, somehow, it cut deeper.

Grimsby winced and turned away. He collected the Wardbox, and they waited in silence until the sirens drew near.

Red fire trucks and men in yellow jackets flooded the scene. First with themselves, then with water. Grimsby vaguely remembered them asking if any of them needed medical attention. He had shaken his head no. They asked him if anyone else was inside. Another no. And then, after a few minutes of frantic motion, they began to contain the fire.

Grimsby watched as the smoldering brick box was doused with water until it was cold and black. He shivered. It had once been his home, but that was a long time ago. So long that he wasn't even sure what it meant.

A black Department van arrived sometime after that.

Peters emerged along with four masked Auditors. The witches were unusually tall and had a cold air that made the emergency service personnel keep a wide berth.

Grimsby felt a nervous urge to run. The last time he had seen the Department, they had tried to arrest him. But they made no aggressive motions.

Instead, Peters only approached them calmly. "I thought it might have been you two."

Mayflower didn't say anything; he only looked at the cracks in the concrete.

Grimsby awkwardly stepped forward. "Sir, Wilson Hives is responsible for the murder of Mansgraf. He admitted it to both me and—"

Peters waved his words away. "Yes, yes. It has become apparent that this is true. A shame, too." He tilted his head at Hives's unconscious body. "The lad had such promise. Ah well." His gaze fell onto the Wardbox in Grimsby's grip. "And I suppose that's our lost bauble, isn't it?"

"Well, technically it's inside of this."

Peters arched a brow at him, saying nothing.

"I mean, uh, yes. Yes, sir, it is."

"Good." He waved to the Auditors behind him, and they approached, collecting Hives and returning him to the black van. Peters held out his hand for the Wardbox.

Grimsby hesitated, glancing over to Mayflower. It had been Mansgraf's last act to try to keep the box from the Department. It felt wrong, like a betrayal—not of Mansgraf but rather of Mayflower—to hand it over now.

Yet what else could he do? It wasn't as though he could keep it from them at this point. Peters and his four Auditors might take issue with it. Besides, the Hand was still in the Wardbox. It'd be useless, and safe, without Mansgraf's key, and who knew where that went after Wudge used it.

Peters seemed to sense his hesitance. "You know, you don't at all act like you're described in your file."

Grimsby pursed his lips, taken aback. "Excuse me?"

"Mansgraf. She wrote a personal note in your report. Just seven words. 'Mediocre witch. Decent person. Not Department material.'"

Grimsby felt his mouth go dry. Seven words. Seven scribbled words had kept him from pursuing his dream. From joining the Department. Seven words had left him scrounging for enough money to have a roof and a meal a day.

Seven words had ruined his life.

Just seven words.

His face twisted, though he tried to keep it straight. *Mansgraf,* he thought bitterly, *what did she know?*

He held out the Wardbox to Peters.

He smiled. "Thank you. Like I said, I think she was all wrong. You might be Department material after all."

Grimsby's heart skipped. "Really?"

Peters nodded. "Tell you what, give this a few days to calm down, and submit another application. I'll handle it personally."

"Thank—you?" he said. His gratitude was genuine, but so was the shock. He hadn't thought it might really happen, that he might actually be given a new chance.

Yet here it was.

His face was flushed and his eyes wide. He reached out blindly, feeling for the wall to help keep his balance.

Peters chuckled. "Of course. Now, go home and get some rest. You've earned it."

"Yes, sir. Thank you—sir."

Peters nodded and walked away. He climbed into the Department van and drove off.

Grimsby could hardly breathe. He had another chance; he had another *life*. Everything was going to get better, absolutely everything.

Mayflower grunted beside him and managed to climb to his feet. "Congratulations," he said, in the same tone with which one greets the bereaved at a funeral.

"Here, let me help you," Grimsby said, reaching out to help steady the wobbling Huntsman.

Mayflower's arm lashed out sharply, the palm striking Grimsby's chest and pushing him away. "I'm fine."

"You're a mess. Let's get you to a—"

"I'm *fine*," he repeated, then said, so low that it might have only been meant for himself to hear, "I'm always fine." He began stumbling toward his jeep.

"You're not fine," Grimsby insisted, following him. "You're in no shape to drive. I'll call you a cab to take you home."

Mayflower ignored him and reached the driver's-side door of the jeep. He stumbled in and shut it firmly behind him.

Grimsby's brow furrowed as he spoke through the missing windshield. "Mayflower, let me help you."

Mayflower looked at him, and when he did, his eyes were as cold as the burnt-out husk of the building they had left behind.

"Peters was right. Mansgraf was wrong about you. On every point. Congratulations."

"What are you saying?"

The jeep coughed to ragged life. "I'm saying goodbye, Grimsby."

He watched as the hunk of bullet-holed scrap metal jumped forward and groaned out of the alley and onto the road. And then it was gone.

Grimsby was alone, and he felt it more keenly than he had since he was a child.

THIRTY-EIGHT

GRIMSBY FELT THE EXHAUST FROM THE PARTING JEEP burn at his eyes, making them water. It was definitely the exhaust. He coughed and tried not to watch it rattle away, but he did a poor job.

He wasn't sure how long it was until a pair of police officers approached him and asked him a few questions. Most of them involved who he was and what he'd been doing there. Grimsby instinctively gave vague answers that drew some frowns but no further questions. It must have been clear from his battered face that he had been a victim of whatever had happened.

When the officers had recorded all his information, they offered to give him a ride home. He declined and began walking instead. He needed time to think. Besides, each step drew a palette of pains from his exhausted body, and he felt he deserved each and every one of them.

Home, or rather his apartment, was a couple of hours away. The night was cool but not cold, and the air felt soothing on his scratches, bumps, and burns, both new and old, and the growing bruises on his face and neck. He was tired. He was hungry.

But most of all, he was hurting.

He had everything he had hoped to have, just two days before. He was no longer the suspect of a murder case. He had discovered the true killer and brought him to justice. And, perhaps greatest of all, he was going to have another shot at joining the Department.

So why did he feel like breaking down altogether and curling into a ball in the middle of the sidewalk?

He knew the answer before he even knew the question.

It was Mayflower.

The man had saved his life numerous times since Grimsby had met him, albeit for his own reasons. He had believed Grimsby was innocent when no one else had, albeit grudgingly. And he had been the closest thing to a friend Grimsby had known for years, though the Huntsman likely hadn't known it.

And while Grimsby had gotten everything he had wanted, Mayflower had gotten nothing, and had lost even more.

He had been a decent man to Grimsby, more so than most anyone ever had. But when the reins changed hands, and Grimsby was in control, he had been so focused on what he wanted for himself that he didn't stop and consider what the Huntsman was due. Let alone what he owed him.

So, even though he had everything he wanted, he didn't deserve a scrap of it.

And it made him sick.

But what could he have done differently?

He couldn't have just stood aside and let Hives be killed in cold blood, yet that was the only justice the Huntsman would have accepted. It wasn't Grimsby's fault that the old man was so determined to shed blood. Why should he feel guilty for stopping him?

"Because he was your friend, idiot," he muttered to himself. "And you let him down."

He could have helped Mayflower find a solution that didn't

involve vigilante execution, but he didn't. He handed Hives over to the Department without hesitation or question.

And the Wardbox, to boot.

Mansgraf's last acts were to keep it from the hands of everyone, including the Department, and Grimsby had not honored her dying wishes. He could have hidden the box, denied all knowledge of it, maybe even given it to Wudge to conceal somewhere. Instead, he handed it over. All for a job he wasn't sure he deserved.

And all it cost him was a friend, though he wasn't sure he deserved that, either.

He focused on keeping his feet moving for a time. His shins burned with his pace and his body jolted against the sidewalk with every step. His muscles were exhausted and begging for a reprieve, but all he gave them was more work. More pain.

And all he could think was, *Good.*

He reached Saul's Sandwiches sometime after full dark. But something made him pause. He turned, and in the faint moonlight, he saw the words that had been scratched into the wall two days ago:

THIS ISN'T OVER

His mind flashed to the human familiar. Blackskull, Hives had called it. It was still missing, still loose. It had found him in this alley once before.

It could find him again.

He ducked into a shadowed corner and hid for a long time outside his home, looking for anything suspicious. But nothing revealed itself. He wasn't even entirely sure what suspicious might look like.

Mayflower would have known.

He winced as something pained his chest for a moment.

After a few more minutes, his aching body demanded action.

And at this point, he was so tired and sore that being torn apart might be a slight reprieve.

He crept toward his own stairs, ears and eyes as alert as his body allowed, but all was quiet. He took the opportunity to dart up the steps and frantically duck inside, closing the door behind him.

It took a moment, and the fading beat of his frantic heart, for him to realize he heard something.

It was crying.

And it was coming from his couch.

He froze in the darkness of his own studio apartment, listening to the snuffling, sobbing sounds. Something was in here with him, and the only other people to ever step foot in his apartment had been Mayflower, his landlord, and an overly aggressive salesman who didn't understand that someone living in a studio apartment couldn't afford a whole set of overpriced knives.

He summoned up an inkling of Impetus, although even that was an effort after his trials over the last few hours. He tugged at the Bind attached to his corner lamp. The drawstring pulled, and the light clicked on.

He waited for the crying form to transform into something monstrous and turn on him, but it remained in a lump on his couch. He nervously approached, and only then did he see a pair of long, leather-wrapped feet poking out from under his pile of blankets.

"Wudge?" Grimsby asked.

The blankets stirred, and a large pair of bloodshot, goatlike eyes glared out at him with yellow irises. A croaking voice sniffled before grumbling, "What."

Grimsby felt his heart slow down a few beats per second. "Oh jeez, it's just you." He let himself take a breath, then frowned. "What are you doing here? I thought you'd be long gone by now."

Wudge didn't answer in words, but he howled a bemoaning cry and buried his face back into the blankets.

Grimsby winced. "Sorry, sorry!" He felt his sympathy rise for the tiny creature. It was hard not to pity anything that could cry, even if it had tried strangling him not so long ago. "What happened, Wudge?"

"W-Wu-Wudge—" he stuttered, his voice muffled by the blankets. "W-Wu-Wudge—"

Grimsby waited patiently for the small creature's stuttering to form actual words.

Wudge finally raised his head. "Wudge's door was—it was—" He took a deep, shuddering breath and howled again. "It was empty! It was fake!" His words broke down into more burbling sobs, and he buried his onion-helmed head in the blankets.

Grimsby frowned. "What do you mean it was empty?"

"W-Wudge tried to open it," he stammered, "and wh-when he did, the key vanished. Then he opened the door and—and—and there was nothing on the other side!"

"You mean it just opened onto a concrete wall?"

Wudge's head trembled in something that might have been a nod.

"The—the she-bitch lied to Wudge. She—she never had the door!"

Grimsby felt some measure of sympathy grow within him. Mansgraf had taken what Wudge had wanted most as well: the door, wherever it led. She was quite good at that, it seemed.

He sat down on the couch beside Wudge. He gingerly patted the top of the blanket mound in a gesture he hoped was comforting. "I'm sorry, man. That really sucks."

Wudge froze for a moment at Grimsby's touch, then took a few shuddering breaths and muttered, "Y-yes. It *does* sucks."

"Here, here's something that helps me when things suck." Grimsby leaned forward and clicked on his small tube television.

He flipped through the channels until he found one that wasn't static. It looked to be playing an old Western of some kind.

Wudge's eyes widened. "Tiny pictures?"

"Tiny stories. Are you hungry, Wudge?" he asked. "Er, do you even eat?"

Wudge's eyes peered from the pile of blankets but didn't pull away from the television. "Wudge eats."

Grimsby climbed to his feet and walked the few steps to the kitchen. He opened the fridge, but the only edible thing inside it was half a bottle of water. The only other thing inside was a paper take-out container, and that was closer to a war crime than it was to food.

"Old reliable it is," Grimsby muttered. He opened the pantry to reveal salt and a bulk package of ramen noodles that was nearly empty. Only one package remained. His stomach growled, and he stared at it forlornly for a moment. Then he grumbled and shook his head. He grabbed the last square package of ramen. "Do you eat ramen?"

"Raw men?" Wudge asked. "Wudge prefers them cooked."

Grimsby opened the package and held the brick of compressed noodles over the couch for Wudge to see. "No. *Ramen.*"

Wudge's spidery fingers snatched the noodles from his hand, and he heard heavy crunching noises.

"No, you're supposed to cook—" He sighed and shook his head.

There were more noises, frantic chewing, and small grumbles. Finally, Wudge spoke. "Wudge likes raw-men," he said begrudgingly.

Grimsby found his mouth cracked in a smile. "Good."

He noticed the closet door was open, yet again, and he kicked it shut as he returned to the couch.

Wudge was sitting upright now, the blankets clutched tightly around him like a hooded robe. He held his ears bundled up in his knobby fingers and glared at the television. His eyes were blood-shot, and nearly entirely red, save for the yellow irises around his horizontal pupils.

Grimsby was struck again with how small Wudge was. "So, Mansgraf ripped you off, huh?"

Wudge shook his head. "No, no. She didn't rip anything off Wudge. She cheated him. She used him. She *lied* to Wudge." He said the word like a curse, in a harsh whisper he seemed to fear others might hear.

Grimsby nodded. "Yeah, we all lie sometimes."

Wudge shook his head. "Humans are bad-terrible things."

"Hey now, not all of us are so bad!"

"But all humans lie."

"Well . . ." Grimsby began, then faltered. "That's not the exact metric for bad-terrible I'd use. Haven't you ever lied, Wudge?"

Wudge's eyes stared straight ahead and his fingers brushed against his onion-helm. "Once," he finally said.

Grimsby felt questions rise in him but pushed them away. It wasn't the time. "Sometimes lying isn't so terrible."

"How?"

He struggled for a moment. "It's—it's just that sometimes knowing the truth doesn't help. It only hurts. Sometimes a lie brings comfort, even when you know it's a lie."

Wudge frowned. "Lies are wrong," he said. He spoke as if Grimsby had suggested stone was soft.

"Usually, yeah. But once in a while, they're all right, I think."

"Like when?"

He thought for a moment. "Like when both people know it's a lie."

"That's not a very good lie, then."

He shrugged. "Depends on what you're trying to do. What Mansgraf did was a bad lie. She lied to you to trick you—"

He froze.

"Mansgraf lied to Wudge why?"

Grimsby hardly heard him. "Mansgraf lied," he said, like he'd seen a ghost and it had just stolen his wallet.

"What is half-witch blabbering about?"

He looked at Wudge. "Mansgraf *lied*!"

Wudge frowned. "Wudge thinks we were just having words about this fact."

"No! No, no, no! She lied! To you, to me, to *everyone*!"

"Wudge is getting confused."

"She convinced all of us the Hand was in the Wardbox. That it was where it would make the most sense. Not because that's where it actually made sense for it to be, but because that's where we'd believe it was."

Wudge frowned and continued munching on ramen.

Grimsby stared at his three-legged coffee table as his mind raced. How could you hide something everyone wanted, when they all knew where it was?

The answer was simple: not in that one place.

The more he thought about it, the more sense it made. Otherwise why wouldn't Mansgraf leave a message for Mayflower telling him where the Wardbox was, rather than to find Grimsby? It had to be because the Wardbox didn't hold the Hand. At least, not anymore. She had convinced everyone it had, so they'd spend all their time looking for the decoy. A decoy that required a miracle, or a smart Huntsman and a lucky witch, to find. Plus, that decoy needed another decoy to even open it, one that teleported away after it was used.

Without Mayflower's knowledge of the Wardbox's creator, it would take nothing short of a miracle to have found the suitcase. Combine that with Wudge's mysterious locating of the key, and that was two miracles the Department or Hives would have needed to get the Hand.

Imagine their surprise when they finally managed those two

miracles and the Wardbox was empty. How much time would they have wasted?

He jumped to his feet and began speed-walking laps around his couch.

But what would she have done with the real Hand? She would have to find a place to hide it where no one would ever look. Except that was inevitably temporary. It would one day be found. She needed to get it to someone to safeguard it for her.

Someone like Mayflower.

She had left a death note, and it must have been directed at him. But she had to have known others would see it. She had to disguise her message. *Kill Grimsby* was an obvious way to convince anyone that he was involved. They'd arrest him and waste time with interrogations. He would just be another distraction. But if he was the distraction, what was the real message?

Her script of choice was ogham, an alphabet of hard lines in stone. To write it in squiggly lines of blood might mar the message. And even a slight tilt might change the meaning of a line.

But if she hadn't said *Kill Grimsby*, what had she said?

He noticed the closet door was open again, and he pushed it firmly closed until it latched. He had been meaning to use a Bind to keep the thing closed, but he was too excited to worry about it now.

He wracked his brain, trying to remember the exact lines for old ogham. He frowned, finding them getting jumbled in his addled memory. He took the photograph Mayflower had given him when he first confronted him from his pocket and stared at it, leaning on the scarred kitchenette counter. He had to be missing something.

He felt Wudge waddle up and leap onto the counter as easily as a cat, despite being tightly wrapped in a long, flowing robe of blankets. Wudge glared at the photo in Grimsby's hands and scoffed, "Half-witch is a bit full of itself, yes?"

"What?"

Wudge ignored him and grabbed the photo, crumpling it up into a ring.

"Hey—stop!" Grimsby said, but Wudge ignored him.

He set the paper crown on Grimsby's head. He laughed, a throaty, croaking chuckle. His voice was more hoarse than usual, but the laugh was fuller for it.

"What are you doing?" Grimsby demanded, frustrated and distracted by his own racing thoughts.

Wudge looked confused. "It is like you have written. King Grimsby."

Grimsby stared in confusion. Then it struck him. In a direct ogham transcription, *kill* and *king* would be almost identical.

King Grimsby.

And suddenly, he knew where the Hand was.

Mansgraf hadn't named him at all. He was a coordinate. And so was her other chosen word. The Hand was where Grimsby and king met, and there was only one such place.

Mighty Magic Donald's Food Kingdom.

He picked up Wudge and squeezed him into a hug. The stumpy creature was so stunned that he barely had time to struggle before Grimsby let him go and rushed to his phone. He pulled out Mayflower's crumpled phone number and began to dial.

THIRTY-NINE

MAYFLOWER HAD FORGOTTEN HE WAS OUT OF WHIS-
key by the time he got home, and he was so drained that
the idea of going out and getting some was more of a pain in the
ass than it was worth.

The kid had turned on him.

He should have expected it. Hell, he had from the jump, but
he'd let himself get soft. The only witch who had truly shot
straight with him from the start had been Mansgraf. She had lied
to him, sure, but she'd lied to everyone. When it came to what she
wanted, and what it might cost, she had always leveled with him.

Grimsby had not.

He didn't care that he got the credit for bringing down Mansgraf's killer. Mayflower had long stopped caring about reputation.
What he cared about was that her killer was still breathing. Punk
or not, by familiar or his own hand, that Hives boy had killed an
honorable woman, and he should have a few holes poked through
his chest as a consequence.

Instead, the killer was in the Department's hands.

He dropped himself in his worn recliner and listened to the
creaks of his old house. There wasn't one he didn't recognize by

now, as he'd spent a great deal of time sitting in the dark and listening to them.

Hives would be tried by Department law, and those pansies rarely handed out a death sentence. He'd be locked away somewhere, probably for an extended sentence that would be shortened based on how useful he was. He'd be sentenced to eighty years, but for him it might only be five or ten. Witches could mess with time like that. He didn't know how, but they could. It wasn't natural, and it made any sentence short of an execution into a slap on the wrist.

The kid probably hadn't known that part. Most folks didn't. If they knew witches could pluck at time like that, it'd make them awful nervous. So far as most folks knew, witches just lived longer than Usuals.

Regardless of what Grimsby knew, the fact remained that Mansgraf's killer was still breathing because of the kid's call.

Not to mention he had handed the Wardbox straight over without a fight or fuss. Mayflower's partner had died to keep it away from everyone, Department included, and Grimsby had just given it away. And got a special invitation to join up as a result.

It was everything the kid wanted, and Mayflower couldn't help but be bitter that it had cost him everything he had fought for. He would have no vengeance, no justice.

Just another dead friend.

He growled.

No. It wouldn't end like this.

Hives was still vulnerable. He'd be transported and held for a time. If Mayflower reached him, maybe he could gun him down before anyone could stop him. It was too late to save the Wardbox and honor Mansgraf's last act, but it wasn't too late for Mayflower to avenge her.

All it would cost was a bullet and his life.

At any price, it'd be a bargain.

He went for his house phone but forgot he had destroyed it after Grieves's original call. He grumbled and flicked open his cell and pecked in Finley's number on the infernal device. He hit the wrong buttons more than once but managed to get the right combination on his third try.

The receiver rang twice before Finley picked up. "Hey, Les," she said. "What's up?"

"I need to know where Auditor Hives is going to be held before his trial."

She chuckled awkwardly. "Uh, you feeling all right, Les?"

"Just get me the damn info!"

"What info? Why would Hives be on trial for anything?"

"Peters and a few others just pinched him for murdering Mansgraf. It should be in the system by now."

"Okay," Finley said, though she sounded doubtful. Dutifully, her heard her tap away at her keys with inhuman speed. "Les, there's been nothing about any arrests of Department personnel."

Mayflower's eyes narrowed. Something was off. "Then where is Hives?"

"Best guess? Stalking that hot partner of his. I'd be lying if I said I hadn't done so myself."

"You mean there's nothing? No arrest, no file, no report? Nothing?"

"As much nothing as if it never happened. Are you sure you're feeling okay? You sound . . . off."

"I'm fine."

"Way off. Something bad happened, didn't it?"

"Yes."

"Do you want to talk about it?"

"No. I want to shoot someone in the goddamned face," Mayflower growled, and snapped shut the phone.

No arrest report or record whatsoever. How could this have happened?

Then it struck him.

Peters hadn't arrested Hives.

He had extracted him.

He felt his own blind foolishness fall away like a scab. Of course Hives hadn't killed Mansgraf. The fool boy lost a fistfight to *Grimsby*. Mansgraf would have eaten him alive.

But Peters, that was a man with the knowledge and skill to get the job done. Though why risk himself when he could send a lackey? Perhaps one who knew too little to incriminate him. Better yet, why even give him the chance? Let him do the work, then remove him from the equation.

But that didn't quite make sense, either. Why hadn't Peters simply let Hives take the fall? The boy must know something important, too important to risk letting him talk. So, make him disappear. But that didn't work, either. Mayflower and Grimsby both knew what had happened. When nothing came of Hives's arrest, they'd ask questions. They'd prod.

His skin prickled with a cold wave of fear.

Peters's actions would make a lot more sense if he didn't intend for Mayflower or Grimsby to survive long enough to ask questions.

The old house creaked in the quiet night.

But not in a way he recognized.

He caught a reflection of movement in the windowpanes beneath his curtains.

He sprung forward out of his recliner, crashing into the coffee table, snapping two of the legs clean off. He rolled to a halt, drawing his gun as he did.

Behind him, a ragged figure slammed its clawed hand into the chair where his throat had been, ripping clean through the upholstery. The creature twitched in annoyance that it had missed, and flung the chair across the room like it was an empty whiskey bottle.

Mayflower felt a grim coal of anger burn in his gut. The familiar. This *thing* had come into his house and brought destruction to his home.

He decided then and there that this would be this creature's last act.

He leveled his gun and opened fire.

The keening peal of the hollow-point rounds tore through the air. The creature flung up its arms to protect its face. The shot struck square in the crux of the thing's forearms and flung it backward into the kitchen. It crashed into the dining table, shattering a dozen empty bottles of whiskey.

Mayflower climbed to his feet and pursued, finding the thing scrambling on broken chunks of its own shattered arms as it tried to stand.

It looked up at him and its hood fell away, revealing a bleached human skull.

"Please, don't do this," it whispered in an echoing, pained voice. Its last words from when it was human.

Mayflower shot it between the eyes.

The skull shattered, exploding shards of bone everywhere. The familiar fell limply to the ground, its body now little more than scrap.

Mayflower kept his weapon trained on it for a few moments as he caught his breath. This must have been how Peters managed to kill Mansgraf. A disguised familiar might have had enough time to get close to her before she realized what it was. Especially with the help of some punk Auditor who was looking to be a hero.

His chest buzzed, and he thought for a moment he'd taken a hit. He growled and snapped open the phone. "What?"

Grimsby's voice played tinnily over the speaker. "Uh—hi, Mayflower. It's—it's me. I know you're mad. And you've a right to be. But listen—"

"Grimsby, I don't have time for your limp apologies. Peters just—" Mayflower's voice caught in his throat for a moment.

Peters needed both witnesses dead for his plan to work. The first was Mayflower.

The second was Grimsby.

"No, listen!" Grimsby persisted. "The Hand isn't in the Wardbox! 'King Grimsby' isn't a typo; it's coordinates. It's where a king and I meet. Don't you get it? She hid it at the restaurant!"

"Grimsby," Mayflower said, trying to keep calm, "where are you?"

"At my apartment, why?"

He was already climbing into his jeep when he spoke. "Get out. Get out right now."

"What? Why?"

"Because I think Peters is behind this, and he just tried to have me killed, and I think you're next."

"Peters?" Grimsby asked, his voice growing slightly distant as he turned away from the phone. "Oh. Oh no."

"Grimsby, just start running," he said, slamming the accelerator harder. "I'm coming—"

He was interrupted by Grimsby's scream on the other side of the phone.

FORTY

G RIMSBY HAD FROZEN AT MAYFLOWER'S WORDS.
That's when he noticed the closet door was open again.
Normally, this annoyed him, but just then it sent a chill through his marrow in an instinctive wave.

Get out. Get out right now. Mayflower's words echoed in his ears, but too late.

The cracked door creaked open wide. At first it was too dark to see within, but then he caught the reflective glimmer of blade-like claws somewhere inside.

On the inside of the open door were thousands of tiny scratches, forming into twisted drawings of mutilated stick figures, like those of some poor kid in serious therapy.

Between the awful illustrations, four words had been carved over and over again in harsh, deep scratches.

IT HURTS SO MUCH.

Grimsby dully felt the phone drop from his hand and fall to the floor. How long had it been there, waiting? The thought frightened him almost as much as the thing itself.

The familiar emerged from the closet, unfurling its long, ugly limbs of twisted metal. Its body was covered in ragged cloth that hid all but the faint ghost of a bleached skull, buried deep within its hood.

"Oh," Grimsby muttered. "Oh no."

It tilted its head sharply to one side in a disturbingly human motion, like cracking one's neck after being cramped for too long. It splayed its long, bladed fingers out with almost cruel deliberateness. Something told Grimsby that it had come to the same conclusion as he had: there was no place to run.

The closet was adjacent to the front door, putting the familiar squarely in the path of his only exit. He briefly felt the urge to run and jump through his window, but he knew he'd never be able to outrun the thing after falling two stories.

He felt his knees grow weak beneath him, and he found himself stumbling numbly backward toward the wall.

With each step back he took, the familiar took one forward.

The difference was that when his back hit the wall and he ran out of steps to take, the familiar kept coming.

It finally stopped, its body seeming to coil in anticipation, and Grimsby felt his own voice bubble up from his throat in an anticipatory moan of primal fear.

The familiar leapt.

Grimsby screamed.

And had this been two days before, that might have been all he did.

But that was a different Grimsby.

Whether it was because he'd been so afraid for so long that he'd grown accustomed to it, like an ill-fitting shoe, or because he had actually gained some measure of frantic courage, it was hard to say.

Either way, the familiar leapt. Grimsby screamed. And then he struck back.

His scream turned to a spell halfway through, and he half yo-deled a strained, *"Bind!"*

If he had been trying to create a new pair of Binds and apply them, he would have been too slow. If he had been outside of his home, he would have been too weak. But, for once, he wasn't slow, and he wasn't weak.

He reached out toward his nearest Bind, one that had been in place for weeks.

A blue thread of light formed between his lamp and the front door. He poured Impetus into the spell to push it past what it had originally been meant to do, and the strand thickened to the width of his pinky and drew taut.

The lamp was ripped from the floor and flung across the room, colliding with the familiar in mid-leap. The force wasn't as much as Grimsby had hoped for, but combined with the speed the famil-iar was moving at in the opposite direction, it made a satisfying crunch.

The impact twisted the lamp into an unrecognizable knot of scrap, but the familiar was more durable. It spun in the air, thrown off course by the blow, and toppled into a heap. It thrashed and clawed madly, digging deep furrows into Grimsby's floors and ripping out chunks of drywall as it flailed.

He winced, trying not to think about his deposit, and made a break for the front door. He was so distracted watching the famil-iar and its deadly claws that his foot caught on the trailing cord of the lamp he had thrown. It jerked under his stride and tangled around his ankle, nearly tripping him.

"Toadstone tonsils!" he cursed, grabbing at the cord to free himself.

Just as he had nearly loosed the cable, he saw something flying toward him in the corner of his eye. He feared the familiar had positioned itself for a second pounce. He turned just in time to feel relief that it wasn't the familiar, followed quickly by surprise as he saw it was his own coffee table.

He tried to dodge out of the way, but one of the remaining legs caught him across the brow, causing the leg to break off completely.

He felt the floor hit the back of his head before he realized he was horizontal.

The familiar climbed to its feet, having run out of coffee tables to fastball at his head, and stalked over to him. Its hood had fallen, revealing an ivory skull and empty eyes.

This wasn't Blackskull, Grimsby realized.

That meant there was more than one familiar. But how many?

He had no time to ponder. This familiar had scrap-wrought metal that climbed all the way to the bridge of its nose, like a steel junkyard muzzle. It loomed over him and stared down the length of its armored face at him.

Grimsby watched, still dazed, as it placed a two-pronged foot of steel on his chest and pressed down, crushing him into the floorboards. It raised its clawed hand to slice across his face, throat, and chest all at once.

"Hey, bonehead!" a voice croaked from above the familiar.

It turned in a strangely genuine gesture of confusion, and a wad of tear- and snot-soaked blankets struck it in the face, stickily clinging to its skull. Wudge swung from the blankets, wrapping them tightly around the familiar's head like a tiny Tarzan swinging from a vine.

The familiar reeled for a moment, tearing the blankets away and sending Wudge flying. Grimsby felt the pressure lift from his chest. He sucked in a breath and brought forth his Impetus. He reached out toward the slowly spinning ceiling fan and shouted, "*Torque!*"

The fan shuddered as the enchantment was turbocharged with

magic, and ratcheted its speed up dangerously quickly. By the time the familiar tore apart the wet cloth around its head, the fan blades were a whirring blur leaking green sparks.

Grimsby pumped as much juice into the spell as he could, and within a moment, something in the fan snapped. The whole contraption fell in a dizzying torrent, more or less straight down onto the familiar.

It leaned back, dodging the initial fall, but a blade's edge caught it in the temple, where the bones are thinnest, and cracked straight through into the eye socket and partway through the nose, scattering chips of human scaffolding everywhere.

The familiar froze, its body only twitching in mute pain and shock. Then it crumpled to the ground, landing heavily on top of Grimsby and knocking the wind out of him once more.

He struggled and managed to get into a position where he could breathe, but he couldn't lift the heavy weight of the familiar off himself. It must have weighed several hundred pounds. How many times were things going to fall on him?

"Wudge," he asked in a strained voice, "a little help?"

Wudge raised a brow at him. "Does the half-witch have any more raw-men?" he asked.

"No, but I—"

"Then Wudge has helped enough," he said, climbing on top of the fallen familiar and settling in to stare at the TV. "Wudge wants to watch the tiny stories."

Grimsby growled and struggled some more but eventually just ran out of energy. He instead let himself relax under the familiar's weight. At least as much as anyone could relax, being under the corpse of a monster that had just nearly killed him.

FORTY-ONE ✳

GRIMSBY HEARD SOMEONE KICK THE DOOR DOWN, BUT he couldn't see over the mound of shaped metal bearing down on him.

For a brief moment, he feared whoever had sent the familiar had come to finish the job, but then he heard Mayflower's guttural growl.

"What the hell is this?" he said.

Grimsby craned his neck to see Mayflower approach and stand over him, his gun held ready but at his side. "Hey, Les. Mind giving me a hand? Wudge is being no help at all."

"Wudge helped! Now he is finished helping," he said. He had wrapped himself up in his now-shredded blankets, though technically they were Grimsby's shredded blankets. He sat perched on the familiar's back, and by extension Grimsby's chest, staring at the television.

Mayflower glared at Wudge, then at Grimsby. "You—you killed it?"

"Technically, it wasn't really alive, right?" he wheezed.

Mayflower had a strange expression on his face, one Grimsby

didn't recognize. "I thought you'd be dead by the time I got here," he said quietly.

"Nope, but I may be soon if somebody doesn't get this jabberwocking thing off me!"

Mayflower shook away whatever his expression was and heaved the familiar aside.

Wudge toppled from his perch and rolled to the ground. He turned and hissed at Mayflower, baring countless needle teeth.

The Huntsman pointed his gun at Wudge, and the little thing scoffed and returned to watching TV.

Grimsby sat up for a moment, blood returning to his numb limbs, his ribs aching from having to move so much weight to breathe. "We need—to go—to MMDFK," he wheezed.

Mayflower glowered. "What?"

Grimsby groaned. "Mighty Magic—Donald's Food—Kingdom."

"Why the hell do we need to go there?"

He finally managed to catch enough breath to say a complete sentence. "That's where she hid it. The Hand."

"What are you talking about? It's in the Wardbox."

Grimsby shook his head. "No, it's not. Mansgraf just wanted people to think it was there. She wanted to buy time for you to find it."

"How do you know?"

He looked around for a moment at the ruined mess of his apartment. He felt a brief pang of pain at the state it was in, after all he had done to clean it not long ago. Finally, he found the photograph of Mansgraf's note, hidden underneath a heap of fallen books.

"Here, look. We were both wrong. It doesn't say *Kill Grimsby*. It says *King Grimsby*."

"Are you sure?"

"Wudge!" Grimsby called. "I'll get you more ramen if you tell Mayflower what this note says."

Wudge's ears twitched. He waddled over and snatched the crumpled photo from Grimsby's grip with his own spidery fingers. "It says King Grimsby," he said firmly. "This is older than most stone writing, but Wudge has seen it before."

Mayflower glared suspiciously at the creature. "How?"

Wudge frowned. "He was there when man-things were still using it."

Mayflower looked like he might argue for a moment, then shook his head. "All right, fine. King Grimsby. Why would she write that? You got a royal cousin I don't know about?"

"It's not a message; it's coordinates. Like X and Y on a map. King and Grimsby. And where do the two meet?"

Mayflower nodded, understanding. "Your food town."

"Food Kingdom," he corrected. "And I think I know just where she hid it."

The Huntsman looked at Grimsby for a long moment, and Grimsby could almost see the reluctance in his face, the unwillingness to trust again. After all, Grimsby had betrayed him by turning over the Wardbox. He hadn't known it was empty then, but that didn't matter.

Mayflower turned to leave, and for a moment Grimsby thought he'd have to watch him go again. But he finally glanced over his shoulder and said, "You coming?"

Moments later, they were in the jeep, roaring down the midnight road. Grimsby felt almost out of place in the passenger seat. It had never been comfortable, but it had also never been this cold before. He was sweating despite it, and the night air rushed in through the missing windshield, making him shiver and clutch himself.

Mayflower hadn't said a word since they got on the move. His eyes were affixed to the road, his darkened glasses tilted down so he could see over them into the night.

Grimsby couldn't help but squirm with guilt. "I'm sorry," he said, "about Hives."

Mayflower said nothing.

"And about handing over the Wardbox to Peters. I didn't know—I couldn't have known—he was somehow involved."

More stony silence was all the Huntsman offered.

"But it's not all bad, right? We'll get the Hand, and you can decide what to do with it. We'll tell them about Peters, and maybe they'll still catch him."

Nothing.

"So it's not all bad, right?"

Mayflower drew a deep breath. "Grimsby," he said, "shut the hell up."

Grimsby balked as if he had been struck.

"I don't want your apology. I don't want you to tell me that things will be all right. I'm old enough to know better."

"But I—"

"You lied to me. You told me you had my back, and when the time came you stabbed me in it instead."

"That's not fair, I—"

"You what?" he asked coldly. "You. What."

Grimsby didn't know what to say. He wouldn't have trusted his voice to stay steady if he did. Mayflower was right. He had made the call to hand over Hives, and that had backfired. He had handed over the Wardbox as well, and that had blown up in his face, too. All for what? To prove his innocence? To get a false promise for a chance to join the Department?

Turns out, it had gotten him nothing. But it had cost Mayflower's trust, something he didn't even realize he'd had.

Yet even though he had only just realized it was gone, he had rarely missed something so much.

"I'm sorry," he said again in a small voice.

"I don't care."

The rest of the drive was cold and quiet.

They pulled up underneath the tall sign bearing the crown and alphabetism of the Food Kingdom. The building was dark, save for the ever-lit kitchen, and not a car was in sight. Yet something was off nonetheless. Grimsby felt it in the back of his head, like a spider braiding his neck hairs.

He debated saying something to Mayflower, but he was still too hurt by the Huntsman's words to speak. So instead, he ignored the feeling, falling quietly into line behind Mayflower as they approached the Food Kingdom.

A poster of Mighty Magic Donald was taped to the front door, declaring the business hours, which had long since passed. Mayflower tested the door, and it swung open easily.

Grimsby frowned; that wasn't right. Carla was strict about locking up. It was the only thing she seemed to like doing. Either this was a fluke or there was something else at play.

"I don't like this," Grimsby said.

"Quiet, witch," Mayflower growled, though he drew his revolver in any case. "Which way?"

Grimsby gestured to the playroom.

They walked through the sitting area, their shadows cast long by the streetlamps outside. They reached the door to the Food Kingdom playroom and the sign of King Donald, holding out his hand to determine the maximum height of potential entrants.

Mayflower took the cardboard king and tossed it across the room.

Inside the playroom, it was dark. The skylight let in a small amount of light from the cloud-cast moon, and it splayed gaudy shades of color over the Food King's realm and his court of mannequins. They weren't where Grimsby had last left them, but that was common enough. Children often absconded with them throughout the day, and not one of them had clothing unmarred by chocolate or grease. And not one of them was without one of Grimsby's Bind runes, blended right into the weave of their costuming, though some he hadn't used in weeks.

"Well?" Mayflower asked.

Grimsby closed his eyes and removed his glasses, then peeked briefly into the Elsewhere.

He ignored the black figures of mannequins and moving shadows that pervaded the world, as his eyes were drawn directly to the statue of Food King Donald.

The king alone was unfazed by the Elsewhere.

Just as the Wardbox had been.

He hadn't realized it during his performance a couple of days before, but it was likely why his Bind spells on the statue had failed. Mansgraf had hidden the Hand inside the hollow statue, and whatever protective magic she'd used had dispelled Grimsby's own.

He quickly replaced his glasses. "That's it," he said. "The statue."

Mayflower nodded and they moved toward the castle. Its french-fry walls were surprisingly tall, and they wrapped around the tiered platform that led to the king. They crossed the cookie drawbridge and climbed up a staircase that led around the shadowed courtyard. Grimsby stumbled more than once in the dark, drawing a muttered curse from the Huntsman.

They walked around the battlements, which towered seven or eight feet off the ground, an impressive height for children. However, Mayflower's tall form made the castle feel oddly disproportionate in a manner Grimsby had never really noticed before.

The final steps led to the Food King's throne and the statue that sat upon it.

Grimsby had rarely gotten this close before, save for when he'd put his Binds on the king originally. He peered hard, straining his eyes, until he saw that the king's hand, which held a royal scepter of licorice, was askew. He got closer and saw that it had been hacked off and quickly reattached with duct tape. He reached out to tug at it, but the tape sparked and snapped at his hand, like a broken transformer.

He winced and stuck his burnt finger into his mouth. "I think this is it."

"Can you open it?" Mayflower asked from behind him.

"Maybe. Let me see."

He removed his glasses again, and the room bloomed scarlet with eerie Elsewhere light. He ignored the crumbling stone keep beneath his feet and the scurrying forms that crawled in the corners of his eyes. The duct tape, unlike the king, was different in the Elsewhere. It glowed with faint amber light in the shapes of runes, drawn in the increasingly familiar hand of Mansgraf.

He couldn't make out most of it, but he could see two things: it was a spell, and Mayflower's name was in it.

"I think you have to open it," he said, his voice warbling strangely in the second world.

He glanced back at the looming shadow behind him and found relief to see the gun in its grip identifying it as Mayflower. The shadow pushed past him and leaned in to examine the spell.

Grimsby then noticed a strange smell. It struck his nose like a mixture of damp clothes and rotting meat. His face twisted in disgust and his eyes fell to the courtyard.

It was full of corpses.

He reeled for a horrified moment and looked away to see the members of the king's court all standing at attention and staring up at him from beyond the castle walls. Nearly two dozen lords, ladies, and knights, all standing in eerily identical positions, and all waiting for something.

He shuddered and fumbled his glasses back on, and the world returned to blessed darkness.

Then the bank of clouds that covered the moon passed, and the silver light of the night grew brighter, distorted into ugly colors by the skylight.

Grimsby looked down to assure himself that there were no corpses, and he saw that he was right.

They weren't corpses. They were mannequins. Piled in a naked mass, the plastic bodies scarred with deep scratches and idle mutilations.

His mind didn't fully grasp what was happening until he saw that the king's courtiers were still just where he had seen them moments before: all standing and staring at him.

Except they were taller than he remembered. Their skin shone and reflected the light of the warped moon. And they all had claws that were idle at their sides.

Familiars.

Each and every one of the mannequins had been stripped and replaced by a human familiar.

Grimsby made a horrified gasp, but Mayflower must not have noticed. The Huntsman peeled away the tape as easily as if it were mundane, and Grimsby felt a small pop of magic as the spell vanished.

"Les—" Grimsby whispered, not daring to move more than was strictly necessary. "Les!"

"What?" Mayflower growled, turning around. He held a small box in his grip, though this one was no Wardbox, but rather just simple wood. From inside, even without his Elsewhere sight, Grimsby felt a sickly tinge of energy.

Grimsby felt the man freeze the instant he turned. The Huntsman hadn't needed witch sight to see what had happened, just light.

Though it would have been nice if that light had come before they had stranded themselves atop a plastic castle in a field full of Halloween-reject murder monsters.

FORTY-TWO

"ARE THOSE . . . ?" GRIMSBY ASKED, BARELY ABLE TO manage words.

"Familiars," Mayflower spat.

Grimsby ducked down behind the plastic battlements in the vain hope that they hadn't seen him. "What do we do?"

Mayflower crouched beside him, checking his weapon. "We get torn up," he said, "and take as many as we can with us."

"I mean what do we do to survive?"

He gave Grimsby a frank look that did not inspire much in the way of hope. "We don't."

"There's gotta be something!"

"One of those things is fast and strong enough to rip you in half before you realize what happened. There's near twenty of them out there."

"I managed to beat one!" Grimsby said defensively.

"That was a fluke. Think you can manage seventeen more flukes in a row?"

Grimsby gulped and peeked over the wall. The familiars were still standing, waiting for something. They looked like a court of malformed monsters, frozen in time.

Then he remembered they were wearing the outfits of the man-nequins. His mannequins.

"Actually," he said, "yes. I think I might be able to manage a few more flukes."

"What?"

"Each of those outfits is covered in my Bind spells. For the show. I may be able to use them to help deal with the speed factor of those things. At least long enough that you can—"

"That I can take my shot," Mayflower finished. "Might work."

"Why aren't they, you know, murderfying yet?"

The moonlight from the sitting area of the restaurant caught the movement of a nearby shadow.

Mayflower growled. "I know why." He shouted, "Peters! I know you're here! Show yourself!"

The was a long silence. Grimsby watched the familiars twitch their claws with sharp anticipation.

A shadow appeared in the doorway to the restaurant, and Director Peters revealed himself. He was dressed in his usual trim suit. Professional, but not stylish. He wore a pair of shaded glasses that hid his eyes. He walked forward through the waiting familiars, undisturbed by them, and clasped his hands behind his back.

"Gentlemen," he said, as though greeting corporate bigwigs at a hostile takeover meeting, "I believe you have something of mine."

Grimsby glanced at the box in Mayflower's grip. He could still feel the Hand inside, and it made his skin crawl. It was like the Hand had invisible fingers beyond the five real ones, and they were all trailing over his flesh.

Mayflower saw Grimsby staring and narrowed his eyes. He stashed the box in his coat and looked down at Peters, drawing his gun. "I do have something for you, but I don't think it's what you're expecting."

Peters smiled flatly. "You are not unpredictable, Mr. Mayflower—"

He was interrupted as Mayflower shot him in the heart.

At least he tried to.

Inches before his chest, the round struck and drew sparks from nothing. The shot flew wide and burrowed into the cinder-block walls of the former warehouse.

Peters brushed sparks from his coat and cleared his throat. "As I said. Not unpredictable."

"I've got more bullets," Mayflower growled.

"Not enough, I can assure you. Besides, I'm not here to speak to you."

"Let me guess, you're here to kill me?"

"No, don't be so dramatic. I'm here to speak to Mr. Grimsby."

Mayflower's eyes narrowed and flicked down to where Grimsby was crouched.

"The kid? He's gone. It's just me here, witch."

"No, I don't think so. Come on out, Mr. Grimsby. I know you're here as well."

Grimsby poked his head up over the french-fry wall.

"Aha, there you are," Peters said. "I thought we had an understanding, Mr. Grimsby."

"You lied to me!" he said.

Peters shrugged. "Did I? How? My offer still stands. You give me the traitor and the Hand, and I'll give you a job."

"Traitor? You don't work for the Department at all."

"Untrue. I very much am the head of the Boston branch of the Department. It is simply more of an aesthetic title than a functional one. However, that is more than enough to enact you into a position of employment."

"I don't want anything from you!"

"I think that's quite untrue. You want purpose? I can give you it. You want a life? I can give you that, too. You want to live?" He flicked a look around at his waiting familiars. "At the moment, I seem to have a monopoly on such allowances."

Grimsby swallowed the lump of fear in his throat. "You say that, but I doubt you own Boardwalk."

Peters's brow twitched in annoyance. "In any case, you've proven to be a resourceful young man. And your little scuffle with Hives has taught me that wit and determination defeat talent and strength."

"What are you talking about?"

"Simply put, I'd rather employ you than kill you. You as well, Mr. Mayflower, but I take it such an option isn't on the table."

Mayflower shot him again and growled a curse as the bullet ricocheted away from whatever spell protected him.

"I thought not. So, Mr. Grimsby, what do you think of my offer?"

Grimsby wanted to reject Peters out of hand, but he found himself hesitating. He was in a bad situation, and someone was quite literally offering him a way out of dying, alongside his lifelong dream.

He was ashamed to say he was tempted.

He was not ashamed, however, to say he had no intention of betraying Mayflower again. The first time still wrenched at his insides, and the guilt weighed on him like an iron yoke. He couldn't imagine doing so twice, even if Mayflower had yet to forgive him.

"I think you can take your monopoly and shove it," Grimsby called down, his voice high-pitched with fear, but with an unwavering air that surprised even him.

He looked over to Mayflower and found the Huntsman had been pointing the gun at Grimsby's heart. Mayflower's brow was deeply furrowed, but he nodded once and turned the barrel away.

Grimsby was slightly less confident he had made the right choice but decided he could hardly blame the Huntsman for doubting him. He had doubted himself, after all.

"A shame," Peters said, seeming genuinely disappointed. "Then I suppose you have forced my hand."

"Looks that way," Mayflower called down.

"Very well." He turned away from the castle and waved dismissively. "Kill them."

The familiars lurched into sudden motion. Some dashed forward with long strides; others fell to all fours and loped toward the plastic battlements. All had claws bared and eyeless sockets focused on the witch and the Huntsman atop the castle before them.

Mayflower drew a bead on the closest target, and after a moment that seemed to Grimsby to stretch on forever, he fired. The round caught a familiar dressed in a peasant's garb square in the skull, shattering the bleached bone and dropping it lifelessly to the ground.

Then he aimed again, just as he had done before.

"Any chance you can shoot faster?" Grimsby asked, trying not to sound frantic and failing at it.

"I've only got five rounds left," Mayflower said.

"But there's sixteen more!"

The gunshot cracked the air and made Grimsby wince. "Fifteen. So you better lend a hand."

Grimsby made a frustrated and fearful groan. He peered over the wall and saw the familiars drawing dangerously close. One had just leapt across the ball-pit moat.

He focused on his Impetus and drew it forth. The warmth poured into his chest and began coursing through him. He ignored the flaring sparks that began to erupt from his scarred arm and focused on his Binds. The nearest familiar was linked by dormant Bind runes to the first one Mayflower had gunned down. Grimsby sometimes made the two characters dance to warm up the kids before a show. He felt out with his Impetus for the threads, and once he found the right one, he pulled it taut.

The familiar was lying still on the ground when strands of light appeared between it and its oncoming partner. The limp body suddenly lurched forward, and conversely the familiar on the far side of the moat was jerked backward. Its body was off-balance from the jump, and it fell back into the moat, sending plastic balls of every color flying outward.

A moment later, just as it regained its footing, the second familiar's corpse crashed into the moat on top of it. The first familiar thrashed against the corpse of the second, entangling the two together.

Another gunshot, and another familiar dropped like scrap metal.

Grimsby found another Bind to pull and managed to force one familiar's mindless charge to collide with a metal set of monkey bars, causing both to bend horridly.

"We need a plan," Grimsby wheezed, his exertion of Impetus draining him. "We can't do this forever."

"Our plan is to do this until we die," Mayflower said, dropping a fourth familiar.

Mayflower had put down four, and Grimsby had delayed two, but that still left too many.

A thought struck him.

"The Hand!" Grimsby said, pulling at another Bind, causing two sprinting familiars to crash into each other. Azure light flared and metal screamed as they collided, sending broken shards everywhere before the two climbed to their feet. "We can use the Hand!"

"What are you talking about?" Another shot, another condemned familiar dropped.

"'Controls those who cannot control themselves,'" Grimsby repeated the words Mansgraf had used to describe the item. "If that's not these guys, I don't know what is."

"No!" Mayflower growled. One familiar had reached the base of the wall and begun to climb. Its claws sank easily through the plastic siding, allowing it to gouge new handholds as it climbed.

Mayflower put a bullet through its skull.

"It's the only way!" Grimsby said, managing a Bind that ripped a familiar from its perch on the wall, pinning it for the moment on its back like an overturned turtle. "Trust me!"

Mayflower glanced at him, and Grimsby saw in the Huntsman's eyes that he didn't trust him. Not anymore.

Even through the noise and the chaos and the fear, Grimsby felt the pain from that look more deeply than anything else. He had broken Mayflower's trust, and it seemed he wouldn't have the time to make it right.

"Grimsby—" Mayflower began, but his eyes flicked over Grimsby's shoulder and widened.

He had no time to look to see what Mayflower had seen, and instead he threw himself forward. He felt something hard strike him in the side, hard enough that something in his chest gave way with a wet crack. His dive turned quickly into a mad tumble, and he found himself falling from the wall into the courtyard of mutilated mannequins.

Had it been a true castle they were in, he would not have survived the fall.

However, it was Mighty Magic Donald's Food Kingdom, and the fall was less than ten feet. He landed on top of the mannequins, though whether that hurt more or less than the rubberized concrete might have, he was uncertain.

Pain flashed through him, like someone had detonated a claymore into his side. It was so severe that his vision warbled for a moment, and so did his focus.

Above, he saw Mayflower standing across from the black-skulled familiar that had stalked Grimsby on the train and outside his apartment. Blackskull climbed over the wall and stood equal to the Huntsman in height.

Grimsby saw Mayflower raise his weapon and fire, his barrel trained directly for Blackskull's right eye socket.

The shot struck, and sparks flew wide. Blackskull's head kicked back. Grimsby felt hope spark in him for a brief moment.

Then he realized that the familiar's skull was wholly intact. The familiar twitched, then leaned forward, and a warped bullet rattled out of its eye socket.

Mayflower was as shocked as Grimsby. The Huntsman let his guard down.

Blackskull struck. Claws raked across Mayflower's chest, flinging him to the side.

Mayflower fell from the wall, landing in a still heap a few feet away from Grimsby.

His gun fell from his grip.

Grimsby felt his skin ice over with fear as Blackskull turned its empty gaze toward him.

More familiars clambered atop the wall, almost desperate to get to their prey, but a raised claw from Blackskull held them back.

The familiar leapt down from the wall, making the ground shudder with its weight. It flexed foot-long claws and started toward Grimsby.

FORTY-THREE ✳

GRIMSBY WATCHED AS BLACKSKULL DREW NEAR. THE towering familiar loomed before the gaudy backdrop of the skylight-obscured moon.

Peters appeared in the drawbridge's gateway, looking for all the world like he was impatiently awaiting the end of a boring meeting. "Stop," he commanded.

Blackskull half turned back to him, then took another step toward Grimsby.

"I said stop!" Peters said, raising his voice.

The familiar twitched with something like emotion and then ceased moving. Its hollow voice echoed from its skull. *This isn't over.*

"Yes, yes," Peters said, waving annoyedly at it. "Touchy things, anthro-familiars. Repeating their last words again and again. So tedious." He shook his head and looked to Grimsby. "Last chance," he said. "The Huntsman is dead, or soon will be. But you don't have to die here. I don't mean to spill any more witch blood than I have to, Mr. Grimsby."

Grimsby struggled to his feet, cradling his injured side. He wasn't sure what broken ribs looked like, but he was fairly certain he now knew what they felt like.

"You're strong. That's good." Peters turned his eye to Mayflower's body, extending his hand to Grimsby like he was making an offering. "Bring me the Hand, and I will help you."

Somehow, Grimsby actually believed Peters was being honest with him. Whether because he actually was, or because he was a good liar, he didn't know. But he did believe that Peters was offering him a chance to survive the night, and that by itself was appealing.

He turned to Mayflower, who still lay in a motionless heap nearby. He felt the pain in his side shift toward his chest. Was he even alive? Any ordinary man, and Grimsby would have had no hope. But Mayflower was no ordinary man.

Yet, alive or dead, what choices did he have left? He was outnumbered, outclassed, and out-practically-everything-else'd to boot. Even if the Huntsman clung to life, what could he do? With no gun, no bullets, and countless wounds, Mayflower was far from being in a position to save anyone.

Unfortunately, so was Grimsby.

That left a lot of saving to be done, and no one around to do it.

He gulped and began limping toward Mayflower and the fallen box that contained the Hand.

"Good," Peters said, urging him on. "Very good."

Grimsby wasn't certain what he was going to do. Peters's offer was shadowing his every thought, and his growing fear at the hopelessness of his situation screamed at him to accept. He pushed the temptation away. Before all else, he needed to know if Mayflower was even alive.

He got close enough to see Mayflower's face, and his body seemed to grow twice as heavy. The Huntsman was a mess. His face was hardly visible through the curtain of blood that covered it. Claws had lacerated his chest, leaving three wide gaps that were closer to black than red. His skin was pale, too pale, and he was utterly still.

Everything grew distant.

The Huntsman had seemed so unstoppable, so powerful.

And yet he was gone.

It hardly seemed possible.

Grimsby's numb legs carried him to Mayflower's side, and he looked down at his fallen friend. His back was to Peters and his minions, and though he could feel their gazes burning into him, he didn't care. Not in that moment.

Fear, pain, and exhaustion seemed to all vanish.

All that was left was an ugly, hollow feeling in his stomach and twin burning coals in his eyes.

Then Mayflower's eye cracked open, like a single marble orb in a field of blood and ash. He glared at Grimsby and bared his red-stained teeth.

Relief flooded through him, and he knelt at the Huntsman's side.

Peters called out from behind him, "Quickly, Mr. Grimsby."

Mayflower flicked his gaze toward the director, then back to Grimsby. He coughed in barely a whisper, "Do it."

"Do what?" Grimsby asked.

"Take it. Save your own skin." He tried to spit the words, but instead they just dribbled out red from his lips.

Grimsby gently touched his fingers to Mayflower's chest, making him wince. He lifted his jacket and revealed a box within the inside pocket.

"Witch," Mayflower accused.

Grimsby's lip curled. He pulled the box containing the Hand from Mayflower's pocket. Then he noticed the other item, hidden in the lining of Mayflower's jacket. He found a spark in his throat, something like hope.

The claymore, paired with its detonator.

He withdrew them both and quickly took the Hand from the box and returned it to Mayflower's coat. It was cold when he touched it, like dirty ice beneath his fingers. He felt it press into his skin, like it was reaching out for him. All he had to do was reach back. He shuddered, glad to get it away from him. He placed the claymore in the box in the Hand's place.

"What are you doing?" Mayflower growled, his voice faint.

"Something stupid," Grimsby said. "Very, very stupid."

He summoned up a breath of Impetus, enough that it would make do but not so much that it would be noticed. He placed the first of the Bind runes on the claymore, right on top of the *FRONT TOWARD ENEMY* imprint.

Grimsby took a shaking breath. "You're only going to get one shot," he whispered, pressing the detonator into the Huntsman's grip. "Wait until it's close. That shield of his might stop it otherwise."

Mayflower glowered at him; then his eyes widened in realization. "You'll have to get clear," he said. "Ten meters at least."

Grimsby grunted and placed another pair of Binds, this one between his own belt and the ground beside Mayflower.

Mayflower nodded in the strictest of motions, then fell still again. If it weren't for the fire in his lone eye, Grimsby might have thought him dead a second time.

He stood and turned to Peters, the box in his grasp, the claymore waiting within it.

Peters had a professional smile on his face. "You made the right decision, Mr. Grimsby. There's much you and I will need to discuss."

Grimsby walked slowly, purposefully, toward Peters and Blackskull. It was likely to be his last walk, and he didn't mind taking his time.

After all he'd been through, this was it.

His last stand.

All he had to do was get close enough to Peters to Bind the

claymore to him, pull the cord on his Bind, and maybe get away before Mayflower detonated the claymore.

"Yeah, simple," he muttered. "Just pie the veteran witch in the face with a claymore. Easy enough." Though he supposed aiming for the face would be a bit unnecessary. Location was usually important in business, but marginally less so in demolitions.

He just had to get close.

He drew a deep breath as he neared Blackskull, and it took every ounce of his self-control to make himself walk into the thing's reach. He saw it twitch with anticipation, but Peters made a warning sound that stayed its claws.

Grimsby was nearly close enough to reach him, but before he could come within a few feet, Blackskull extended an arm to block his path.

"That's close enough," Peters said. "Open the box."

Grimsby felt his muscles freeze. Peters knew something was off. Somehow, he knew. He wasn't close enough. If he dropped the box now, and triggered his Bind, which would pull him out of range, the explosion might not be enough to break through Peters's barrier. If he survived, even if the familiars didn't rip them apart, Peters certainly would.

"The box, Mr. Grimsby," Peters said, as calm as a surgeon. "Open it."

He needed to do something, now, before it was too late. He couldn't get close enough to Peters, and that just left one other option.

"Before I do, tell me something," he said.

Peters let loose a brief, weary sigh, then gave Grimsby a calculating look. Somehow Grimsby felt acutely aware that the man was measuring if it would save time to humor him or simply kill him. Fortunately, he must have leaned to the former.

"Of course, I'm sure you have many questions."

"What did the magician say to the witch?"

Peters's eyes narrowed. "What?"

He slapped Blackskull on the chest, placing the second Bind.

The director's gaze grew to a glare, and Grimsby saw immediately that his spell had been noticed.

He flipped open the box and yelled. "Ta-da!"

Peters's mouth opened, but before he could utter a spell, Grimsby managed his own.

"Bind!"

As he shouted, a single strand of blue light appeared between Blackskull and the claymore. The mine flew out of its container and stuck to Blackskull's chest, burying the raised letters into the ragged cloth.

Peters yelled something, but Grimsby was too distracted to hear as he triggered the second Bind and felt himself jerked quickly backward toward Mayflower.

But before he could get away, something hard and strong wrapped around his chest and held him fast. Sharp blades dug into his skin, sinking deeply enough to both draw blood and squeeze the wind from his lungs.

The sudden flurry of movement was over in an instant, and Grimsby found himself trapped in Blackskull's grasp, his Bind pulling painfully at his belt while the familiar held him in place.

"Mayflower! Do it!" Grimsby shouted, but his choked voice was hardly enough to echo across the room. He looked over and saw Mayflower, propped up on one elbow, bloody hand wrapped around the detonator.

But the Huntsman didn't press the button.

He only stared, one white eye unblinking in the sheen of red across his face.

Peters scoffed and shook his head. "A valiant effort, boys, but I'm afraid even this wouldn't be enough to defeat my spell." He turned to Blackskull and gestured at the claymore, being careful to stay several paces away, despite his shield. "Remove that thing."

Blackskull scraped at the claymore with its free hand, but every time it was pulled away, the Binds pulled it right back like a rubber band. The familiar actually seemed to grow frustrated as it batted at the explosive to no avail.

"*This isn't over*," it echoed.

"An annoyance, nothing more," Peters said. "Besides, your dear Huntsman wouldn't pull the trigger. Not with you so close."

"Don't be so sure," Grimsby wheezed, feeling blood soak his shirt from the familiar's claws.

"I'm quite sure, as he would have already, wouldn't you, Mr. Mayflower?"

Mayflower shook his head a few degrees and let his hand fall to the floor.

"As I suspected," Peters said. "This has gone on long enough." He stepped forward and raised his hand. With a wave of Impetus it began to glow with fiery light. "The two of you are apparently useless, and so you must be disposed of."

"You shouldn't have gotten so close," Grimsby whispered.

"And why not?" Peters demanded.

He triggered the first Bind he had placed, the one neither Peters nor Mayflower had noticed.

A strand of gossamer appeared, with one end linked to Grimsby's palm.

And the other tied to the detonator.

"Because in this Mighty Magic Food Kingdom . . ."

The small plastic device flew across the room silently, and he managed to catch it with the help of the spell.

"Good guys always win."

Peters's eyes widened and he tried to leap away from the now-explosive familiar.

Grimsby pressed the button.

The world went white.

FORTY-FOUR

GRIMSBY WAS ALMOST SURPRISED TO OPEN HIS EYES. HE immediately regretted it. His head felt like someone had shoved a crew of jackhammers into it while he was out. There wasn't even much to see anyway. Just a bunch of floating blobs of color and the fuzzy outline of the skylight.

He almost rolled over and closed his eyes again, until he turned his head and saw Blackskull's severed arm, which had been wrapped around him, lying in front of him.

He suddenly remembered where he was, what was happening, and was almost frightened to look down at his own body, expecting to see it end unexpectedly at the waist.

But he was oddly intact.

Somehow, he'd survived the explosion.

He was almost excited, until he glanced around and saw the dozen or so of Peters's familiars that still remained. They stood, motionless, just where they had been, awaiting their master's orders.

But Peters lay in a heap nearby. The explosion must have caught him as well.

Grimsby felt his stomach begin to shimmy and slur in his guts at the thought that he'd killed Peters. He felt like retching up his food-starved innards then and there. So much so that, when Peters stirred, Grimsby was relieved.

Until he realized what that meant.

The spell that saved Peters from Mayflower's bullets must have protected him from the mine, and likely had been close enough to save Grimsby as well.

But as Peters stood, shaking his head and adjusting his cracked glasses, Grimsby realized that it was over.

They had lost.

The Department director still had a handful of familiars, his health, and almost certainly no shortage of magic.

While Grimsby had little more than a headache and a positive attitude.

He managed to struggle to his feet, hardly keeping his balance. He thought he heard something odd, which at this point included just about anything that wasn't a high-pitched ringing sound, but he couldn't locate the source.

Peters, meanwhile, turned to him, venom in his eyes. His hand extended out to his side, and a blue fire appeared in his palm like a pilot light.

Grimsby tried to summon some measure of Impetus, but it was spent. Sparks flickered and leapt from his scars, but no warmth flowed through him. He was tapped out.

That sound came again. Familiar, yet warped.

He turned to see Mayflower shouting at him. The Huntsman had struggled a few bloody feet from where he'd been, leaving a red trail on the concrete, but he hadn't managed to get to his feet. He was holding something in the air, waving it.

The Hand.

Grimsby was still in such a fugue that he almost waved back.

Then the ringing in his ears calmed enough that Grimsby heard Peters speak behind him.

"Kill him."

The dozen familiars charged as one, and ten times a dozen clawed fingers all extended out toward Grimsby.

Mayflower threw the Hand.

The glossy preserved skin glistened in grotesque shades as it soared through the air.

Grimsby reached out, almost instinctively, to catch it. And, whether by the skill of Mayflower's throw, the immensity of Grimsby's dumb luck, or some small measure of both mixed with a miracle, he caught it.

The dense dead flesh struck his palm, and he gripped it tight in his left hand.

Peters screamed and extended his burning palm toward Grimsby. A serpentine torrent of fire rushed forth, past the charging familiars.

Grimsby felt the icy tendrils reaching out from the Hand and into him, veins of cold power that were eager but just out of reach. He had felt them before, and recoiled.

This time, he reached back to them.

Grimsby had never touched a snake, but he expected he now knew what it felt like. The cold spread from the Hand in his grasp, wrapping around his forearm in a braid of ice. The skin of his scars didn't spark with this magic; it grew frigid and gray.

Sickly blue light shone from his scars, a hue he had never seen before, but one that made his stomach quail all the same. Mist rolled off his flesh, and the room quickly dropped in temperature.

It all seemed so calm, so numb. He had time to languish in every arctic moment before he remembered Peters's oncoming spell.

The torrent of blue fire flooded forth, but when it struck the mist that pooled around Grimsby, it splashed out and around like it had struck a wall. The fire shrieked and squealed as the mist consumed it greedily, and more clouds of cold formed.

Grimsby felt his exhaustion vanish, replaced by something ugly, brittle, and unrelenting. He felt his chest swell with power, as though his every word could shape reality.

He turned to the familiars, all still madly rushing toward him, and uttered a word, mist flowing from his mouth.

"*Stop.*"

He found himself unsurprised when they did.

Peters's face twisted with unbridled emotion, the first Grimsby had seen from him since he snapped in the restaurant the day before. But this time, it wasn't rage or frustration.

It was fear.

Grimsby felt some gross, grim satisfaction to have elicited such terror in the man. Yet even below the feelings of whelming power and control, he felt sick.

Peters's fear turned to panic, and he raised his hand and shouted, loosing forth another volley of fire. It was as harmless to Grimsby as the first.

He pointed the Hand, *his* hand, at the familiars and gestured toward Peters. The fingers curled until a single dooming pointer remained. "Stop him."

The familiars turned at once on their former master.

Peters screamed, scrambling back and turning his spell toward his once allies, but though the costumes burned away, their metal bodies were unharmed.

The first reached Peters, and the spells stopped.

More reached him, and the screams turned from desperation to hideous, wrenching cries of agony.

The human familiars, creations of cruelty, took their time.

Grimsby felt a smile curl on his lips. But it wasn't *his* smile.

It was someone else's.

Horror flooded through him. Horror, fear, and revulsion like he'd never known. Until this moment, all the monsters he'd seen had been on the outside.

This monster, though, this new one, was inside him.

The most frightening part, however, was he wasn't sure if it was the Hand that had put it there or if it had been there all along.

And he didn't think he could beat this one.

It was too strong. It was too much. And he was alone.

A hand gripped his shoulder, one that may as well have been made of fire.

He turned to see Mayflower, his body battered and bleeding, his eyes hard and bright.

The cold in Grimsby recoiled at the warmth, and he felt the urge to lash out, to turn his newfound minions onto this painful source of heat.

Mayflower must have seen something in Grimsby's face. His grip tightened and his eyes burned. "Fight it, kid. *Fight.*"

Grimsby felt emotion roil in him. Boiling emotion starkly at odds with the cold satisfaction that oppressed it. He felt a spark in his belly, one ephemeral mote of warmth in a body grown corpse cold.

He seized it, cradling it, wrapping his Impetus around it to protect it from the hungering ice. The spark caught into a flame, and he felt his Impetus grow in kind. The blue light and mist that rolled off his arm spat and hissed as tongues of orange fire welled in his scars.

The numbness began to give way to heat. It was painful, but it was a familiar pain. It was Grimsby's pain. Perhaps, more than anything in the world, it was *his.* And suddenly, in that heat, he found himself again.

He turned to the familiars and commanded them, *"Stop."* The voice was his own. It was too shuddering to be the other's.

Even as the familiars did as he commanded, he felt the cold presence in him surge in rage. Veins of rime crawled over his skin as it fought back. They brought blessed numbness with them. They offered him an escape. From pain, from fear, from everything.

The cold light in his scars began to take hold, choking out the embers of warmth he had fought to create, the motes of pain he had harnessed all his life.

For a moment, flanked by agony and salvation, Grimsby almost let the cold overtake him. It would have been so easy, so painless.

Then he wondered what would be left of him if he let the cold take his pain away. What would remain of Grimsby if he let the cold take his fear and his struggles from him?

The answer was obvious. And it frightened him.

Nothing.

Then, as though in response to his fear, the presence within him flinched. It was as though the emotion itself, perhaps any emotion, was like a hot iron that had been thrust forth.

Grimsby redoubled his assault of emotion, calling forth every burning memory.

His tenebrous friendship with and guilt-stricken betrayal of Mayflower.

The fear and thrill of his rivalry and overcoming of Hives.

The heat in his face whenever he saw Rayne.

The empathy he felt for Wudge and his lost home.

The loss of his mother.

Each wondrous and painful moment brought newfound flame to his scars, driving back the chill light and mist.

The fingers of the Hand spread and writhed in his grasp, and he could feel the agony of this other inside him.

The fire of his scars reached out and spread, burning away mist and rime. He felt the Hand squirm, desperate in his grasp. It pushed the power and ice back toward him, promising things he scarcely comprehended in a wordless voice.

A woman's voice.

He shook his head and said the most powerful word he knew.

"No."

He dropped the Hand from his grip. It fell, palm up, and the fingers curled in like a dying spider. Then it lay still.

He stared at it for a moment, his body shivering almost uncontrollably.

He would have collapsed, but he felt Mayflower's hand of iron hold him up.

"I—I—" Grimsby said, his voice hardly discernible from the sobs.

"You did good," the Huntsman said. "We're gonna be all right."

Grimsby nodded and managed to get some semblance of control.

A choked cough splattered across the room, and he turned to see Peters at the center of the frozen familiars. Their last order, to *stop*, still ruled them.

Blood spread from Peters in a sickening pool, and Grimsby felt the full realization of what he'd done come over him. He couldn't stop staring at the brutality. The spreading red. The rent flesh.

It was his fault.

Mayflower saw him and turned him around. "Don't look," he said. "Stay here."

Grimsby listened. He was so battered and hurt and tired that it seemed the only option.

The Huntsman walked away with a heavy limp and recovered his fallen gun. He tapped open the cylinder and dropped the six spent casings to the ground. He dug in his pocket and withdrew another bullet. This one was simple, plain copper, unlike the old ugly ones he had used before. He loaded it and walked past Grimsby toward Peters.

Grimsby felt the urge to watch the Huntsman, but the sputtering gasps from Peters kept him turned away. He watched Mayflower pass from his vision but kept his gaze focused solely on the Hand, lying on the floor in a gesture of frozen agony.

Peters's dying gasps halted.

Mayflower's gun went off a moment later.

Grimsby winced, but he didn't look. He heard Mayflower return to his side. "Is . . . is he?"

"Dead." Mayflower confirmed.

"Did I—I—?" He couldn't even manage the words.

"No," the Huntsman said firmly. "I killed him."

"But—"

Mayflower's rough hands seized him and pulled him to look eye to eye. "You didn't kill him, Grimsby. I did. Hell, if anything he killed his damned self. But this is important: *you* didn't kill him. Understand?"

Grimsby's gaze fell again to the Hand, and he knew he didn't really understand. He also wasn't sure he believed the Huntsman.

Mayflower was about to speak, but he stopped, head turning like an old hound's.

"Department's here," he said.

"What? How do you know?"

He tapped an ear. "I know."

Grimsby thought of the Hand falling into anyone else's possession and shuddered. "We can't let them take it."

"It might be our only bargaining chip to get you out of this mess," Mayflower said.

"I don't care."

Mayflower hesitated but nodded. "What do we do?"

Grimsby knelt and begin tracing a circle around the hand, keeping a wide berth between his fingers and its pale flesh. His hands were so stained with grime and blood that they left a brown trail behind them. When the circle was complete, Grimsby touched its edge and whispered.

"*Chute.*"

The concrete vanished into a black void, and the Hand fell through.

"Where does that go?" Mayflower asked.

"I don't know."

He thought for a moment, then nodded. "Good."

The portal vanished, leaving empty concrete.

The glass doors shattered and people began shouting as black-suited Agents and white-masked Auditors flooded the realm of Mighty Magic Donald.

Grimsby sat down and held up his hands until somebody finally cuffed him and carried him away.

FORTY-FIVE

"So you're claiming that Mansgraf's note was a distraction for us, while Mayflower pursued the real lead?" Rayne asked, her pen scribbling endlessly.

Grimsby groaned, and the sound echoed in the tiny concrete room. "Yes. The only reason she named me was because I was near where she hid the Hand."

He looked over at the mirror that covered one wall as he spoke. Rayne was sitting at the table across from him, but she was merely conducting the interview. He was sure whoever was in charge was behind the glass.

"And what happened to the Hand, Mr. Grimsby?"

"Eyes aflame," he cursed. "Again, I don't know."

"You've said that several times, but you haven't elaborated."

"Yeah, because I don't know! Peters showed up, there were monsters and explosions, and no shortage of me getting my butt kicked. I was lucky to survive. How the blue blazes can I be expected to keep a ledger of any body parts involved in the situation that weren't my own?"

Rayne only nodded placidly. "Of course, Mr. Grimsby, of

course." She jotted more notes. "And this . . . black-skulled familiar you saw. What happened to it?"

"I think the explosion turned it to scrap metal. You should have found its body."

"Mm-hmm," she said, jotting more notes.

"You did find it, didn't you?"

"I'm afraid I'm unable to reveal that information."

They hadn't found it. Grimsby felt a chill. Had Blackskull managed to crawl away with just one arm? Where had it gone? And why hadn't it been frozen like the other familiars?

He shivered as the familiar's words echoed in his head.

This isn't over.

He shook the feeling away. Time for worrying about that later. "So am I going to be charged with what happened to Mansgraf?"

"It has become apparent to the Department that Director Peters was somehow involved in the ordeal, and until we conduct a more thorough investigation, we will be declining to press any charges."

"Yeah, well, I doubt Peters is in any shape to testify in any case."

"That is correct." Her voice was cool and calm and as calculated as a machine, though Grimsby thought he saw some cracks in the casing as she looked up from her notepad. "And what of Wilson Hives?" she asked. "Do you have any knowledge of his whereabouts?"

Grimsby stammered, taken aback by the sudden question. "What? No. You mean—you mean you guys couldn't find him?"

She shook her head, her teal eyes searching his own.

He felt guilt worm into his stomach. He hadn't even spared a thought for Hives since Peters had taken him away. He thought of the tall figures that accompanied the director when he collected Hives, realizing they must have been familiars in disguise. He shuddered, then described the scene to her.

She said nothing as she noted his words, though her expression grew taut.

Grimsby felt his stomach twist and braid. Hives was, in all likelihood, dead. He had been an ass, but he hadn't deserved that.

"I'm—I'm sorry," he said. "I know he was your partner—"

She shook away his words, her face becoming a mask once more. "Thank you, Mr. Grimsby."

He balked, her coldness drawing him to silence on the matter. Finally, he said, "So what's going to happen to me?"

She held a hand to her ear and didn't say anything for a long moment. Grimsby could tell she was listening through an earpiece, though he had no idea what was being said.

It had been nearly two days since the Department had arrested him, and he had found it more boring than anything else. Long hours of sitting in a moderately appointed cell, waiting. He had given his testimony probably a dozen times, and he had been careful to keep his story straight. He told no lies, and that made it easier.

The hard part was leaving out the important truths.

Like what had happened to the Hand, or Wudge's involvement altogether.

The second had been Mayflower's suggestion, as Wudge's very description might undermine the legitimacy of his story. That, coupled with the idea of the erratic creature testifying in court, and Grimsby had agreed.

All that time, and he still had no idea what was to be done with him. He felt like he might be developing stomach ulcers from so much tense waiting.

Rayne nodded to no one and turned back to him. "You are to be released."

"Released?" Grimsby repeated, stunned at the simplicity of her statement.

"Yes, pending your remaining within Boston for the foreseeable future. We may uncover new evidence that may change things, but for the time being you will return to your life."

Grimsby wasn't sure whether to feel relief or despair.

Return to his life.

What did that even mean anymore?

He was fairly certain the Department would have closed down MMDFK after the incident, and even if they hadn't, his last shift had ended with him evading the authorities and leaving a chaotic mess in his wake. And that was nearly three days ago. The likelihood that he could even return to his job was near nil.

Even if he could, how could he go back to living his old life after all this?

He was changed, scarred, and in ways beyond just his flesh.

It had been a nightmare, but it had also been something more somehow. Something bigger. Something important.

How could he go back to his old life when he hardly recognized himself anymore?

He looked at Rayne, and something of his emotion must have shown on his face. She tilted down her glasses for a moment, her teal eyes meeting his. She didn't say anything, but her expression itself was an apology.

There was nothing more she could do for him.

He felt himself shrink, almost as if he was deflating. He looked away from her eyes, shame in his gut and despair crawling up his neck. He didn't know what he'd do, but he wasn't going to break down.

Not here, in front of her. Not here, in front of that mirror.

If he did, he'd just be proving their doubts about him right.

Rayne stood and said a goodbye before leaving, but Grimsby barely heard it. He only stared at the table and tried to be strong.

He knew he was failing.

FORTY-SIX

MAYFLOWER GLARED HARD THROUGH THE GLASS, HIS lips twitching with anger. "The kid deserves better than that, Grieves."

Damien Grieves stood beside him, his hands folded professionally behind his back. "Keeping him out of prison is as good as I can manage in such circumstances, Les."

Mayflower's muscles tensed, and his arm immediately twinged in pain, hanging from the sling around his neck. "You and I both know that's bullshit."

"I'm merely assistant director; my hands are tied."

"And who the hell becomes director when they replace Peters?"

He straightened his stylish suit jacket and shrugged with his eyebrows. "I wouldn't dare to assume—"

"You. We both know it will be you."

"Why, Les, I didn't know you had such faith in me."

Mayflower felt the urge to sock Grieves in the side of his face but managed to resist. It wouldn't do Grimsby any favors. Nor his own numerous stitches. Though it might have done wonders for the Huntsman's temper.

He forced the urge back down. "You think I'm an idiot?"

"Why, Les, of course not."

"You knew about Peters. The whole goddamned time, you knew."

For the first time, Grieves looked him in the eye, his expression as level as if an engineer had laid it out on a schematic. "I don't know what you're talking about."

"Why else would you involve me? Tell me about Mansgraf against Peters's direct orders?"

"Informational oversight on my part."

"Bullshit. You knew Peters was involved. Maybe you didn't know the dirty details, but you knew enough. Enough to know that involving me would better the odds Peters was discovered and revealed. With him gone, you'd be the obvious successor."

Grieves's face was as much a mask as those worn by his Auditors. He flicked a gaze around the room, ensuring it was empty aside from Mayflower and himself. "I'm only happy that a man who would abuse his position has been relieved of it, and if it is decided that I should be a suitable candidate for his replacement, then I shall be happy of that as well."

Mayflower felt something foul on his tongue and resisted the urge to spit. "You're a damned snake, Grieves. If you're not going to admit you used me, fine. But you're a dumbass if you throw an asset like that kid out on the street." He pointed to Grimsby on the other side of the glass. He sat in his cushionless chair, his head hung on his neck as he stared at the table he was cuffed to.

"I've read Mansgraf's report on him. 'Mediocre witch. Decent person. Not Department material.' Brief and to the point, just as she liked to be."

"She was wrong."

"Was she now?"

Mayflower glanced at Grimsby, then nodded firmly. "Mostly."

Grieves shook his head. "I can't be employing dangerous rogue assets like Grimsby. What will people think?"

"Whatever you tell them to," Mayflower said grimly.

"Perish the thought," Grieves said. Then he smiled for the first time.

"You owe me," Mayflower said.

"Do I?"

"Without me—hell, without Grimsby—Peters would still be around. And you'd still be his peon."

Grieves's smile faded as quick as it had come. "I don't recall any such agreement."

"You're a real son of a bitch, Grieves."

He clicked his tongue. "Such shameful decorum. In spite of that, I'd still like to hire you, just as before."

"I told you no once," Mayflower said. He had to keep his tone level, though he felt a growl bubble in his throat as his hand trembled the slightest twitch. If not for Grimsby's intervention, Mayflower would have killed Hives and Peters would have gotten away with murdering Mansgraf. His old intuitions were as rusted as he feared them to be when this all began, and it was a miracle he hadn't gotten anyone killed who hadn't deserved it.

No, he thought, shaking his head firmly, *I can't go back to this life.*

No matter how much he wanted to.

"You certain about that?" Grieves asked, his expression tinged with the barest hint of smugness.

"You think I'm the type to change my mind easily?" Mayflower said, temper simmering as he tore his attention away from his own twisted guts.

Grieves flicked a glance to Grimsby, and his smile returned. "Oh, I think you can be reasoned with."

Mayflower realized the director's meaning and felt a hot coal in the pit of his stomach. "You're a real son of a bitch, Grieves."

FORTY-SEVEN

GRIMSBY SAT ON HIS BROKEN COUCH, STARING THROUGH the old TV set. Some old black-and-white Western was playing, though he didn't pay it much mind. Beside him, though, Wudge sat eagerly on the edge of the couch, munching on a square of dried ramen.

"Wudge likes the part when they shoots each other," he said, bouncing a little on the cushion.

"That's all the parts, Wudge," he said distantly.

Wudge cackled in agreement.

Grimsby turned his stare to the hole in the ceiling where the fan had been.

The Department had dropped him off the night before with hardly a word. He hadn't slept since, and not just because Wudge hadn't budged from his sleeping couch.

He had called Carla at MMDFK but only got an automated message. Apparently, the Food Kingdom would be closed for the foreseeable future for "development," whatever that meant. Regardless, it left him officially unemployed.

He didn't know what he would do, or how he'd get by, and

he'd been staring at a blur of old Westerns trying to figure it out since he got home.

Now, however, he was doing little more than staring. He'd seen no tunnel, let alone a light at the end of it. No solutions, no hope.

Just grainy pictures of good guys chasing bad guys.

He had once thought things would be so simple, but not anymore.

Three knocks sounded at his door, stirring him from his dazed stupor. He automatically stood and made his way to the entry, stepping over the body of the familiar he'd destroyed. It had been too heavy to move on his own, and Wudge had demanded more ramen to help remove it than Grimsby could afford.

He made his way past the open door of the closet. After he had gotten home, he'd lifted the door off the hinges and tossed it into the alley below. The scrawled pictures the familiar had left on it still gave him chills.

He turned the dead bolt, leaving the chain in place, and cracked the door open to reveal Mayflower.

Grimsby felt his brain lock up for a moment. He hadn't seen the Huntsman since they had both been arrested. He quickly unlatched the chain and opened the door wider, trying to think of something meaningful to say.

Instead, he just said, "Uh, hi."

Mayflower nodded. "Grimsby." He looked over his shoulder at the television and nodded. "That's a good one."

"Is it?"

"Yeah."

There was a long moment of silence that Grimsby felt the urge to break. "So, glad to see you're doing better."

Mayflower lifted his slung arm briefly and shrugged. "Yeah. Department's got decent docs."

"So . . . what are you doing here?"

For the first time, Grimsby realized Mayflower wasn't dressed in his usual careless manner. His mismatched suit had been replaced with a dark blue one that was well tailored. His flannel shirt was replaced with a suspiciously clean white one. Only his brown motorcycle boots remained the same.

He rocked his head back and forth in annoyance. "Department code. You know how it is."

Grimsby felt his gut twist and an acrid taste grow in his mouth. "No, I don't."

"Well, you'll be sick of it soon enough." He offered a small black square of leather to Grimsby.

He took it, more by confused autopilot than by choice. It was a bifold. He opened it to reveal the silver star of the Department. Below it was an engraved metal plate.

It read: *G. G. Grimsby, Auditor.*

He was so shocked that he dropped it onto the floor. He stared down at it, the wheels in his brain somehow caught on themselves. "That—that—that—"

"Is yours," Mayflower said, grunting as he knelt to retrieve the badge. "If you want it."

"Mine?"

He nodded. "Fair warning, though. You're to be partnered with the hardest, meanest, and grumpiest old bastard they have in the Department."

"Who?" Grimsby asked, still numbly dumbfounded.

Mayflower sighed and shook his head. "Me, dumbass. Now, the offer's on the table. There's only one question left: do you still want it?"

There was something dire in the Huntsman's face, some tangled burden that Grimsby could not discern, though he could hardly spare it a thought as he stared at the badge, suddenly uncertain. All he had ever wanted, for as long as he could remember, was to be an Auditor.

Now it was right here before him, and a question rattled around in his head. But it wasn't if he was ready. And it wasn't if he was good enough. Mayflower had been right; the only question left was simple.

Did he still want it?

After all he had endured the last few days, after all the close calls and closer calls, he had managed because he had no choice. He had to manage, or he would die.

Now there was a choice. And it was one he never knew would be so hard.

Two paths: one dangerous, the other sad.

Mayflower saw the indecision in his face. "The path unchosen is the path most regretted," he said. "But that doesn't make it the right path."

"How do I know what the right one is?" Grimsby asked. "How could I know?"

The Huntsman curled a smirk at him. "That's the trick, kid. You don't find the right path. You *make* it. Whichever one you choose, walk it, and walk it hard, and you'll do all right for yourself."

Grimsby felt his words run out.

The time to talk was done, and the time to choose had come.

He took a deep breath and then took the badge the Huntsman offered.

Mayflower nodded, something heavy in the gesture. "All right. Let's go."

"Where?"

"To get your suit, Auditor Grimsby."

EPILOGUE ✳

"ARE YOU CERTAIN?" DAMIEN GRIEVES ASKED. HE FORCED his tone to remain cool and composed, though he felt his throat tighten as he stared past the two-way mirror and into the darkened room.

"I think it would be best, Director," Auditor Bathory said, her furrowed brow difficult to see in the dim light. "Seeing someone it knows well might trigger unpredictable responses."

Damien said nothing. Auditor Elizabeth "Rayne" Bathory was as sharp as they came, despite her young tenure at the Department. He never trusted anyone entirely, but he trusted her assessment when it came to this matter.

"Very well," he said, ignoring the heavy tread of his own pulse. "You may proceed."

Auditor Bathory nodded and stepped into the sealed chamber that formed an airlock between observation and interrogation. He could barely see her in the dim light. She had suggested that less stimulus would be ideal for not upsetting the subject.

At the room's center was a steel table, bolted to the floor. Rayne approached it and sat in the seat nearest Damien's window. The room was quiet and still. The only sound was the rustle of cloth as the Auditor took her place, played over speakers from microphones placed all around the room. Across from her, a shadowed form remained motionless.

"Subject appears unresponsive," Rayne said. "Requesting permission to proceed."

Damien bit back his initial reply. It was a risk, their plan. The subject—he had to call her that to keep his head level—had been unresponsive to everyone, aside for occasional scant movement. They were uncertain she—it, he corrected himself—was even aware.

He took a breath, then nodded, leaning forward to press the intercom button. "Proceed."

Auditor Bathory produced a black plastic bag from which she drew two items of patchwork cloth: a robe and a limp pointed hat.

In the darkness at the far side of the table, something moved.

Rayne placed the items on the table, then slid them to the middle of the table.

The figure across from her twitched.

There was a long, tense pause. Then the sound of metal squeaked against metal.

Damien felt like he could almost see its eyes in the dark, like twin holes in space, more deeply black than any void.

"Response confirmed," Rayne said. Her voice was level, but Damien could see fear creep into her posture. Like a true Auditor, she suppressed it immediately. "Permission to proceed?"

Phase two was even more dangerous. It could well be that at his next word, Auditor Bathory would die horribly, her body torn open and spilled upon the very window he now peered through. The Agents standing at the ready outside would be too slow to help her, and even Damien's own magic would likely come too late.

He felt his reserve falter for a moment but steeled it down as one might lash a madman to a ship's mast. Bathory—Rayne knew the risks. Yet she had volunteered to face the danger because she also knew what it might mean to the Department.

What it might mean to him.

His finger was white, numb, and bloodless as he pressed the intercom button. "Proceed."

He then pressed the button near it—a button that released the shackles that held the creature in place.

The table buzzed loudly and shuddered as the shackles built into it released. Auditor Bathory flinched, albeit barely, at the sudden noise. She braced herself, but there was no flash of motion, no blur of violence. Only silence.

Then, slowly, a hand reached out of the dark, one made of twisted metal overlaid with silver plates, oddly slender and beautiful. It clamped down on the robe and hat and pulled them back into the dark. There was more movement, and the rustle of cloth over steel. Then, silence.

Damien felt his mouth go dry as he pressed the intercom button. "Proceed to final phase."

Rayne nodded without turning around. She withdrew a pad and pen and set them on the table.

"Can you hear me?" she asked.

For a moment, there was no reply. Then a solitary ping rang out as a metal finger tapped on the table.

She jotted a note, then pressed again. "Do you know where you are?"

There was another tap on the table.

"Do you know who you are?" Rayne asked.

There was another pause, one so long that Damien thought they'd receive no reply at all, until finally another tap came, this one softer.

Damien found himself leaning forward, his body tensed.

Rayne gathered herself for the last question.

"Is your name Samantha Mansgraf?"

The figure across the table leaned forward until the patchwork hat came into view. Beneath it lay a skull, still fresh and pink, webbed with dark veins of congealed blood. Black runes marked the skull, somehow written in Mansgraf's own hand.

A sepulchral breath echoed into the room, like a winter wind through an abandoned city, all emanating from the familiar and its hollow skull.

Damien felt his blood run cold and his hand tremble as he heard the thing whispering Mansgraf's final words in a grave tone caught between a cackle and a curse:

"Flesh and blood."